HEART OF
OBSIDIAN

A PSY-CHANGELING NOVEL

NALINI SINGH

First published in Great Britain in 2013 by Gollancz
An imprint of the Orion Publishing Group
Orion House, 5 Upper St Martin's Lane, London WC2H 9EA
An Hachette UK Company

A CIP catalogue record for this book is available
from the British Library

ISBN 978 0 575 11097 7 (Cased)
ISBN 978 0 575 11102 8 (Export Trade Paperback)

1 3 5 7 9 10 8 6 4 2

Printed in Great Britain by Clays Ltd, St Ives plc

The Orion Publishing Group's policy is to use papers that are natural,
renewable and recyclable products and made from wood grown in
sustainable forests. The logging and manufacturing processes are expected
to conform to the environmental regulations of the country of origin.

www.nalinisingh.com
www.orionbooks.co.uk
www.gollancz.co.uk

HEART OF
OBSIDIAN

Darkest Part of Night

IN THE YEAR 1979, the Psy race made the decision to embrace Silence and condition all emotion out of their young; to become without hope or despair, anger or fear, sorrow or joy.

Mothers and fathers sentenced their children to lives of icy control out of a soul-deep love those children would never feel in return. They told their babies that Silence was a precious gift, that it would save them from the madness and violence that so often came intertwined with the staggering beauty of their psychic abilities.

Without Silence, said a leading philosopher of the day, *we will cannibalize ourselves in a storm of blood and death and insanity, until the Psy race becomes nothing but a terrible memory.*

In 1979, Silence was a beacon of hope . . . but 1979 was more than a hundred years ago.

Those first children are long dead and the PsyNet has been rocked by the initial volley of a civil war that might yet tear it apart, taking the changelings and humans with it. A civil war that has awakened a whispering understanding in the populace about the ugly irony of Silence: in creating a society that rewards lack of emotion, the Psy have created fertile ground for the rise of psychopathic personalities to the leadership of their race.

An individual who feels nothing is, after all, the perfect graduate of Silence.

Ruthless. Cold-blooded. Without mercy . . . without conscience.

Chapter 1

KALEB KRYCHEK, CARDINAL telekinetic and a man no one wanted to meet alone on a dark night, had been searching for his quarry for seven years, three weeks, and two days. Even while he slept, his mind had continued to hunt through the sprawling psychic network that was the heartbeat and the cage of the Psy race. Not for a day, not for a second, had he forgotten his search, forgotten what they'd taken from him.

Everyone involved would pay. He'd make certain of it.

Right now, however, he had different priorities, his search complete, his target huddled in a corner of a small, windowless room in his isolated home on the outskirts of Moscow. Crouching down in front of her, he held out a glass of water. "Drink."

Her response was to crush herself impossibly further into the corner and tighten her arms around the knees she hugged to her chest. She'd spent the hour since he'd retrieved her from her prison rocking to and fro in brittle silence. Her hair was a tangled rats' nest around her face, her upper arms bearing both fresh scratches and marks of older gouges.

She was still a bare five feet, two inches . . . or so he judged. She'd been in a huddled position pre-teleport, had only curled further into her shell in the past sixty minutes. Her eyes—a blue so deep they were midnight—refused to meet his, skittering away if he entered her line of sight.

Now she ducked her head, the matted waist-length strands that should've been a rich black interwoven with unexpected strands of red-gold, dull and greasy around her down-bent face. That face was all bone under pallid skin of palest brown, the nails on her hands gnawed to the quick yet embedded with dried blood that said she'd used the stubs to viciously scratch either her own skin or another's, perhaps both.

At last, he understood why the NetMind and DarkMind, the twin entities that knew every corner of the vast psychic network that connected all Psy on the planet but for the renegades, had been unable to find her—regardless of how many times he'd made the request or how much information he'd given them in an effort to narrow the scope of the search. Kaleb had been *inside* her mind during retrieval, had needed to be to complete the teleport, and even then, he wouldn't have known it was her if he hadn't had incontrovertible evidence to the contrary. The person she'd been was gone.

Whether what remained was anything more than a broken shell was yet an unanswered question.

"Drink or I'll leave you to wallow in your filth."

He used words that would've once caused her to react—but he didn't know if that part of her existed any longer. The file he'd so meticulously put together over the years, the file he'd studied until he could recite the contents in his sleep, was going to be useless. She was no longer that girl with her hair brushed straight and shiny, and midnight eyes that seemed to see far beyond the skin.

"Perhaps you enjoy smelling like something from the garbage."

The rocking increased.

Logic said he needed to get a Psy-Med specialist in here as fast as possible. But Kaleb knew he wasn't going to do that. He trusted very, *very* few people, and he trusted no one when it came to her. Since his current approach wasn't bearing the results he wanted, he shifted focus with the ease of a man who had no emotional attachment to a decision.

"Your lips are cracked and it's clear you haven't had enough fluids for at least twenty-four hours." In the split second that he'd teleported into the white-on-white room where she'd been held, the overhead light cutting in its torturous brightness, he'd seen the bottles thrown at the wall, the liquid soaked into the floor.

His initial assumption had been that the painful brightness was a normal part of her existence, but it may have been a punishment, her captors attempting to break her will. That it wasn't already broken. . . yes, it said something about the woman who refused to interact with him on any level.

"If you wanted to kill yourself," he said, watching for even the most minor response to the brutal words, "there are easier ways than dying of thirst. Or aren't you intelligent enough to work that out?"

The rocking accelerated further.

"I can as easily pin you to the wall and force the water down your throat. I won't even need to touch you."

She hissed at him, dark blue orbs glinting behind the tangled mass of her hair.

He didn't move, didn't betray any reaction to the fact that she'd responded in some fashion at last, even if it was nonverbal. "Drink it. I won't ask again."

Still she resisted. Unexpected. Her mind might be broken, but it wasn't—had never been—unintelligent. No, her intellect was so piercing, her teachers had struggled to keep up with her. She had to be aware that refusing him wasn't an option. The power of a cardinal telekinetic was vast. He could crack every bone in her body with a fleeting thought, crush those bones into dust if he so chose. Even if she no longer understood that, she'd experienced his strength when he teleported her from her cell and to his home; she had to comprehend her precarious situation.

Her eyes flicked to the glass in his hand, teeth biting down on her badly cracked lower lip. Yet she didn't reach for the water she so patently needed. Why?

He took a moment to think, consider the circumstances in which he'd found her. "It's not drugged," he said, talking to a face that held no recognition, no sign that she remembered their final blood-soaked encounter, an encounter where she'd screamed for so long and in such agony she'd caused damage to her throat that would've needed medical attention to repair.

"Infused with the minerals and vitamins that you need," he continued, "but not drugged. You're no use to me in a coma." Holding her gaze when it finally connected with his, he took a healthy swallow of the water, then held out the glass.

It was snatched from him a second later. He'd teleported in another full glass from the kitchen before she finished the first. She emptied them both. Getting rid of the glass with a negligible use of his telekinesis, he rose from his crouched position in front of her. "Do you want to eat first or shower?"

She stared up at him, eyes narrowed.

"Fine, I'll make the decision for you." He brought in a plate of fresh, uncut fruit, as well as a thick slice of bread spread with butter and honey. It wasn't the kind of food he ate—like most Psy, he lived on nutrition bars, for Silence thrived in the absence of sensation, and taste was a powerful one.

His guest's Silence, however, had been shattered a lifetime ago. Sensation might well be the key to bringing her back from the mental wasteland where she'd retreated, her personality and abilities entombed. Teleporting in a knife, he sliced the bread into four smaller pieces, then, going down on his haunches, held the plate out to her. She stared for over a minute before selecting a piece not in the quick jab he'd expected, but with measured deliberation.

So, her captors hadn't starved her. She'd chosen not to eat.

It took no effort to reach out with his mind, set the water to boil in the kitchen, prepare a mug of tea just hot enough that she could sip it. He dumped three teaspoons of sugar in the mug before bringing it in for her. This time, she didn't hesitate, cuddling the mug to her chest.

Heat.

Realizing she was cold, he adjusted the thermostat to further warm up the already warm room. She didn't react except to take another quarter of the bread. As she ate with slow neatness, he had the sense he was being evaluated. It would've been easy to jump to the conclusion that she wasn't as broken as she appeared, that this was all a clever act, but the fleeting moments he'd spent in her mind told a far different story.

She'd been splintered from the inside out.

The intelligence that judged him at this instant was more akin to the primal hindbrain that existed within every civilized being, the part that knew how to identify predator from prey, danger from safety. It wasn't the level of function he needed from her, but it was better than total catatonia or actual physical brain damage.

Her brain was fine. It was her mind that was broken.

Picking up an apple, he went to cut it, but her eyes flicked left to the grapes. He didn't say a word, simply put down the apple and turned the plate so the grapes were close to her hand. She ate four, took a sip of tea, and stopped.

Half a slice of bread, four grapes, two glasses of water, and a sip of tea. It was a better result than he might have initially predicted.

"I'll leave this here for you," he said, rising to put the plate on the small table on the far side of the bed. "If you want more, or something different, you'll have to get it from the kitchen yourself."

That got her attention.

The subtle rocking that had restarted when he rose to his feet stopped, and he knew she was listening. He had read *Psy-Med Journals* in preparation for the eventuality that she was broken when he found her, had even sat in remotely on countless lectures on the subject, but where the specialists recommended quiet, calm, gentle interaction, he knew the primitive mind behind those eyes of midnight blue would see right through such an act.

He was the monster that stalked nightmare, and they both knew it.

"You can move around the house as you please," he told her, calculating how many years it had been since she'd been allowed any kind of freedom. The entire span of her captivity? If so, in this he could understand the impact on her psyche better than any stranger with psycho-medical training.

"The reason this room has no windows," he said, answering the question she hadn't asked, but that had to be at the surface of her consciousness, "was to negate the possibility of panic on your part at being removed from a closed environment."

Her shoulders stiffened. Perhaps, he thought, there *was* more than an animal mind present within the fragile shell of her body. Perhaps. "If you prefer another room, choose it. For now, the bathroom is through there." He pointed to the door on the other side of the bed, having deliberately

chosen the smallest suite in the house for the same reason he'd given for
the lack of windows.

He'd built the suite for her, for this exact possibility.

It was impossible to predict how she might react to the wide-open
vista that encircled the house. He had no neighbors within screaming
distance . . . further. The one side not bounded by grassy fields housed the
terrace—and it was flush up against a jagged gorge. A terrace, he realized
all at once, that had no railings and could be reached by any number of
rooms in the house, including the bedroom across from this one.

He was already retrieving the supplies to fix that oversight as he
spoke. "If you wish to continue to smell like a pigsty, that's your choice.
However, when I get sick of the stink, I'll simply teleport you into the
shower, clothes and all, and turn on the water while pouring liquid soap
over your head."

The rocking had stopped totally by now.

"There are civilian clothes for you in the closet." Not every piece
would fit her emaciated frame, but she'd have enough for the time being.
"If you're attached to your institutional uniform"—a white smock, white
pants, both filthy—"there's a clean set in the dresser." He'd sourced it a
few minutes ago from a medical facility that would never notice the lack.

The woman in the corner remained mutinously silent.

Turning, he walked to the door, his fingers playing over the tiny platinum star in his pocket. "It's after midnight. Sleep if you wish—if not,
the house is yours to explore. I'll be on the terrace." He left without further words. This chess game was the most important of his life, each
move as critical as the next. Those who'd held her captive had treated her
as one might a dumb animal, but she was not that. No, she was far more
gifted a prize. One he would do nothing to jeopardize.

As he would make no final decisions.

Not yet. Not until he knew how much of her they'd broken.

KALEB could've built the barrier between the terrace and the gorge
using his telekinetic abilities, but he stripped, changed into thin black

sweatpants designed to keep the body cool, and took on the task manually. As a Tk, energy was his lifeblood, but right now, he had an excess of it—not on the psychic plane, but on the physical.

Had he been human or changeling, the sudden spike in his energy levels might've been put down to excitement in achieving the goal that had been his driving force for seven years, in having her in his home and within reach. But he wasn't a member of the emotional races. He was Psy and he was Silent, his emotions conditioned out of him when he'd been a child. His path to that Silence had been erratic at times, but the end result was the development of a coolly rational mind that held no shadow of fear or hope, anguish or excitement.

He had once had a large structural flaw in his conditioning, a bone-deep fracture in his Silence, but that had been in another life. The fracture had sealed to adamantine hardness, the weak spot morphing into the strongest part of his Silence, but he knew that behind the stone, the fault remained.

The day it no longer did . . . it was better for the world if that didn't come to pass.

Wiping the sweat off his brow with his forearm, he turned up the voltage on the outdoor lights and began to drill in the screws that would ensure the metal barrier he was putting in place wouldn't collapse even in a major earth tremor. He hadn't searched so long for his quarry to lose her through a lack of preparation.

Even as he concentrated on the task, he kept an ear open for his guest. Some would say "prisoner" was the more apt term, but the words didn't matter. Only the fact that she was in his grasp.

CRASH!

Drill abandoned, he'd teleported into her room before he consciously processed the violence of sound.

Chapter 2

THE DRESSER MIRROR against the wall opposite the bathroom door lay smashed, shards of glass on the carpet, on the bed, on her as she sat hunched in the center of that bed. A smeared streak of wet red sliced her cheek from where a splinter had flown directly at her, but she appeared otherwise uninjured.

Not far from the mirror lay the broken pieces of the mug she'd used to shatter the glass, the spilled tea a rusty stain on the dresser itself and on the pale rug that covered the polished wood of the floor.

Kaleb didn't ask for the reason behind her behavior. "Stay still." Gathering up the larger fragments of glass, he teleported them out into the waste receptacle. He knew a teleporter who could take blood itself out of carpet, but Kaleb's ability worked on a larger scale. He could cause an earthquake that would devour a city, rip an airjet out of the sky with his mind, even create a tidal wave—what he could not do was pick up every tiny sliver of glass.

"You can't stay in this room," he said. "Not until it's been cleaned."

She shifted to press her back against the headboard in silent rebellion. Since forcing her compliance would run counter to his intention to win her trust, he reworked the situation, came up with another viable solution. "Hold on."

His guest let out a surprised gasp, grabbing at the sheets as the entire bed lifted a foot off the floor. Holding it and the other furniture aloft, Kaleb used his Tk to roll up the thick rug that ran the entire length of the room and covered ninety percent of the floor. There appeared to be no shards on the floor itself, but he walked around the room to make certain before returning to his position by the door, the rolled-up rug at his feet.

Gauging the impact of the stains caused by the tea, he accessed a visual file he made certain to keep up-to-date and, using the image as a lock, teleported the rug straight into the incinerator of the region's central waste processing and recycling plant.

Neither his DNA nor hers could be permitted to fall into the wrong hands.

He had her lifted off the sheets and the bedding rolled up and in the same incinerator before she realized what was happening. Placing her back on the now-stripped bed, he brought in a spare rug from the storage space under the house and rolled it out. "Try not to damage this one," he said as he resettled the bed. "It's hand-knotted silk."

A vivid blue swirled with cream and a hint of indigo, he'd bought it five years ago, when his companies first started turning profits that went well beyond what even the most conservative individual would consider a healthy safety margin. "Is there anything else you'd like to destroy? Do it now so I can catch the shrapnel."

The woman on the bed stared at him, before doing something he hadn't anticipated. She picked up the small vase on the bedside table and threw it at something above his head. He ducked, turning just in time to stop the projectile from impacting with the tiny sensor light that gave away the position of the fire alarm.

As the vase hovered in front of the blinking red light, he began to comprehend the very rational reason behind her apparently irrational act. "It's not a camera. And the mirror was just a mirror." Even as he spoke, he understood that she wasn't going to believe him. The alarm would be in pieces the instant he walked out the door, even if she had to use every projectile in the room to smash it.

Returning the vase to the table, he reached up to remove the alarm from the wall, his height—unlike hers—more than sufficient for the task. The removal wouldn't compromise her safety; he'd make certain of that fact. Task complete, he got rid of the device and once more faced the woman who hadn't taken her eyes off him since he'd appeared in the bedroom. "Anything else?"

Her gaze went to the recessed ceiling light.

"I take that out," he said, "and you'll be in the dark."

No change in her focus.

Since the battle wasn't a crucial one in this war, he 'ported in a small table lamp from another part of the house. "Go over that."

She took her time doing so, but when she turned it on rather than attempt to destroy it, he judged her satisfied that it wasn't rigged with surveillance equipment. Dismantling the ceiling light, he scanned the room for anything else that might read as suspicious to her mind. Nothing stood out, and given the areas on which she'd focused, it was likely she'd already checked the walls and visually examined the ceiling.

Categorically not a mind functioning on the animal level alone, regardless of what he'd seen of her twisted mental pathways.

Walking into the bathroom on that thought, he removed both the light and a ceiling-mounted heat lamp, replacing them with a tall, free-standing waterproof lamp she could take apart if necessary. The mirror went, too, and he removed the fine grille on the airflow system so she could see there was nothing beyond but a silent fan meant to mitigate condensation.

By the time he returned to the terrace, his skin had cooled, but it heated up quickly enough, even in the light breeze coming off the trees on the other side of the gorge. With each screw he drilled into place, he considered the room where she'd been held, the probable response of her captors when they'd lost the feed from her cell to sudden static. It would've lasted mere seconds, left them staring at the image of an empty room after it cleared.

The static was a useful tool he'd discovered as a teen while experimenting with his abilities. The sheer strength of his telekinesis meant he put out a low-level "hum" that wasn't discernible to humanoid ears, but that made animals uneasy and messed with technology. He had it under control now, of course. The only time he permitted the hum to escape his shields was when he needed to obfuscate his presence in front of a camera or to otherwise disrupt technological surveillance. It was an aspect of his abilities known to only one other living individual aside from Kaleb.

Nevertheless, given the speed of the teleport, his guest's captors would suspect the involvement of a high-level Tk, and there were very few of them in the pool, but no one would know it had been Kaleb. Not until he was ready.

And then they would beg for mercy.

Even the most powerful, most Silent begged in the end, the conditioning cracking in the face of a scrabbling panic that blinded them to the fact Kaleb had no mercy in him.

The final screw in place, he packed up his equipment and teleported it away. It was odd to see the terrace surrounded by metal railings—they allowed a view out from between the bars but no entry to the black maw of the gorge. Not even his guest was thin enough to fit in the spaces between the bars.

Sir.

The polite telepathic knock belonged to Silver, his aide and a member of the quietly influential Mercant family.

He opened the telepathic channel. *What is it?* He didn't remind her that he'd asked not to be disturbed—Silver wouldn't be going against his express orders unless it was necessary.

There's been an attack against a small think tank in Khartoum. The think tank had just announced the parameters of its next research project: the benefits to Psy of greater political cooperation and social interaction with humans and changelings.

So, he thought, the next volley had been shot in the civil war that loomed over the PsyNet. *How many dead?*

All ten of those in the building at the time. A poisonous gas introduced into their air supply.

Has Pure Psy claimed responsibility? The radical pro-Silence group had gone quiet in the aftermath of its decisive defeat in the California region at the hands of a force comprised of the SnowDancer wolves and the DarkRiver leopards, as well as Psy who looked to the two Councilors in the area—Nikita Duncan and Anthony Kyriakus—for guidance. The humans, too, had joined in the resistance to Pure Psy's attempt to seize control of the greater San Francisco and Sierra Nevada region, leading to an alliance that crossed racial boundaries Pure Psy wanted to maintain at all costs.

Such a motive seemed to run counter to the group's avowed focus on the PsyNet, but underlying Pure Psy's outwardly "rational" rhetoric was the belief that the Psy were superior to the other races, that if their people would only seal the cracks that had begun to appear in the foundations of the Silence Protocol, they would once again be the most powerful race on the planet.

Any attempt to better integrate the Psy populace with the humans and changelings was thus seen not only as an attack against the Protocol, but as a threat to the genetic superiority of the Psy race. It was an unsound premise. Kaleb knew the Psy were as flawed as the humans or changelings—he'd come of age in rooms ripe with the scent of congealing blood, screams echoing in his ears; he knew the dark underbelly of their race had simply been buried, not erased.

Confirmed, Silver said after a short delay. *Pure Psy has taken responsibility for the poisoning, and the claim was public.* She sent him a visual, her telepathy strong enough that it was crisp, clear.

The side of the building owned by the think tank had been emblazoned with the image of a star with the letter *P* at the center. The *P* was white, the area around it black. Below were the words *Absolution in Purity, JOIN US.*

Absolution in Purity
JOIN US

This is new, he said to Silver.

Yes. It's the first appearance of this decal.

A decal. That explained how the Pure Psy operatives had been able to put it up so fast. He wondered if the religious undertone was intentional. Vasquez, the faceless man at the head of Pure Psy since Councilor Henry

Scott's demise, might be a fanatic, but he was a smart fanatic, as evidenced by the fact that no one had been able to dig up any verifiable details about his physical appearance. Now, even as he decried those whose Silence was fractured, who believed emotion was not the enemy of the Psy race, he used an emotive call to arms.

Clever.

Or psychotic.

Why hasn't this news hit the Net? Kaleb might have been distracted over the past few hours, but his mind continued to scan the pathways of the Net, and he'd heard nothing of what was a significant act of aggression.

Bad timing, answered Silver's mental voice. *Pure Psy operatives must've finished putting up the decal seconds before an Enforcement vehicle cruised down the street and spotted it. The officers became suspicious, checked the building, and discovered the bodies.*

As a result, the external processing is being completed while the city sleeps, the decal removed. The only reason I have the data is because of a cousin high in Enforcement Command in the country—they've managed to black out the incident as far as the media are concerned.

The failure to gain Netwide exposure would only incite Pure Psy to further acts of lethal violence. *Is your contact any closer to infiltrating the inner circle?* While Pure Psy was doing an excellent job of creating the instability he needed for his current endgame, the group was a rogue element. Kaleb preferred iron control in all things.

No. Vasquez is very, very careful.

Continue to monitor the situation in Khartoum. Keep me updated.

Yes, sir.

Hearing a tiny sound at his back as he closed the telepathic link, he walked to the railing instead of turning, his eyes on the impenetrable depths of the gorge.

The lights went off a second later, leaving the terrace lit only by the stars, the moon at full dark tonight.

Bare feet padding on the wood of the terrace, a whisper of scent, clean and fresh, a flutter of green as she came to stand beside him— though she left a good three meters of distance between them. Dressed in a green T-shirt and soft gray pajama pants, she'd clearly washed her hair, but it hung tangled and knotted around her face, hiding her profile from him as she closed her fingers around the bars, squeezing the cold of the metal so hard her skin turned ghostly white.

"It's only a prison," he said, "so long as you aren't in control of your mind." If he dropped the shields in which he'd encased her, she became vulnerable to even the weakest of their brethren, her mind shorn of its protective coating. "Rebuild your shields and I'll set you free."

It was a lie.

He would never let her go.

Chapter 3

IT WAS DIFFERENT here, the harsh, cutting light that had hurt her eyes until her head throbbed nowhere in evidence. Everything was soft and unobtrusive. No, not everything. Not the man who had brought her to this place. He was hard.

Like black ice.

He spoke to her in a voice that made her skin prickle, said words that sometimes made sense and sometimes became lost by the time they reached her through the twisted labyrinth of her mind. She'd created that labyrinth, she knew that. What she didn't know was why. Why would she sabotage her own mind? Why would she consciously hobble her own abilities?

The labyrinth was why they'd kept her in that white room for so long she couldn't remember the beginning anymore, couldn't think of the last time she'd truly been able to *sleep*. The glare had beaten down on her like a vicious hammer, even if she curled up into a ball and hid her face in her arms. Her jailers had promised to turn off the lights if she would unravel the labyrinth and be useful again, *do* things for them.

Mind clearing for a fraction of a minute as the labyrinth reset, she realized she should've been executed when it became obvious she had no intention of cooperating. That she'd been permitted to live told her that whatever it was she could do, it was important and powerful enough to keep her safe, if only half-alive, trapped, and chained. Her last attempt—

The labyrinth twisted, changing shape as it did a thousand times a day, and her thoughts warped out of all comprehension, shredding the gossamer weave of reason and memory. Fingers tightening on the iron bars of the railing that kept her from falling into the black abyss on the other side, she breathed through the change, blinking away the spots of light from in front of her eyes. But the spots didn't fade, and it was with a sense of dawning wonder that she realized those dots were the stars in the night sky.

They glittered and shimmered until she reached out a hand, wanting to touch. But they were too far away . . . and in her hand, she held a book. Startled, she almost dropped the unexpected item, but the cushion of solid air around her hand told her the man of black ice wouldn't have allowed the book to plummet into the abyss.

She couldn't read the words on the cover in the dark, didn't know if she could read words at all. But drawing the slender volume back through the bars, she held it against her chest as if it were a treasure, and when she was certain he wasn't watching her, she chanced a look at the man.

He wasn't like the guards in the white place full of painful light that had been her prison. They'd hurt her, but this man, he could slit her throat and not blink. She knew that with the same part of her brain that had birthed the labyrinth, the part driven by the relentless will to survive. It cared nothing for the quality of her life, only that she remain alive. That brutal pragmatism was why she'd lived long enough to be here under the stars beside a man who possessed eyes of the same starlight, icy white on a background of black silk.

Cardinal, whispered a hidden pocket of memory, *his eyes are those of a cardinal.*

She k—

The labyrinth twisted again, wrenching the thought out of shape and turning her mind into a kaleidoscope; a million vivid images splintered and spun until nothing made sense and beauty was a creation of shattered glass. At times, she gave in to her fascination for the kaleidoscope for untold hours, allowing it to take her away into an inner world where the acute white light didn't hurt and her mind wasn't a crab without a shell, soft and vulnerable and exposed. So horribly exposed. It *hurt.*

But . . . she had a shell now.

Frowning, she poked a psychic finger at the adamantine black shield around her mind. No give. None. Intrigued, she stroked her fingers along the inner surface and found that it "tasted" of black ice. Of him. The dangerous, beautiful man with the hard voice who'd stolen her from the place where they wouldn't let her sleep, where they demanded she do things that would bleed away her very being.

The same man who had put her in a place with bars.

It was the last coherent thought she had before the labyrinth reset once more, tearing words and sentences into confetti that dazzled her senses and blanked out the reality around her.

KALEB watched his guest leave the terrace two hours after she'd arrived. Except for when she'd reached out into the night and he'd taken the risk of giving her the book, she'd stood motionless, her eyes lifted to the stars. It could be that part of her remembered the starlit night that was the PsyNet, as visualized by the vast majority of the populace, each Psy mind a spark in the darkness, or perhaps she'd been hypnotized by the openness of the sky after having spent so many years in a cage.

The sound of metal straining.

Twisting, he saw one of the heavy iron bars had bent almost in half. He fixed it with a glancing thought before walking into his bedroom via the sliding doors that opened directly onto the left side of the terrace. His room was located across from hers, meaning he'd be able to keep an ear open for her even in sleep.

It took only a few minutes to shower off the sweat.

Lying down in bed after drying off, the sheets crisp against his naked skin, he set his mind for exactly five hours of sleep. He could survive for long periods on less, but five hours was the optimal amount of rest he needed to recharge his physical and psychic batteries. The entire house was already locked and alarmed, but, setting a psychic alarm that would go off the instant she made any noise, he went to sleep.

He dreamed.

Dreams denoted a sublevel failure in his conditioning, but Kaleb had long ago learned to compensate for those failures, though he couldn't control his subconscious. However, the dreams were no longer as all-encompassing as they'd been in his teens—then, he'd often woken so stressed it had taken him at least an hour to regain his concentration. As an adult, he woke alert and with full memory of every aspect of the nighttime visions conjured by his subconscious.

Psy-Med would draw some interesting conclusions from his dreams, he thought the next morning as he dressed in work-ready suit pants of black along with a white shirt, leaving the collar open for the time being; but as none of their number would ever be invited inside his mind, that was a moot point.

The door across from his own was closed when he exited the bedroom, and he didn't disturb his guest's rest—he had all the patience in the world now that he had her under his roof. Entering the kitchen, he came to an abrupt halt. She was curled up in a chair in the sun-drenched breakfast "nook" he'd embedded into the design during the custom build by several human corporations—though he'd never planned on using it.

The humans had seen nothing wrong with features that would've alerted a Psy architect to the fact that something was not quite right with the house, not when it was meant for Kaleb Krychek, considered one of the most Silent individuals in the Net. As it was, the humans had done a stellar job, and with each firm privy to only a strictly limited slice of the construction process, with Kaleb himself having put in the final security features, they had no knowledge of the advanced systems that protected it.

As his guest had no knowledge of the psychic alarm he'd set—yet it hadn't activated, in spite of the fact she'd left her room. He checked the alarm, found he'd made a basic miscalculation. Because he was the source of her shields, and though his mind was separated from hers by an impenetrable firewall, his consciousness considered her a part of him. Resetting the parameters so the mistake wouldn't be repeated, he walked to the counter and, after 'porting in breakfast pastries from the kitchen of a highly successful hotel he owned, prepared a cup of hot chocolate.

He had never tasted the sweet liquid himself, but he'd done his research on sensations and tastes that were considered to offer "comfort" in the emotional races. Given the current state of mind and physical health of the woman who sat in the sunshine, such items might be effective in breaching the wall of her distrust.

Walking over to place the mug in front of her, he asked, "Are you hungry?"

Dark blue eyes peered at him from behind the tangled but clean strands of her hair, and he had the disconcerting sensation she was looking right through his shields. Not that it mattered—she already knew his darkest secret, had tasted the iron rich scent of it as she screamed.

Breaking the eye contact with a sudden shift of her head, she bent closer to the hot chocolate. As she examined it, he mixed up the nutrient drink he preferred as breakfast, and mentally went over his schedule for the day. Whether he took the upcoming comm meeting here or at his central Moscow office made no difference to the eventual outcome—Kaleb would come out on top. He always did.

Failure was not an option.

Right then, the woman for whom he'd searched for seven years slid out of her chair to walk toward him. When she stopped a meter away, he stepped back, saying nothing as she reached for the food he'd teleported in, the remote 'port a simple matter: that particular hotel kitchen was run by a chef who liked everything exactly in its place, including the baskets of fresh pastries individually wrapped in distinctive paper sleeves. Kaleb's image file of the kitchen gave him a location lock, the paper sleeves a detail lock within that specific location. Now, he watched as his guest chose a warm apricot Danish, put it neatly on a saucer, and took it back to her seat.

He'd expected her to eat the pastry, but she returned to the counter, picked up another Danish—blackberry—put it on a second saucer, and took it back to the table. It wasn't until she placed it on the other side of the table and pushed the hot chocolate to the middle that he realized he was being invited to breakfast.

Lenik, he said, waiting only long enough for Silver's subordinate to open the telepathic pathway before saying, *reschedule my meeting with Imkorp.*

Sir. They're already unsteady about the agreement.

They'll wait. Kaleb held the power in the negotiation, a fact of which he'd be happy to remind the Imkorp CEO should he have forgotten.

I'll contact them immediately.

That done, Kaleb poured himself a glass of water and took it to the table. "Thank you," he said, pushing the mug back to her, "but that's for you."

She continued to examine him, a sudden, incisive intelligence in the deep, deep blue of her irises that had his instincts on full alert. "Who are you?" The words were a rasp, as if she hadn't used her vocal cords for months . . . or years.

"Kaleb Krychek."

A pause. "Kaleb Krychek." Bending her head after repeating his name in the same flat tone he'd given it, she picked up her Danish and bit in. When she stared at him, he echoed the action.

The taste was a violent insult to taste buds accustomed to flavorless nutrition bars and drinks designed to deliver the necessary calories and minerals, with the occasional bland meal thrown in to balance his diet, but he swallowed the bite he'd taken of the pastry, drinking some water to wash it down. Seemingly satisfied with that, the small woman on the other side of the table continued to eat her own Danish in neat, precise bites until the entire thing was gone.

Good. She's eating.

She'd always had a slender and graceful body, as befit the dancer she'd been, but she no longer carried the supple muscle that screamed health regardless of low body weight. Her frame was now fragile, her shoulder bones protruding through the green T-shirt she continued to wear, her cheeks sunken. When he teleported the remainder of the tray onto the table, she stared at it with considering eyes before choosing a banana muffin.

Taking a butter knife from the tray, she cut the muffin in two and put half on his plate. "Thank you," he said again and took a bite of the soft, too-sweet item to pacify her.

She ate her half of the muffin and drank most of her hot chocolate before speaking again. "Kaleb Krychek. That's a long name."

"You can call me Kaleb," he said, and they were words he'd spoken to her before, when she hadn't understood what he was, why she should run from him.

"I have your shell, Kaleb."

He processed her words, could make no sense of them. "Do you?"

"It's black and hard."

"You're talking about the mental shield I've put over you." He finished his water. "It was necessary. Your mind was exposed." Naked, vulnerable—a fact unacceptable to him on every level. "The obsidian shield conceals all trace of you from the Net."

Open concern on her face, she whispered, "Are you exposed now?"

Her empathy didn't surprise him; it was what had led to her torture. "No," he said, "I have the capacity to maintain dual shields without problem." He was the most powerful Psy in the Net, of that he had no doubt, his psychic strength enough to destroy the very fabric of their race—or to control it. As to which he chose to do . . . it depended on her.

If she demanded vengeance, he'd turn the world bloodred.

She reached for his abandoned muffin, cut off a piece, and ate it. "Can you see me?"

"Your thoughts are your own." He hadn't invaded her mind past that instant of contact required for the teleport.

Piercing intelligence again. "Does sharing your shell mean I can see your secrets?"

"No. You don't want to see inside my mind." It was a warning. "The rumor in the Net is that I can drive people insane."

No terror, no fear, just unwavering attention that said she heard far more than he said. "Can you?"

"Yes." He wanted to ask her what she saw when she looked at him, whether the nightmare was apparent to those midnight eyes. "Until they see phantoms and hear terrible voices, until they can no longer exist in the rational world and become broken facsimiles of who they once were."

"Why?"

"Because I can."

Chapter 4

SHE HEARD HIS answer, this man as unreadable as a cobra about to strike, his voice raising every tiny hair on her body, but she knew he wasn't telling her all of it. The reason for her certainty, and for the inexplicable violence of emotion that drove her to strip away his icy facade, was not anything she could articulate. One fact, however, was suddenly crystalline in its clarity in this instant when she could think, could reason—she needed her abilities against the cold strength of him.

There was no other way she'd survive.

Unlike those who had kept her in a cage while they attempted to break her, the cardinal across from her wouldn't be forced to a halt by the labyrinth. He'd dig, go deeper, drag her out of hiding with vicious determination. He would be ruthless in his pursuit, brutal in his purpose. Nothing and no one would stop him—least of all a Psy who had hobbled her greatest strength.

Drinking the rich, sweet liquid he'd given her in a gesture of care she knew had to be calculated to earn her trust, she—

The labyrinth twisted.

However, this time, she twisted with it, unwilling to lose her train of thought. The food in her belly, the warmth of the chocolate in her throat, the fresh bite of scent that was Kaleb's newly showered body . . . different from the clean, masculine sweat she'd smelled the previous night as his skin gleamed in the moonlight . . . it all served to convince her that this wasn't a hallucination.

Kaleb could never be a hallucination—he gave off a sense of power that was a near-gravitational force, a silent reminder of the strength that lived in his veins, a strength that had taken her from her prison to this house that might be another prison, in the blink of an eye. No, she couldn't survive him in her current condition, her psyche in pieces, her ability barricaded behind a tangled maze so intricate, none of her captors had ever come close to navigating it.

"I created a key to unlock the labyrinth," she murmured.

He went utterly, absolutely still, a sculpture carved in clean lines. "Where?"

"Inside my mind." She spoke more to herself than to him as the labyrinth continued to alter shape, but in a way that no longer shredded her thoughts . . . as it hadn't truly done since she woke from the first true hours of sleep she'd had for an eon. Her thoughts had been lucid for over an hour, her sense of self, of memory, becoming ever more coherent.

And she understood what she'd done.

There was no manual way to unlock her mind and reverse the creation of the labyrinth. Not even she could undo the intricate tapestry of the psychic trap on command. Torture, bribes, mental force—they had only served to strengthen the twisted forest that protected her. Her captors could've beaten her to death, could've burned her alive, and it would've gained them nothing.

The *only* way to reverse the ruinous effects of her own creation was for her to be put into an environment her subconscious recognized as "safe."

It was impossible that this situation fit those parameters—the male with hair of jet-black who smelled of ice and pine in a way that made her want to rub her face against his skin, and whose eyes never moved off her, was clearly not safe in any way, shape, or form. He was a predator: he'd told her of his ability to cause madness, displaying his utter lack of remorse in committing such a heinous act. More, his motives in appropriating her from her former prison were worse than opaque.

Yet the labyrinth continued to unstitch itself, her mind brushing off cobweb after cobweb as she came out of her long hibernation, splintered memories merging into a moth-eaten stream. So when Kaleb's eyes went pitch-black without warning, she had the knowledge to understand he had to be using a great deal of power . . . and since he *was* a power, that meant something very, very bad was about to happen or had already done so. "Kaleb."

THE psychic surge impacted Kaleb's mind with the force of a slamming blow.

The velocity of the wave made it deadly clear the damage that had produced it was catastrophic. Locking down the house with a single telekinetic command, he shot out into the PsyNet to see hundreds of thousands of minds flickering in a way that denoted stunned shock at the sudden insult.

It was the one vulnerability of the Psy, their need for the biofeedback provided by the psychic network that connected their race. That connection meant Psy could go anywhere in the world on the psychic plane, could share data with an ease the other races couldn't imagine. It also meant they couldn't escape the devastating aftershocks of a fatal event that had happened on another continent—in a city called Perth, Australia.

A city he'd now reached.

The black fabric of the PsyNet, the minds within it flashing red in panic as their conditioning shattered with the onset of agonizing pain, was crumpling inward here, in a pattern he'd witnessed only once before. Hundreds had died then—men, women, children—but Cape Dorset's population was minuscule in comparison to Perth's.

Throwing out a protective telepathic shield the instant he was close enough, he halted the collapse. And knew that thousands were already dead, their minds severed from the Net at implosion in a brutal punch of pain that would've ended the lives of children at once. The adults would've lived a few seconds longer, the toughest lasting perhaps a minute.

The anchor network in Perth has been compromised, he communicated to the leader of the Arrows, covert operatives who were the most highly trained and dangerous in the world. *Initiate secondary backup.* That backup system, put quietly in place after Pure Psy began to target the anchors, the linchpins who kept the Net from collapsing, was still a work in progress.

Initiated, Aden replied within a split second. *I'll assist with the shield.*

Unnecessary. Kaleb could seal up the breach on his own. *Find out how this was done.* The telekinetic behind the earlier murders was dead, gutted by a changeling during another attempted killing. Every other anchor in the world had been notified, and the majority were now in hiding, their locations known to only a select few in each region.

There are reports of fires in several parts of Perth, Aden said after a short pause. *Vasic and I are teleporting to the affected area.*

Suturing the bleeding gash in the psychic fabric of the Net with measured efficiency, Kaleb spoke to the minds whose lives hung by a thread he held in his grasp. *This is Councilor Kaleb Krychek,* he said, using his now-defunct title because it would foster calm. *I am in the process of stabilizing this region. You are safe.*

Simple. Matter-of-fact. Effective.

None of these people would ever forget who it was that had come to their aid when their world turned to hell.

ADEN looked across the road at the pile of burned timbers belching black smoke in the noon sunshine, the beams glowing dark red from the fire that continued to lick at the remains of what must've been a small cottage. One of his people in the region had just confirmed the cottage had been home to an anchor, regardless of the fact that it was in a suburban area when the majority of anchors were known to prefer solitude.

It had been thought the locality would provide better camouflage.

Eyes on the destruction that bore silent testament to the failure of the strategy, he said, "What did you use to facilitate the teleport?" to the man who'd brought him to the location.

Vasic nodded at the gathering of neighbors in the distance, many with sleek camera-enabled phones in their hands. "One of them is live-broadcasting and panned the area. I saw this building."

"It was a good choice." The whitewashed wooden church where they stood sat across the road from the burning house. It provided both privacy and an excellent vantage point. "This appears to have been a brute attack." No finesse, nothing but the intent to take a life on which hinged the lives of thousands of others.

"Accelerant and a Molotov cocktail to set it off, if I'm reading the signs right."

"Cheap and effective." Aden considered the mechanics of the attack. "It's the accelerant that's the issue—how did they get enough of it on the house to trap the target inside?" Glimpsing a small sign on the mailbox of one of the neighboring homes, he had his answer. "Gas. They tampered with the gas lines, somehow initiated a leak—gas also explains the localized explosion reported by neighbors. Victim could've already been dead by the time the fire started."

"Doable . . . especially if Pure Psy had a believer in the utility company." Vasic's cool gaze took in the fire crew's attempts to contain the ravenous flames, and suddenly the retardant was doing a much more effective job.

"Don't waste your power," Aden said, aware his partner had used his kinetic energy to fight the energy of the fire. "All of the nearby homes have been evacuated and we need to check out the other sites."

Vasic glanced at the computronic gauntlet that had become part of his arm, fusing into his very cells in an experimental process to test biocompatible hardware. There were significant risks in the procedure, and Aden had advised Vasic against it, but the other male had made the decision that if someone in the squad needed to test it, it should be him.

Vasic wasn't too concerned about his future life span.

"I have image locks for all of them," he said now.

"Go."

Each site proved identical to the first—a flaming and collapsed building. In two cases, the fire had consumed a number of neighboring houses, the inferno spreading before the crews could reach the scene, though their response times proved to have been impeccable in spite of the sheer number of simultaneous targets. The likelihood of gas and the violence of the fires also meant there was no chance of survivors—little chance of even finding a body still in one piece inside.

Outside was another story. A man identified as a worker with a gas utility had been discovered in the cul-de-sac in front of one of the sites, his body flung violently outward by the force of the blast when the house exploded. "He didn't clear the scene fast enough," Aden said. "Or he made a mistake."

"He was only a pawn."

"Yes."

As Vasic again used his telekinetic abilities to subtly assist the fire-fighters at the most dangerous location—the fire only a street away from a hospice, the patients too unwell to be evacuated—Aden made his report to the former Councilor who had almost completely sealed the tear in the Net using a vast telepathic ability that marked him as an impossible dual cardinal.

The region has suffered a significant information leak, he said. *The locations of at least half of the anchors and their failsafe networks were fatally compromised.* Pure Psy couldn't have reached this many people at one time without a specific road map. *No chance of survivors.*

Track down the individual responsible and make an example of him or her.

Aden and the Arrows had aligned themselves with Krychek, but it was understood that they would not blindly follow his orders. The members of the squad had learned their lesson after their experience at the hands of Ming LeBon, understood that loyalty was a coin easily spent outside their own. It was only because of Kaleb's track record of never turning on those who had offered him their loyalty that they had chosen to work with him. Trust was a different matter.

This particular order, however, didn't require much thought. *I'm already working on it.* Aden had no ethical problem with assassinating the traitor in a bloody, public way that would make the consequences of betrayal clear, not when one of the murdered anchors proved to have lived a hundred meters from a nursery school used by Psy parents. All of those children had been connected to the PsyNet in the region that had imploded. All of those children were dead.

PSYNET BEACON: BREAKING NEWS

PsyNet collapse in Perth, Australia, caused by attack on local anchor network. Pure Psy claims responsibility. Eight thousand confirmed fatalities and rising. Councilor Kaleb Krychek able to seal the breach, allowing anchors from nearby regions to buttress the weakened section.

> DO NOT VENTURE INTO COLLAPSE ZONE. REPEAT. DO NOT VENTURE
> INTO COLLAPSE ZONE. ANCHOR NETWORK IS STRETCHED THIN AND
> CANNOT SUPPORT ADDITIONAL MINDS.

*This feed will continue to be updated as further news becomes available.**

PSYNET BEACON: CURRENT EDITION
LETTERS TO THE EDITOR

I write in regard to your correspondent's recent extended essay in relation to the violence in California. I have been a supporter of Pure Psy since it was first formed. I believe Silence is the reason for the survival of our race and that without it, we would've long sunk into murderous depravity.

However, I now find myself conflicted. I agree with your correspondent's argument that violence such as that mounted by Pure Psy against the changelings runs counter to the aim of Purity espoused by the group and is in direct violation of the founding tenets of Silence.

It has left me in a position where I do not know if I am any longer a supporter of Pure Psy. I remain very much a proponent of the truth that Silence is the reason for the survival of our race.

Yours sincerely,
Name withheld by request
(Prague)

Your correspondent's reporting was extremely biased in pitching the battle as being against the changelings.

The truth, as every intelligent mind in the Net realizes, is that the violence was unfortunately mandated by the coterie of defectors in the region who act as agitators in attracting and encouraging others to break conditioning. This cannot be permitted to continue, and I, for one, am in full support of Pure Psy's actions in this regard.

E. Miller
(Mexico City)

I would like to congratulate you on your continuing unflinching and critical coverage of recent events. Pure Psy's intimidation tactics are now a matter of public record, and it is to your correspondent's credit that he did not give in to such threats—threats that, as he says, strike at the very heart of the protocol Pure Psy says it seeks to uphold.

C. Prasad
(Nairobi)

Chapter 5

KALEB'S THOUGHTS TOOK an instant to normalize when he returned to his body. It was a predictable result of the amount of power he'd expended to seal the breach while continuing to function on a basic level in Moscow—to the point where he was never vulnerable to a physical or psychic attack.

Blinking to clear dry eyes, he reached for the glass of water beside his hand, the glass positioned beside several nutrition bars. None of it had been on the table when he entered the Net. "Thank you," he said and began to methodically eat his way through the tasteless items of food, his energy levels already nearly back to peak efficiency. Most Psy couldn't recover as quickly, but Kaleb had long been aware that he wasn't "normal" in any way, his DNA holding a thousand secrets.

Finishing the third nutrition bar, he looked across at the woman for whom he might yet cause a massacre that'd make today look like the merest incident. And saw that she'd changed in a fundamental way—her back was no longer bent, her head no longer ducked. Rather, she sat straight up, her hair tucked behind her ears, the dark blue of her eyes focused on him with a vivid intelligence that had always tested his own.

If he hadn't had such granite control over his body and mind, his heartbeat might've accelerated, his breathing might have turned ragged. *She was coming back.* "The labyrinth," he said through the primal scream inside him, "you've navigated it?"

"There was no need. It has dissolved."

Her response was unexpected—the mind he'd glimpsed during teleport had been so chaotic a mess that it seemed impossible the strands had untangled themselves. "Have you regained your memories and abilities?" *Do you remember?*

"My abilities, yes. The entirety of my memories, no." She folded her arms on the table and he saw again how thin they were, how fragile her body.

Rising, he mixed up a nutrient drink flavored with her favorite, cherry. She accepted it and took a sip. Eyes widening, she took another. "Cherry." A sigh heavy with pleasure. "Thank you."

He gave a curt nod before retaking his seat.

"The duration of the labyrinth," she said, her voice still husky from disuse, "may have caused permanent damage to my memory centers. I was very young when I created it, not yet fully trained, and the construction was rough."

Sixteen. That's how old she'd been when she had disappeared. "What is your name?" he asked, every cell in his body motionless as he waited for her answer, waited to see how much of her had come back.

Midnight blue caught his own, his image reflected in the opaque depths. "Sahara Kyriakus, of the PsyClan NightStar."

SAHARA'S revelation incited no visible change in Kaleb's expression, not even the flicker of an eyelash. His Silence, she thought, taking another sip of the cherry-flavored drink he'd given her, must be pristine. Wholly unlike her own. Yet her responses . . . she knew they weren't quite right, weren't quite rational, given her precarious situation.

I am, she realized within her strange calm, *not yet truly awake.*

"What do you know about NightStar?" the dangerous man across from her asked in that chill-as-frost voice that resonated inside her in a way she couldn't understand—as if she heard things in it he didn't say, knew him in ways that were impossible. Even in her current state, she recognized that a man like Kaleb Krychek would trust no one with his secrets.

And if someone had the misfortune to discover them?

That person would not live long enough to share the discovery. With his black hair, cardinal eyes, and honed physique, Kaleb might be almost shockingly handsome, but the beauty was nothing but a mask for the deadly mind within. The knowledge should've made her afraid, but she found herself fighting the strangest compulsion to cry, her eyes burning as the eerie calm threatened to splinter.

"NightStar is an F-Psy clan," she said, her voice rough from the effort it took to hold those unfathomable tears at bay—for a stranger who might well end her life when he realized she had no intention of cooperating with him any more than she had with her previous captors. "But I do not carry the PsyClan's name as my last, as I am not a foreseer, do not see what will be."

"No." The black silk of Kaleb's hair glinted in the morning sunlight, and she had the disorienting sense that she'd been here in this moment before, sitting across from this man while the sun played over his hair. "You see the past."

Fighting her way through the sticky threads of a web seductive in its insistence she trust Kaleb, she fell back on facts burned into her long-term memory. "Sahara Kyriakus, Clan NightStar, custodial parent Leon Kyriakus—Gradient 7.7 M-Psy with recessive F genes.

"Biological mother Daniela García, Gradient 8.2 telepath, part of a small but highly regarded family group based out of Cuba." Her skin tone, she thought as her eyes fell on her arm, came as a result of the mix of maternal and paternal DNA, would turn a deep golden brown with further exposure to the sun.

"Daniela García also possesses markers for recessive F abilities, the latter the reason she was considered a good genetic match for my father." Foreseers ran in the NightStar family tree, and the clan did everything it could to maintain that lucrative line. "While I am not a foreseer, I am placed in the same designation, subdesignation B."

Considered a rare offshoot of the F ability, backsight, her mind recited, bore enough similarities to the kind of telepathy utilized by Justice Psy that there was continuing debate within academic circles as to its proper placement. The most significant difference between the two designations was that unlike the J-Psy, those in subdesignation B did not go into a living mind and retrieve a particular memory.

Rather, they could be hit by flashes about the past without warning, independent of their physical proximity to the locations or individuals involved—though, like their F brethren, a B could "prime" her mind to seek knowledge about a particular past event. And similarly to a J, they could project the entire piece of backsight to another mind. As a result, one of their uses was that at times, they could act as witnesses to events that left no survivors. Subdesignation B had also been consulted in situations where critical data had been lost due to a sudden injury or accident.

"Testing," she added as the facts continued to scroll in her mind, "puts me at 8.1 on the Gradient."

Kaleb nudged her forgotten glass and waited until she'd drunk half of the cherry-flavored supplement before saying, "Those were your stats at sixteen, but you hadn't plateaued and been assigned your permanent position on the Gradient. I'd guess you're now between 9.5 and 9.7."

"Is that why you want me?" she asked, the tears inside her forming into an aching knot. "For my backsight?"

The clean line of his jaw caught her eye as he spoke, her fingers spreading on the table. "I have no use or need of a B."

His words gave her pause, her mind on the dangerous shadow ability that existed below her backsight and, unbeknownst to those who had tested her, was the true reason for her position on the Gradient. Her backsight was, at most, only a 3 on the scale used to measure psychic ability. However, the error didn't speak to the skills of the testing staff but to the stealthy nature of what existed inside her—to the extent that she herself hadn't become aware of it until she was twelve. And then, she'd learned to hide it, because it made her a target.

"If you don't need my backsight," she said to Kaleb, "then why am I here?" Regardless of her question, she was dead certain he knew what she could do—there could be no other reason he'd gone to such lengths to find and capture her.

The black depths of his eyes devoid of stars once more, an endless night that threatened to suck her under, he rose to his feet and, placing his hands on the table, leaned toward her until she could've reached out and run her fingers along his freshly shaven jaw. "You are here," he said in a tone that made her heart thump wildly against her ribs, "because you belong to me."

TEN minutes later, Sahara sat on the edge of the bed that was her own, Kaleb's words gleaming against the wall of her mind. They made as little sense now as they had when he'd spoken them. One thing, however, was patent.

She was not free to leave this house. Neither was she free to enter the PsyNet.

Considering those facts in the abnormal calm that insulated her from her perilous situation, she decided she didn't want to do either at present. The instant she slipped outside the obsidian of Kaleb's mental protection, she exposed her naked, vulnerable mind. Further, she had no idea of where she'd go, what she'd do upon escaping him. As proven by the hazy distance between her and her emotions—until it felt as if she were looking out at the world through a wall of water—her mind remained bruised, her thinking processes flawed.

NightStar.

An option for sanctuary, except, with her fragmented memory centers, she had no way of knowing if her clan hadn't in fact worked hand in glove with her captors to harness her ability to their own ends, giving her up to soul-destroying loneliness. The guards in her prison hadn't seen her as an individual, hadn't even seen her as a sentient being. She'd simply been a task, nameless and without identity.

Had one shown her even the smallest kindness, would the labyrinth have begun to unravel? Sahara would never know, because the instant the individual in charge of her incarceration had discovered the labyrinth— too late to halt the process—her normal guards, who occasionally spoke to her, had been replaced by men and women so icily Silent it had never occurred to them to deviate from their assigned duties . . . whether those duties were to force-feed her or to strip her to the skin while lowering the room temperature to freezing.

Kaleb, in contrast, had thus far done nothing to cause her harm. He'd given her *privacy*, free access to clean clothing and a shower, as well as food that made her taste buds sing and her parched soul shudder. Neither had he commented on or challenged her broken Silence. It would be stupid and premature to leave his protection until she was in a better mental state, able to judge friend from foe.

As for Kaleb himself . . . the responses he aroused in her were raw, disturbing, painful. Even now, the knot of tears lay rigid against her breastbone, as if simply waiting for her to surrender to an emotion that was wholly without reason. To cry for Kaleb, she would have to know him, and he was a stranger . . . who knew she adored cherry-flavored drinks and that she felt the cold more acutely than most people. It hadn't escaped her notice that the entire sprawl of the house was now at a temperature she found most comfortable.

Taking a deep breath in an effort to fight the compulsion to go to him, to demand answers to questions she couldn't articulate, she picked up the book he'd given her the previous night and decided to walk to the terrace. The sunshine, the cool autumn wind, she craved it against her skin . . . as she craved contact with another living being, her body starved for far more than food.

Her thoughts scattered when she caught the fleeting reflection of a woman with a tangled dark mane. Blinking, she stared at the window, but it wasn't the best mirror and only served to frustrate. Since her room had no mirrors—a vague memory of shattered glass, shards slicing a fine, bright line across her cheek—she walked back down the corridor and entered the room across from her own.

The clean, fresh scent of soap and aftershave that held a hint of pine.

Since Kaleb had left the door open, she decided it wasn't off-limits and continued deeper inside, placing the book on the bed while she explored. Barren of anything but the bed and a small bedside table, the closet built into the wall opposite the sliding doors that led out onto the terrace, the room was military neat, not a single piece of clothing or other ephemera scattered around.

The bathroom was the same, Kaleb's personal grooming gear stored efficiently inside the mirrored cabinet above the granite countertop that housed the sink. Fascinated, she picked up his aftershave, drew in the scent that made her skin ache, then examined the slick black device he used to shave, unable to imagine the ice-edged man who considered her his doing such an intimate act.

Touching her hand to her own jaw, she thought back to when he'd leaned over her in the kitchen. It had taken every ounce of her will not to brush her fingers over the hard angles of his face.

It had been so long.

She shook off the bone-piercing thought, knowing it to be a creation of her damaged mind. A cardinal Tk would have had no reason to be in the circumference of her life as a girl—NightStar was famously insular, and Tks were trained in special schools for reasons of safety. No, she had never touched Kaleb Krychek, regardless of what might be termed the birth of a dangerously obsessive compulsion toward the man who was effectively her jailer.

Putting the shaver back in its spot, her fingers lingering longer than they should have, she closed the cabinet doors . . . and looked at who she'd become. At sixteen, she'd had a little more fat in her cheeks, a softer curve to her jaw. Right now, she was all bone. Her increased calorie intake would ensure a return to a healthier appearance—but not to the extent that she'd carry the baby fat in her cheeks again. The finer line of her face was a natural result of adulthood and she liked it.

Her hair, however . . .

Taking a tangled hunk, she brought it to her nose, caught the scent of citrus and something softer. So, she hadn't imagined taking a shower and scrubbing her hair three times over. Clean though it was, it was also knotted to the point of making her appear a madwoman—

"That was the goal." The labyrinth had been only part of her plan to hide herself from those who would turn her into a trained animal poised to perform on command. "It's not necessary any longer," she whispered and clawed back another piece of herself.

Chapter 6

IT TOOK SERIOUS concentration, her arms aching by the end, but her hair hung straight and thick down her back an hour later, as she made her way through the house again. Peeking inside the large room situated right beside the main doors to the terrace, she saw Kaleb sitting at a desk. In front of him was a transparent—from her point of view—computer screen apparently functioning in comm mode.

Steel—platinum?—cuff links at his wrists and a tie of chrome blue at his throat now, a sharp contrast to his white shirt, he was focused on someone on the other side of the screen, but he curled his fingers to her in a "come in" motion. Drawn toward him on a level that threatened to overpower her ability to reason, until it felt as if they were connected by an invisible thread, she walked in.

His desk was a hunk of highly polished wood, the edges jagged, as if the roots of a forest giant had been cut in slices then smoothed, the flowing lines within telling the story of centuries past. It was beautiful, and not what she might have expected of him . . . but there was something in the primal nature of the choice that suited him. As did the bitterly clean surface of the desk, unmarred by even a single pen or piece of paper.

The walls opposite that desk held shelves that housed a number of expensive hard-copy books on a myriad of subjects, from changeling society to physics to construction manuals and geological research, with a number of separate volumes dealing with earthquakes and volcanoes.

She could understand the eclectic collection compiled by an intelligent mind, could even comprehend the reason a cardinal Tk might be interested in the movement of the tectonic plates—though the idea that he might have that much power made her heart stutter—but here and there on the shelves sat things jarring in their incongruity. Like a polished blue pebble beside the book on South American volcanoes. Lapis lazuli, she identified after rubbing the pebble between her fingertips.

On another shelf sat something as inexplicable: a flat piece of wood carved with his name and the spindly image of a tree. The workmanship was rough, nothing unique about the wood itself. Not far from it, and slipped in between a thick textbook on earthquakes and one on undersea currents, was a tiny volume of poetry. It was so thin, she only saw it by chance, and from the look of the spine, she could tell it was cheaply bound, in ragged condition, unlike the other books on the shelves.

Curious, she took a second look at the shelves and found several more unexpected volumes hidden in plain sight. All were of relatively flimsy construction, and they contained everything from further poetry to plays to a reprint of a nineteenth-century classic written by a human. Then there was a twisted piece of metal that wasn't identifiable as anything in particular, except that her mind kept telling her it had once been part of a bullet train.

Shaking off the odd sense of knowing, she focused once more on the cardinal currently ripping his opponent to shreds with cold-blooded precision, taking in the dark hair cut with brutal neatness, the clean lines of his face, his skin tanned enough that he couldn't spend all his time indoors, those incredible eyes. But in spite of his beauty, he was harshly masculine, his every action marking him as quintessentially and fascinatingly male.

Her breath hitched, her fingers worrying the lapis lazuli pebble she'd never returned to the shelf. Forcing herself to return it, *because* she wanted to steal it, captivated by the feel and shape of it, she attempted not to stare at Kaleb. The majority of her guards had been male—and a number had undoubtedly been chosen because of their looks in an effort to manipulate her youth and splintered Silence. Not once had she forgotten the fact that they were a threat to her very existence.

And yet she saw primal beauty in this merciless, no doubt manipulative, and bitingly intelligent male who clearly lived for power, for control—all things her shadow ability would make it ruthlessly simple for him to acquire. The individual who controlled Sahara Kyriakus could control the PsyNet, and Kaleb Krychek, her ears told her, was the kind of ruthless man who would use every advantage at his disposal when it came to the dance of power.

Disturbed by that realization on an elemental level, an ache in her chest, she walked toward the open glass doors to the right of his desk. It was instinct to stay out of the line of sight of the aggressive-voiced man on the other end of the comm who, it was clear, was about to lose the skirmish. For now, it was better she remain a ghost in the eyes of the world.

The polished wood of the terrace was smooth beneath her feet, the sun a languid caress against her skin. Tilting her face upward, she drank it in, her skin greedy for the kiss of heat, of light.

You'll burn.

Startled by the cool words that had traveled along a telepathic pathway she hadn't been aware she'd opened, she twisted her head to look inside the study. The man who continued to both intrigue and confuse her had his eyes on the comm screen, still involved in a business negotiation that was more akin to a deadly play of razors, each word designed to inflict maximum damage. Sliding the doors shut, she padded to the sun lounger in the far corner, an item that hadn't been there earlier this morning, and sat with her legs stretched out on the cushioned fabric, toes reaching for the sun.

A large outdoor umbrella stood above her a second later, shading her face while leaving her feet exposed. *Stop doing that,* she said along that same telepathic channel, and it didn't feel new, didn't feel awkward. No, it felt as if the pathway was carved into her mind, the groove worn in over countless years. As if she'd known Kaleb longer than she'd known herself. *It's showing off.*

A pause that might've indicated surprise before a small table appeared at her elbow. On it sat a plate of cookies and a long glass filled with what turned out to be mango nectar. Drawn by the cookies, she ate two different kinds and took a sip of the thick, refreshing drink before pointedly ignoring her beautiful captor and opening the book in her lap.

It was a math textbook.

Such physical books, she remembered, were no longer part of the education system, but this one had been well used. Employing black ink, someone had written in concise explanations of the equations and corrected the frustrated mistakes—lines crossed out, rewritten—made by a writer who used blue ink.

It hurt her to touch the black writing, made her throat thicken, so she shut the book.

The texture of the cover, the tear on one corner, the stamp that denoted the book had come from a used-goods dealer, each was so familiar it was like hearing music just far enough away that it was impossible to identify the tune. Touching her fingers to the faded stamp, she imagined what she might see were she a Ps-Psy, born with the ability to sense memories left behind on physical objects.

HANDS in the pockets of his pants, Kaleb stood at the glass doors to the terrace, looking through them to the woman who sat on the lounger, her feet bared to the still-warm sun of early fall and her fingers stroking the cover of the textbook he'd originally found in a junk store that sold dubious "antiques." As evidenced by her tart reply a few minutes ago, there was no fear in her, no sense of panic at being in his control.

He knew that lack was a momentary lull—this woman who spoke to him without concern and who seemed to be shocked or unsettled by nothing was not the real Sahara Kyriakus. No, she was a sleepwalker whose task it was to ready Sahara's body and mind for the true waking.

She wouldn't be calm once that happened, wouldn't look at him with dark blue eyes untainted by fear. Then, she'd either use her ability against him—or she'd run, terror in her every jagged breath. Which was why he'd retrieved the dirty smock she'd thrown in the laundry and vacuum sealed it to preserve her scent. He would never use his mind to leash hers, but he would track her through rain, hail, fire itself. Never again was anyone, even Sahara herself, taking her from him.

!!!

He threw up his strongest shields at the wordless warning from the NetMind and DarkMind both, connecting with the twin neosentience at the same time. *What has occurred?* This wasn't another anchor collapse, not with the roaring force of the shock wave that had just passed—as if it had gathered momentum across the entire breadth of the Net.

Images of crumbling houses, ripped walls, a torn dress fell into his mind, at a speed that told him the twin neosentience that was born of the Net was confused and in pain. Grabbing hold of each image, he separated them, found the common denominator. All of the damage had been caused by rot, fungus, mildew.

Show me.

Entering the psychic network that was as familiar to him as the streets of Moscow, he cloaked himself and shot to the location they'd pinpointed . . . except it was no longer there.

The region was black, but that was the only similarity it had to the rest of the PsyNet. This blackness not only held no stars, it effectively repelled light. Though he was immune to the rot that was crawling through parts of the network that connected millions of Psy around the world, seeping insidiously into the minds of the population, he took care approaching the pulsing emptiness.

Halting at the very edge, he sent an exploratory tendril of psychic energy into the blackness. The nothingness sucked it in, and if Kaleb hadn't already cut the tendril loose, it would've continued sucking until it stole every drop of energy from his mind and body both. Death would've been an excruciatingly painful process.

Can you go there? he asked the NetMind.

A sense of desolation, of terrible pain from the half of the twin neosentience that was recognized by the populace and considered the librarian and guardian of the PsyNet. It only communicated, however, with a very, very short list of people. And it communicated with no one like it did with Kaleb.

His connection with the ancient, yet childlike neosentience, and its twisted, broken twin, had been formed in a chill, isolated childhood composed of physical pain and mental torture that had shaped him into the man he'd become. For a long time, the NetMind and the DarkMind had been his only friends.

He no longer thought of them in that way, hadn't done so since he was a boy of nine or ten. Though chronologically far older than Kaleb, having come into being at the dawn of the PsyNet, they were yet young, children to his adult.

Where the NetMind was an innocent, the DarkMind was akin to an ignored, abused child who sought only to bully and abuse others, knowing no other way in which to interact. In Kaleb, it had found acceptance, a darkness that welcomed the malignant violence and anger at the core of its being.

And you? he asked that dark twin.

It slid sinuously into the blackness, rolling in it like a cat.

Initiate a barricade, he ordered the NetMind as the DarkMind slid back to twine affectionately around him, its touch cold as the death Kaleb had meted out more than once. *Ensure a wide buffer zone. I don't want anyone coming in contact with this.*

Images of building blocks cascaded into his mind and he realized the NetMind was already working on the barricade. *Good*, he said, giving it the praise it needed.

Shifting position once the twin neosentience turned toward its task, the DarkMind choosing to assist the NetMind for reasons of its own, Kaleb located the mind of Subject 8-91. The male was infected with the same disease that had just devoured a chunk of the Net and, thus, was meant to act as Kaleb's control as to the progression of that disease, his "canary in a coal mine."

Some would term that a cruelty, but 8-91 was too far gone to be helped—and he was expendable, his contribution to the world negligible. He was contributing far more, helping his fellow citizens, by acting as a barometer for this disease without a name.

Subject 8-91, however, remained alive, functional, and with no awareness of the disease that had eaten into his frontal cortex. Clearly, the infection advanced at a different rate in an individual than it did in the psychic fabric that connected ninety-nine-point-nine percent of Psy on the planet.

Kaleb's cell phone rang.

He'd been expecting the call. "Nikita," he said, dropping out of the Net to speak to the woman who had been a Councilor before the Council imploded, and who now held power in a region that had become a focal point for those whose Silence was fractured.

"I assume," she said, "you're aware of the shock wave that just rolled through the Net?"

"I've seen the cause. One minute." Hanging up, he stepped out to check on Sahara, saw that she'd fallen asleep, her hair a silken pool of black as she lay curled on her side. It wasn't as vivid and as glossy as it should be, but he saw the promise. Yet she was nowhere near to the Sahara she was meant to be—tiny, her skin too pale, she looked as if she'd disappear any second.

Reaching out, he lifted a single strand of hair, rubbed it between his fingertips. Real, very much so. And safe in the home he'd turned into an impregnable vault.

Resetting the perimeter alarms to remote alert, and changing the angle of the sun umbrella so that she was fully protected, he pulled on his suit jacket, thought of Nikita Duncan's high-rise office in San Francisco, and was there, his mind making the transition with a speed and an accuracy that the dead Councilor Santano Enrique had once considered a tool for his exclusive use.

"No one has any explanations," Nikita said to him the second he appeared, her voice as businesslike as the skirt-suit she wore, the lights of San Francisco bright in the midnight darkness behind her. "Yet you said you've seen the cause."

He saw no reason not to share the truth—it was one that would become apparent soon enough if his theory about what was happening proved correct. "Part of the Net has ceased to exist."

"Another anchor attack?" The blunt edge of Nikita's hair swept over her jaw as she leaned on her desk, hands flat on the glass and almond-shaped eyes steady with an icy intelligence that had led to her position as one of the wealthiest women in the world. "I've heard no reports—"

"No. The Net itself has disintegrated."

Nikita stared at him, barely containing a jerk when the comm panel on the wall chimed an incoming call. "It's Anthony," she said, touching the discreet pad built into her desk to accept the call and bring the other man into their conversation.

Kaleb considered what Anthony Kyriakus would do if he knew that his niece was currently in Kaleb's care. Likely unleash the full force of Night-Star's power in an attempt to retrieve her—Sahara's clan had been searching for her with quiet, relentless persistence since her disappearance. Kaleb knew that because he'd had to take care to skirt their trackers more than once, and because he'd hacked into their files. Had they pinpointed her location before he did, he would've appropriated and used that information without compunction—Sahara belonged to him, no one else.

"The outbreak at Sunshine Station," he said after Nikita had brought Anthony up-to-date. "Do you recall the details?"

"Of course." Anthony's reply was immediate. "One hundred and forty-one lives lost to a sudden psychosis—they attacked one another in brutal, bloody ways."

Nikita picked up the narrative with a flawless ease that told Kaleb the two were in telepathic communication. "The outbreak was deemed to have been an indication of critical problems with the Protocol, as was the incident at the science station in Russia." A pause. "You showed me a 'sick' section of the Net once. It was small, hidden—you're saying the psychosis was caused by this infection? That it's grown big enough to create such a massive disturbance in the Net?"

Kaleb wasn't surprised Nikita had made the connection—mental viruses were her specialty, after all. "Yes." Connected to the psychic network from birth, there was no way for those of his race to avoid the virus—every millisecond of the biofeedback they needed to live carried a potentially lethal payload. "It appears the infection has begun to attack its primary host."

The PsyNet was vast, could take a considerable beating, but it wasn't indestructible. "Tonight's damage," he continued, "caused no fatalities, but only because it was localized in the region that would've supported the minds at Sunshine." And that station was abandoned, an icy monument to death, blood splatter frozen on the walls and meals abandoned half-eaten, no living beings within miles.

"We can't allow the infection to hit a populated zone," Nikita said, cutting to the point as always. "If it has the same impact it did at Sunshine, we'd be looking at a massacre."

A taut silence, and Kaleb knew they were all thinking of a San Francisco or a Moscow overrun with Psy who had given in to murderous insanity. Mindless, their cells factories for the virus, they'd kill anything in their path, hack their fellow citizens to pieces, paint the streets in blood.

Chapter 7

ANTHONY WAS THE one who spoke. "Can the virus be contained?"

"The NetMind is building a barricade to ensure people don't venture into the infected area, but I don't believe it'll hold against the virus itself." Kaleb had a theory about a "cure," but it wasn't one he planned to share with either Nikita or Anthony until he had all the pieces in place for his takeover of the Net.

"You," he said to Nikita, "may have certain useful insights." She'd never confirmed her ability with mental viruses, but everyone in this conversation knew it existed.

To her credit, she gave a curt nod. "I'll do a reconnaissance tonight."

"If it's taken this long to eat up the region of the Net that served Sunshine," Anthony said, the silver at his temples glinting in the light on his desk, "it must be a slow-moving disease."

"Indications are it's grown stronger, but not faster," Kaleb confirmed. "We can't afford not to study it, but the Pure Psy threat is far more immediate."

Nikita shared a glance with Anthony as Kaleb finished speaking, and it was a silent communication that Kaleb knew involved no telepathy. Once again, he wondered exactly how closely the two had begun to work together. Not that it mattered. While Nikita and Anthony were extremely strong, with a massive combined economic and financial reach, they couldn't stop Kaleb. No one could.

Not now.

Two years ago, perhaps. However—and thanks to the leopard and wolf changelings in Nikita's region, though they would never know the role they'd played in his life—his power had matured to its full potential in the interim. The scope of it might have driven another man mad; it was to Kaleb's advantage that he'd had his brush with madness as a child and survived.

Whether or not he was sane was another question.

"If you'll excuse me," he said before Nikita or Anthony could respond to his point about Pure Psy, "I have another matter to attend to." He left without waiting for a response. Ming and Tatiana had contacted him via the PsyNet, and he'd shared the same information he had with Nikita and Anthony. As for the suspiciously quiet Shoshanna Scott, he had an extremely reliable spy in her ranks.

There was no reason to waste any further time on the ex-Councilors.

Sahara was still asleep when he returned to the terrace, her breathing even. He was about to turn on his heel and leave when her eyes fluttered open, the deep blue seeming to look straight through him and to the vicious secrets that marked him as kin to the DarkMind.

"I opened the book," she said, uncurling her legs with the almost feline grace she'd developed as a teen, after taking dance lessons ostensibly to build her muscle strength and sense of balance.

All perfectly satisfactory reasons. All lies. Sahara had simply loved to dance.

"I hate math."

Sliding off his jacket at her sleepy murmur, he 'ported it to his office, then undid his cuffs and began to roll them up, slipping the cuff links into a pocket. It was his left forearm that bore the mark—the scar—and it was a mark he needed her to see now that her mind was no longer confused, as it had been the night before. He had to know if she remembered.

"Math was never your best subject," he said when her eyes lingered on the scar without recognition. "But at last count, you spoke ten languages with a native's fluency. French, Spanish, Hindi, Mandarin Chinese, Swahili, Arabic, and Hungarian, to name a few."

"Do I really?" she asked, a spark in her eye as she shifted on the lounger in silent invitation.

Taking it, he sat on the edge with his back to her and his arms braced on his knees . . . and he remembered the seven years he had waited for her to come back, the countless days he'd stood on this terrace staring down at the gorge as the rational part of his mind tried to convince the obsessive madness that lived in him of her likely death.

The gorge, deep and without end, hadn't existed until the first time he'd imagined her erased from existence. "You're rested?"

"Mmm." Sitting up with that wordless response, she leaned her side against his back, the heat of her branding him through the fine cotton of his shirt.

Kaleb went motionless, touch so rare in his life as to be a nullity.

"My body," she whispered, one hand coming to rest on his shoulder, "it aches, it's so hungry for contact with another living being."

Kaleb forced his muscles to relax one by one. Her trust was critical—and if this was what it took to gain it, he'd handle the sensory overload. "The changelings," he said quietly, "have a concept called skin privileges."

Her fingers brushed his nape, sending a near-painful current over his skin as his body struggled to process the shocking level of input. "How do you know that?" Husky words, her arm sliding around his waist.

No one had held him for . . . an eon. "I," he said, fighting to keep his tone even, "have certain contacts." The fact was, he'd made it a point to discover the inner workings of a changeling pack—information was power and power was control.

Hand flexing against his abdomen, she said, "Skin privileges . . . tell me about them."

"At the most basic level, the term refers to rules that regulate how much contact one changeling can have with another," he said, barely trusting himself to explore the fine bones of her wrist, her skin so soft. "They're a tactile race, but permission to touch is never assumed. It is considered a gift and a privilege." The concept resonated with Kaleb in a way no changeling would ever understand.

Sahara was quiet for several minutes, her breathing the only sound in the universe. "Do you share skin privileges with anyone?" she asked at last, dropping her hand onto his thigh, wrist turned upward, as if inviting him to stroke the vulnerable underside.

Thigh muscles rigid, Kaleb curled his fingers into his palm, flexed them . . . and ran his thumb over the delicate veins he could see through her skin. "I did," he told her, speaking of a past only one other living being knew existed. "A long time ago."

Sahara drew a design on his shoulder blade with her fingertip before smoothing her hand down his back in a caress that sent rocks tumbling into the gorge. "You breached Silence."

He disciplined his Tk at once but didn't release her wrist. "Yes." The cost of his breach had been a slow river of hot red that had soaked the cheap hotel sheets, the smell of scorched flesh scenting the air. It was a memory embedded into every cell of his body, of an event that, when she remembered it, would make Sahara realize exactly who he was beneath the suits and the veneer of civilization.

When the time came, a better man would let her go. But Kaleb wasn't a better man. He'd bring her back again and again. No matter her terror. Until her ability rose to the surface in a raw psychic surge. "You must be hungry." He released her wrist, the cold, hard truth causing the part of him that lived in the darkness to go as adamantine as the shield he'd placed over her. "Are you ready to eat something else?"

"Can I have more of the mango nectar?" Sahara continued to caress his back, and he knew it was an illusionary trust, born of a shattered mind.

Turning slightly after teleporting in the drink she'd requested, he unscrewed the lid and poured the thick liquid into a new glass. "You need solids, too."

Sahara didn't argue when he brought in food, then sat with her while she ate as much as she could stomach. It was a birdlike portion, but aware she'd do better with small meals scattered throughout the day, he didn't make any comment. When she passed him an apple and a knife, he cut it for her, and he ate the piece she gave him.

It was a quiet, unexpected interlude, part of a calm that lasted for the seven days that followed—a week in which Sahara slept often and deeply;

ate nutritional, designed-to-be-appetizing meals that Kaleb made sure were always available; gently exercised her body in stretches he knew she'd learned as a dancer even if she didn't; and talked to him without fear.

He made sure he was home almost the entirety of the time when she was awake, taking care of other business, including meetings with the Arrows, while she slept. It had become clear that the individual behind the Perth leak had had expert help in hiding his trail, but Kaleb had no doubts the Arrows would locate him—or her.

Kaleb had other priorities.

Now and then, Sahara would find him on the terrace and lean her body against his as they spoke. Aware this was a transitory instant that would soon be erased by a past scored in agonizing screams, he made no effort to avoid her. When she didn't press him for more information about herself or the situation, he understood that her subconscious continued to insulate her from reality in order to give her time to heal.

Everything changed on the eighth day.

SAHARA went to bed with the remembered feel of Kaleb's muscled body against her own, as they stood talking under the stars, and woke with a scream stuck in her throat, her heart beating hard enough that it threatened to punch through her sternum. Frightened on the deepest level, she searched frantically for a light, desperate to know what was being done to her.

Her scrabbling fingers somehow hit the touch sensor on the lamp on the bedside table, and soft warmth spilled into the room. A beautiful silk carpet, walls painted a gentle cream, a mirrorless dresser with a hairbrush on the surface, and a large bed covered with a comforter patterned with tiny roses. Not a cell, but she knew in her bones it was still a prison. Even if her captor let her wander the halls as she pleased.

"Kaleb Krychek."

"You belong to me."

"Drink."

A warm wall of muscle under her palm.

Swallowing at the waterfall of memory, she pushed off the sheets and stumbled to the bathroom. Her fingers shook as she threw water on her face and wiped it dry, and she had to grip the edge of the sink for several long minutes to stabilize herself enough that she could think. The calm haze in which she'd existed since Kaleb brought her here had well and truly torn apart, shreds of it fluttering in the nauseating wave of her fear.

How could she have been so serene? Touching Kaleb Krychek as if he were simply a man? He wasn't. Even in her incarceration, she hadn't been totally cut off from news of the outside world—the guards had talked to each other, if not to her, and her mind had catalogued that overheard information in the brief, secret periods of lucidity she'd built into the labyrinth.

Kaleb Krychek, *Councilor* Kaleb Krychek, was a telekinetic so powerful, it was rumored he could sink cities, possibly crack the crust of the planet itself. A male with a mind he'd confirmed could cause true madness in hers if he so chose, one who was whispered to kill with the same ease and lack of concern as another man might draw breath.

On the sink, her bones pushed white against skin that had barely begun to be gilded by the sun after so many years in the dark.

"I heard he was Santano's protégé."

According to the long-term memories she could access at this instant, Santano Enrique was a Councilor, but she knew nothing about him beyond that. Yet the tone of the voices she recalled told her this was an important fact about Kaleb.

Drinking some water, she took a deep breath and tried to figure out her next move.

At least there's hope.

The thought was a glow in her heart. For so long, there hadn't been even a possibility of hope, her mind ripped open with such brutal ugliness that she'd had to curl up within herself to survive. The stripping had been in retaliation for her creation of the labyrinth, but Sahara wasn't sorry. Without the labyrinth, she'd be worse than one of the so-called rehabilitated, her personality erased, her mind that of an automaton who did exactly as her jailers ordered.

The shield.

Breathing in and out at the mental reminder, she opened her psychic eye to the obsidian shield that protected her mind. That *beautiful*, indestructible creation wasn't hers, could never be hers. It belonged to Kaleb. If she attempted to escape him, he might well collapse it in punishment.

Her stomach roiled at the idea of being so naked and helpless once more, panic threatening to seize her senses, but she gritted her teeth, forced herself to *think* the same way she'd done as a scared teenager at the mercy of strangers who wanted only to use her until she was nothing and no one. There might be gaps in her memory, huge chunks lost to the twists of the labyrinth, but some things were hardwired. She knew how to build shields, had done so since childhood.

And Kaleb would never hurt me.

Ignoring the thought that had to be a product of her confusion over his apparent care of her, she began to weave her own shields below his. When he realized she had no intention of giving him what he wanted and withdrew his protection—

He won't hurt me. He'd never hurt me.

Trembling at the thoughts that could well mean she hadn't come out of the labyrinth sane, she decided to shower, in the hope the water would calm her. It did, one thought arrowing through the panic.

I have the tools to escape.

Chapter 8

HER STOMACH REVOLTED violently at the idea of using those tools against Kaleb, but the reminder that she wasn't helpless gave her something to cling to. No longer was she a drugged sixteen-year-old with erratic control over her mind; she was a woman, a survivor. Dressed, she tied back her hair and opened her door, taking care to be quiet. From the way Kaleb never had any trouble locating her, he had to be keeping track of her in some fashion . . . perhaps through a Trojan in her mind.

Bile burning her throat, she scrambled to check her neural pathways for the construct that could give one telepath a back door into another's mind. Nothing obvious jumped out at her, but Kaleb was too powerful not to know how to hide such a leash—and regardless of her subconscious's determination to trust him, he was a man who lived for power. Even as the latter thought crossed her mind, another, more rational part reminded her that no such construct—no matter how subtle—could circumvent the unique natural safeguards born of her ability.

Her mind simply *could not be compromised* by outside forces.

Added to that, if Kaleb had wished to know her thoughts, fragmented though they'd been, he could've easily rifled through them in the days since he'd taken her. The quiet psychic recorders she'd hidden inside her mind long before the labyrinth told her he hadn't. Rather than relief, the realization made her blood chill—because it left only one reason why he wanted her under his control.

And she'd never tested her ability against a man with shields of obsidian.

Her every breath jagged, her heart out of sync, she stepped out of her room to see the door to his own open. Not chancing a look inside in case he was still within, she padded down the hallway to the kitchen, the gentle light coming in through the window telling her the sun had just risen. Once there, she forced herself to eat—she had to rebuild her strength. But her hand shook as she picked up a breakfast bagel so fresh it was still warm, the paper sleeve around it bearing the elegant silhouette of what appeared to be a luxury hotel.

Most telekinetics hoarded their strength for only the most necessary use, but Kaleb . . . that level of power was beyond scary. Except an insane part of her continued to fight her conscious mind, continued to see him as safe and as *off-limits* to the single devastating weapon she had in her arsenal. The irrationality of it frightened her, made her distrustful of her own judgment—how could it be otherwise when it was clear to anyone with a working brain that a man so deep in Silence would only ever "help" another being if it was to his advantage?

The bagel stuck in her throat, but she swallowed it down using the fortified nutrient drink she'd located in the cooler and made a mental note to eat again in an hour, before taking a deep breath and heading toward Kaleb's study.

It was empty.

Palms damp, her gaze went to the computer panel on his desk. The transparent screen was raised up from its resting position flat on the desk, and when she shifted her angle of sight, she could see news reports scrolling across it, so the password had been cleared.

A flicker of movement.

Jerking, she looked through the glass doors to see Kaleb on the terrace. Dressed only in a pair of long black athletic pants, his feet bare, his skin gleamed golden under the sunlight as he went through the elegantly deadly patterns of a martial art she couldn't name but knew instinctively was nothing a civilian should know.

Except, of course, Kaleb was no civilian.

Her fingers curled into her hands as she watched him, the fluidity and grace of his body doing nothing to mask the fact that the beautiful movements could quickly turn lethal. It was hypnotic, the way he moved, the flex and release of his muscles compelling on a visceral level, until she found herself leaning against the French doors, her palms spread on the glass.

The cold was a shock, snapping her back to a reality in which she was a prisoner who appeared to have formed an unhealthy and dangerous attachment to the man who was her new jailer—when she'd survived years in captivity without falling victim to the psychological trap that made prisoners feel sympathetic toward their captors. Yet two days with Kaleb and the labyrinth had unraveled. Not only that, but she'd *cuddled* against that lethally honed body, caressed him with long, slow strokes.

And felt . . . happy.

Throat dry and skin hot, she shot one last look at the male on the terrace before sliding into his chair. Fear crawled up her spine as she brought up the Internet, and she couldn't stop from glancing over her shoulder to check that he remained outside. He did, his hair gleaming blue-black in the soft light of the rising sun.

The search box blinked at her.

Biting down on her lower lip, she entered not Kaleb's name, but that of his apparent mentor, Santano Enrique. Had anyone asked her to explain why she'd done so, she wouldn't have been able to give them an answer—her choice was driven by raw instinct, the "feel" of Enrique's name as she typed it out on the infrared keyboard causing a churning sickness in her abdomen.

Search results scrolled across the screen. Clicking the top hit, she found herself at a news site. Councilor Enrique was dead. The details, reproduced from an official Council release, appeared innocuous enou—

"Are you finding what you need?"

Her blood ran cold.

When the man who stood next to the desk put one hand on the back of the chair she'd appropriated, and the other palm-down beside the computer, she found herself torn between the urge to run . . . and to lean her head against the dark heat of his body, breathe deep of the clean male sweat that made his skin glimmer. Her madness where Kaleb was concerned was clearly deep-rooted and without reason.

"Ah," he said, reading the article she'd pulled up. "So you heard about Santano."

Once, on a nature show, she'd seen a lion playing with a gazelle, allowing its prey to believe it was about to escape, all the while digging its claws deeper into the helpless animal. She knew she was the gazelle right now, just as she knew there was no point in attempting to hide her fear—she wasn't that accomplished a liar.

However, neither was she going to sit frozen and allow him to torment her; she'd created the labyrinth to escape her previous captors, and while she had no intention or desire to entomb her mind in that way again, she would find another way to outwit him, to survive.

"Sahara! I'll come for you! Survive! Survive for me!"

The echo of that primal promise had run in a continuous loop in her mind for the duration of her captivity. Sahara didn't have the memory of the event or the time when the original words had been spoken, didn't know the identity of the speaker, but she knew one thing: her death would mean more, *far more*, than the simple extinguishing of a life.

Some might say the belief was a delusional one her mind had created to survive a nightmare—and perhaps it was—but it had helped her navigate the piercing loneliness of the past seven years. It would help her weather this, too.

"What are you going to do to me?" she asked, proud her voice didn't tremble.

Cardinal eyes devoid of stars met her own gaze, Kaleb's hair uncharacteristically tousled. "Give you your own organizer." A paper-thin tablet computer landed on the desk an instant later. "I need this screen for a comm conference in twenty minutes."

With that, he reached out and entered a URL into the browser—an obscure one to her eyes, created as it was of a string of numbers. "That'll tell you what you need to know about Santano." Pushing off the desk, he walked to the door. "Remember, I need that screen in nineteen minutes."

She stared after him in openmouthed disbelief until she could no longer hear his footsteps. Her mind tried to find some kind of reason in his response, was stymied by the inexplicability of it. Kaleb had to know full well that information was power, and yet he'd handed her the key to it.

Rubbing her fingertips over her temples in a vain effort to clear the confusion, she turned her attention to the page he'd brought up—and found herself on a site run by a self-termed conspiracy theorist. The otherwise anonymous owner identified himself as Psy, and given the amount of information on the site, he was one clever enough to hide his tracks from the Council's enforcers—because the topics he covered were more than taboo.

Skimming past the recent entries, which stated the Council was no longer in existence, regardless of the lack of an official announcement, she found the search box and once more typed in Enrique's name . . . to be directed to a single continuous page that held update after update. The most recent one was dated just over two years ago and stated simply: *Kaleb Krychek now on Council. Acknowledged protégé of Santano Enrique—no evidence for or against theory that he assisted S.E. in the torture murders.*

A stabbing pain in her chest, a cry trapped behind her hand. Scrolling to the bottom of the page, she began to read up from the oldest entry.

According to the author, Santano Enrique had been that rarest of anchors, one who'd not only embraced politics instead of isolation, but thrived in the cutthroat world of the Council. He'd also been a serial killer responsible for the torture murders of a number of young changeling women. He hadn't died of natural causes, as reported in the mainstream media. He'd been executed by the DarkRiver leopards and the SnowDancer wolves in a gruesome fashion, a message to the remainder of the Council left stapled to his tongue.

"You have five more minutes."

Snapping up her head, she saw Kaleb in the doorway. His hair was damp but neatly combed, his shirt a deep blue, his pants charcoal, the belt black—the same shade as his shoes. He held a glass of the nutrient drink in his hand.

Whatever he'd learned at his mentor's knee, it could be nothing good. And yet the compulsion to go to him thundered in her blood, making her distrust her own mind—regardless of the fact she *knew* she was immune to mind control on that level. As no one could compromise her mind, neither could anyone control her, not without her being aware of the interference.

Still, her stomach twisted, her nails digging into the softness of her palms.

"How could anyone outside the Council know all these details?" she said, surprised the words came out sounding calm and rational when her body and mind continued to fight a battle she couldn't explain. "Either he's delusional or he has a source."

Kaleb sipped at his drink, never taking his eyes off her. "What do you think?"

"His accusations are so outlandish, they might well be the truth. A source."

"Likely." Finishing the drink, he teleported the glass away. "He is correct in all particulars."

Her fingers trembled as she picked up the organizer, noting absently that it was far thinner and lighter than had been the norm seven years before. "Santano Enrique was insane?" Even as she asked the question, she was thinking about the statement she'd just read that said Kaleb had effectively been in Enrique's "care" since he was five years of age. It would be the greatest fallacy to assume the experience hadn't warped his development, turning him into a mirror of the man who had been the paternal figure in his life.

Kaleb slid his hands into the pockets of his suit pants, nothing in him speaking of the boy he'd been—a boy who had grown up with a monster. "That," he said, "is a matter of opinion. Some would say he was a perfect creation of Silence. Totally without emotion, without empathy. To him, the murders were interesting experiments."

KALEB saw the slick sheen of fear in Sahara's eyes as she rose from his chair, her hair clipped back to expose a face that had no deceit in it. He wondered if she was even capable of the games he played on a daily basis, using truths and lies interchangeably to achieve his aims.

Though she left the room without taking her eyes off him, he knew she hadn't regained the totality of her memories—she wasn't afraid enough, the wariness in her generalized and not specific to him.

He let her go, not pointing out that if he wanted to hurt her right this instant, there was nothing in the world she could do to stop him. Her bones would snap like matchsticks should he unleash the merest fraction of his telekinetic strength, her blood pouring out of her in a pulse of darkest scarlet. As it had once before, to soak into the sheets on the bed in that cheap hotel room that had burned to black cinders but hadn't escaped Enforcement's eye, thanks to the games Santano liked to play.

Waiting several minutes to give her guard a chance to go down, he walked to the open doors to see that she'd taken a cross-legged position on the sun lounger. The umbrella, unnecessary at this time of day, remained closed, the glossy black of her hair glowing with hints of red-gold in the dawn light.

Those strands were unusual but not totally unpredictable, given the genetic mix of maternal and paternal DNA. Her mother's hair color was a soft black, while her father's was that of wet clay, the otherwise recessive trait for red hair strong in the Kyriakus family tree. It was Sahara's psychic profile that had come out of the blue, rare as that of a dual cardinal.

To Kaleb's knowledge, Sahara was the *only* individual in the Net with her specific ability—one so coveted her captors hadn't executed her despite the labyrinth.

Sahara Kyriakus held within her the potential to make a man into an emperor.

Pure Psy

IF THERE WAS one individual in the Net who had Vasquez's respect, it was Kaleb Krychek. The cardinal Tk had proven his Silence with his cool, calculated ascension to the Council, eliminating anyone who stood in his way, and doing so with a stealth and an intelligence that meant none of the executions had ever been connected to him.

Henry, too, had spoken well of the younger man, but he'd been unsure about trusting Kaleb with the inner workings of Pure Psy. "Krychek's priorities are not our own," the now-dead leader of Pure Psy had said. "He wants to take total, unquestioned control of the Net, of that I'm certain."

That goal had clashed with Pure Psy's—for where Krychek wanted to utilize such control to increase his power, Pure Psy wanted to use it for the betterment of the Psy race. However, the situation had changed since Henry's original decision not to invite Krychek into their inner circle, the most critical being Henry's assassination.

The organization would need a strong man at the helm when it rose to power and Krychek fit the bill to perfection. His involvement would also serve to calm the populace, maintaining continuity with the previous Council.

Vasquez had no issue with giving up his current position to Kaleb for a function more suited to his training. He knew he wasn't meant for leadership. He was a general with the capacity for absolute loyalty to his chosen leader. Krychek, by contrast, took orders from no one. Exactly as it should be for the man at the top of the food chain.

Together, they would make the perfect team.

Chapter 9

SAHARA UNDERSTOOD THE organizer Kaleb had given her could well be set up to transmit her activities to him, but it seemed counterintuitive since he could've withheld the device in the first place. Then there was the fact that her mind remained naked, for all intents and purposes, her shields nascent, and yet he'd made no effort to intrude, done not a single thing to make her feel hunted.

"Worrying about his motivations won't change things," she muttered to herself and began to pull up the major news sites.

It surprised her, how much information she found on Psy-affiliated sites—information that would've been embargoed under threat of severe punishment by the Council at the time of her kidnapping. Fascinated by the references to an armed conflict that had involved Councilor Henry Scott and a group named Pure Psy against the changelings, she read article after article.

What startled her even more than the idea of an open conflict were the opinion pieces.

The Silence Protocol has come to define us as a race, read one anonymous piece in a human-run news outlet, *but is this the legacy we want to leave? Do we not have the strength to face our demons rather than stifling them and pretending that means they no longer exist, all the while knowing that evil walks amongst us?*

Shoving a hand through her hair at words that would've led to a swift rehabilitation order seven years ago, the writer's mind and personality stripped to leave him barely functional enough for menial labor, she continued to read, absorbing everything with the hunger of a mind that had been starved of knowledge for years.

However, compelled though she was by the political changes that had taken place during that time, the subject that fascinated her most was Kaleb Krychek. But setting aside the conspiracy site Kaleb himself had shown her, searches on him brought up only business and public Council biographical data, the only non-Council biography being on a human-run public encyclopedia:

KALEB KRYCHEK

Summary: An unexpected cardinal telekinetic born of two low-Gradient parents whose recessive genes combined with powerful results in the fetus. Trained and monitored by Santano Enrique from age five.[1]

Made first millions at age twenty-three after backing high-risk project that led to a major breakthrough in comm screen tech. Ascended to Council at age twenty-seven.

Resident in Moscow.

Continue to full article

1. Citation needed

After reading through the entire biography, which insinuated that Kaleb had risen to his current position by eliminating everyone who stood in his path—timely natural deaths, people dropping out of nego-tiations without warning, unexplained disappearances—but offered no proof of the allegations, Sahara returned to the conspiracy site. There, she read that he was rumored to be able to cause madness, a fact he'd already confirmed, and that while he had publicly clean hands, he wasn't averse to doing his own dirty work.

Though Krychek is the youngest member of the Council, stated an update made a year ago, *he is the most ruthless and dangerous. No one else ever comes out the winner in any negotiation in which Krychek shows an interest.*

Six months ago, Agro Grav turned down an offer by the Councilor. However, the CEO had a sudden change of heart two days later. At no point did he explain his reversal—but it is notable that he removed his daughters from boarding school at the same time, in favor of home tutoring.

Her hand shook again and so badly that she had to put down the tablet before she dropped it. Inside her chest, her heart raced at a manic pace, as her head spun, her body no longer under her control. Panicking, she swung her legs over the side of the lounger and tried to stand up, only to collapse back down, her bones the consistency of rubber, and her heartbeat was in her mouth now, her breath stuck in her chest, shards of broken mirrors stabbing at her throat and a suffocating blackness creeping into the edges of her vision.

"Breathe." It was a ruthless command, an insistent hand pushing her head between her knees.

She went, her sight limited to two tiny pinpricks of light.

A sense of movement, Kaleb's body crouching down in front of her. "In and out."

She clung to the steady rhythm of the words he repeated in a calm, tempered voice, her chest expanding and deflating until the black began to recede and he lifted his hand from her nape.

Raising her head, she drank the water he gave her before meeting the eyes of this man who might truly be the worst monster of them all. That cardinal gaze was pure black again, no light in the darkness, and for some reason, the sight made her want to sob as if her heart was broken, the knot of tears inside her a painful tightness.

"Thank you," she said, barely managing to rein in the violent need to mourn something that had never belonged to her. "I've never had a panic attack before."

He stayed in his crouched position, looking up at her with that hard, beautiful face she had the haunting sense she'd seen many, many times before, except he didn't appear in a single one of her returning memories.

Perhaps because her mind was playing tricks on her . . . or perhaps because their meeting had been too ugly to remember.

Kaleb had, after all, been protégé to a serial killer, a fact she could not allow herself to forget. Santano Enrique had preferred changeling victims, but who was to say Kaleb hadn't stuck with women of his own race?

Kaleb will never hurt me.

Again that voice from deep within her psyche, that compulsion to trust that sang to the tears locked in her chest.

"Even when they took you?" Kaleb asked, and though she couldn't forget what she'd read about him, neither could she stop herself from brushing her fingers lightly over the warm hardness of his jaw.

He went motionless, but didn't stop her.

It's been so very long.

Holding the mysterious thought inside, she said, "I was afraid," and waited to see if he would react to the evidence that her Silence had always been problematic, but he simply continued to watch her.

"Afraid," she said again. "In a way that made everything inside me turn cold, but I didn't panic. Not like this." Saying the words made her realize that far more than her body had turned fragile in the years she'd been kept like a performing animal in a cage. "I'm broken."

No change in his expression. "Do you believe that makes you irreversibly flawed?"

Frowning, she curled her fingers into her palm when they would've reached for him again. "That doesn't make sense. If I'm broken, I'm flawed."

"That is one interpretation." With that enigmatic statement, he rose to his feet, a male of such ice-cut beauty that he was more akin to a statue than living, breathing flesh.

And yet he was flesh—her fingertips held the echo of the warmth of his skin, her body remembered the strength of his back from when she'd leaned against him on this very lounger . . . and it ached for further contact, reason colliding against a need born in memories she couldn't access, and that might not even exist beyond the realm of the imagination.

"It's near certain," he said, "that you're suffering from post-traumatic stress disorder."

Wanting to test herself, she stood, too. Her legs trembled, but held. "I should probably have specialist help," she murmured, simply to see how he would respond, this man who let her wander the house at will, who protected her mind, who gave her the tools to gain knowledge about the world—but who alarmed the doors so she couldn't leave.

"Would you like to speak to someone from Psy-Med?"

Startled, she stared at him. "If I say yes?"

"I'll make sure you have access to the best specialists in the world."

She couldn't judge him, she realized with a sense of despair out of all proportion to the topic of conversation and the fleeting time she'd known him. He gave off none of the physical or vocal clues that even other Psy did, his control honed to an impossible edge. "How? By taking someone else captive?"

A steady look. "No one speaks my secrets."

Sucking in a breath at the sheer, terrifying emotionlessness of his statement, she shook her head. "I don't want the terror of another living being"—Silent or not—"on my conscience."

His stillness was suddenly so absolute, she'd have believed herself alone if she hadn't been able to see him in front of her. "There are other ways."

She wanted desperately to believe he was attempting to compromise, that he wasn't the cold-blooded murderer the articles had made him out to be. The vicious depth of her need scared her to the bone—she didn't need a specialist to tell her the compulsion she felt toward Kaleb was unhealthy and could turn deadly.

"I'm not ready yet." After years of having her mind splayed open, she couldn't bear the idea of anyone else attempting to divine her secrets. "All I want," she whispered to her jailer, "is to be free."

Kaleb's lashes came down, the world fragmented for a single split second, and then she was standing on the shimmering black sands of a windswept beach, not another being in sight for what appeared to be miles in every direction; the rolling sand dunes to her right home to hardy grasses that waved in the breeze. On her other side, water danced gently to shore, leaving graceful ripples in the sand, the sea foam wild lace entangled with tiny shells that sparkled under the yellow-orange sunlight of late afternoon.

"Is this real?" she whispered, afraid he'd created an illusion inside her mind, one so detailed she could even feel the salt-laced wind against her lips.

"Pain is the best indicator of whether something is an illusion or reality."

She recognized the words from a childhood lesson, one taught to all Psy children.

Reaching up, she pinched the sensitive flesh at the back of her arm, winced. Then she smiled and, turning, kicked off her shoes to curl her feet into the sun-warmed grains that weren't truly black at all, but an amalgam of colors that shimmered in the light.

She knew this wasn't freedom, not when Kaleb stood by the nearest dune, silent and watchful, but to a girl who'd come to womanhood in a cage, it was enough for this sunshine-drenched instant. She would enjoy the beautiful *now* and worry about the future after drinking of happiness.

Running forward, she spread her arms and spun around in circles, the sky a shattering blue overhead, the sun's caress languid against her skin, the sand sugar-fine between her toes. She laughed and laughed, and when she was finally too dizzy to spin anymore, she collapsed on the heated softness of the sand to see that Kaleb had taken a seat at the foot of a dune, his arms braced loosely on his knees, his no-doubt expensive suit utterly out of place in this wilderness untouched by the hand of man.

And yet . . . he fit.

It was nothing she could've ever predicted, but Kaleb Krychek fit here in this wild place, where the sea held the promise of fury even in the calm and the wind stroked possessively through the grasses, tugging at her hair, his own. He appeared as much a part of the landscape as the dunes and the water . . . and as isolated, as alone.

Frowning when she realized her eyes were lingering on him, her thoughts once more circling back to her captor, she got up and started to walk toward the cliffs in the distance. They stayed remote though she must've walked for an hour, but the peace of the water, the lap of the waves, the salt in her every breath, it was better therapy than any invasive Psy-Med exam.

She stopped only when her body protested the unaccustomed level of exercise. Looking back, she could see Kaleb waiting with a patience that somehow did nothing to mute the power of him, but she knew she couldn't make it back to him, her body almost at its limit. Her heart, however, wasn't yet full enough, her skin still soaking in this dramatic, haunting part of the world far from the morning skies of Moscow.

Tucking back a flyaway strand of hair, she sat down on the sand, her arms around her knees in an echo of Kaleb's position, her mind in turns frustrated and fascinated by the enigma of him. There was something not quite right about this captivity, something not quite right about Kaleb's behavior. She'd been imprisoned for over seven years, knew the difference between a cage and . . . whatever this was.

"You belong to me."

An unambiguous statement of ownership that told her he'd come after her if she attempted to escape. Yet so far, he'd given her every other thing she'd requested. It could be a clever ploy meant to cause exactly the confusion that had her so off balance, but that didn't explain why her own mind was split in two on the subject of Kaleb Krychek.

Even now, she fought the wrenching need to go to him, touch her skin to his.

So long, it had been so long.

Accessing the telepathic channel between them, a channel that had been open on his end since he'd found her, she stretched out a hand into the darkness. *Would you like to sit with me?* It disturbed her to see him so alone.

He was seated beside her a second later, his eyes on the heavier waves rolling in to shore as the tide began to come in, the foam kissing the sand a meter in front of their feet. "You like the sea."

"I always have," she said, able to feel the heat of his bigger body in spite of the inches that separated them. "When I was first put in a cell, I used to imagine the motion and the breadth of the sea to keep myself calm."

Kaleb's eyes on her profile, potent as a touch. "You remember everything about the years you were held captive?"

"No," she whispered, refusing to turn, uncertain she could resist the need that drew her to him, "there are gaps." Almost, she told him about the irreversible damage done before the labyrinth, when she hadn't understood the cost demanded by her ability.

"And before?" he asked. "Do you recall the first sixteen years of your life?"

"Not all of it." However, she had the sense that those missing pieces weren't permanent. "I'll remember when I'm read—" She broke off as Kaleb rose to his feet without warning, reaching down to pull her up at the same time.

They were back on the terrace before she could do more than take a breath. Gasping, she swayed, would've stumbled if he hadn't steadied her. "Kaleb? What is it?" she asked, gripping at his upper arms.

But he was already gone, leaving her holding on to air.

Chapter 10

KALEB FOUND HIMSELF surrounded by chaos, screams shattering the early morning hush in Copenhagen. The rescue workers who'd already made it to the scene shouted for people to clear the area, their Danish rapid, fire crews rushing to stifle the flames. However, no one approached Kaleb where he stood in front of the apartment building that had collapsed in on one side from the force of the explosive device, clouds of dust lingering in the air as flames blew out windows to shower bystanders with splinters that sliced and cut.

The building was an ordinary one, filled with ordinary people—but for one thing. It was—*had been?*—home to a scholar working on a thesis that challenged the Adelajas' original theories and proofs on the value of Silence. The scholar's focus had been on the well-disguised disappearance of the Adelajas' twin sons, known as the "firsts," on which the couple had based their entire theory that conditioning emotion out of the Psy would save them from the insanity and violence that threatened to destroy their race.

Kaleb knew that because the NetMind and DarkMind told him everything that might impact the Net—as they'd told him of this explosion—but if this was a Pure Psy attack, then the fanatical group had far better sources of information, and more powerful sympathizers, than he'd guessed.

"Help! Please!"

Glancing up to locate the source of the thin scream, repeated in Danish and again in English, he saw a woman with an infant cradled against her chest in one of the seventh-floor rooms that hadn't collapsed in the initial blast. Judging from the thick gray smoke spiraling around her, he knew she and the child would be dead in minutes.

It took no thought to teleport up to bring mother and child to safety, the woman's coughing drawing the attention of the medics, though it was the child she thrust at them with frantic cries. Wrapping both survivors in a blanket, the medics began to check their distressed patients for smoke inhalation.

"I'll take this side," he said to the teleporter who'd arrived a second before in response to Kaleb's direct request that the Arrows render assistance. "There are people trapped in rooms we can't see from here."

Vasic nodded and disappeared to the back of the building. His partner, Aden, was already organizing the paramedics, including Arrow medics, with military precision. It was the first time in living memory that the lethal squad of assassins, their black uniforms marking them as some of the Net's most dangerous men and women, had so publicly stepped in to offer humanitarian assistance.

Leaving Aden to manage the manpower so that the right people were handling the right tasks, Kaleb zeroed in on the next trapped survivor. As long as he had a viable visual lock, he could get to them.

UNSETTLED by Kaleb's sudden departure, Sahara decided to walk through the house while she got her thoughts in order. As she knew well by now, it wasn't the spartan cube people might expect of a cardinal Tk. Instead, it flowed from level to level, each divided from the other by a single wide step, with the lowest featuring a small internal koi pond filled with bright orange fish and surrounded by foliage that thrived in the warmth created by multiple skylights that occasionally opened to let in the cooler outside air. The temperature in the pond itself, she realized today, was regulated by a separate system, to ensure it remained comfortable for its inhabitants.

It made her so happy, that pond, her eyes spilling over with emotion.

"Silly girl," she whispered, wiping away the tears to kneel beside the jagged stone that bordered the water, emotion thick in her heart.

This place . . . this entire home, it felt so *familiar*, so safe.

It was a long, peaceful time later that she continued her walk through the airy, light-drenched rooms and wide hallways. Yet, regardless of its generous use of space, the house wasn't so big that it felt impersonal. No, it was a home, with a hundred tiny details that denoted thought had been put into the design, with every room but for a limited few having wide floor-to-ceiling windows.

The windows on the level just up from the pond had been coated in something to protect the books that lined the shelves, hundreds of precious volumes sitting neatly in alphabetical order. The bent spines and worn covers told her the books had been read—or used. Many of them were nonfiction, the subjects as eclectic as those in Kaleb's study.

A beautiful room, the rug on the floor ruby red and creamy white, the chairs comfortable . . . and yet it felt unfinished. She knew in her bones that while Kaleb might use the books, he never sat in here. As he didn't sit in the breakfast area, or use the living room. He might sleep in his bed, but his study was the single room in the house that seemed to bear any imprint of the intelligent, lethal, *fascinating* man who was her captor.

Taking the wide step up to the next level, she looked out through the windows to see a haunting vista of empty grasslands. "As beautiful and dangerous and lonely as you," she whispered, her mind filled with the image of Kaleb against the backdrop of the dunes.

Skin suddenly chilled, she wrapped her arms around herself and returned to the sunshine on the terrace. It was an automatic act to check the news sites on her organizer, her mind racing to fill in the gaps about this present that to her was an unknown future.

BREAKING NEWS! Bomb Blast in Copenhagen—Casualties Rising

Immediately searching for live coverage, she clicked on a comm feed fronted by a human reporter, sadness and shock intertwining inside her at the carnage visible behind the ponytailed blonde: broken bricks, fallen timbers, thick black smoke from what must be a secondary fire, dirty and bleeding victims sitting shell-shocked on the road, medical blankets around their shoulders.

"*. . . amazing! I've never seen anything like it!*"

The reporter's inappropriate excitement had Sahara frowning . . . just as Kaleb appeared in front of a medical van with a child in his arms, his shirt covered with soot, streaks of black on his face. He was gone a second later, the screaming toddler safely passed to a paramedic.

"As most of you will recognize, that was Councilor Kaleb Krychek," the reporter said out of frame as her cameraman scanned for the next teleport. "He, with the help of a number of unnamed Tks dressed in what appear to be black combat uniforms, has ensured that the cost of this tragic and unprovoked act of violence will remain limited to those who died in the initial blast."

The camera zoomed in on the side of the building that had collapsed. "According to unconfirmed reports coming out of Australia," the reporter continued, "this is the second time in the past two weeks that Councilor Krychek has been involved in a major rescue."

The camera halted on the seated form of a woman wrapped in a blanket, a field bandage on her right hand. "Ma'am"—soft, sensitive—"you were rescued by the Councilor, were you not?"

"Yes." Sahara caught the trembling of the woman's fingers before she hid both hands in the blanket. "I'd be dead now if not for him."

"You are Psy, but did you have any reason to hope for telekinetic assistance, particularly from Councilor Krychek himself?"

Tugging the blanket more tightly around herself, the woman shook her head. "Councilors don't waste their time on such 'small' incidents . . . but he did, and I don't think anyone in this city will ever forget it."

Sahara froze.

What Kaleb had done today, actions that had the reporter hailing him as a hero, didn't line up with either his reputation or his unmistakable lust for power—unless he was ruthless enough to have planned the entire exercise.

No, no, no.

Ignoring the shaken voice in her mind, she scanned more reports, saw that Pure Psy had claimed responsibility for the attack, but that knowledge did nothing to melt the ice in her veins.

What better partner for a man widely believed to be aiming for a total takeover of the Net than a group whose every action led to further cracks in the structure of Psy society? Cracks that left plenty of room for a "hero" to step in and clean up the mess.

As for the lives lost, they'd be written off as collateral damage.

KALEB returned home without speaking to the news media. It wasn't necessary—he knew word of his actions had gone viral across the world, the images of him with survivor after survivor in his arms far more powerful than anything he could've said. Unbuttoning his shirt as he walked down the corridor to his bedroom, he entered to find Sahara sitting on the edge of his bed.

She jerked up to her feet, her eyes going to his chest, back up, color on her cheekbones. "I'm sorry, I didn't think. I was waiting for you."

The latter words were a punch to the solar plexus, an echo across time, but tasting the fear beneath her embarrassment, he kept his distance. "We can speak after I shower." Smoke and grit coated his every breath.

The color on her cheeks still hot, she said, "Of course," and slipped out.

Closing the door, he stripped and stepped under the pounding spray of the shower to wash off the scent of smoke and flame that seemed embedded in his very cells. The bomb had been expertly placed to do maximum damage, the resulting fire a bonus for Pure Psy. At least a hundred and five confirmed dead, with fifty-seven unaccounted for.

Chances were good that a percentage of the missing had already left for work and would get in touch with the authorities as the news spread, but there was also a high chance that there'd been people inside who weren't on the building manifest. Until the forensic teams were able to get in to scour the building for victims, the final death toll could not be predicted with any certainty.

Scrubbing at his body and hair until the water ran clear, he got out, dried himself off. It was as he was about to put on a suit in preparation for the meetings he'd had Silver postpone that he remembered the way Sahara's gaze had fixed on his bare chest, her breath hitching as her skin heated.

He knew he had a physically attractive body—changeling and human females had made that clear with the silent invitations they sent him on a regular basis. None of them ever approached, realizing who and what he was, but he'd known that should he decide to accept one of those invitations, he wouldn't hear the word "no." His very coldness seemed a lure for certain women, and though he had paused to consider if they would scream in terror when faced with the reality of him, he had never tested the theory.

To him, his body was a tool, and the women who'd sent the invitations had nothing to offer him that would've made it worth his while to put that tool to intimate use. Sahara wasn't one of those nameless women with a heat in their eyes that reminded him of the fever in Santano Enrique's at the moment of the kill. Given that link to blood and torture, Kaleb wasn't certain he wouldn't have snapped the women's fragile necks had he accepted their invitations.

That wasn't ever going to be an issue with Sahara. She fell into a unique category of her own. More, he needed her to bond with him. And regardless of the fact that physical contact caused him acute discomfort, and sex would require him to push himself inside Sahara's body, the primal act was known to create a bond far stronger than any chain. As if the sweat and heat of sex melded the couple together.

His hand flexed, clenched, his body hardening in response to images he wasn't consciously aware of forming. It was a problematic development. While his body was in prime condition, the fact was, he shouldn't have responded—that he'd done so with such faint provocation spoke to deep issues with his control that he'd have to fix before he laid hands on Sahara.

As it was, any such thoughts were premature. Sahara wasn't yet at a point where he could initiate the most intimate level of physical bonding. For now, he'd use her attraction to his body to keep her off balance, allow it to eat into the fear that colored her eyes whenever she looked at him . . . a fear that made his Tk wrench at the reins, ready to break free and destroy everything around them.

Discarding the shirt he'd picked up, he pulled on only a pair of the lightweight black pants he wore while running, his upper body bare. His eye caught on the mark on his left forearm as he threw the towel over the railing in the bathroom. Though Sahara had seen it multiple times by now, she hadn't asked about it.

She would. It was inevitable.

As inevitable as what had taken place seven years ago, what he had done. A boy who grew up with a monster had no choice but to become another monster just to survive. Redemption was an impossibility, a mirage flecked with blood.

Sahara knew that better than any other person on the planet.

SAHARA made it to the kitchen before collapsing against one of the walls for a long, shuddering minute, her heart in her throat. She'd gone to Kaleb's room with some vague idea of confronting him with her suspicions about his involvement with Pure Psy while he was tired, his guard presumably lowered.

Then he'd walked in and her neurons had gone haywire. The sight of him with his shirt unbuttoned to the waist had been an electric kiss to her body, a physical response so deep, it was as if it had had years to take shape, not simply a matter of days. And while the sight of his muscled chest and abdomen had dried up her throat, made her skin burn, it was the *intimacy* implied by seeing him half-dressed that had her heart stuttering in the most erratic of rhythms.

Fisting her hand against her stomach in a vain attempt to control the strange fluttering sensation within, she forced herself to move and prepare the nutrient drink he preferred, as well as a cup of hot chocolate for herself. The sweet drink had rapidly become something she associated with care, with safety.

The fact that Kaleb had given it to her the first time wasn't lost on her.

After a second's thought, she made several sandwiches using a high-calorie spread she found in the cooler, and put the plate on the table, along with four bars of dark chocolate. All of the items were designed specifically for Psy, the tastes muted, and would help Kaleb refuel his body after the massive amount of energy he'd just expended.

The task was complete all too soon, leaving her grappling with the same clawing desire that had gripped her by the throat in the bedroom. "I'm unsteady," she whispered, her skin aching with a sense of acute anticipation. "My judgment is impaired. I was sixteen when I was captured."

"A very mature sixteen," said a familiar masculine voice from the doorway. "You made a meal. Thank you."

She couldn't look away from him, his skin a sun gold that belied the cool lack of expression on his face. If he'd kept his distance, she might have resisted the temptation that had been riding her since the bedroom . . . but he crossed over to her, didn't say a word when she ran her fingers over the tensile warmth of him, her nipples tight points against the thin fabric of her sleeveless lilac shirt.

His own hand was big, warm against her cheek as he cupped her jaw. "Don't be afraid of me, Sahara." Bending his head, he spoke with his lips against hers, the contact igniting a thousand tiny lightning strikes in her blood. "I'd line the streets with bodies before I'd ever hurt you."

Chapter 11

I'D LINE THE streets with bodies before I'd ever hurt you.

The violence of his promise tore apart the misty cloud around her mind, made her aware of how intimately she'd pressed herself against him, his body pushing into her abdomen in a way that screamed of broken conditioning. But his eyes, those cardinal eyes, they were watchful, calculating.

Jerking away, she stumbled into a seat at the table. "What's happening?" The whispered question was for herself, her actions inexplicable to her rational mind. This, after all, was the man she suspected of being unconscionable enough to participate in a plot to commit mass murder in order to gain a stranglehold on power. And yet, even now, she hungered to go to him, to touch, to caress, to hold and be held.

Kaleb braced himself against the table with one hand, reaching out with the other as if to tuck her hair behind her ears. Halting when she flinched, he said, "The door is always open," his voice causing the tiny hairs at her nape to rise in a combination of crushing need, confusion, and fear.

Watching him as he went to take a seat on the other side of the table, his every movement imbued with the lethal elegance of a man who held death in the palm of his hand, she suddenly remembered what he'd said before the madness that was her craving for him had clawed through her senses. "How do you know," she asked, voice husky with the desire that even now lingered just below the surface of her skin, "that I was a mature sixteen-year-old?"

A slight pause that could be explained by the fact he'd just taken a bite of one of the sandwiches she'd prepared. "Your Psy-Med reports," he said after swallowing, "indicate you were at a level of psychological development closer to that of a young woman than a girl."

Cupping her hands around the mug of hot chocolate, though her palms cried out for living heat, she said, "You're lying to me," so certain it hurt.

"I would never lie to you." Eyes of starless night locked with her own.

Breath catching, she held that cardinal gaze so brutal with power she couldn't imagine how he remained sane. "Then you're not telling me the whole truth."

No answer, his face without expression, a sculpture gilded gold by the sunlight.

"How about you?" She sipped at her hot chocolate in a vain effort to warm the increasing cold within, her body aching with a deep sense of loss for which she had no name. "Were you ever a child?" Ever without the vicious restraint that turned him into a man of ice even as his body burned?

"Of course." A toneless response.

One that didn't answer the question. "You know what I mean."

He drank half of the nutrient drink, ate another sandwich before speaking again. "Childhood is an impossibility when you have the potential to kill anyone in your path."

The unvarnished honesty of his words had her halting with her mug halfway to her mouth, her heart a drumbeat, a sudden "push" at the back of her mind—as if something important was struggling to break free. "When did Santano Enrique . . . take you?" she asked, and it wasn't the question she'd meant to ask, her subconscious seizing the reins from her grasp.

"I first remember meeting him at three." Nothing in his voice or face gave any hint that he was disturbed at discussing the murderous psychopath who'd been his trainer. "That was when I was placed in a facility meant for potentially dangerous children; most were earmarked for the Arrow Squad."

Sahara had seen something about the Arrows on the conspiracy site. "They're a covert unit of highly trained soldiers and assassins?" At his nod, she said, "I read that they were formed at the inception of Silence, and that their central aim is the continuance of the Protocol."

To be an Arrow, it had been stated, *is to be Silent. The squad is composed of men and women with the most violent and dangerous psychic abilities on the planet, psychic abilities that cannot be permitted to slip out of their conscious control.*

"The Arrows keep their own counsel," Kaleb said in response to her question, "but there are signs they're reassessing their goals in light of the current situation in the Net."

Even with her memories in fragments and her knowledge of the world yet shallow, Sahara understood that Kaleb and the Arrows had to be linked in some form. There was no way the most powerful cardinal Tk in the world wouldn't have come to the attention of the squad—and vice versa—particularly given his childhood. "You grew up with them."

To her surprise, Kaleb shook his head. "I only spent four years in the facility. Santano moved me to a separate location when I turned seven and it became clear the ferocity of my abilities made me a threat to the safety of the other children."

That made no sense—*all* of those children had to have been dangerous. And yet the monster had taken only one . . . bringing Kaleb, alone and vulnerable, into a nightmare. Horror choking up her throat, she clutched at straws. "Your parents—they came with you?" Psy did not abandon their young, for children were a genetic legacy.

"I never saw them after I was placed in the Arrow facility." Black ice in every word. "They were unequipped to cope with a cardinal offspring and were handsomely compensated for renouncing any future claim on me. It would've made no financial sense for Santano to train me if he didn't have ownership of my skills."

Her heart wept for him, this dangerous man who'd once been a small boy. If he was a monster now, then the seeds had been sown in his childhood—no child should have to grow up knowing he'd been *sold* because he was too much trouble to handle. He must've been so scared to be left behind at the facility, so confused, before the cold truth was hammered into him by instructors who had no reason to be kind.

To be aware so young that he was unwanted, to grow up with no one who was his own, even in the cold way of their race . . . the scars would've been brutal. Because while love was anathema in the PsyNet, family—or at the very least—*genetic* loyalty was part of the bedrock of their race.

Swallowing her feelings, knowing they would not be welcome, she said, "Why aren't you an Arrow?" The words came out unexpectedly taut, until she realized she'd stopped breathing under the intensity of the eye contact she couldn't remember making and yet that held her captive.

"Santano had other plans for me." With that flat statement, he ate his way through the last sandwich with the methodical pace of a man for whom taste meant nothing, food only a source of fuel; then he unwrapped a chocolate bar. "Why don't you ask?"

"What?" It took effort to keep her voice even when a slow-burning fury raged within her veins, her anger directed at the people who had brought a strong, gifted child into this world, then abdicated all responsibility for him.

"Exactly how much of a protégé I was to my trainer."

Frost digging into her heart, jagged and brittle. "Because I'm not ready for the answer." She might suspect him of the most terrible crimes, but if he admitted to helping the dead Councilor torture then murder his victims, it might snap the fragile clawhold she had on reality.

Kaleb's expression didn't alter, and yet she had the haunting sense she'd given the wrong answer, that she'd *hurt* him in some inexplicable way. Another sign of the madness that had her body aching for his no matter what he might've done, how many moral lines he might have crossed, how much blood he had on his hands.

Flexing her own hand on the table until her fingertips brushed his, her eyes seeing her actions but her mind repudiating her orders to withdraw, she whispered, "Why are you holding me?"

Closing his hand over hers, the tanned skin of his shoulders warm in the sunlight pouring through the window, he said, "Because you belong to me."

She shivered at the dark possession in the words, in those eyes of obsidian. "As those changeling women belonged to Enrique?" The words spilled out, bloody rain in the sunshine.

Shifting his hold to cup her hand, lift her palm to his lips, he pressed a kiss to the center that made her womb clench. "No." A hard answer, all razor-sharp edges. "They never gave themselves to him."

Her breath caught. "Did I?" Curling her fingers into her palm, she pulled back her hand. "Give myself to you?" She'd been sixteen, her conditioning never quite right, but the idea that she'd broken the biggest taboo of her race and shared her body with him had everything in her responding in a violent negative.

Yet the way she burned for him, it spoke of an attraction that had had years to ferment, to come to maturity. At twenty-two to her sixteen, powerful and dangerous, he would've been shockingly attractive to her senses . . . as he was now. The idea of those strong hands on her flesh, possessive and caressing, it made perspiration glimmer on her skin, even as she accepted that should he have taken advantage of a teenage girl, it would be an unforgivable act of trespass.

"I," he said, rising to move around and cup her cheek with his hand as he had at the start, "am a virgin."

Of everything he could've said, that was the least expected. Throat dry, she shook her head. "That doesn't answer the question I asked." Didn't tell her who he was to her, who he'd been . . . if he'd been anything at all. This raw attraction could well be nothing but a coping mechanism formulated by her fractured psyche, something Kaleb was smart enough to use to his advantage. No one became a Councilor at age twenty-seven without having a piercing level of intelligence. He'd use her susceptibility to his body as ruthlessly as he'd use any other advantage, the physical contact he permitted apt to be a calculated ploy.

"Whatever I tell you," he said, rubbing his thumb over her lower lip before releasing her, "you'll disbelieve. You don't trust me." With that blunt comment, he headed for the door. "I have to finalize some documents, but we can go for a walk later if you feel rested from this morning."

Startled by the abrupt change in the situation, she nodded, her eyes lingering on the muscled sweep of his back as he left without further words. "This," she whispered desperately to herself, "is a predictable psychological response to the fact he holds me in his power." Her mind, however, flatly rejected that hypothesis. As proof, it offered memories from the start of her original captivity, when she'd still been in a small suite of rooms rather than a cell.

She'd had one main guard those first months. He'd never harmed her in any way, made sure she had extra blankets, reading material, educational games to ensure her mind didn't stagnate—though it had been dulled by the drugs they put in her food. Tall and blond, with aquiline features and sharp green eyes, he'd been classically handsome and, at nineteen, only three years her senior.

He'd no doubt been chosen because of his projected appeal to a scared teenage girl with suspect conditioning, but never, *not once*, had she forgotten that he was her jailer, his aim to keep her content in her pretty cage. She certainly hadn't craved his touch, had in fact actively avoided even accidental contact. In helping to steal her freedom, he'd negated every other act of apparent kindness.

None of that seemed to matter with Kaleb.

Her body ached, her senses drinking in the lingering freshness of his aftershave until it was all she could scent, until the need to go to Kaleb, this stranger wrapped in darkness and painted bloodred, was a stranglehold around her throat. All she wanted to do was strip herself to the skin and wrap herself around him so close that nothing could ever separate them again.

Mad, she thought, face flushing, *I'm truly going mad.*

Shivers after the heat, a rush of tears burning the backs of her eyes, a staccato heartbeat that was in her mouth, in her ears, a roaring rush. *BOOM! BOOM! BOOM!* The world began to crumble at the edges under the rage of sound, the walls liquefying into pools of gleaming white, the floor a dazzling kaleidoscope.

Stumbling out of the chair, her balance lost in the trembling mirage that was the world, she banged into the counter in her attempt to get to the door, to escape the insanity eating away at her senses. "I need to breathe." Her throat was strangling, the air too thick to draw into her lungs.

The door shifted just as she reached it, breaking into pieces splattered with sticky red. And suddenly, her mind was filled with the scent of iron, hot and rich, a thin feminine scream echoing in her ears as a man with cardinal eyes sliced a blade into her flesh, the blood welling over the sides of the wound to run down her bruised and torn skin in a river of warmth that made him laugh.

And laugh.

Chapter 12

STOP! YOU'RE HURTING me! Stop!

The scared, pain-drenched words crashed into Kaleb's mind in what had to be an unconscious telepathic cry. Cutting off his audio-only discussion with brutal abruptness, his mental state too unsteady for a teleport, he ran into the kitchen to see Sahara clawing at the door, her hair hanging around her down-bent face and her fingers bloody, her fingernails broken and torn.

No!

"Sahara." Gripping her shoulders, he turned her around to face him, the contact initiating the same dangerous response it had earlier; his Tk shoved at his skin, wanting to punch out, to break and shatter and savage. As he had then, he choked it into vicious submission. "Look at me."

She flinched at the cold command, her eyes wild, skittering. Those of a trapped creature. His breathing accelerated, his blood boiling under his skin as his mind clouded in a way that could be lethal. Shifting his grip to her right wrist, he pulled her now-rigid form to the alarm panel beside the door.

While she stood mute and barely breathing beside him, he input the voice code, then lifted her hand to place her palm on the scanner. "Sahara Kyriakus, full and unrestricted authorization."

A query popped up on the small screen below the palm plate. *Authorization to include Krychek properties outside current location?*

"Yes." Never again would she be locked in a cage.

The computronics hummed, a green glow lighting up the panel as

Sahara's palm was scanned. *Authorization successful,* scrolled the message a second later.

Dropping her hand, he pushed open the door. She remained where he'd left her, that panicked, trapped expression slowly replaced by one he recognized as fear. Scanning the area for a threat, he saw only empty fields that sprawled to a dramatic blue horizon. He kept them that way to ensure his enemies had no place to hide, should they manage to skirt the perimeter security, but to her it likely seemed an endless blue-green sea.

Not leaving her side but staying silent to give her time to become used to the vista free of walls and fences, he wet a towel using his Tk and used it to wipe off the blood from her hands to reveal she hadn't done as much damage as he'd first believed. Still, he coated the torn and bruised sections with a salve before shifting into her line of sight until she could no longer avoid his presence.

"I saw things," she whispered, the dark, dark blue of her eyes drowning in confusion, "and now I can't remember." Haunting vulnerability, her skin translucent in the light. "Am I going mad, Kaleb?"

He could guess the memories she'd glimpsed, and from her response, it was clear her mind was in no way ready to handle the ugly truth. Thrusting his hands into her hair to hold her head, the contact arcing through his nerves, he said, "No," his tone coolly matter-of-fact because she needed him to be sane at this instant. "According to Psy-Med reports, flashbacks and blackouts are common occurrences in patients suffering from PTSD." For some it never ended, the scars too deep, but he had no intention of sharing that fact with Sahara.

Taking a shuddering breath, another, she shifted her gaze to the wide-open doorway. "No locks?"

"None." He'd made a near-fatal error in not disengaging them the instant she came to full consciousness. "You're an intelligent woman. You know you put yourself at risk if you leave the secured perimeter. However, that perimeter extends a mile in every direction." He'd bought out all remaining properties within that circumference six months ago, soon after discovering Sahara was alive. "You're safe inside that zone."

Throat moving as she swallowed, Sahara reached out to fist her hand in the fine cotton of the shirt he'd put on after leaving the kitchen. "Who *are* you?"

"A caretaker," he said, and it was *a* truth, if not everything.

Frown lines on her brow, her fingers flexing and clenching against his chest in a way that challenged his already unsteady control. "Of this house?"

"Yes." It was an anchor, a physical symbol of his search, of *her*.

"Who owns it?"

"You do." He'd had it built according to specifications she'd outlined at fifteen, watched over it all the years of her captivity, using lethal force to repel anyone who meant it harm. "Welcome home."

PSYNET BEACON: BREAKING NEWS

Copenhagen situation contained. One hundred and five confirmed dead, with number expected to rise once site is cleared for excavation by forensic teams.

Councilor Kaleb Krychek, and a team of unnamed operatives rumored to be from the Arrow Squad, responsible for ninety-five percent of rescues. None accessible for comment.

*This feed will continue to be updated as further news becomes available.**

PSYNET BEACON: CURRENT EDITION
LETTERS TO THE EDITOR

Your recent op-ed piece about the rumored disintegration of the Council sinks this highly regarded news bulletin to the level of a human tabloid.

Such sensationalism can only lead to confusion and destabilization at a time when it is integral we remain calm and rational.

Be assured I will be taking my complaint to the News Media Oversight Committee.

R. Vrruti
(Turin)

Bravo to the *Beacon* for finally stating what many in the populace suspect to be true. If the PsyNet is to survive in the absence of the Council, a new ruling order must be anointed.

Pure Psy are clearly setting themselves up as a choice, but their mindless attacks against the anchors aside, their recent loss to the cobbled-up forces in the California region does not bathe their martial abilities in a competent light. And it is clear that in the current climate, our new leadership must be willing and capable of using force to ensure the peace and Silence so necessary to our survival.

Name withheld by request
(Sioux Falls)

If the Council is in fact no longer in existence, then war among the former Councilors is not a possibility, as per the op-ed, but an inevitability.

As they are some of the most powerful Psy in the world, it is certain that each will seek to gain control of a piece of the Net. Civilians would do well to stay out of their way—collateral damage is apt to be in the hundreds of thousands.

K. Ichikawa
(Fukuoka)

Chapter 13

WELCOME HOME.

"How can this be my house?" Sahara whispered, hotly conscious of the muscled planes of Kaleb's chest beneath her palm. "I was sixteen at the time of my kidnapping." Telling herself not to give in to the craving that lived in every cell of her body, a craving that had just led her into a terrifying fall into blackness, she took a deep breath . . . but didn't let go. Instead, she spread her palm over the cotton of his shirt and, tipping back her head, looked into the pitch-black of his gaze.

"It was a gift," was the frank yet unfathomable answer. "For your nineteenth birthday."

Sahara had no need to ask him who had given her such a lovely home as a gift, a home that seemed to have been plucked out of her very thoughts. Her heart a hugeness in her chest, she said, "Tell me," aware of a vast gulf beneath her feet, a storm of knowledge that pushed at her mind but couldn't penetrate. "Tell me you aren't evil." *Please.*

Kaleb's thumbs moved against her temples. "I'm sorry."

Shaking her head in a mute refusal to accept what he was trying to tell her, she lifted trembling fingers to his jaw. "What have you done?"

"Too much that can never be undone."

Crying in earnest now for a man she didn't know, and yet who was in the most secret part of her heart, she wrapped her arms around his neck and held on, just held on, all the while knowing that he might already have slipped out of her grasp.

His arms came around her, locked tight, his breath harsh against her ear. "I'm sorry," he said again, voice rough as sandpaper and body rigid, as if he'd clenched every muscle he possessed.

"It's okay," she said through her sobs. "It's okay." Cupping his nape, she murmured the words over and over, having no conscious knowledge of why she did so—but aware in her bones that while he might be the dangerous one in the room, right this instant, she was the strong one. "It's okay, Kaleb. I'm here."

And I won't let it be too late.

The silent vow a glowing brand on her heart, she was staring at the window over the breakfast nook when it fractured diagonally down the middle with a loud crack. The unexpected sound nudged loose another memory, one that had her struggling out of his hold. "I'm *hurting* you!"

Silence, she remembered too late, was built on a system of punishment for incorrect behavior, and while her conditioning might have been shattered out of existence, Kaleb lived within it. For him to touch her, hold her, was to lay himself open to an excruciating backlash of pain that had him wiping away a drop of blood from his nose, the color scarlet on the sleeve of his shirt.

"No, it's—" Whatever it was he might've said was lost as there was a flicker at the corner of her eye that wrenched his attention sideways.

KALEB didn't recognize the thickly muscled man who'd teleported into the room.

Flinging the intruder to the wall, he pinned the other man there with a telekinetic grip on his throat, sweeping out his shields at the same time to choke off the male's mind so he couldn't send any telepathic messages. The ability to stifle communication on that level wasn't one possessed by most telepaths; Kaleb had learned it from a monster. "Identify yourself."

The man's mud-colored eyes went to Sahara, blood beginning to bubble out of his mouth as he clawed at the invisible hand that had cut off his airway. When Kaleb turned his attention to Sahara, he glimpsed a sickening fear that had her taking a trembling step backward, her hands in bloodless fists at her sides. "This man hurt you?"

A swallow, a jerky nod, one hand rubbing absently over the upper part of her other arm. And he knew that arm had been broken. Slamming the intruder's head against the wall once more, he walked over to finish the execution by manually gripping the male by the neck and beginning to squeeze the life out of him. Eyes awash with panic begged for him to stop, never realizing that some things were unforgivable.

Sahara came to sudden life behind him. "Kaleb, stop."

The man hanging on the wall in front of Kaleb was now unconscious, most of his bones shattered from the way Kaleb had thrown him against the wall, blood pouring out of his ears, his nose, his mouth.

"*Kaleb!*" Sahara cried, hearing another bone snap in the body of the man who had once tortured her until she'd gone so deep into the labyrinth, she'd felt no pain, no touch, nothing, the numbness absolute.

The look on Kaleb's face when he turned chilled her blood. He was in a place of such darkness, it had not even a hint of light. "No," she whispered. "No." Haunted by the depth of his fury, and terrified at the price he'd pay, she dared put her hand on his forearm.

"Go." A cold, hard command. "Get out of this room."

"Not until you come with me." She would not abandon him, absolving herself of all responsibility.

The darkness glided through his eyes, a living entity. "Such soft bones you have, Sahara, so easy to break."

It was meant to scare her. It did. Oh, it did. "Tell me why. Why kill this man? What reason could be good enough for this torture?" she whispered as he allowed the intruder to rise to consciousness before tightening his hold again.

He raised a hand, and she barely stopped herself from flinching, deadly certain the action would push him over the fine edge on which he currently stood. But he didn't hurt her, his finger breathtakingly gentle as he traced the curve of her cheekbone. "This was broken once."

A flickering montage of snapshots, the hazy years when she'd been pumped full of drugs and put in environs designed to shatter her spirit:

—*blackness, a room without light or air*

—*being treated with a false solicitousness*

—the sound of bone breaking, and pain, such terrible pain when she didn't retreat into the heart of the labyrinth fast enough

—lights even brighter than the white room from where Kaleb had taken her

—cruel cold on her naked body

"I . . . I think I remember." No matter the ugliness of the memories, she couldn't move away, couldn't break this painful, intense connection that tied her to the deadly Tk with eyes of obsidian.

Kaleb traced her cheekbone again. "He used a baton on you." A whisper so soft, it was a creation of purest rage. "He shattered your cheekbone, left you unconscious. The memory is at the forefront of his mind. I only had to punch through the first level of his shields to get to it. A pity his mind is now destroyed, his other memories shredded."

Nausea roiled in her stomach, flooded her mouth at the detached remoteness of that last sentence. "No," she said, the echoes of the past dulled by the pharmaceuticals they'd dosed her with at the time, but the *now* terrible. "No, Kaleb. He was no one, just a guard. There were—" She caught herself before she made a horrible error.

The cardinal with one hand crushing another man's airway kept tracing her cheekbone with his free hand. "Others. There were others. They'll all die, one by one." Then he turned, taking one look at the limp man in his grasp, and it ended.

The guard's neck snapped, his body falling to the floor, a discarded bit of trash.

Sahara fought the urge to throw up, to back away. "Why?" she asked again, a shivering cold in her chest. "Why take vengeance for me?"

His hand dropped off her cheek, his eyes continuing to roil with a sinuous darkness that spoke of hidden places of madness and death. "He wanted to steal you." *And you belong to me.*

A sharp pain in her chest at the dangerously possessive telepathic coda, the cold escalating to turn her blood to ice . . . because even faced with the bloody, broken reality of who he was, she wanted only to lay her face against Kaleb's chest, wrap her arms around him, and forget the world. Never had she felt as safe, as real, as when she'd held on to him, the peace in her a contradictory tempest of emotion. It was as if he were her own personal madness.

Swallowing to wet a throat as dry as bone, she tried to focus on something practical, something that didn't make her question her sanity. "How did he even find me?"

"His Tk was like mine; he could lock on to people as well as places." Kaleb's tone made it clear he'd taken that information from the guard's bruised and bleeding mind before that mind crumpled under the pressure of the brute-force intrusion. "However, he was much weaker on the Gradient, with a severely limited teleport range. It means he had help tracking you to this immediate area."

Teleporting in a scanner, he began to run it over her body before she'd connected the dots. The slim black device made a high-pitched beeping sound when he passed it over her lower back. "I need to push up your shirt."

She gave a shaky nod and waited, skin clammy and pulse oddly muted, as if her hearing were damaged, the world heard through a wall of water.

"There's a tracker embedded under your skin here"—a light touch to the right of her spinal column just before it curved into her sweats— "about the size of a grain of rice."

"They tagged me like an animal." It came out a harsh whisper, the numbness that insulated her from the reality of the violation holding by a wire-thin filament. "Like a piece of property."

"Wait." Dropping her shirt back down, Kaleb continued to scan her body.

He found five trackers. *Five.*

"They aren't difficult to remove." Black ice coated the rage she'd earlier glimpsed. "I should've checked for trackers when I first brought you home. We could've taken them out before the Tk was close enough to get a lock on you."

"Do it now," she ordered, the water crashing around her in a roar of pain and anger and revulsion. "I want them out now!" Her voice broke. "Get them out! Get th—"

Kaleb squeezed her nape. "I'll have them out in the next five minutes."

His assurance was enough for her to hold on to the shreds of her sanity . . . because Kaleb never broke his promises.

"Sahara! I'll come for you! Survive! Survive for me!"

Of course it was Kaleb who had spoken those words to her, made that vow. She was that important to no one else. Why that was true, and when he'd made the promise, those were questions she couldn't answer, but at this instant it mattered nothing. Not when, having led her into his bedroom, he placed his hand on her hair and said, "Lie down on your stomach and dampen your pain receptors while I 'port in a sterile medical kit."

Climbing onto the bed, she did as directed.

"I'm using a laser scalpel," he said, pushing up her shirt again to make a fine cut in her flesh. His hand was warm and strong against her skin where he braced himself, his knees on either side of her body as he straddled her. "You may feel the tweezers going in."

A cold push that burned, then nothing.

"Is it out?" she asked, skin continuing to crawl at the idea of what she'd had inside her all this time.

"Yes." Pressing a small thin-skin bandage over the wound, he asked her to flip over, then moved on to the next one. Placed just under her right hip, it really hurt when he used the tweezers, the whimper escaping her lips. It was strange. She remembered never, ever crying when they'd hurt her so much during her captivity, but here with Kaleb, her lower lip trembled, her eyes burned. As if all her defenses had fallen.

Kaleb paused, head jerking up. "Sahara"—a whip in his voice—"why haven't you done as I asked and dampened your pain receptors?"

"I don't remember how," she admitted, fingers flexing and clenching on the sheets. "I'm used to retreating into the labyrinth to escape pain. Please get it out. Please, Kaleb."

"I have it." Pulling the second tracker loose to her muffled sob, he telepathed a set of step-by-step instructions about how to temporarily numb her pain receptors. "Try—I can't give you any pain medication without it impacting your psychic state."

It was hard to concentrate, but she made a fumbling attempt, managed to lower the pain a fraction.

"I'm not destroying the tracking devices," Kaleb said, head bent as he concentrated on marking the exact location of the third bug, which had been inserted under her right armpit—a location she would've never thought to check.

"Why?" It made her skin crawl to think they might remain in the house.

"I'm teleporting each to a different hard-to-reach location around the world."

Her horror abated under the cold reasoning apparent in his voice. "That's smart," she said as he pulled out the tiny piece of technology. "It'll confuse them." Focusing her eyes on his chest so as not to see what he held in his hand, she made a conscious attempt to keep her breathing even.

The fourth bug was implanted between two of her toes. But the fifth . . . "I'll do it," she said, gorge rising at the knowledge that she'd been so thoroughly violated. That it must've been done by a medical team made it no less repugnant.

"You can't. It's too deep inside you." Putting down the medical tools, Kaleb retrieved the scanner he'd originally used to detect the bugs. "If I can see it in enough detail, I may be able to get it out."

Sahara bit down hard on her lower lip as he focused the scanner on her navel . . . lower. It was such an ugly thing they'd done to her that she couldn't quite bring herself to think about it. Instead, she kept her attention on her lethal, enigmatic captor, his silky black hair sliding over his forehead as he said, "Hold the scanner in this position."

She reached down without looking to do so.

"I have it." Kaleb's eyes locked with her own, the connection painfully intimate. "I'll have to tear it out through your flesh, but the damage will be minor as it's embedded relatively close to the surface of the skin. It'll hurt."

"It's okay," she said, tightening her grip on the scanner. "I'm ready."

Kaleb's jaw clenched at the gasp that escaped her. "It's out and buried inside a mountain deep in the heart of SnowDancer wolf territory, where only the very stupid would attempt to trespass."

Her skin felt suddenly clammy. "Thank you."

"The wound should heal on its own within the next two days," he said, tugging the scanner from her bone white grip to place it on the bedside table, "but if you feel something is wrong, I can have you in front of an M-Psy in seconds."

"It doesn't really hurt anymore." Shivers wracking her frame, she curled into herself. "Others will come eventually," she managed to say through her chattering teeth. "When they cross-check their readings with the Tk's report, they'll realize the trackers were all in one place here."

Chapter 14

KALEB LAY DOWN in front of her, tugging her close.

She resisted, though her skin ached for contact. "This hurts you."

"No." His hand closed over her throat in a dark possessiveness that was paradoxically calming. "I can turn off the dissonance."

The words made no sense, and then they did, her stomach dropping. If he could switch the pain controls on and off at will, there was *no restraint* on his telekinetic strength. It made him beyond lethal. "Impossible," she whispered, her eyes searching his expression for some sign that she'd misunderstood. "You wouldn't have survived to adulthood without the dissonance." It was what kept powerful offensive Psy from inadvertently causing harm to themselves or others.

"A child can learn many things." He gave her no chance to respond to that flat statement, before saying, "No one will come for you. Before his brain collapsed inward, I learned the Tk hadn't shared data because he wanted to use your recovery to increase his status."

The cold ruthlessness of him continued to shock her, and yet she allowed him at her throat, her pulse beginning to beat in time to his. "The trackers?"

"The devices only broadcast within a radius equal to that of a large city. No one else came toward this part of Russia."

So she was safe. As safe as she could be with a cardinal who had taken a life without remorse and with a calculated cruelty designed to prolong suffering. That she hadn't run screaming in horror, but into his arms, made her consider if her captivity had caused far more damage

than she realized. This compulsive, brutal attraction that had her opening the top buttons of his shirt to splay her fingers on his skin had to be
a creation of her no doubt powerful survival instinct. What better way to
survive than to make her captor believe her in his thrall?

The abhorrent thoughts slammed up hard against the raw emotions
that had torn her apart in the kitchen as they'd had a conversation that
had been missing so many parts, the words unspoken far more painful
than those they'd said aloud. Nothing so deep, so painfully passionate,
so *old*, could be the work of a mind bent on survival alone.

Yet, regardless of the mysterious emotional tie that bound her to a
cardinal Tk who could be a sculpture in Silence one minute and driven
by blackest rage the next, the fact was, *he appeared in not a single one of her
returning memories.* Either she had never before met him and she was
going mad, or their previous meeting had been so horrific, her mind
protected her from it even now . . . kept her from realizing that she was
at the mercy of a man groomed to adulthood by a psychopathic murderer.

"Did you help Enrique murder his victims?" she asked, the words
torn out of her.

Kaleb's eyes swirled with a blackness that seemed deeper than ebony
as he shifted position so that he was looking down at her, his hand still
at her throat. "I," he said, brushing his thumb over the flutter of her
pulse, "was there for every second of their torture and deaths."

HOURS after she'd finally run from Kaleb, her stomach convulsing as
she fought the urge to retch, Sahara lay in a fetal position in her own
bed, beneath three blankets that did nothing to negate the frigid cold in
her chest, in her bones. She should've been long asleep, but she couldn't
get Kaleb's voice out of her head.

I was there for every second of their torture and deaths.

The way he'd said it, it was simple, absolute fact. No room for negotiation or subtlety. Even if he hadn't actively helped—and she knew that
was a vain hope, no matter how much she wanted it to be true—he'd

known what Enrique was doing long before it had come to the attention of the changelings who had eventually executed the Councilor. She'd never blame the innocent child Kaleb had once been, but he'd kept this silence even after he became an adult with full access to his telekinetic strength; he'd protected his mentor, his teacher.

"Loyalty is everything."

A fury of backsight spun into her mind on the heels of that distorted vocal echo, and as always when her mind saw the past, she was an uninvolved bystander . . . except this time, the subject of her vision was a younger version of herself. Her just-above-the-knee-length tunic a sedate gray over a neat white shirt, black ballet flats on her feet, she walked down a leafy avenue shaded with cherry blossom trees in full bloom, the light tinged a soft pink by the delicate flowers.

Sahara recognized the uniform as that of her junior high school. From the way she'd done her hair—a single neat braid that reached the middle of her shoulders—as well as the type of satchel she wore over her shoulder and the bruise on her arm, she knew she was fifteen and on her way home after a vigorous game of baseball in her last-period physical health class.

One of her schoolmates had thrown for the plate, caught her on the arm instead as she slid home. He'd been very apologetic, but Sahara had been truthful when she assured him she was fine. Simply because, as a Psy, she had slightly weaker physiology than humans or changelings, didn't mean she was easily breakable, or that she couldn't take the normal wear and tear of life. As it was the body that supported the mind, physical exercise was a routine part of every Psy student's life.

It was the official reason why Sahara took dance classes three times a week.

"Memory," Sahara whispered in a bed far from the school where she'd once played baseball, understanding the fragment of backsight had segued into a hereto hidden memory.

As she walked on that far-off day, she took in everything around her, from the falling petals of soft pink to the occasional hover-capable car on the road. She'd always liked the dappled shade created by the heavily blooming trees, though to admit that would have been to sentence herself to corrective conditioning, so she'd hidden the fracture in her already unsound Silence and continued to take pleasure in the myriad hues of spring.

The fact was, she was temperamentally unsuited to the Protocol. It just couldn't sink its hooks into her, no matter how hard she tried. And she had tried. As a small child, she'd wanted to be like everyone else, had been diligent in practicing her mental exercises. The latter had had some effect—she'd been able to pass for Silent, though she had always thought Faith suspected.

Faith! Red hair. Cardinal eyes. Her gifted cousin who had kept her secret.

Fifteen-year-old Sahara nodded hello at a passing human classmate when he waved to her from his bicycle. Such actions were permissible in order to maintain social harmony, but the truth was, Sahara enjoyed interacting with different types of people. It was why she'd chosen to attend a school that wasn't specifically geared toward Psy, though when she'd made the request to the head of her family unit, she'd focused on the school's world-class foreign-languages program.

She wasn't the only Psy student, the school's academic track a brilliant one, but they were a definite minority. It gave Sahara countless opportunities to mix with people who lived outside Silence. The girl she liked best in her class was a gifted human pianist. The music Magdalena could create carried a haunting passion that went beyond notes and keys.

Sahara also had a changeling classmate who could do things on the sports fields that should've been impossible. Though Sahara's mind was scalpel sharp, her educational workload far more advanced than that of the rest of her class, her fingers couldn't create music that made the soul soar, her body couldn't move with the grace of a changeling's. But that didn't matter when she danced. It felt like flying.

That was who she was as she walked home from school that day— flawed, happy, smart enough to know that intelligence wasn't everything—and who she was when she chose to turn off the road in favor of a path through a quiet park. No other students walked here, but there was birdsong in the air, sunshine in the sky. She felt no concern, was utterly confident of her safety, and excited.

So excited!

SAHARA sat up in bed as the memory dissolved, leaving her with a single luminous piece of knowledge that tore apart her earlier doubts about her mental health. Her and Kaleb's relationship might be a thing of darkness, but it hadn't come into being because she was sick and damaged and struggling to survive.

She *had* met Kaleb before. A long time ago.

Not once.

Many times.

Every year on her birthday, he'd waited for her in a hidden curve of that pathway, and . . .

Her eyes went wide. Pushing off the blankets, she went to the right side of the bed, lifted up the mattress, and pulled out the small treasure she'd concealed there out of habit, she'd been protecting it for so long. She'd gone so psychotic when a guard tried to take it from her as a punishment that he'd been fired—because Sahara's hysteria had left her useless to her captors for days.

She'd still been cooperating to a certain point at that stage, in the hope that she could lull them into a false sense of security. That plan had failed, but after the mania of her reaction, no one had ever again tried to take her treasure from her, even during the worst punishments—as if they were afraid of fatally breaking her. Still, she'd stopped wearing it, hiding it in knots she created in her clothing.

Now, it glittered in the lamplight, a charm bracelet of shining platinum.

"Thirteen," she whispered and touched the key she knew was meant to represent the endless choices open to her.

"Fourteen." An open book. That was the year her ability for languages had become apparent, French as easy for her to understand and use as

Cantonese and Hungarian—as long as she was taught by a fluent speaker of the language, rather than using computronic aids. Intrigued teachers had theorized she had some type of unheard-of psychic ability that allowed her to unconsciously absorb languages from those around her, never realizing how close they skated to the perilous truth.

"Fifteen." A tiny globe that represented her dream of seeing the world.

"Sixteen." She touched wondering fingers to the dancer who leaped into the void with abandon, her arms raised above her head, pure joy in her expression.

Four, only four.

All from the man who now held her captive.

She sat on the edge of the bed, the bright metal warm in her palm, the charms of exquisite workmanship. It was the kind of gift that could be taken in many ways, the majority of them troubling, given Kaleb's connection to Santano Enrique, as well as the six-year age gap between Kaleb and Sahara. It mattered nothing now that they were both adults, but at the start, Kaleb would've been nineteen to her thirteen.

Except . . . for her the bracelet was associated with hope and a rare, incandescent joy. There was no hint of a taint, none of the ugliness that might mean Kaleb had been grooming her as a future victim. Even the idea made her stomach revolt, as if she'd done a terrible insult to something indescribably precious.

Kaleb would never hurt me.

Closing her fingers over the lovely present given to her by a familiar stranger wreathed in shadows, Sahara realized she had a choice to make: to trust in the emotions engendered by this bracelet—a bracelet she'd guarded and treasured for seven long, agonizingly lonely years, or to listen to the coldly rational part of her that reminded her Kaleb had walked hand in hand with a murderous monster since childhood.

IN spite of the late hour, he was working at his desk, his dark hair pristine, his steel gray shirt unwrinkled in the slightly yellow-tinged light from the table lamp that provided the only illumination in the room.

Looking up when she came in, the roiling darkness she'd glimpsed in the bedroom yet visible in his eyes, he said, "Yes?"

The dead calm of his voice had her hesitating, the decision she'd made a painful hope she couldn't bear to have crushed.

"Sahara," he said at her silence, "if you're here for a reason, speak. If you're not, leave."

Swallowing at the cold warning that told her not to push him, she took a seat in the chair on the other side of his desk. He watched her with the unblinking gaze of a predator so deadly, the world had never seen anything like him. "Where"—she wet a throat gone dry as a desert sun—"where are the rest?"

His eyes didn't move off her.

Trembling within, she lifted her fisted hand in front of her. Platinum shimmered in the golden light as her fingers fell open. A moment of absolute, endless silence, and then Kaleb blinked and the stars were back in his eyes.

Not breaking the eye contact that threatened to brand her from the inside out, he laid his right hand palm-up on his desk. Seven charms lay on his skin between one heartbeat and the next. Biting back tears as the most secret part of her keened in joy, she leaned closer, hand rising.

He drew the charms away.

Anger flashed, hot and raw. "They're mine."

"That's not how it works."

Scowling, and *wanting* the charms, she sat back in the chair as he stood and moved around the table with that deadly grace that always drew her eye, her body taut with a very adult tension. Breath shallow, she slipped the bracelet over her wrist, snicked the clasp into place, and held out her arm toward him. "Now."

Leaning against the desk in front of her, he lifted his hand and a single charm appeared between his fingertips. "Seventeen."

"A compass." *To find my way home.* Heart breaking, she looked her fill of him as he finished hooking the charm onto the bracelet, and again, she asked herself who he was to her. Who had he *been* to her, this beautiful man who might be so deeply damaged as to be forever broken?

Chapter 15

HE GLANCED UP, a lock of hair falling across his forehead, midnight dark against his golden skin. For a fleeting instant, she saw the boy he'd once been, all silky hair and quiet eyes, and she knew the memory was true. Her and Kaleb, whatever it was that tied them together, it had begun long before she was thirteen, begun when they were *both* children.

"Hurry," she whispered, helpless as her other hand rose to push that errant lock off his forehead.

He didn't move away, didn't repudiate her touch. "Eighteen." A second charm appeared between his fingers.

She twisted her head this way and that to try to see what it was as he hooked it into place, but he deliberately blocked her sight. She saw the reason why when he straightened. "An unsheathed blade." *What he had become the day she vanished.*

"Nineteen." He began to hook the charm on before she saw the telekinetic fetch.

A small home.

The rock that was her heart grew heavier. "Twenty."

"Twenty." This one, he let her see.

A tiny heart formed of a deep blue stone, so very beautiful it made her breath release in a sigh. "Sapphire?"

"Tanzanite." His eyes met hers. "Rare. Unique."

A frozen heart, she thought, her wonder swirled with a haunting sorrow. His heart or hers?

"Twenty-one."

An hourglass.

"Twenty-two."

A fragment of jagged obsidian, edges smoothed only enough not to cut her skin.

"Twenty-three."

A single, perfect star.

Frowning, she looked up at him. "I don't understand."

He hooked the charm into place. "Only this star matters." His thumb brushing over her inner wrist. "Should it be erased, no other has the right to live."

"I'd line the streets with bodies before I'd ever hurt you."

A wave of black rushed through her in a nightmare of understanding. "What's twenty-four?" she managed to ask through the roar, curling her wrist close to her chest.

"As yet undecided."

"I know what I want." This battle was one she had to win, not only for the future of the world, but for herself, for Kaleb, for what they might have been . . . what they could be.

A waiting silence from the man who would've annihilated an entire civilization in vengeance for her, ending the lives of millions, innocents and sinners alike.

"A sheath for the blade," she whispered.

The stars faded into black. "That might not be possible."

It can't be too late, she thought again. She *refused* to let it be too late, refused to believe he was forever gone, the damage permanent. "I want jewels on the sheath, bright and colorful." *And hopeful.*

"It'll require considerable work," he said softly, the obsidian of his gaze holding her own, "might even be an impossible task."

"Are you surrendering, then?" It was a question as soft. "Walking away?"

Kaleb's response held a possessiveness that might yet keep her a prisoner. "I will never walk away from you."

. . .

KALEB didn't go to bed after Sahara left his office following an interaction he hadn't ever thought would come to pass, not given what she'd
learned of him, and the injuries done to her in the years of captivity. He
should've known not to attempt to predict or judge her—Sahara Kyriakus
had always had an unexpected and stubborn will. No other woman
could've survived seven years in hell and come out of it with the strength
to challenge Kaleb.

He waited an hour to give her time to fall into deep sleep, before getting up and rolling down the sleeves of his shirt to do up the cuffs. Picking up his jacket from where it hung behind the study door, he shrugged
into it. His choice of clothing was another mask—it gave people a certain impression of him, an impression he intended to use tonight to
ensure Sahara's future safety.

No one was ever again taking her from him.

Ready, he discovered himself unable to leave before making dead certain she was safe and undisturbed in her rest. If he lost her now, after
she'd returned to him at last, eyes of midnight blue holding a fragile
trust he'd never again expected to see, there would no longer be any
question about his sanity or lack of it. The world had no knowledge of
the delicate hands that held its fate.

He made sure to position himself in the shadows by the door when
he teleported into her room, not wanting to scare her if she wasn't lost in
sleep. Fear in Sahara's eyes, he'd learned when she'd run from him earlier, burned worse than any acid Santano had poured on him when he'd
been a boy. It was dangerous, that pain, could drown the world in blood,
but Sahara had been the first, would always be the deepest, fracture in
his conditioning.

It was a truth as pure and as inescapable as the wind.

The room was pitch-black, but his eyes had learned to adapt in the
darkness of his childhood, and he had no trouble seeing her. Risking
going closer when her breathing proved quiet and steady, he saw her face
was turned sideways on the pillow as she lay on her back, the black

strands of her hair silky and thick across the Egyptian cotton of the pillowcase.

It was the best money could buy. He'd made certain of it.

Hand rising, he almost touched the sleep-warm curve of her cheek before realizing it would wake her . . . scare her. He couldn't risk that. Not now, when she'd remembered just enough to trust him on a basic level but not enough to brand him the monster he knew himself to be.

"You are what I made you. There is nothing else."

Visions of blood, bright and hot, spraying across his retinas, he teleported out and manually checked every door and window. Rerouting the perimeter alarms to feed into his cell phone once he was satisfied the house was secure, he made sure the siren remained active. If a breach did occur, he didn't want Sahara caught unprepared. The filleting knife she'd hidden under her pillow would work fine as a weapon if he was delayed by a second or two, especially since he'd quietly sharpened it until it would take only a single swipe to sever the carotid or jugular.

Security check complete, he looked in a mirror to confirm his mask remained in place, hair combed neatly and suit jacket buttoned, before accessing his Tk to build the framework for a teleport more complex than his usual split-second shifts. As the search for Sahara had thrown into dark focus, his ability to lock onto people wasn't foolproof. If the individual in question didn't know who she was, the attempt would fail. It was no coincidence the enemy Tk had found Sahara *after* she came out of the labyrinth.

A small number of telepaths in the Net—not necessarily the strongest, but the most intelligent—had figured out that weakness, too. If Kaleb had to guess, he'd say that was how the entire Lauren family, now part of the SnowDancer wolf pack, had ensured the success of their defection.

Tonight, he had to locate another individual who understood telepathic camouflage: Tatiana Rika-Smythe, fellow ex-Councilor and a woman who knew how to lay false trails so complex, it had taken him years to navigate the twisted pathways and retrieve Sahara . . . and days to unravel the blueprints of the psychic vault that had concealed Sahara's mind, *hidden* her from him.

He'd taken the blueprints apart piece by piece, and the more he saw, the more he'd recognized Tatiana's meticulous brand of psychic construction. "Do you know the name of the person who held you captive?" he'd asked Sahara earlier that night, as she sat curled up in the chair across from him, the star finally on the bracelet where it belonged. "The one in charge."

A shake of her head. "I was always blindfolded, my psychic senses leashed, and my hands tied when she came to visit."

She.

Another nail in the coffin, but it wasn't enough. The fact that he'd identified the man he'd executed today as being attached to one of Tatiana's shell companies was even more persuasive, but Kaleb needed to be certain beyond any doubt before he meted out this punishment. Baiting the trap, however, required only a little effort.

Tatiana had been very, very careful about protecting the location of her bolt-hole, which was why Kaleb had concentrated his attention on her finances. As expected, she had a multilayered and profitable empire. He'd long ago stripped away the phantom corporations that owned her assets per the official records, then sectioned the properties into business and personal.

He'd known her hidden base of operations would be in those files—Tatiana's biggest weakness was that she couldn't let go of anything she owned, not even to a shell company of which she had full control. Dig deep enough and her name *always* turned up as the true owner. That digging required considerable patience—and when it came to punishing those who had kept Sahara from him, Kaleb had an endless amount.

Australia had flashed up multiple times in his initial search, but he'd disregarded it as Tatiana had previously retreated to a remote part of that country. It would be unlike her to choose the same location twice. Only later had he considered the fact that Tatiana was intelligent and cunning enough to play everyone by doing exactly that. If not the same exact place as her previous headquarters, then close enough to it that she'd have access to the infrastructure she'd already put in place.

After that, it hadn't taken him long to discover the hidden property two miles from her known base. Getting an image he could use for a teleport lock had cost him over a hundred thousand dollars, but the man he'd turned in her employ had come through. Using that image to 'port himself to the fringe of the property, his Tk strength unshielded, he scanned the area bathed in the misty gray of early morning.

A single light burned in the apparently ordinary cottage set in the midst of a huge plot of land, the house surrounded by sparse native foliage. He saw footprints that suggested animals had passed near his current position—kangaroos from the shape—but the area closer to the house was apt to be alarmed and set with booby traps.

Retrieving the high-powered binoculars he'd slid into his pocket, he focused on the single square of light until Tatiana rose to get something, crossing the window, then back. Target confirmed, he worked with the binoculars until the focus was sharp enough to pick up a very specific knot pattern in the pine paneling opposite the window.

It was time to exact payment for seven years of Sahara's life.

Since perception was often everything when it came to the dance of power, he slid away the binoculars. He wanted Tatiana to know he could find her wherever she went; wanted her to taste fear, acrid and acidic.

He wanted her to beg for her life.

Seated behind the desk in front of which he appeared, Tatiana had a gun pointed at his head before he finished the teleport, but he'd long ago worked out how to compensate for the split-second vulnerability that came with entering an unknown situation. He avoided the laser fire with a fluid shift, then knocked the gun out of her hand, blocking her vicious telepathic strike at the same time.

"An unfriendly welcome for a colleague who wishes to talk business," he said to the brunette, undoing the buttons on his suit jacket before taking a seat in the chair on his side of the desk.

Though Tatiana's hazel-green eyes remained flat with suspicion, she didn't attempt to go for another weapon. "What are you doing here, Kaleb? We didn't have a meeting scheduled."

"I came across an item I thought might be of particular interest to you."

Relaxing into the black leather of her chair in a show of indifference, Tatiana picked up and tapped a stylus against the electronic blotter in front of her. "Really?"

Kaleb smiled and it was a calculated act. He'd learned to mimic the facial movement to placate the humans and changelings with whom he did business, but knew full well that it had the opposite effect on those of his own race. "Why such a violent welcome?" he asked, shoulders relaxed and arm lying loosely along the armrest.

"I wasn't conscious this location had been compromised," she said with just enough of a hesitation that he knew it had been as deliberate as his own actions.

Tatiana, he thought, would not pause at playing wounded prey if it got her what she wanted. "Ah."

"How did you penetrate my defenses?"

"I'm a teleport-capable Tk, Tatiana," he said with a gentleness that was a threat. "Do you honestly believe any security could keep me out if I wanted to get into a location, in the PsyNet or out?"

A flicker of comprehension, flawless olive-toned skin tightening over the razor-sharp blades of her cheekbones, but it wasn't enough. He needed absolute and categorical confirmation of her guilt, because this punishment would fit the crime in ways Tatiana couldn't comprehend.

"So," she said, continuing to tap the stylus in an unsteady rhythm he guessed was meant to distract him—because Psy did not make such "unconscious" nervous movements, "the business you have to discuss."

He smiled again. "I think you know."

"This will be an interminable negotiation if you don't put things on the table."

Yes, Tatiana was clever, but Kaleb had expected the demand. "I have in my possession," he murmured, "an item that may belong to you. It was retrieved by an Arrow"—a lie with just enough of a possibility of truth that she wouldn't question it—"after he became suspicious of a section of the Net that was blocked off for no rational reason."

"Really?" A thoughtful pause. "What makes you believe this item is of any value to me?"

"Your telepathic work is unmistakable in its complexity and dexterity."

"You flatter me."

"The truth is not flattery."

Tatiana responded with a smile as practiced and as false as his own. "I've heard that you're doing business with Nikita and Anthony as well."

He shrugged, the movement another one he'd copied from the more emotional races, and answered with the absolute truth. "It makes logical sense to create and utilize multiple strategic partnerships. Unlike the changelings, we do not blood-ally ourselves to one another; fidelity is understood to be a fluid concept." By some.

"That," Tatiana said, putting down the stylus, "is why we'd make an unbeatable team. Neither one of us has any flaws in our Silence."

Kaleb thought of the woman who slept in the house he'd built for her, of the man with a broken neck who had burned to ash in a crematorium incinerator hours ago, and knew his Silence was far more complex than Tatiana could imagine. "I insist on loyalty in my partners," he said. "I do not believe you capable of it." Even Nikita, ruthless as she was, would not stab him in the back as long as he kept his end of their bargain.

"I've never had a partner who deserved loyalty," Tatiana responded. "You, however, would."

"Now you flatter me."

"Truth is the best defense." The stylus in her grasp again, tap-tapping. "What do you want in exchange for the item?"

Chapter 16

"NOTHING YOU CAN'T afford," Kaleb said, his blood calm and as cold as death as he gave Tatiana more rope with which to hang herself. "A piece of information."

She waited.

"I want to know why you had the item in such a secure lockup in the first place." No privacy, no air, blinding light. "Backsight isn't, after all, a particularly useful ability."

"Backsight? You've lost me."

Clever, so clever, not to fall for his trap. "Exactly." As if making a decision, he rose, doing up the buttons on his jacket as he did so. "It appears I was mistaken. The item isn't yours—there is only one individual left to whom it could belong."

Tatiana continued to maintain her relaxed pose, but he saw the fine lines form at the corners of her eyes. "Who?"

"Anthony, of course," he said, well aware Tatiana utilized NightStar's forecasting services on a regular basis to increase the financial status of her empire. She could not afford to be blacklisted. Not only would it put her at a severe disadvantage in the Psy financial world, but her current investments would dive in value once the news leaked. And NightStar—Anthony—would make certain it did. The F-Psy clan understood loyalty, too, in a way Tatiana never would.

The tapping paused, the tendons in Tatiana's hand standing out against her skin. "No."

"No?"

Eyes connecting with his, chips of agate, she nodded at the chair. "Perhaps we can do business after all."

"I'm glad to hear it." He sat down, waited.

Tatiana took her time in replying. "I acquired the item intending to use it as a hostage should NightStar ever attempt to blacklist me, but it was never needed."

A lie, but that didn't matter. What mattered was the confirmation.

Tatiana gasped as she was shoved backward, her chair crashing to the floor as invisible manacles pinned her to the wall, her feet at least a half meter off the ground. One sleek black pump landed on the carpet with a dull thud, while the other drummed against the wall as she struggled to break free.

He hadn't expected such useless panic from Tatiana.

Put immediately on alert by her uncharacteristic lack of control, he looked into his mind—and saw the insidious tendril that had already penetrated the first three layers of his shields. Slamming outward with violent force, he sealed up the surgical holes she'd created as a drop of blood, dark and viscous, dripped out of her nose.

"Very smart." He'd made a near-fatal error in the grip of the black rage that lived below the shell of his Silence. Another half a minute and she'd have been inside his mind.

"What do you want?" she said when her ruse failed to distract him, her body now motionless and her voice frigid.

"I want to know why you took her," he repeated, relaxing into the chair without ever taking one eye off his shields.

"She's malfunctioning, of no use to you."

Kaleb sighed. "That's not the question I asked."

"You can't kill me," Tatiana said in that same icily composed tone. "Regardless of the rumors of the Council's demise, the psychic shock wave caused by the death of another Councilor will cause the Net to destabilize to a dangerous extent, especially given the current violence."

"Yes, that's true." And Kaleb hadn't yet decided if he wanted the Net to fracture on that level. "But there are worse things than death." With that, he used his telekinesis to dislocate her left knee the same way Sahara's had once been dislocated, according to the information caught by the scanner when he'd inspected her for tracking devices.

"I apologize," he said after Tatiana stopped screaming. "Where were we? I believe you were about to answer my question."

"She was given to me," Tatiana gasped, her left knee beginning to swell up.

"And who was your generous benefactor?"

"You know."

He didn't bother to warn her this time, simply dislocated her left shoulder exactly as Sahara's had been three years ago. That piece of information he'd gained when he pulverized the mind of the pathetic excuse for a male he'd executed in the kitchen. His lack of restraint had cost him a large amount of useful data; the guard's mind had broken split seconds after Kaleb smashed through his shields, leaving Kaleb a very short window in which to sweep up information, but he found he felt no remorse.

As he didn't now, watching Tatiana's head loll forward. She'd blacked out. "Weak," he said, having stayed conscious through far worse as a seven-year-old. He gave her a minute, and when she didn't awaken, picked up the glass of water on her desk without moving from his position in the chair and threw the contents into her face.

She came to with a whimpering jerk, wet strands of hair sticking to her skin and a glint of fear in her eye. Her Silence might have been pristine until this moment, her will ruthless, but for all her deadly cunning and strength, Tatiana Rika-Smythe hadn't been trained as Kaleb had been. She didn't know how to hold on to the conditioning—or a convincing reproduction of it—in the face of excruciating pain, with no end in sight.

Shivering from the onset of shock, she rasped out, "Santano Enrique gave her to me."

Her answer was no surprise, but Kaleb had needed to hear it from her mouth. "Why?"

"We were . . . partners of a kind. He respected my ambition, and I respected the fact he'd cut my throat if I ever turned that ambition in his direction. We trusted each other."

It was the ugliest definition of trust he'd ever heard. "Did you know she was mine when you took her?"

Tatiana shook her head. "No. I didn't think he allowed you to pick victims."

No, it wasn't then that Santano had needed him. "What are you doing, Tatiana?" He shifted the majority of his attention to his own mind as several alarms activated at once and found a secondary, near-invisible telepathic worm seconds away from penetrating his final shield.

His rebuff this time made blood vessels burst in her eyes, but she hissed out a breath, holding his gaze with the crimson of her own. "You aren't unbeatable. I almost had you."

"Almost is never good enough with someone like me, you know that." Shutting her up by constricting her diaphragm to the point that she had to shunt all her concentration toward the task of drawing in enough air to survive, he leaned back in the chair and said, "You never should have taken what was mine."

Despite her diminished oxygen supply, Tatiana began to struggle in earnest, striking at him with aggressive telepathic blows as vehicles running dark screamed to a halt outside. "Calling in reinforcements? Tut-tut." With that, he walked unhurriedly around the desk and teleported them both out.

The blackness inside the old cement bunker was broken up only by a single long-life bulb hanging from a rusty chain in the ceiling. The dull light didn't penetrate the shadows that gathered in deep pockets around the circular room, but it was enough to illuminate the yellowed and stained concrete beneath the steel table on which he dumped Tatiana's body, the shoe still on her foot clanking against the metal.

Stepping back, he watched her struggle up into a sitting position and look carefully around. No feigned emotion, nothing but the frosty will of a woman who had always been able to negotiate or manipulate her way out of trouble. It was an admirable trait, one Kaleb appreciated for the way it would extend and intensify her torture.

Tatiana would spend countless hours plotting escape, only to realize her hell was permanent.

"What is this place?" she asked.

"You don't know?" He waited for her to discover what he'd done.

It only took her a second. "Why can't I access the PsyNet?" she asked in a tone an octave higher than her normal voice, the first true hint of panic she'd betrayed. "You have a shield over me."

"I have other uses for my abilities. The DarkMind, however, finds it fun to play with a mind whose Silence promises to crack slowly and with great pain." It had sucked Tatiana into itself, blocking out everything, including her telepathic channels, in endless nothingness. If it then began to feed off her ensuing terror, first she'd go slowly, insidiously insane, then she'd fall into a coma where terror would continue to be her sole companion, and from there, death wouldn't be far behind.

That little habit of "eating" people was one tendency of the Dark-Mind Kaleb had never been able to stem—so he'd directed it at those who deserved a slow, maddening death. Kaleb did his own killing when it came to power and politics, but he had no compunction in setting the DarkMind loose on the other vermin. The last one had been a would-be pedophile with a collection of photographs that should have never existed, a man who had just gained a job as a nursery-school teacher.

However, the DarkMind knew not to feed off Tatiana. She was Kaleb's, and the dark neosentience was delighted to help him hold her. Kaleb, after all, understood the cruelty and rage and malevolence that had created it . . . because he'd been created of the same ugly components. "The DarkMind," he told Tatiana, "will keep you isolated in that black cocoon as long as I please."

"If I disappear from the Net," Tatiana said, not understanding that there was nothing she could say that would alter her fate, "it'll have the same effect as my death. The resulting shock wave—"

"Tatiana, Tatiana." He shook his head. "You disappeared from the Net when you created such beautiful shields to conceal your location."

She had made it so easy for him. "Soon after I leave, your security team will receive a sharply worded note ordering them to do a full security audit, since they failed their recent 'test.'"

Again, she had paved the way for her own imprisonment—she was so paranoid about her enemies that she rarely used telepathy these days, preferring to communicate via secure e-mail. "As for your companies, as long as they continue to receive instructions from 'you,' no one will be any the wiser."

Tatiana's hand gripped the edge of the metal table hard enough to make her bones push against her skin. "Kaleb, I didn't know she was yours."

"That's irrelevant." Rage rolled through his bloodstream in a pitiless wave, cold and unforgiving. "You still damaged her to the point where she may never fully come back." Sahara had screamed in that bloody bed during their last meeting, but she had never begged, somehow managed to stay whole. Then had come Tatiana, and a captivity that had forced Sahara to entomb herself to survive.

"What does it matter to you, if you intend to kill her anyway?" Tatiana asked, a desperation in her tone that was too ragged to be feigned.

Psychic isolation had a way of doing that to Psy. Sahara had lived the same nightmare for seven years. "My intent makes no difference to your culpability."

Strolling around the circular room, he glanced at the food stores to make sure she had enough to survive on. The medical supplies were basic, but she'd be able to do some first aid. He'd been very careful about the injuries he'd done her—none of it was life threatening, and she could fix the dislocations herself.

It wasn't difficult. Kaleb had learned to do so as a boy.

Tatiana followed him with her eyes. "You're not planning to leave me here." Swinging her legs off the side of the table that had channels on either side meant for blood and other bodily fluids, she bit down on her lower lip, her left knee grotesquely swollen. "Kaleb, you can't. You're not Santano Enrique."

"Aren't I?" He smiled again. "The food will last for six months if you don't gorge. I hope you enjoy the accommodations."

"Wait! Wait! What is this place?"

Closing the distance between them, he leaned in to whisper the truth in her ear. "It's Santano's oldest playroom, of course." A room no one else knew existed, the stains on the floor created by the blood of countless victims Kaleb had watched scream and plead and break.

HAVING woken early to find Kaleb's door closed, Sahara dressed in jeans paired with a floaty rose-colored top, made herself a hot drink, then padded down to visit the koi, before curling up in her favorite armchair in the living room. She loved the way the pale gold morning sunshine made the room glow, the grasslands beyond shimmering with light, until they weren't desolate but achingly beautiful.

Her intent had been to read further articles on her cousin Faith's spectacular defection from the PsyNet, but the light kept hitting the bracelet she wore on her right wrist, and each time it did, she'd think of a man kissed by darkness, of the single star and a history she couldn't remember. She was rubbing her finger over the final platinum charm when Kaleb walked into the room. Dressed in the same business suit she'd seen him in last night, it was clear he hadn't been asleep as she'd assumed.

Her first thought was that he was a dangerously seductive predator in a flawlessly cut mask. Her second was that something was very, *very* wrong. "Kaleb, what is it?" Putting aside her organizer, she shoved aside the lap blanket she'd found folded on the back of the armchair and ran to him. His expression was as remote and as inscrutable as always, and yet her blood ran cold, the tiny hairs on her body standing up in alarm.

"Kaleb, please." Desperation had her daring to touch the fingertips of both hands to his cheeks. "What have you done?" It came out a near whisper.

"Nothing that didn't need to be done." Closing his hands around her wrists, he tugged her own gently off his face and to her sides, where he broke contact. "You don't want to touch me right now."

"Why?" There was a wildness inside of her, a screaming, panicked girl who said she had to fix this, fix *him*, though she knew, she *knew* that she couldn't turn back time, couldn't undo that which had made him into this shard of obsidian. "Are you afraid whatever you've done will rub off on me?"

"Do you think I'm sorry?" He gave her a smile that was lazy and perfect . . . and horrifying. "I'm not and I never will be."

Chapter 17

WALKING AROUND HER trembling form, he moved to the windows that overlooked the grasslands. "Why are you so certain I've done anything at all?"

Sahara swallowed around the chilling fear incited by his otherness. He had always been lethal, but now it was as if he'd gone so far into the abyss that he'd become a living, breathing part of it. At this instant, she wasn't certain the intelligence behind those eyes of darkest night was anything she could comprehend, so cold as to be inhuman. "I just am," she said at last, the gut-deep knowledge rising from the hidden part of her in which lived the girl she'd once been. "Talk to me."

"Perhaps your backsight has evolved," he said, his tone gentle . . . and heavy with the same black rage she'd witnessed in the kitchen when he executed the guard. "Your cousin Faith's visions are now apparently no longer limited to business."

Unable to bear seeing him all alone by the window, though he scared her down to her bones right now, she walked to stand close enough that their clothing brushed. "Faith," she said, picking up on the topic he'd raised simply to keep the line of communication open, "helped me refine and build my firewalls." Such shielding would be critical should she set foot in the PsyNet.

"Unusual for a cardinal F."

"When she was much younger, the M-Psy in charge of her believed contact with another child might help develop her lagging speech." Delayed speech was common in the F designation, but Faith had been three before she said her first word. "I was younger than her, but they chose me because I was so vocal."

"And perhaps because a child closer to her age may have resented the extra training and attention mandated by her cardinal status."

"Yes." Sahara had been too much in awe of her cardinal cousin, with her pretty red hair, to feel any such envy. "She was older than her years, her Silence faultless, but she was never unkind to me—she made me feel important." Strictly supervised at all times, they had never had the freedom to become friends, but Sahara had felt the promise of it. "I was sad when her power spiked after eleven months and further contact was deemed disruptive and unhealthy for her mental state."

The justification was one Sahara had been too young to doubt. Clearly, however, since Faith had ended up mate to a jaguar changeling, a predator with very sharp teeth, she was in no way fragile. "Did our PsyClan betray her for money?" Had they locked Faith up to milk her of visions, and the millions those visions brought into the family's coffers?

"Unknown." Kaleb turned at last, his gaze crashing with her own.

The power that burned in the black depths was staggering, a near-physical force.

"I grew up with a cardinal," she whispered, suddenly conscious of how tightly he usually shielded himself. "You're *more*." It should've been impossible: to be a cardinal was to be off the scale, but she'd never felt such power.

The force of it was terrifying. Even more so was the fact that her need for him had in no way been diminished by the darkness that encased him. It made her consider exactly how much she'd accept, how much she'd forgive, how far she'd walk into the abyss for this deadly Tk who had a claim on her so deep, reason had nothing to do with it.

"I was there for every second of their torture and deaths."

Chest a painful tightness, she broke the agonizing intimacy of the eye contact and took what felt like her first clear breath in hours. When she glanced back at him, he was looking out through the window once more, his aloneness an opaque shield. And she knew that if she chose to walk away and ignore this, he wouldn't stop her. Kaleb was used to answering to no one, but the flip side of that was that he had no one who cared if he ever came home.

"Tell me," she whispered, heart twisting with the tumult of her emotions, because the idea of a world without Kaleb in it ignited a panic that obliterated her fear of what he was, to replace it with nerve-shredding horror. "What you did."

His eyes, black as a moonless night, remained on the empty grasslands. "Why?"

No denial. It struck her that he was far too intelligent for that to have been a mistake. "Because you said you'd never lie to me." The words came from that girl, the one who had gritted her teeth and clawed her way to the surface of Sahara's mind, and who held within her the secrets of the past that linked Sahara to Kaleb.

His head snapped toward her. "I also told you not to trust me."

Sahara leaned her shoulder against the window, her body turned toward his. "If not you, then who?" A sense of déjà vu, as if she'd said the words before, as if they'd already had this conversation. "You promised." With those whispered words, she gave in to the madness and brushed back the silken black strands that had fallen across his forehead, the fleeting contact breaking her heart.

This time, he didn't push her away. But the black ice, it remained as he spoke. "I went to have a discussion with the woman who held you captive."

It was the last thing she'd expected him to say. "Who?" A rasped-out question, her gut roiling at the memory of her hours with the stranger who had urged her to "cooperate" in a gentle tone that was an ugly counterpoint to the torture being inflicted on her flesh.

"Tatiana Rika-Smythe."

The name meant very little to Sahara except for what she'd read in recent news articles. She'd been a teen at the time of her abduction, had had little interest in the Council and the politicking of those aspiring for it. "It makes sense," she said, feeling not rage, but a nauseating sense of revulsion. "As much as anyone else hungry for power."

Kaleb reached out to touch a tiny scar on her left cheekbone, the impact lightning in her veins. "You didn't have this when you were six-teen."

"What?" Raising her hand, she closed her fingers around the strong bones of his wrist. "No. I must've been around eighteen when . . . you know what happened."

"Yes." A flat statement, his hand cupping her jaw. "They hurt you."

Sahara's skull echoed with the sound of bones breaking as Kaleb flung her former guard against the kitchen wall, a potent reminder of the deadly possessiveness that drove Kaleb's actions where she was con-cerned. "What," she asked again, "did you do to Tatiana?" It wouldn't, she knew, have been the relatively quick death he'd meted out to the guard.

Kaleb stroked the forgotten scar with his thumb once more before dropping his hand, his wrist sliding out of her grasp. "She's in a hole," he said. "I'll make sure she spends a lifetime in that hole. It seems a fitting punishment."

Sahara wrapped her arms around herself, rubbing at her flesh in a vain effort to warm it up. "Have you cut her off from the PsyNet?"

"What use would the punishment be otherwise?" No hesitation, no give, no change in his tone or expression.

Sahara wanted to smash her fisted hands against the invisible black ice, even knowing that it was too hard to shatter, that the effort would only bloody her hands and leave him untouched. "She'll go mad." Under all the rhetoric and the lies, one truth remained—that the Psy were not the least, but the *most* social of all three races. As a changeling wolf needed his pack, those of her race needed the connection and stimula-tion of a psychic network peopled by other minds. "We aren't built for such isolation."

"You survived." Anger so cold, it masqueraded as pure Silence.

"I wasn't completely cut off, not to that extreme." She had no loyalty to Tatiana, didn't care if the other woman lived or died, but this was costing Kaleb a piece of his soul, and he couldn't afford to give away any more. "I could always hear the guards talking to one another, if not to me. It was enough to remind me the world existed."

The darkness prowled in Kaleb's eyes, a living entity. "I'll make sure to visit her every three or four months. That should even out the field."

KALEB saw the torment in Sahara's expression and knew that whatever Tatiana had ordered done to her during the years she'd spent in captivity, it hadn't destroyed her conscience. It was not unexpected. That had always been the difference that kept them on opposite sides of the line that separated dark from light, good from evil—his ability to feel empathy, feel anything, had been eradicated before it could ever take root, with a single, limited exception.

"I," he murmured, "can never permit her freedom. She would find a way to harm you."

Sahara's eyes were haunted when they met his. "Am I so important to you?"

"Yes," he said. "You're everything." The entire reason for his existence.

A single tear trailed down Sahara's cheek. "Why can't I remember you?"

"You're not strong enough yet." For the horror, the pain, the realization of the betrayal that had splattered blood around a cheap hotel room when she'd been a girl on the brink of womanhood.

Stroking her fingers along his jaw, she said, "Come back, Kaleb," and stepped closer, moving her hands to his lapels to push the unbuttoned suit jacket off his shoulders. "Walk out of the dark."

He could crack the earth's crust for her if she wanted, cause the Ring of Fire to ignite and the world to tremble, but he could not give her this one thing she asked. The darkness was inside him now, part of the very cells of his body, as indelible as the life that had shaped him.

She heard his silence but didn't put distance between them, didn't cry. Instead, she brushed away the remnants of her earlier tears and, undoing the silk of his tie, slid it out from around his neck to drop it to the floor with his jacket. When her fingers began to work on the buttons of his shirt, he removed his cuff links and threw them on a nearby table.

The clinking sound as they landed had her lashes rising, the incredible midnight blue of her eyes drenched with emotion. But she held her words still, lowering her gaze to pull his shirt out from his pants and finish unbuttoning it. He stood motionless, each flicker of contact a shock to his senses, but it was a pain he craved—until her, he had believed himself immune to the need for skin-to-skin contact, contact that defined intimacy for the humans and changelings.

Now he knew his need was more vicious than theirs could ever be.

Shrugging off his shirt at the push of her fingers, he hissed out a breath when she wrapped her arms around his waist to lay her cheek against his chest. When she would've pulled back, he put a hand to the back of her head and said, "No. I've disabled the dissonance."

Thanks to Santano's ego and arrogance, Kaleb, a deadly dual cardinal, had never been fully indoctrinated with the programming that dealt out painful punishment for any hint of emotion. Designed not only to bolster the individual's Silence, but to suppress any response that might trigger a catastrophic lack of psychic control, the brutality of the punishment was tied to the intensity of the breach. Given the experiences Kaleb had undergone as a boy, the resulting dissonance would've killed him. So Santano had leashed his abilities through the application of another kind of pain.

Now the only restraint on his abilities was the one he'd put in place.

Assessing the risks, he spread his fingers in the heavy silk of Sahara's hair, wrapping his other arm around her shoulders to hold her to him. Her breath was soft over his skin, her body thin but no longer so fragile as to be easily breakable, her warmth a reminder that she was alive and with him.

It wasn't enough, the bond between them nascent at best. She might wear his bracelet, but she remained wary, her eyes watchful—he needed her committed to him before she remembered the ugly truth that connected them.

Tugging back her head with the hand he had in her hair, he wrapped his other one gently around her throat and, looking into her eyes, leaned down to brush his lips across her own. It was a calculated act, his every sense concentrated on Sahara, on judging her responses in order to offer the correct feedback.

"Kaleb." A gasp, her fingernails biting into the flesh of his back.

SAHARA ached deep inside, and it wasn't an ache that had in any way abated since she'd walked out of the labyrinth. No, it had only grown deeper, day by day. Today, she'd touched Kaleb in a last-ditch attempt to bring him back from the dark place where he'd gone, but now that his skin brushed against her own, she hungered for more. This, in spite of the fact that the darkness remained in his gaze, the inhuman intelligence of him watching her with eyes of obsidian.

It was madness to permit this to continue, to make herself ever more vulnerable to a man she might never understand, but reason had long slipped out of her grasp. Pressing her hand to his cheek, she closed her eyes and parted her lips under his in an instinctive invitation that he accepted without hesitation, one hand gentle at her throat, the other tight in her hair as the taste of him—hot, male, inexorably dark— infiltrated her every sense.

The caress felt raw, unpracticed, but no less addicting for it. The realization that he'd done this act with no other, that it was as new a pleasure to him as it was to her, was heroin in her bloodstream, a shocking punch of sensation, the world a study in passionate red. Stretching her body upward, her weight balanced on her toes, she kissed him with a wild desperation that lacked any sense of finesse.

It didn't matter.

Kaleb took what she gave and demanded more, until her heart ricocheted in a hard drumbeat against her ribs and air was something she gasped in between indulging in the heated recklessness of the kiss. A kiss that had her pressed between the cool glass of the window and the hard ridges of Kaleb's body, one of his hands still at her throat.

The physical reminder of his deadly possessiveness did nothing to throw cold water on the conflagration that threatened to consume them both. Kaleb wasn't cold now, his skin hot enough to burn, the arm he'd braced over her head trapping her in a prison she had no desire to escape. Thrusting her hands into his hair, she held him to her, sinking her teeth into his lower lip in a feral act of passion that should've shocked her.

It didn't. Not in the madness.

His hand tightened the barest fraction on her throat before he echoed the act, and she wanted to scream at the electric burn the primal caress ignited over her body. Too much, this was too much too soon, but she couldn't stop, couldn't bear to let him go. The sound of something crashing to the kitchen tiles made her jerk back, chest heaving. "Kaleb?"

"It's nothing." His mouth was on hers again the next second, the muscled width of his shoulders hiding the rest of the room from her view . . . but she felt it when something hit the wall with enough violence to make the house vibrate.

Wrenching away her mouth, she shoved at his chest.

He didn't budge, the look on his face leaving her uncertain if he was rational in any way, his eyes gleaming a black so deep, she'd never seen it in nature. Only in the darkest, most twisted recesses of the labyrinth.

Chapter 18

"KALEB, SOMETHING IS wrong."

His expression didn't alter, the flush of passion on his cheekbones and the perspiration that glimmered on his shoulders in the morning sunlight doing nothing to soften the hardness of him. Even the hair she'd mussed with her fingers only made him appear more dangerous, a predator who'd removed his mask to reveal the harsh truth.

Breath still short and shallow, she pressed her fingers to his lips when he would've claimed her mouth again, the addictive heat of him pressed up against her breasts. It took a level of self-control that was staggering in its intensity—this man, he could make her his slave, her body his to command. *"Kaleb."*

Stroking his thumb over her pulse once more, he finally released her and turned to face the room. Sahara looked around him, felt her eyes widen.

The room was trashed.

It had been the sofa smashing into the opposite wall that had finally broken through the desire that had had them both in its grip. The piece of furniture had created a hole in that wall, but that wasn't the worst of it. Every single window in the room, aside from the one on which she'd leaned, was spiderwebbed with fractures so deep it felt as if a breath would cause the shards to fall, while the floor was *rippled*, and a large table lay in splinters near the wide doorway into the kitchen, as if it had been thrown at the doorway and not made it through.

"A kiss," she whispered, staring at Kaleb's profile as he took in the damage done by his telekinetic strength with a clinical eye. "One kiss."

Kaleb, his upper body gilded by the sunlight, angled his face toward her. "I'll have to refine my shields—they failed against the intensity of the contact."

Sahara released a shuddering breath, her breasts heavy and almost painful. "Are you safe on the PsyNet?" If his shields failed on the mental plane, his mind would become as vulnerable as hers had been before he'd extended his shields to protect her. "If any of what we're experiencing leaks—"

"There's been no breach." A pause before he shifted to face her, one of his hands lightly cupping the side of her jaw, his eyes a black inferno. "I want more."

Caught off guard at the realization that his arousal hadn't been tempered by the interruption, Sahara's lips parted in a gasp. Kaleb took the silent invitation, his mouth on hers as he pressed her back to the glass, his erection pushing into her abdomen in hard demand. Moaning, she sucked on his tongue as his hand came up to cover her breast . . . and the world turned to shards of glass, the windows exploding in a glittering shower of deadly snow.

KALEB had Sahara out on the terrace before she could be hit by a single splinter of glass. Her eyes huge, she watched the glass collide in the middle of the room before the shards fell to the floor in an oddly musical crash. Ignoring the sight, Kaleb found his gaze locked on the slick wetness of her lips.

A single thought and he could have them in the bedroom, could have her naked, the skin-to-skin contact total.

"You're bleeding." Sahara's fingertips skated over his shoulders, where he'd been hit by a few stray splinters.

Blood. She had bled more than he'd thought possible.

The cold whisper of memory succeeded in doing what the glass hadn't, reminding him of the damage that could be done by an out-of-control Tk. Forcing his fingers to release her arms, he turned away to look out through the bars of the railing and into the gorge, the air cool against his skin, the sun not yet at full strength.

With each breath came another piece of reason. Both his PsyNet and personal shielding, he saw when he checked on them, were over half-gone. They hadn't collapsed—they had exploded one by one, going outward from his core. Not a fatal failure, three of his outer shields holding firm . . . but close. Closer than he'd come since he was a child.

A few more minutes and his abilities would've gone rogue.

"This is dangerous." Sahara came to stand beside him, but she didn't attempt to touch, leaving enough distance between them to prevent accidental contact. "For both of us."

Already rebuilding his shields, Kaleb reached out to grip the iron bars, his arms spread wide. "You were never at risk." The obsidian shield he'd placed around her was impregnable.

That very impermeability was the reason he couldn't go obsidian himself. It would leave him cut off from the data streams of the Net, a deadly blindness. Now, his renewed shields fractured before reaching maximum strength, Sahara's proximity problematic. Fixing an isolated location in his mind, he said, "I'll return in an hour," and teleported out.

SAHARA didn't attempt to stop Kaleb, the glitter of glass when she turned to look into the living room proof enough of why he needed to distance himself from her. Staring at the sunlight as it was refracted by the shards, creating beauty out of destruction, she leaned her back against the iron bars that encircled the terrace.

You were never at risk.

"Wasn't I?" she whispered, thinking of the madness of her surrender. Even after recognizing how far he walked in the darkness, even after hearing the chill inhumanity in his voice, even after seeing the calculation in his gaze before he kissed her, she had given in to the rage of need that lived inside her.

And in him.

Kaleb may have begun the kiss with a calculated motive—but he had been her partner in the madness by the end, his body as aroused as her own, his mind as enslaved as hers. Fingers trembling, she pushed back her hair and took a seat on the lounger, her eyes trained on the smooth wooden planks that made up the terrace. It wasn't healthy, this obsessive need she had for Kaleb, not when her trust in him was born of a past she couldn't consciously remember.

Even more, when she didn't know who she was, who she'd *become*.

She was still there when Kaleb returned, walking onto the terrace through the doors of his study. It was clear he'd showered, washing off the blood and sweat both. His hair was in place, his suit pants a crisp black, the same color as the silk tie at his throat, a fresh white shirt covering his upper body. He hadn't folded back the sleeves as he often did at home. Instead, cuff links glinted at his wrists.

The mask was back in place.

"I've organized damage repair," he said to her, sliding his hands into the pockets of his pants. "I'll need to relocate you for a few hours tomorrow to give the human crew time to get the work done."

Sahara, her body in a kind of shock at the rawness of what had passed, tried to find some hint of the same in Kaleb and failed. "Aren't you afraid they'll sell information about your home?"

"No." It was said with the brutal confidence of a man who knew he scared people far more than could be alleviated by any monetary incentive.

The tiny hairs on her arms rose in shivering warning, though the sun shone overhead. "I can't think here," she said, the glinting shards of glass continuing to catch her eye, the bars around the terrace suddenly stifling. "The beach. Will you take me to the beach?"

She kicked off her shoes the instant they arrived at the isolated stretch of water, the endless horizon unlocking the chains around her ribs. Sucking in gulps of the sea air, she rolled up her jeans and waded into the shallows, her thoughts calming and settling with each lap of the waves against her shins. It was a long time later, her decision made, that she came to sit beside him on the sun-warmed sand, taking care to make certain their bodies didn't touch.

As she'd learned in the house, the ice that encased Kaleb *wasn't* indestructible. And if he crashed through it again, she'd fall with him. Regardless of her reasoned, rational thoughts, one thing she'd accepted as she stood in the water: Kaleb was an addiction so visceral, she could never hope to control it. Not while the past that connected them remained a smudged mirage.

"I want to ask you for something," she said quietly. "But first, I need you to tell me what's happening in the PsyNet." It was critical she have that information if she was to enter the psychic network on her own in the near future.

KALEB had been primed to deal with the fallout from his significant loss of control, but this was one question he hadn't expected. However, he didn't even consider shielding her from the truth. Sahara's strength was indisputable—she had survived seven years of captivity and, before that, she'd survived a monster and his apprentice.

"It's being attacked on two fronts," he said, the walls of his mind scrolling with images of a chipped blade as it sank into soft feminine flesh. "Pure Psy is the first and obvious aggressor, but the more dangerous one, long term, is a disease that's causing the psychic fabric of the Net to rot and die."

Seeing her interest, he gave her the full details, before adding, "In a Psy host, infection leads to mental degradation, including outbreaks of violence and, eventually, death."

Expressive, her face hid nothing as she worked through the ramifications. "It's us," she said, her intelligence as acute as it had always been. "The Net is created out of the minds of our race, and we're broken on a fundamental level." Sadness lingered in the midnight blue. "If it's a Netwide problem, it must be manifesting in more subtle ways even in areas that appear free of infection."

She had understood in a single minute what others had not seen after months of exposure, even people who should know better. "There are those who are becoming more and more innocent"—almost childlike—"while others are turning twisted and dark to the extent that their future rampages will eclipse the insanity and serial killing that made Silence seem the better choice."

Sahara hugged her arms around her raised knees. "That's bad, but not as bad as what the infection is doing to the psychic fabric of the Net."

Kaleb said nothing, his attention on the scent of her hair as the wind swept the strands across her face and over his arm.

"If the rot creates enough points of weakness," she whispered, "the Net will fragment and eventually collapse. *Everyone* will die."

"It won't fragment, won't collapse." If it did, Sahara would die and that was unacceptable. "I have the power to ensure it maintains its integrity."

Sahara had already begun to understand what drove Kaleb. "You plan to seize total control." She knew she should be horrified—Kaleb was an avatar of darkness, in no way the right man to trust with the fate of an entire people. But she couldn't argue with his reasoning; his power was vast. He might be the only one capable of saving their race from the day of reckoning coming ever nearer with every infection, every inch of rot. "What will you do with it?"

"That has yet to be decided."

Beads of cold sweat rolled down her spine, and suddenly the declaration of possession she'd taken as a sign of an obsession that could entomb them both in black ice was something else altogether. "That's why you want me, isn't it?" she said, her pain so deep, it had no name, no ending. "You know what I can do."

Kaleb stared out over the water, his profile limned by the sun. "I've always known what you could do." Had been aware of the vast potential locked within her slender frame since she was a child. "I won't use you or hurt you." The promise was one he'd made long ago, one she could no longer remember . . . though she'd kept her own promise.

Sahara had no comprehension of the power she wielded, of the empires he'd destroy for her, the blood he'd spill. All she saw was the

monster he'd become. "I would never hurt you." Every man had a breaking point, and Sahara was his—and though he knew his declaration to
be the wrong move on the chessboard, her trust in him wavering, he
could no longer stand the wariness of her.

Sahara's eyes were of infinite depth when she looked at him, the clarity of her gaze seeming to strip away the mask until she saw the ugly
truth of his becoming. "I want to go home," she said, "to Tahoe. To my
father."

Every muscle in his body went rigid. "I've told you, you belong to
me." She was the only person in the world who did, and he would never
surrender his claim.

Not unless and until she did the one thing that would forever separate them.

"You also promised me you'd never hurt me." It was a quiet reminder
of the vow he'd just remade. "This—us—I'm being subsumed in it."
Acrid fear, the line of her jaw taut as she turned her gaze to the water. "I
can't become who I'm meant to be in your shadow. I'm afraid of waking
up one day and finding there's nothing left inside me but this furious
need for you that wrenches away my sanity."

The cold void in him, the part that spoke to the DarkMind and found
satisfaction in Tatiana's terror, saw in her confession—in the memory of
the way she'd held him to her, both of them out of control—a submission
that gave him the power to bend her to his will. If he held her long
enough, Sahara would be his in every way. But even the part that was the
void, merciless and without conscience, knew one thing: the woman
who remained would no longer be Sahara, her murder a quiet suffoca-
tion.

"There is no guarantee NightStar will be safe for you," he said, the
waves crashing to shore with increasing force as his telekinesis threatened to slip its bonds. "You had your suspicions about what they did to
Faith."

"My father, I remember him now." She blinked against the spray of a
wave that slammed to the sand with enough force to reach them both.

"He's not just a name, was never just a genetic donor. He would've missed me."

Seeing the flecks of water on his shirt, Kaleb was reminded of the shards of glass that carpeted the living room. "Your father is Silent." As he spoke, he switched on the dissonance at the highest level, wracking his body with a nerve-shredding pain that he bore in expressionless quiet. He could not risk losing lethal control while Sahara sat next to him, asking to walk away. The pain itself did nothing to halt the Tk—no, it was simply a reminder that he could never, ever let go.

If he struck out and ended her, he would become a nightmare in truth.

"He might be Silent," Sahara said, her mind filled with images of a big man who had picked her up and dusted her off after countless childhood accidents, "but I was more to him than a biological legacy." In front of her, the waves remained aggressive but no longer violent, and she knew the Tk beside her had found the black ice again. Passionate anger bubbled below her skin, her hatred directed at the very remoteness that might make him open to reason.

"My father treated me with care"—she tightened her grip around her own wrists to stop from reaching for Kaleb—"even when my only known gift was backsight at a level far below my standing on the Gradient. He never once made me feel as if I were a disappointment. My whole life, I knew I was important to him."

Glancing at Kaleb when he remained silent, the wind whipping her hair off her face, she said, "Did he search for me?"

Kaleb's eyes remained on the water, his gaze that blackness so absolute, she couldn't imagine what he saw. "Yes. Leon Kyriakus has led the NightStar search since the day of your disappearance, to the present day."

Hope struggled to life inside her. "Tatiana is . . . out of the picture"—tightening her stomach muscles to contain the roiling in her abdomen—"and there is no reason to believe anyone in my family was ever sympathetic to her. NightStar is a very tight-knit clan." They'd had to be. Foresight was not a gift that allowed for the survival of the individual without the support of the group. "Even if they did sell out Faith"—it hurt to think that—"it shows a profit motive. There is *no* possible economic advantage in giving up my ability to another."

No response from the deadly Tk who considered her his possession.

"I want to go home, Kaleb," she said again, and watched the waves turn murderous.

Chapter 19

SAHARA THOUGHT THE sight magnificent, the crashing thunder of the water a dark music. There was no fear in her blood because, foolish though it might be, she believed him when he said he wouldn't hurt her, this fascinating and lethal male her subconscious saw as safe, and who held the power to enslave her body. There was a haunting hardness to his beauty, as if he had been carved of pure iron, but that only made the temptation worse—because he burned for her, as he burned for no other.

"I want to sit in my father's kitchen," she whispered, tasting the salt of the spray thrown up by the waves, "and I want to sleep in the bed that was mine." She was no longer the teenager who had once shared the small, neat house with her father, but that teenage self was the only template she had for who she might've been. It was her starting point.

Kaleb's response was scalpel sharp and as cold. "Your shields are paper-thin."

"Yes." Wanting desperately to hold him, to scream at the injustice of what had been done to them both, she tightened her grip on her own wrists until her hands threatened to go numb. "I'll need help to hide my broken Silence, as well as my vulnerabilities."

"Are you asking me to help you?"

It was a ridiculous request of this man who had confessed to having been an apprentice to a serial murderer, and who had kept her prisoner in a home far from civilization, and yet she said, "Yes."

Heart thudding at the risk she took, but no longer able to fight the hunger for contact, she touched her fingers to his forearm, directly above the mark that was less a scar and more a brand, the fine and slightly damp cotton of his shirt not thick enough to conceal the raised ridges she traced with her fingertips.

She wanted to ask him about that mark until it hurt, but every time she went to open her mouth on the question, her heart began to pound loud enough to drown out all other sound, her throat lined with grit so hard and rough, it threatened to cut. It was a key to the past, that terrible brand, but it was a key her mind wasn't yet ready to turn.

"You can reach me, take me, at any time." It was a simple fact, his power vast, and one she could not ignore, even as she fought for her freedom.

Her own power was as vast . . . but irrational though her decision might be, it was one she *would not* use on Kaleb. "All I'm asking," she said as that silent repudiation sang in her blood, "is that you give me time to become who I'm meant to be." Instead of this fractured facsimile. "It hurts to be so broken."

KALEB had spent seven years searching for her with ruthless focus, and now she asked him to set her free. Once again, the void, the part of him that he knew was perilously unbalanced, held in check only through the power of his will, responded with a primal negative.

Mine. She is mine.

No one else had any right to her.

That unbalanced part, however, was also insanely protective where Sahara was concerned, and it had already accepted that to hold her would be to break her. He had to let her go. Her gratefulness, the rational, manipulative part of his mind murmured, would serve to strengthen the embryonic new bond between them. Already, she'd asked for his help— if he played this right, she would always turn first to him.

As for her safety, NightStar was safe enough. The PsyClan might lock up its mad, but it did so in serene surroundings meant to offer the fragmented foreseers some quality of life, complete with a rotation of caretakers that meant they were never lost in isolation and never at risk of harming themselves. Anthony Kyriakus, the head of the clan, understood loyalty—no NightStar, even their most famous defector, had ever been publicly hung out to dry. As such, Sahara's broken Silence would be noted in-house and kept scrupulously out of public view.

"I'll continue to shield you." His own power was enormous, but as Tatiana had discovered, he also had the resources of the NetMind and DarkMind at his disposal. "No one will be able to enter your mind."

Sahara nodded, her profile delicate against the background of the windswept dunes. Alone, desolate. In a way that he hadn't considered, and one that might be causing her excruciating pain. "Are you having trouble with the continued separation from the PsyNet?" he asked, conscious that to release her from his shields while her own were paper-thin would be to paint a target on her back.

Pure Psy would term her an abomination in her broken Silence, and then there were the other predators. If, however, the separation was starving her mind as Tatiana's cage had done, he'd quite simply eliminate anyone who posed a threat. Soon enough, people would come to understand that to attempt to harm Sahara was to sign their death warrant.

"No," she said, playing the shimmering black sand through her fingers with the concentration of someone for whom such sensation had been out of reach for an eon. "It's safer and healthier for me to remain inside your shields until my own are at full strength." A smile directed at him, one that held an open and deep tenderness. "And I'm not alone—you're there, but you never intrude, never take what isn't yours to take."

Even in the darkest part of his psyche, the part covered in blood and death, he recoiled at the idea of violating her. "I'll maintain the shields until you say otherwise."

Sahara watched him with those eyes of blue midnight, and he wondered if she could see the ugliness that had shaped his stance. It was better for her if she didn't. Some memories couldn't be erased, some depravities too sickening to forget. Kaleb had survived by slicing away his capacity for empathy, for pity.

Sahara wasn't built to make the same choice, and so the memories would eat her alive. "Don't," he said. "You'll regret it."

"I would never," was the soft answer. "I would *never*."

Some part of her, he thought once again, remembered the promise she'd made him before the night a knife slid over and into her flesh and blood smeared his skin. And Sahara had never once broken a promise she'd made him. He was the one who'd done that, his betrayal unforgivable.

Continuing to maintain the intimacy of the eye contact, her gaze holding a haunting sadness that he knew was for him, Sahara touched her fingers to his jaw in a featherlight caress, but when she spoke, it was to say, "Tatiana may have shared the truth about me with others—another reason for me to avoid the PsyNet for now."

"I could take you to her." Subject Tatiana to the power of the very gift she'd tortured Sahara in an attempt to harness. "You can do whatever you like to her."

"I never want to touch that woman in any way, even on the psychic plane. She's evil." Quick, jagged words thick with revulsion. "She always spoke to me in such a cool, cogent way, but it was her orders the guards followed when they—" She cut herself off with vicious suddenness, the edges of her words torn raw.

"I'll find out what was done to you," he said, knowing she'd stopped herself because of him, because of what he'd done to Tatiana and to the guard who had dared enter his home with the intent of taking Sahara. "Whether you tell me or not."

Sahara set her jaw, her expression no longer haunted but fierce. "I won't push you deeper into the darkness."

He didn't tell her it was too late, that it had been too late the first time they'd met. Because Sahara hadn't wanted to believe him then, and she wouldn't want to believe him now. That was who she was, as he was a man who had no compunction committing murder when it was necessary.

Shifting his gaze to the wind-lashed waves thundering to shore, he said, "I'll take you home." He rose to his feet and accessed his memory banks to locate an image he'd updated three weeks before. Retrieval was simple—a mental trick that came naturally to most telekinetics—and an image of a tree trunk with an idiosyncratic pattern of knotholes was at the forefront of his mind a second later.

"Wait," he said to Sahara when she got to her feet, and, activating the low-level hum of his ability, he did a test 'port. He appeared in the night darkness beside the tree at the back of Leon Kyriakus's home between one thought and the next, the tree large enough to provide concealment for a Tk who should have never set foot on this land. But he had, and in so doing, he'd altered the course of Sahara's life, coloring it in suffering and isolation.

The well-kept house at the edge of the NightStar compound appeared quiet, but a light glowed in the room he knew to be Leon's study.

Returning to Sahara, he said, "Are you ready?" as the void screamed its denial of what he was about to do, the madness threatening to suck him under.

A deep breath before she slid her hand into his. "I'll be able to reach you?" The question was quiet, her hand clenching on his.

"At will." His telepathy was agonizingly strong, would amplify her own abilities to allow them to speak as they wished. "If you feel at risk at any stage, just call. I'll come." He would always come to her call.

An unexpected uncertainty, her throat moving as she swallowed. "What if the clan disowns me because of my broken Silence?"

"They didn't disown Faith, and it's highly unlikely they'll do so when it comes to a family member they've been searching for for seven years." When her breath trembled, he said, "A single word and I'll get you out." It was keeping his distance that might yet prove an impossibility.

Pulse fluttering in her throat, she nodded. "Let's go."

He made the teleport with that slender hand curled around his, the connection causing his already raw nerve endings to bleed. Though he'd planned on using sex to bond Sahara closer to him, he hadn't realized the brutal impact intimate touch—extended touch of any kind—would have on him when it was Sahara whose skin slid against his, Sahara whose taste was a drug in his system. To everyone else, he would appear as stable as always. He wasn't. And that could be devastating when it involved Kaleb's level of power.

Sahara's fingers flexed in his hold, causing another tiny rupture, another spike in the dissonance he'd initiated. "I never thought to check if he still lives here. This unit is meant for a parent and child, not a man alone."

"He does." Kaleb knew Leon Kyriakus had never stopped waiting for his only daughter to come home. He hadn't paused for a suitable period, then organized another fertilization and conception contract to replace his genetic legacy. He hadn't cleared out her room and thrown away her belongings. And he hadn't ever stopped searching for her.

Having no experience of parental loyalty, it had taken Kaleb years to accept that Leon would never give up on his child—and he would certainly never hand her over to Kaleb, should it be Leon who located her first. Not without a bloody fight. Such fidelity was something Kaleb respected, and he'd had every intention of permitting Leon to see his daughter—*after* she had bonded to Kaleb in a way that could not be severed by any power on this Earth.

The one thing he hadn't factored into his strategy was that Sahara was the greatest, deepest fracture in his psyche. He would do things for her he'd do for no one else, but while he'd empty the sky for her so she could spread her wings, fly, he would not set her free. She belonged to him, would always belong to him. "Your father," he added, "leaves an electronic key for you in the small hollow below the last step."

Wet in the deep blue eyes he'd waited seven long years to see again, Sahara took a step toward the house, halted. "You won't leave me yet?"

He stepped forward in silent answer.

AS Sahara raised her hand to knock on the door, however, Kaleb's palm broke contact with her own. She felt stunningly moorless, her heart aching with a sense of loss beyond all proportion to the act, but she knew he'd made the right choice. Her father was about to find his kidnapped daughter on his doorstep. Any further source of stress would be untenable.

A sound from inside that sent her heart into her throat. *Kaleb.*

Call and I'll come. Always.

The door opened to spill golden light onto her feet, on the heels of a promise that felt etched in stone, the man on the other side as tall and as wide as in her memory—her father had never had the body of the stereotypical Psy. He looked more akin to the old-fashioned lumberjacks she'd seen on the comm once, his face square, and his hair a deep auburn . . . though it now bore more than a few strands of silver.

New, too, were the deep grooves that marked the sides of his mouth and spread out from the corners of his eyes. Those eyes were identical to her own, a genetic accident that made their familial connection unmistakable. As she looked into them, her throat thick, she expected to glimpse confusion. It had been seven years, after all, and she no longer appeared the girl she'd been at sixteen.

"Sahara." Blinding recognition before he dragged her into his arms, holding on so tight she couldn't breathe. Her heart splintered with love. No, she wouldn't be disowned, not by this man who held her as if she were a treasure, the scent of him a mingling of the clinic where he treated the children of the clan and the smuggled coffee he drank in secret.

It was the scent of home.

"It's you." Voice hoarse, he relaxed his hold enough that he could look into her face. "It's you."

"Hello, Father." She let the tears fall, the knot choking up her throat making her voice near soundless. "I'm not the same as I was."

"You're home. That's what matters. And your father," he murmured, a sheen in his own eyes, "is not the same as he was, either. Losing a child alters a man in ways that can never be undone."

Tears turning into sobs, she clung to him, as she couldn't cling to the years forever lost. She didn't know how long they stood there, but when he pulled her into the house, Sahara turned to say good-bye to Kaleb . . . except the night stood desolate and alone, the deadly telekinetic who'd brought her home gone as if he'd never existed.

Chapter 20

ADEN WAS IN Venice, having completed a discussion with the leader of the rebel Arrow cell in the city, when his cell phone rang with an incoming call from Kaleb Krychek.

"What progress have you made in discovering the identity of the individual behind the leak in Perth?" Kaleb asked, and it was a question Aden had expected earlier. However, and but for his recent rescue efforts, Kaleb had been uncharacteristically quiet over the past two months.

"Considerable," Aden replied, thinking of all the Arrow tails the cardinal Tk had eluded in those months as he slipped in and out of distant parts of the PsyNet. "His name is Allan Dawes and thirty-six hours ago, just as we were closing in, he disappeared both from his physical life and from the PsyNet. It's certain he's being hidden by telepaths with more advanced training within Pure Psy." It wouldn't save the middle-aged male, simply delay the inevitable.

Kaleb's response made it clear he had the same expectation. "I'm changing my earlier order. Bring him to me. I want to have a personal discussion with Mr. Dawes."

"I'll arrange the transfer once he's in the custody of the squad." Hanging up, Aden relayed the request to his partner.

"You think Kaleb may be working with Pure Psy," Vasic said, his eyes on the canal not far in front of them, the water a broken mirror as a result of the early morning rain that fell in hard sheets.

Protected from the downpour by the overhang of the building where they stood, Aden slid away his cell phone. "Krychek is driven by power," he said, having never had any illusions about the other male's motivations. "If Pure Psy succeeds in totally destabilizing the current power structure, it'll leave a vacuum only Krychek will be strong enough to fill."

Vasic was silent for a long time, the sound of the rain hitting the canal water muted thunder. "Krychek," he said at last, "has the strength to wrench control of the Net on his own."

"But then," Aden pointed out, "he'd have to fight to hold on to it. Far better to come to leadership as a savior, a hero."

Vasic nodded. "We watch him. Even a dual cardinal can be killed if it proves necessary."

Aden knew that if that decision were ever made, they'd have only a single shot at taking Krychek unawares. Failure would mean death for the entire squad. "We watch him," he agreed as the rain slanted to hit the ground at his feet, flicking droplets onto his regulation black combat boots.

Chapter 21

SAHARA COULDN'T HAVE better timed her return.

Sleep was out of the question for either her or her father that night, both of them unable to let one another out of their sight.

"I have a scheduled day off today from my duties at the medical center," her father told her the next morning. "No one will come looking."

By silent agreement, they stayed inside, putting off the moment they'd have to speak to Anthony—her paternal uncle and the head of NightStar. Though they discussed a myriad of subjects, her father didn't ask probing questions, didn't force her to speak of things she didn't want to speak about.

He was simply happy to have her home.

They talked of family, and of the changes in the world that had led to the clan setting startling new protocols in place when it came to the gifted and troubled F designation. "Faith's defection taught us that we were wrong to follow the rules handed down to us after the inception of Silence."

Voice somber, he drank a sip of the nutrient drink he'd mixed for them both. "As a medic, I genuinely believed the actions we took lowered the risk of mental degradation for the Fs. So did Anthony. It's why he permitted Faith to be trained as she was. To find out that we might have been driving her, driving all of the Fs, toward the madness we intended to thwart . . . it shook the foundations of the family."

Sahara trusted her father in this as she'd trust no one else—he was a true healer at heart, had long ago adopted the human oath of "first do no harm," the plaque with the complete pledge hanging in his office. "I've missed so much," she said, anger bright and new awakening in her blood. "Had so much stolen from me."

"You have a lifetime ahead of you," her father said, closing his hand over her own. "You also have a father, and a PsyClan who will back you every step of the way."

Her father, she realized, her eyes on the freckled cream of his skin against her own, had always made casual contact, especially after the discovery of her shadow ability. Never had he treated her as a leper, and in so doing, he'd helped her maintain her sense of humanity. Kaleb, too, she realized with a sense of wonder, had never repudiated her touch, though he'd always been aware of the risk she posed.

"Don't. You'll regret it."

"I would never."

Her answer hadn't changed, would never change, but examined in the cold light of day, the unadulterated emotional fury of her refusal was a mystery. Not once—*not once*—had she been tempted to use her ability on him, though it would've fundamentally altered the balance of power. Even the idea of it made her feel nauseated.

"Your memories," her father said, cutting through the visceral reaction. "How damaged are they? There are medical telepaths who may be—"

"No," she interrupted. "I don't want anyone inside my head." At her father's immediate nod of understanding, she added, "And I have almost everything." It was a lie, but how could she tell him that the biggest, most important piece was missing?

A piece named Kaleb.

It was hours later that they gave in to tiredness at last. Entering her bedroom, Sahara found a box of clothing Kaleb had clearly 'ported in, along with a cell phone encoded with his direct lines.

"Thank you," she whispered.

Changing into a loose T-shirt that happened to be at the top of the box, she slipped into her old single bed. Her rest was dreamless, and she woke the next morning ready to face the clan. Soon as she and her father had both breakfasted, they headed to Anthony's office. The

central NightStar compound, the homes built to blend into their surroundings, had always had larger areas of open and green space than was
usual in Psy complexes, but those areas had been further expanded during her time in captivity, a number of leafy trees providing dappled
shade.

Eyes widened when they landed on her, the shock too great to suppress, but no one attempted to stop their progress. When they reached
the office, Anthony's assistant, an older woman Sahara recognized from
before her abduction, waved them in without questions. The head of the
PsyClan, black hair silvered at the temples, came around his desk as they
entered, his gaze direct, unwavering.

"Leon." A nod to acknowledge his younger half brother before he
returned his attention to her. "Sahara. You look well."

Yes, she did. Thanks to the care of the most deadly cardinal on the
planet, her face wasn't gaunt, her body slender but healthy. She knew,
however, that her physical health wasn't at the top of Anthony's list of
priorities. "I don't know," she said, "if my rescuer embedded any treach-
erous tendencies in me, but I believe not." Kaleb didn't need to control
her in that fashion. And—"My ability means I would've been aware of
any such attempts at mental coercion."

"Does your rescuer have a name?"

She told him, having informed her father ahead of time.

"I see." Walking back around the desk, Anthony retook his seat,
waving for them to do the same. "According to the PsyNet, you don't
exist."

"Good." Her father's response was fierce. "It means she's safe from
any further attempts to abduct and cage her, even if it is Krychek doing
the protecting."

"Agreed." Anthony leaned back in the black leather of his chair. "Do
you know the identity of the individual or individuals behind your captivity?"

Sahara hadn't discussed this with Kaleb but saw no reason why he'd
want the truth kept secret—and it *was* the truth, of that she had no
doubt. Kaleb did not lie to her. "Tatiana Rika-Smythe."

No surprise in Anthony's expression, nothing but the penetrating intellect of a man at the head of one of the most influential families in the Net. "Did Kaleb mention why he rescued you?"

Sahara hesitated . . . and then she lied. "It was a challenge, and NightStar now owes him a significant favor." What was between her and Kaleb was between her and Kaleb. She'd allow no one else to interfere with the raw, passionate relationship formed of hidden memories and the charm bracelet she wore concealed under her simple white shirt, a talisman of strength from a man who might be her greatest, deepest weakness. "The psychic cost of the exercise, he decided, would be worth the gain."

From the way Anthony's eyes, a rich brown, lingered on her, he knew she was hiding something, but Sahara didn't flinch. *Secret*, the girl she'd been whispered. *Secret.*

"The secondary benefit of your lack of visibility in the Net," Anthony said into the heavy quiet, "is that your splintered Silence remains hidden from the pro-Silence lobby."

Fingers trembling, she gripped the arms of her chair. "Are you planning to order me to undergo a program of reconditioning?" No one was ever again going to attempt to mold her mind to their liking, and if that was what Anthony planned, she had to know.

"No." Her father's gaze locked with his half brother's, his loyalties clear. "No one touches Sahara's mind."

Anthony's response was a calm "Yes. It's too late for that," but his eyes continued to watch her. "Kaleb may not have attemped to hack your mind; however, Tatiana had you for an extended period. How certain are you that you haven't been compromised?"

"Absolutely," Sahara said without hesitation, conscious Anthony would continue to keep an eye on her regardless. That was part of his mandate as the head of the PsyClan and she didn't resent him for it. She also knew he'd find nothing of concern—even before the labyrinth became a barrier of chaos Tatiana couldn't navigate, Sahara's unique natural safeguards had acted as an impenetrable firewall against any attempts at mental manipulation.

"It's why," Sahara said, her stomach twisting, "Tatiana resorted to such unsubtle methods as ripping my shields apart to leave my thoughts exposed and inflicting physical torture." By then, Sahara had already created the labyrinth; it had not only helped her protect her secrets and sense of self when her mind was torn open, it had given her a place to go where nothing hurt, negating the danger that she'd break under the psychic and physical torture, cooperate, simply to avoid the pain.

"You're right," Anthony said, somewhat to her surprise. "Tatiana never uses open force if she can utilize a telepathic worm or other similar methods." Pausing a beat, he added, "You're safe inside the family when it comes to your broken Silence. As for the outside world, I'd suggest caution. Learn to pretend and pretend well." The words were coolly practical, the message unexpected in spite of what she'd learned about the events that had shaped the clan in the years since she'd last sat in this office.

"One more thing, Sahara," Anthony said as she was walking out the door a half hour later, "Kaleb might have rescued you, but don't make the mistake of trusting him. He's never done a selfless act in his life—and he's more than manipulative enough to set you free as part of his strategy to win your loyalty."

Unspoken were the words that the person who had Sahara's loyalty would also have access to her ability: an ability so quiet and so terrifying that no one and nothing could stand in its path, and yet one that left not a single trace. No bodies, no anger, no embers of rebellion. The perfect weapon for a man who wanted to seize control of the Net.

ANTHONY spent several minutes considering his next move after the door closed behind Sahara and Leon. Though he'd joined in the search for his niece on multiple occasions as his duties permitted, the last as recently as two months ago, he'd known the chances of locating her were low. She was far too valuable a prize for her captors to be in any way careless.

Now not only had she been located, but returned. Despite the warning Anthony had given Sahara, it was near certain Kaleb hadn't understood the power he held in his grasp, or he'd never have given her up. Unlike Nikita, however, Anthony had learned not to ascribe motives to the cardinal Tk that couldn't be backed up by cold, hard fact. Kaleb played political games with the skill and ease of a man who'd begun grooming himself for the position long before adulthood.

In the end, the only viable choice was to open a line of dialogue and see if he could divine the true reason behind the other man's actions. One thing was categorical—it wasn't because tracing her was a challenge that Kaleb had begun hunting Sahara in the first place. A man with Kaleb's lust for power did not waste his energies.

Inputting the other man's code into the comm, he waited.

Kaleb's face appeared on-screen almost immediately, the glass of the wall behind him presenting a view of Moscow Anthony had seen on multiple occasions. The distinctive onion-shaped domes of the cathedral in the distance glowed in the lights set up to highlight the structure, the Moscow night smudged with what appeared to be light rain. "Anthony, I've been expecting your call."

"I seem to owe you thanks for returning a member of my clan." Anthony preferred not to be beholden to anyone, and when it came to Kaleb Krychek, the obligation was one he wanted cleared as fast as possible. "NightStar wishes to discharge the debt."

"I assume you know from whom I retrieved Sahara?" the cardinal Tk said instead of making a demand.

Anthony nodded. "The clan will take care of that matter." Tatiana was very good at going under when she didn't wish to be found, but NightStar could destroy what mattered most to her—money, power, status—without ever laying a finger on her. "Death isn't always the most fitting punishment." It was too quick, over too soon—and Tatiana had stolen more than seven years of not just one life, but two: Leon had never been the same after his daughter's disappearance. And Sahara was a Kyriakus child, a NightStar. Nothing and *no one* was permitted to harm Anthony's family and walk away unscathed.

"On that point, I have no argument," Kaleb said, his expression a gray wall of Silence. "However, you should know Tatiana is no longer a threat to Sahara. I had certain . . . issues of my own to discuss with her."

"I see." Even if Tatiana was dead or otherwise out of the picture, it did nothing to alter Anthony's resolve to obliterate her empire, crushing and publicly humiliating her in the process. NightStar had always been a quiet power; it was time the Net learned exactly how far they'd go to protect and avenge their own. "Was your discussion productive?"

Kaleb angled his head in an unusual moment of distraction. "I apologize," he said when his gaze returned to Anthony. "I've just had a report from the Arrows that may interest you."

"Perth or Copenhagen?"

"Perth. The conspirator behind the fatal information leak, previously identified as Allan Dawes, has been traced to Argentina. Retrieval is expected within the next forty-eight hours."

"And then?"

"He'll become an example to others who believe assisting Pure Psy is in any way a good career move."

Anthony didn't flinch from the cold-blooded response. He'd seen the carnage in Perth, had watched a recording of his daughter convulse from the vicious force of her visions minutes before the first fires. Faith's foresight had been specific enough that they'd gotten word out to the city, successfully saving countless lives, but they hadn't been fast enough to save everyone, and he knew the resulting losses had left Faith distraught.

"We must," he said, "be careful not to create martyrs of the insurgents."

"You think that might be Vasquez's plan—to solidify the sense of alienation and fear that drives his membership under the Pure Psy rhetoric?" Kaleb leaned back in his office chair, his attention never shifting off the screen. "I assume you know about him."

Anthony gave a nod, the name of the otherwise anonymous man at the helm of the pro-Silence organization having come to him through his sprawling network of contacts. "He is extremely intelligent, and this way, we do the work for him."

Kaleb considered the point. "You're right—it may not be worth a public execution. I'll handle it quietly. His disappearance will make the point as well."

Anthony thought of everything else Kaleb had been "handling" lately and knew the cardinal was far, *far* more dangerous than Vasquez would ever be, but right now, he had to work with Kaleb. Because the other male hadn't *yet* turned murderous on the scale of Pure Psy . . . though Anthony's suspicions on that point were starting to increase.

Had he, for example, just been led by the nose when it came to Allan Dawes? It was possible Kaleb had never intended to execute the man, but now he'd made Anthony complicit in the decision. "If you require assistance in the matter of Dawes," he said, his reservations about Kaleb's possible involvement with Pure Psy not yet critical, "NightStar is prepared to step in."

Kaleb inclined his head in silent acceptance. "You understand that does not wipe the debt in the matter of Sahara Kyriakus."

"Of course."

"I would rather have you as an ally than not," Kaleb said, "so there is no reason to be concerned I'll ask for the impossible. At this stage, all I want is your public backing."

"You want NightStar to support your bid to take over the Net?"

"Consider the alternatives, Anthony." Kaleb continued to speak in the same tone he always used, ice-cold and composed. "Either Pure Psy rips the Net apart or our fellow former Councilors attempt to set up fiefdoms while fighting to eliminate one another and us. The ensuing wars will devastate our race."

Anthony knew that to be true. What Kaleb wasn't saying was that no one knew what the cardinal would do with the Net once he had it in his grasp. "I can't back you on current facts," he responded. "I will, however, make no open move against you before first giving you a warning." It was a major concession.

The Tk on the other side of the comm gave a slight nod before signing off. It was far easier a capitulation than Anthony had expected and it made him even more chary of Kaleb's motives. The problem was, Kaleb Krychek was the most opaque individual in the Net. Anthony's foreseers, when instructed to hone in on the cardinal telekinetic, saw only a destructive, roiling darkness.

"Nothing," one F-Psy had gasped, shivering so hard her teeth clattered. "When I look into the future with Krychek as a focus, all I see is the death . . . of everything."

PSYNET BEACON: CURRENT EDITION
LETTERS TO THE EDITOR

Starred Letter

I refer to the covert viral discussion profiled in the *Beacon*'s previous edition, to do with the future viability of the Silence Protocol.

I believe the fact that such discussions were able to—and continue to—take place, without the minds of the individuals involved being shut down by the application of embedded pain controls, speaks to critical problems in the structural integrity of the Protocol. Even two years ago, such a topic would've been stifled before it ever grew to the point where it was circling the globe in clandestine chat rooms and in-person discussions.

While Pure Psy's tenets are fanatical in the extreme, hidden in their rhetoric may be a critical point: that this freedom is not necessarily a fact to celebrate. Our race chose Silence because our minds skew toward insanity and violence without such strictures. This is not my opinion, but a fact written into our history in blood.

A hundred years ago, we were on the verge of total annihilation, our young murdered in their thousands by other Psy, while hundreds of thousands more sank into the splintered worlds created by broken minds. We were more violent than the changelings whose physicality we now deem makes them a lesser race, and more vicious than the humans we've come to consider our inferiors.

Yet once again, it is our "superior" race that is on the verge of a cataclysm.

I, for one, do not wish to live in the world of the past, but it cannot be denied that Silence has lost its way in the last ten years. Some whisper it was never as effective as successive Councils would've had us believe, that the defective members of the population were simply eliminated before they became a problem. Others, as we've seen, are willing to commit murder to Silence us all.

Who is right? Who is wrong? I have no answers—all I know is that we stand at a crossroads. The decisions we make will either save us, or end us.

Professor Eric Tuivala
Anthropologist
(New Zealand)

Chapter 22

SAHARA SAT UP in the narrow single bed that was her own, unable to fall asleep as she had the previous night. Pushing off the sheets, she padded to the window to stare out at the landscaped gardens below, the blades of grass kissed silver by the moonlight. She felt disconnected, out of sync with the world . . . as if this were a dream created in the depths of the labyrinth, her body trapped in the hellhole where she'd spent so many years.

It was a certainty that she was being foolish in her refusal to talk to a Psy-Med specialist, but even now, with her senses confused and her mind struggling to hold on to the world, her fear of mental violation was worse than her fear of madness. Pressing her fingers to the glass, she tried to use the smooth coldness as an anchor, but the glass melted beneath her fingertips, the world twisting sideways in a smear of silver and black, as her consciousness attempted and failed to hold on to what was.

Clawing her way to some semblance of reason, she found a sliver of hope in the memory of a man who had promised her he would always come to her call. *Kaleb. I need you.* She knew without a doubt that reality wouldn't waver with him here. He was too powerful a force, speaking to parts of her she didn't know existed until he was in the room.

He stood beside her a heartbeat later, dressed in black suit pants and a crisp white shirt, no tie, the collar open to expose the strong column of his throat. The cuff links at his wrists caught the moonlight as he slid his hands into his pockets, and the world righted itself, only for her breath to catch, her body recognizing his.

"Why are you awake?" he asked.

Though he wasn't touching her, the heat of him branded her through the T-shirt she wore on top of a pair of gray sweatpants. "I need to be doing something," she said, struggling to explain the frustration that had her unable to sleep.

"I know I'm not functional enough to go out into the world, but I feel as if my skin will burst if I just stay here." Shaking with the clawing ferocity of the anger and helplessness inside her, she closed the inches between them and began to unbutton his shirt, her skin a fever. If she drowned herself in sensation, in Kaleb, it would hold the other emotions at bay. Nothing else existed when—

"Sahara." Kaleb's hands closed over her wrists. "Put on clothes suitable for temperatures in the higher elevations," he said, eyes pitch-black. "I'll be back in five minutes."

Sahara didn't stop to reason, to consider the fact that she was about to go off into the darkness with a man who *was* the darkness. She simply stripped, pulled on jeans, a thin long-sleeved mohair top, and a heavy zip-up hooded sweatshirt. Slipping her feet into socks, she'd just finished tying her sneakers when Kaleb reappeared.

He'd changed into black cargo pants and a black T-shirt, his feet in scuffed boots that appeared worn in. Looking her up and down, he nodded—and then they weren't in her room any longer, but at the foot of an imposing rock face under a huge silver moon that cast a spotlight over the firs that sprawled a dark green sea in every direction, majestic against a backdrop of snowcapped mountains familiar to anyone in this region. "We're in the Sierra Nevada." Changeling-wolf territory.

"Yes. We'll remain in a satellite shadow as long as we don't move past the tree line."

"The live patrols?" The SnowDancer pack was rumored to kill intruders first and ask questions of the corpses.

"I'm scanning for any minds in the vicinity, but the wolves rarely patrol this section—there's nowhere to go from this point where sentries won't spot an intruder." Pulling out something from one of the pockets of his cargos, he held it out.

Half-gloves. Leather. To protect her palms from the rock. Exhilaration bursting through her bloodstream, she slipped them on, then moved to the rock face, took a grip on the first handhold, and began to climb. Finally, *finally* she felt alive again!

The wind was quiet and gentle against her face, the rock hard under her fingertips, the chill night air so clean and pure it almost hurt. Drawing it in, she found another hold, then another, and when her foot slipped, said, "No!" to halt Kaleb's help, and got herself out of the situation on her own.

Heart thudding and sweat pouring down her temples, it took her over an hour to climb a puny increment of the jagged rock face, but she laughed in unadulterated delight as she pulled herself to a seat on a slight outcrop. "My arms are crying!"

Kaleb looked up from the foot of the rock. *Takes practice.*

As she watched, he began to climb, his body moving with such fluidity she couldn't separate move from move. She knew without asking that he wasn't using his telekinesis—Tks were generally physically adept, a known side effect of their ability. But Kaleb was better than adept. He climbed with a wild grace that hypnotized.

Stunned at the lethal beauty of him, she watched in silence until he was almost lost to her sight. *Come back.* She was frightened, though she knew he was a Tk, would never die in a fall. But the fear, it was so profound, it clenched bony fingers around her heart and squeezed. As if she had witnessed him fall once, knew he could be hurt. *Kaleb, I can't see you.*

He reappeared into view seconds later, backtracking with that same hypnotic grace. Halting beside her, he hugged the rock with a one-handed grip, his feet on a whisper-thin ledge, the muscles of his arm hard and defined. With his free hand, he drank from a bottle of water he'd had in another pocket, before passing it to her.

She took a drink . . . and the cobwebs fell away from her memories of the first night she'd spent with him. He'd given her water then, too.

"Was I really that bad?" she asked. "You said I smelled like a pigsty." The thought embarrassed her now as it hadn't then.

"I was attempting to incite a response." Taking back the bottle with that matter-of-fact response, he held out a hand. "Can you climb back down?"

Sahara considered the jellylike state of her limbs and forced herself to be realistic. "I don't think so." A second later, she found herself on the ground.

Lying on her back on the soft grass, she watched him climb down to land on his feet beside her, strong and muscled and dangerous. When he turned and met her gaze, her thighs clenched, a sheen of perspiration breaking out over her skin that had nothing to do with the climb and everything to do with a hunger that was no longer the desperation she'd felt in her bedroom, but a hotter, deeper ache.

It had been so long.

Breath turning shallow, she parted her lips. "Kaleb."

KALEB had intended to keep his distance from Sahara until he was dead sure his shields were adamantine. Except now she looked at him with desire a red flush on her cheekbones, her chest rising and falling in a rapid rhythm, and it was a siren call to his own body. She had no comprehension of the power she wielded, didn't understand that when he told her he'd line the streets with bodies for her, he meant every word.

As far as Sahara Kyriakus was concerned, he was a weapon she could point in any direction she chose. There was *nothing* he wouldn't do for her . . . except let her go.

"Kaleb," she whispered again. "I've missed you."

He broke.

Gripping her wrists together as he came down over her, he pinned them above her head. "You can't touch me." Her fingers curled at his low-voiced order, but there was no panic, her lips soft under the hard demand of his mouth, her thighs spreading to cradle him.

Even as slender as she remained, there was no doubting her femininity. Gentle curves under his free hand, her breasts crushed against his chest, lips plump and wet. Until Sahara, he hadn't understood why men murdered to possess a woman. Now the rage of it was a black fire in his blood, a deadly inferno that would engulf the world should anyone dare take her from him again.

When she began to struggle under his weight, he tightened his hold on the delicate bones of her wrists before he could rein in the violently possessive response. Opening his hand a second later, he waited for her next move. Should it be a rejection, he'd give every indication of accepting it, then strategize his next play—Sahara was as physically susceptible to him as he was to her, and it was an advantage he'd use without hesitation.

"I'm too hot." With that complaint, she reached between them to unzip her sweatshirt and twisted to get it off. It left her dressed only in a warm but thin white top that hugged the mounds of her breasts, the curve of her waist.

"Don't," he said, when she would've put her hands on him. "We don't want that rock face coming down over us."

Dropping her arms to the lush green grass, Sahara's eyes went to the huge slab of rock at his back. "You're not exaggerating, are you?"

"No." He had no need to exaggerate.

A subtle movement of her throat as she swallowed. He followed it with his gaze, aware of her pulse gaining in speed, her breath hitching. "I'll keep my hands to myself," she promised, voice rough. "But you can't look at me like that."

Gripping her jaw in silent answer, he braced himself with his free arm beside her head, and then he branded her mouth with his own. *You are mine.* It was a statement telepathed along the private pathway that had formed years ago. *Mine to touch. Mine to look at. Mine.* Releasing her jaw, he stroked his hand down her throat to close over her breast.

Sahara shuddered.

Able to feel the pebbled hardness of her nipple under his palm, he took care in learning the shape of her. A gasp, her body attempting to shift restlessly under his. Sensitive, extremely so. Filing away the piece of knowledge, he rubbed his thumb over her nipple and she almost twisted out from under him, breaking the kiss to sob out a breath. "Please, please. More."

Kaleb felt his closest PsyNet shield fall in a crash that almost took out the second. But he wasn't dangerous to her. Not yet. "I'll give you anything you want." Holding her gaze, he slipped his hand under the bottom of her top to spread it on her abdomen. It quivered under his touch, her teeth sinking into her lower lip.

"That's for me to do," he said in a quiet rebuke that had her sucking in a breath.

His mouth was on hers an instant later, his teeth biting down on her lower lip a fraction too hard. Back arching up from the ground, she broke the kiss . . . only to return for another, her tongue stroking against his with an intimacy that went straight to the rock-hard erection pressing against the zipper of his pants. As if she were licking her tongue along the rigid length of his penis and not inside his mouth.

This time, it was Kaleb who broke the kiss. "No," he said when she would've initiated another kiss.

Chest heaving, Sahara licked her lips, and he had to look away before he broke his own rules and asked her to put her hands on the painful hardness between his thighs, to squeeze and stroke his naked flesh. He focused instead on his exploration of her body. Her pulse fluttered under his hand when he moved it to lie over her ribs, the moonlight shimmering on her skin. A little further up, he found lace, fine and silky.

"It was in the box," Sahara whispered on a hitched breath. "Thank you."

The fact she wore his gift against her skin pleased him, but it wasn't enough.

Removing his hand, to her frustrated "No," he pushed up her top to bare her breasts to the night . . . to him.

Her body went utterly motionless.

Do you want me to stop? he forced himself to ask, the fury to possess a turbulent storm inside him. Below that was an old and vicious rage, incited by the sight of the fine silvery scars that marked her flesh and that she likely no longer noticed. He did. He'd been there when each and every cut was made, remembered exactly how deep each wound had been, knew how much medical attention she must've needed to heal.

"No." Her skin gleaming with the finest layer of perspiration, her breasts rising and falling as if in invitation, Sahara's voice pulled him out of the blood-soaked past. "No, don't stop, Kaleb."

Wrenching his anger under control, and slamming down ice-cold shields around the violent surge of arousal provoked by the sound of his name on her lips, he concentrated on the creamy flesh cupped in delicate pink lace. It wasn't what he wanted. Pulling first at one cup, then the other, he pushed the lace down until the heavy weight of her breasts spilled free, the soft pink providing a frame for the lush curves that melted the black ice around his pounding erection as if it didn't exist.

SAHARA dug her nails into the earth in an effort to fight the urge to beg for Kaleb's touch as he watched her with those eyes of madness. It should've scared her, the possessive darkness she saw in them, and perhaps part of her was terrified, but not enough to back away, not enough to end this raw wave of sensation, vivid and wild and alive.

Shifting position, Kaleb straddled her. The next instant, he placed his hands under her upper back, lifted her slightly, and put his lips around one aching nipple. She shoved a fist against her mouth to stifle her scream, the wet suction of his mouth as hotly erotic as the hard strength of his grip.

He moved to her neglected breast without warning, the night air cool on the wet of her other nipple. Whimpering, she twisted under him, but there was no way for her to gain contact with the hard ridge of his erection, his knees planted on either side of her thighs. Teeth scraped her highly sensitive nipple an instant later, making her bite down on her fist. *Stop! It's too much!*

Kaleb released her nipple, his lips wet, his eyes so dark they were akin to black pearls, a shimmer of midnight color in their depths. "Are you certain?"

The quiet question raised every hair on her body.

Not in fear. In the blinding realization of how tight a leash he had on himself.

Dear God. What would he do to her if he slipped that leash?

The damp folds between her thighs grew slick with a melting heat. Squeezing those thighs in a vain effort to find relief, she removed her fist from her mouth and whispered, "No. I can take more." Wanted more. Wanted everything.

Not asking a second time, Kaleb looked down at her breasts, his hair falling across his forehead. Sliding a hand from under her back, he gripped one breast with a firmness that felt like a brand and lowered his mouth to her flesh again. Her mind went red, her back arching as if to thrust her breast farther into his mouth. *Kaleb, I need—*

Tell me. Another scrape of teeth that scattered her neurons, her nails clawing the earth, crushed grass under her palms.

Touch me, please. I can't—

Here? He cupped her between the thighs in a raw intimacy, pushing up with the heel of his hand.

And the world splintered.

SAHARA opened her eyes to find Kaleb still straddling her body, her top shoved up her chest and the cups of her bra pushed down to expose her breasts. The Tk on top of her had his gaze on her bared flesh, the intensity of his focus such that it caused her pleasure-lax muscles to twinge in renewed arousal.

As she watched, he reached out and fixed her bra, his fingers brushing her nipples. Sucking in a breath, her abdomen taut, she stayed silent as he tugged down her top. His every action was careful, that of a man who knew he could be pushed off the edge and into the abyss with a single wrong move.

"Teeth," he said in that same frigid tone she'd heard earlier, "are not always used in sexual play."

Sahara's chest rose and fell in a shallow rhythm. "No?"

"It is a matter of preference, according to the papers I've read on intimacy." Lashes rising, obsidian eyes looking into her own, the black fire in them as hot as his voice was cold. "What is your preference?"

"Yes." The confession felt as intimate as what he'd just done to her body. "With you."

His expression altered to a hardness that made it clear who and what he was, his arms coming down on either side of her as he lowered his face until their breaths kissed. "It will," he said in a silken whisper, "only ever be with me."

Chapter 23

TWENTY MINUTES LATER, Kaleb returned to the rock face, Sahara now safe in her bedroom. She hadn't run from him even after he'd exposed his murderous possessiveness where she was concerned. But then, they both knew she had the power to stop him, the only individual in the Net who could.

"If you ever do it," he'd said when she touched her fingers to his cheek in a tender good-bye, "make sure you go all the way and end me." Should he be left breathing after Sahara's power sliced through him, taking the only thing that mattered, he'd become the monster Santano had groomed him to be. "Serial killer, mass murderer, there's not a name for the evil that lives inside me."

Jaw set and eyes fierce, she'd shaken her head. "I won't let the darkness have you."

Her promise echoing in his head, he climbed with single-minded focus, his muscles straining to hold him to the wall as he fought to overcome the physical frustration that was a pulsing grip around his erection. It wasn't until halfway through the third ascent that he could think again, his mind coldly rational.

His campaign to win Sahara's trust, he thought, was progressing according to plan. She'd not only called him when she felt under threat, she'd invited physical contact. The fact that physical contact was causing severe damage to his shields and his thinking processes was a side effect he'd have to handle. Backing off was not an option—her memories were becoming more lucid with each passing day, her psyche healing at a rate that spoke to a remorseless internal strength.

Soon she would be ready to remember him, and why her subconscious had blocked him from her conscious mind in the first place. There were some things no one could take, some betrayals too reprehensible to forgive.

"No! Don't! Kaleb, stop!"

Scraping the skin off his palm as he lunged for a grip, he blew out a harsh breath and continued to climb until it was only the cold stone and the next grip that mattered. And still he heard her screaming at him to stop.

IT was the creak that woke Sahara in the pitch-dark early morning hours, intruding on hazy dreams of a boy she couldn't quite see.

Snapping to full alertness with the speed and silence of someone who'd been at the mercy of others for too long, she nonetheless kept her eyes closed, listening with every cell in her body. It was a trick she'd learned during her years of confinement, a way to gather information while the guards thought her asleep.

She flicked her eyes open only once she was sure the intruder wasn't in the room. Her attention locked on the door, her pulse a drumbeat. Releasing a quiet breath, she listened . . . and just barely heard the stealthy movements of someone attempting to disengage the lock she'd flicked on for no reason but that she was obsessed with her privacy.

Father?

No response along the old telepathic pathway to her call, nothing but a dull silence that made enraged fear ripple through her blood. Reaching under the bed, she retrieved the butcher's knife she'd stolen from an unused set of kitchen tools her father had been given by a patient who was an F, and as such, received goods from businesses as a matter of course. The idea of ever again being caught unarmed and vulnerable was her worst nightmare.

Pushing off the sheets with care, she shoved the pillows underneath to create the illusion of a person and pulled the sheets back up, just as the lock snicked open. Heart thudding and eyes on the knob as it began to turn, she padded across the floor to press her back to the wall. She knew every inch of this house, her feet silent on the old wood that had given the intruder away.

When the door opened, she waited only long enough to make sure she hadn't made a mistake, that it *wasn't* her father, before she struck. It might have been cleaner to use her ability, but Sahara had no intention of getting any closer to the stranger than she had to be before he was immobilized. All indications were that no one had any effective means of defense against her ability; however, she wasn't going to bet her life on that assumption so soon after leaving the labyrinth.

Screaming as the butcher's knife buried itself between his shoulder blades, the darkly-clad intruder spun around, reaching for her with his arms and no doubt his mind. She felt nothing of the telepathic assault inside the obsidian shields that protected her, and it took little skill to avoid his hands, his balance destroyed by the blow she'd struck, the heavy blade lodged in his back.

The man's feet skidded in his own blood right as she caught a flicker at the corner of her eye, and suddenly the unknown male was thrown across the room.

"Wait!" she screamed an instant before his back hit the wall, realizing Kaleb had to have detected the attempted attack on her shields.

The man froze in midair, blood dripping to the floor in fat droplets.

"Don't kill him. We need to know who sent him." Sahara went to step closer, but she was too slow.

"Done." The intruder's body slammed into the wall, the blade thudding home against his breastbone with a sickening crunch as it all but cut him in half. He crumpled to the floor, blood pouring out of his mouth.

Her stomach might have lurched at the sight at any other time, but she was already running out of her room and into the one down the hallway. "Father!" Leon Kryiakus's big body lay limp beside his bed, a necklace of sticky red wreathing his throat. "No, no. Please no. Father, please." Fingers trembling, she searched for a pulse. "Kaleb! He's alive!"

"Move." Gathering her father's body in his arms with telekinetic ease, Kaleb teleported out with the terse instruction to keep her telepathic pathways open.

He returned less than three minutes later, to find her seated on the bed, staring at the smear of blood on the carpet. She snapped up her head. "Is he—"

"Your father's in emergency surgery, watched over by a temporary guard from one of my units in the area. I've notified Anthony, and NightStar's people will be at the hospital within the next half hour."

Hand shaking, Sahara went to thrust it through her hair when the iron-rich scent of blood hit her nostrils. Her fury reignited as she realized it was her father's blood on her fingers. Shoving past Kaleb to the attached bathroom, she washed it off with jagged actions before wiping her hands clean. "I want to go to him."

"You'd just be waiting outside surgery," Kaleb said with grim pragmatism. "My man knows to contact you should there be a change in your father's condition."

She couldn't bear the idea of her father slipping away just when she'd found him again. "I want—"

"The hospital has multiple exits and entrances; the risk of someone getting to you is much higher." Hard words, no hint of tenderness. "You know Leon wouldn't want you in the line of fire."

Conscious he was right, she forced herself to think past adrenaline-fueled anger tangled with gut-wrenching worry and walked back to her own room—and to the body of the man who had nearly taken her father's life. "Who was he?"

"A freelance operative, not a particularly adept one or Leon would be dead and you'd be in his grasp."

"You tore his mind open? You know that compromises data," she said, turning on him in a fury. "That was irresponsible and reckless."

A shrug as false and as remote as his eyes were not. "I offered him a quick death in exchange for the information," Kaleb said, as if speaking of a business negotiation. "He kept his end of the bargain; I kept mine."

Eyes of starless night pinned her to the spot. "It appears you have a bounty on you."

"What? Who? Tatiana?" The other woman was in no position to give orders, but she had people who might well do so for her.

Kaleb shook his head and spoke the last name she had ever expected to hear. "Santano Enrique."

Ice in her blood, choking up her throat. "He's dead," she forced past the sudden, overwhelming rage.

"It appears he has risen from the ashes." Kaleb tucked her hair behind her ear. "He was involved in your abduction."

Sahara knew she should follow that thread, should ask him exactly why a serial killer with a predilection for changeling victims had turned his attention to her, and whether Kaleb had had anything to do with it, but she couldn't. The idea of bringing up the topic made her stomach hurt, her breath stick in her throat. *Not yet. Not yet.* She wasn't ready to know, wasn't strong enough to face the dark truth.

If Kaleb had betrayed her, the knowledge would break her.

"The bounty," he said when she remained silent, "must've been a failsafe in case of your escape." Halting at the sound of the front door opening, he waited until Anthony stepped into the room.

The head of her clan examined the dead bounty hunter with an impassive expression before shifting his attention to Kaleb. "I assume you got the information we need before you executed him?"

Kaleb told Anthony the same thing he'd told Sahara. Anthony's response was, "Not even the most bumbling bounty hunter would hunt a target for a dead man. Payment is everything."

"Santano may have been a psychopath, but he was a smart one. The considerable fee for this bounty is held in trust by a certain mercenary organization. To be paid on delivery of Sahara Kyriakus—dead or alive—to either Santano or the current head of his operations."

"Santano kept his interest in you quiet," Anthony said to Sahara and hidden in the words was a question. "I never suspected him of involvement in your abduction."

She spread her hands, not sharing the fact that Enrique's protégé had apparently always been aware of her ability.

"NightStar has a leak," Kaleb said at the same time.

"I'll handle that situation."

Kaleb inclined his head in silent agreement—Anthony had come by his reputation honestly. Unlike certain others in the Net, the other man did not mind getting his hands dirty. And if he failed to take care of the matter, Kaleb would do so. He'd permit no threat to Sahara to exist, much less live and breathe.

"You need to move immediately into a safe house."

Sahara's back went stiff at Anthony's statement, her muscles rigid. "No. I won't be caged again."

"There is no other option," Anthony responded. "As long as the bounty exists, you stay a target."

"Are you certain a safe house will provide any better protection?" Kaleb had no intention of allowing Sahara to go anywhere aside from the home he'd built for her in Moscow. "This hunter, inept and young, managed to evade your perimeter guards."

"That will be investigated." A flint-hard promise. "Our safe houses are fortresses."

Sahara, hands fisted, shook her head. *"No."* Backing away from them until her spine hit the wall, she began to bump her fists against it. "No. No. No."

Recognizing the danger, Kaleb reacted before Anthony could figure out what was happening. "No safe house, no cage," he said, cupping her face and forcing her to meet his gaze until she stopped bumping her fists against the wall, though she continued to rock back and forth.

You risk losing her if you push this, he 'pathed to Anthony as he released her. *Her mind isn't fully healed.* It was why Kaleb had scared information from the intruder instead of permitting her to exercise her ability.

I can't leave her unprotected.

I can protect her.

"So can the cats."

Kaleb was still trying to digest that wholly unexpected statement when Anthony shifted to enter Sahara's line of sight. "I'm sending you to Faith."

Sahara's body stopped moving, eyes of midnight blue shifting to Anthony. "Faith?"

"Even the best bounty hunter in the world won't think to look for you in the midst of a changeling pack."

"The connection with Faith," Sahara began, her intelligence plainly pushing past the visceral reaction that had sent her tumbling back into her personal hell.

Anthony shook his head. "No one expected NightStar to jettison the most powerful F-Psy on the planet, regardless of her personal choices. That was business and expected. This is family."

Kaleb knew Anthony wasn't saying everything, but he could guess. NightStar had been very, *very* careful to maintain a line of demarcation between its business dealings with Faith and her lack of status as a member of the family—in public at least. Privately was another matter: Anthony remained in regular, direct contact with his daughter.

The latter suspicion was one it had taken Kaleb a year to confirm.

"You're ready to trust the changelings with Sahara's life?" The only reason he was willing to consider the proposal was because of Sahara's response to the mention of her cousin—and because he knew Anthony was right about the prospect of any bounty hunter venturing onto Dark-River land.

"If they accept her as family, the leopards will close ranks. With Faith certain to vouch for her, as well as Sahara's broken Silence, there is no reason to assume they won't treat her as one of their own." Anthony's next words were directed at Sahara. "You'll be safe within their borders, and you'll have the forested part of their territory to roam."

That territory is vast, Kaleb added, sending Sahara a number of telepathic images. *You'll be as free as any leopard changeling, so long as you don't go into a city.*

Deep blue eyes met his before moving to Anthony. "Yes."

"I'll clear it with the DarkRiver alpha." Anthony glanced at Kaleb. "You seem to be treating my territory as your own." It was a warning.

Kaleb slid his hands into the pockets of his pants. "Would you rather I let her die?" he said aloud, even as he spoke to Sahara along their private telepathic channel. *Why didn't you call me?*

I had it under control. I am a grown woman.

Anthony's stare bore into him on the heels of Sahara's tart reply, but Kaleb hadn't been intimidated by anyone for a long time. "I can transfer Sahara to leopard territory."

"Thank you but that won't be necessary."

"Very well." He looked to Sahara. *The knife was a nice touch.*

Her scowl faded into a frown. *Someone once told me I must always be prepared. I don't remember who it was, but it was sound advice.*

If only, Kaleb thought, she'd followed it when she was sixteen. But then, Santano had been a cardinal Tk, an adult male who found pleasure in the pain of young women who couldn't fight back. Sahara had never stood a chance.

Chapter 24

SAHARA KNEW THE black-garbed man who stood beside her as the clock ticked over four a.m. was an Arrow. She also knew he was a teleporter, one with cold gray eyes and a computronic gauntlet on his left forearm. Yet regardless of the single silver star on the shoulder of his combat uniform that said he was aligned to Kaleb, Anthony trusted the male to transport her to DarkRiver territory.

"I've been sent the image for the transfer." The Arrow looked up from the small screen built into the gauntlet. "Are you ready?"

Sahara had never once hesitated with Kaleb, but she had to take a deep breath before nodding when it came to this Arrow with his steely eyes that seemed as distant as light on a storm-dark horizon. If Kaleb was at times encased in black ice, this man was as chill as frost, his Silence metallic in its perfection.

He was, however, as fast as Kaleb—and since he wasn't a cardinal, he had to be one of the *extremely* rare true teleporters, designation Tk, subdesignation V. While those of subdesignation V were telekinetics, with the attendant abilities depending on their level of power, it was said they came out of the womb with the ability to 'port, no practice or study necessary, the talent independent of their standing on the Gradient.

As a girl, she'd once heard that Tk-V children were GPS chipped as babies. Sahara didn't know if that was true, or only a story made up by young Psy who had never met anyone from the near-mythical subdesignation V, but it made sense. Like all telekinetics capable of teleportation, they had to have steel-trap geographic memories. So a baby or a toddler could conceivably teleport himself to a random location he'd glimpsed from a car, for example, then become too distressed to teleport back home.

Now the teleporter, a man she simply couldn't imagine as a child, glanced around the pine-needle-carpeted clearing made distinctive by two royal blue scarves hung from thick branches. He inclined his head at the woman with hair of scarlet silk who ran toward Sahara, then was gone.

"Sahara. It's really you!" Cheeks stained with tears, the lovely woman cupped Sahara's face, her smile luminous through the wet. "I thought I'd never see you again."

"Faith." It was a whisper as she took in the woman her remote, composed cousin had become. Alive and stunningly *vibrant*. "You're so beautiful."

A startled light in the cardinal starlight of Faith's eyes before she gave a small cry and removed her hands. "Forgive me. I didn't—"

"It's all right." Sahara took the slender hands that had touched her with an unhidden affection that made her throat thicken, brought them back to her cheeks. "My Silence is far more than broken."

Wrapping her arms tight around Sahara, her cousin whispered, "I never forgot you," into a quiet filled with the music of a thousand leaves rustling in a passing wind. "Father . . . it wasn't until after my defection that he told me about your abduction, and that the family had never stopped searching for you."

Returning Faith's embrace, emotion burning her eyes, Sahara said, "I know you tried to find me, too, through your visions." It was something her own father had shared with her that first day they'd spent together.

A shaky breath as Faith drew back. "I'm so sorry about Leon. He was kind to me whenever our paths crossed."

"He's strong, he'll be okay." Sahara refused to believe in any other outcome. "He didn't give up on me, and I won't give up on him." A future without her father's big, solid presence in her life was incomprehensible.

"If it helps," Faith said, "when I look into the future with Leon as a focus, I constantly see him in his clinic, talking to a patient, or at his desk. I feel no sadness, no sense of loss."

Sahara squeezed her cousin's hand. "Thank you." To hear that from the most gifted F-Psy in the world was no small thing, the glimmer of hope one she held on to with both hands. "I'm sorry, too," she said softly, "about Marine." Faith's younger sister had been a cardinal telepath, her studies rarely crossing with Sahara's, but they'd been cousins all the same.

Sadness in Faith's eyes, her fingers brushing Sahara's cheek. "Marine lived an extraordinary life, did things I only found out about after I was no longer in the PsyNet. She left her mark." Unhidden pride, a water-logged smile. "I like to think she would've cheered and said 'Finally!' when her toe-the-line sister rebelled at last."

Sahara's responding smile was just as shaky. "I'm so happy you made it out, Faith, that you have a life full of joy. Thank you for inviting me into it."

"You can stay forever as far as I'm concerned." Tender warmth in every word. "We can finally be friends as we always wanted to be."

Sahara wanted nothing more than to accept the offer of sanctuary and just *be*, but she couldn't do it under false pretenses. "I may be danger-ous to your pack. Kaleb Krychek can find me at any time."

The warm welcome in Faith's expression didn't falter. "We've already thought of that. Fact is, if Father is right and Kaleb is a teleporter who can lock on to people rather than simply places, he can find any of us." Smoothing Sahara's hair, she continued. "Still, he's never shown any aggression toward the pack, and you're *family*. If he does turn hostile, we'll handle it."

Even as Sahara's heart warmed at Faith's protectiveness, another part of her whispered that Kaleb had no family, no one to call his own, no one who would welcome him with the unconditional love with which Faith had welcomed her. "But," she said through a deep sense of desolation mixed with anger at the parents who had given up a defenseless boy to a monster, "you will put me away from your vulnerable?" Kaleb might not harm her, but she couldn't promise the same when it came to others.

"Yes." Faith's eyes were gentle as she said, "Don't worry, Sahara. We've been playing these games a long time." It was the firm reassurance of an older sister. "Your aerie is close to our place, but far enough away to afford you your privacy."

"I have my own aerie?" The idea of a house in the treetops made the damaged girl inside her gasp in wonder.

"Yes, but only if you prefer it that way," Faith assured her.

"I think I'd like my own place." It felt disloyal to say that when Kaleb had built her a graceful, light-drenched home that sang to her soul—but that home wasn't what she needed at this moment, wasn't a place where she could stretch her long-stunted wings.

Kaleb was too protective . . . too much an addiction.

Her breasts ached at the memory of how he'd touched her, his eyes an obsidian storm. Every time he came near her, she wanted to dance in the storm. Even now, so far from him, the pine in the air reminded her of him with every breath she took. "Did your mate come with you?" she asked Faith, making the conscious decision to turn her concentration away from the cardinal who'd kissed her under a wolf moon.

Faith's face glowed. "Vaughn."

A tall man with amber hair caught neatly in a queue at the nape of his neck and eyes of near gold appeared out of the shadows. "It's good to meet you at last, Sahara." Quiet and deep, his voice was honey over her skin.

"I'm so happy to meet you, too," she said, fascinated by the way he moved as he pulled down the scarves that had acted as markers for the teleport; she'd never mistake him for either Psy or human.

"He's magnificent, isn't he?" Faith whispered, lips to her ear.

"Yes." But no matter his golden beauty, he didn't make her skin burn, her heart beat out of rhythm, and her soul hurt.

"Let's get you home," her cousin's mate said, throwing one of the scarves around Faith's neck, the other around Sahara's.

The knit was soft against her skin and the pine needles thick underneath her feet as they began to walk. Sahara tried to take in everything at once, until Vaughn teased her gently about spinning her head off her neck. Liking this jaguar who was her cousin's, Sahara made a face at him that caused his cheeks to crease in feline amusement, and continued to drink in the wildness around her.

When she turned her gaze upward, it was to see a stunning sky still dotted with countless stars . . . but her eyes kept being drawn to a star situated away from the others, lonely and hard and bright.

The canopy closed overhead a minute later, hiding the star from sight. It wasn't long afterward that she stood in front of a tree so immense, she couldn't see all of it. *"Oh."* Running to the bottom of the forest giant, she stared up at the neat little house perched among the branches. It was connected to a second house by a pathway along a wide branch.

Light, yellow and rich, spilled from the windows of both.

"Who lives there?" she asked, pointing to the second one.

"No one," Faith said, hand linked to Vaughn's. "It's for when you want us to stay over."

"A guest treehouse!" Delighted, she sent the image of her aerie to the man who was that lonely star, ice hard and cold, the act coming from the same part of her that had turned to him when the world skewed sideways, finding aching pleasure in his touch, unrivaled safety in his arms. And she knew he was too deep inside her, meant too much for her to keep a rational distance, that it would be futile to try. *Look!*

A hesitation before the dark music of his voice flowed into her mind, wrapping around her senses to curl her toes. *You like it?*

Yes, Sahara said and, though she knew it was foolish with a man as powerful as Kaleb, felt as if she'd wounded him. *The house you built,* she whispered in a gentle confession, *it sings to me in ways I don't understand, but I'm not ready for it yet, not whole enough.*

Vaughn lunged up the tree with dangerous feline grace as she added that last, claws slicing out of his hands and feet to anchor him to the trunk. Eyes wide, she watched him climb to a rolled-up rope ladder at the top without causing anything more than surface scratches on the trunk.

"I can't do that," she said when he jumped back down after freeing the ladder, cat-quiet in spite of the muscled strength of his body.

A sharp grin, the jaguar who was his other half in his eyes. "You don't have to." Reaching into his pocket after retracting his claws, he pulled out a small gadget. "It's a remote to bring the ladder down and roll it back up."

Faith slapped her mate playfully on the shoulder. "Why didn't you just use the remote in the first place?"

The changeling male gave his mate a long look, eyes wild gold. "Red, if you expect me to use a *remote* to get up a tree, we need to have a serious talk."

Sahara bit back a laugh at the affront in his expression. "Thank you for the remote. I'm very much not insulted."

"You can thank Dorian—he's another one of the sentinels," Vaughn said, tucking a grinning Faith to his side. "He came up with this a while ago, but couldn't get anyone to use it. I think a few packmates even threatened to excommunicate him."

"Predatory changeling pride," Faith said in a stage whisper, "is a sensitive thing."

The laughing tease had Vaughn fisting his hand in Faith's hair to pull her into a kiss as playful as it was sensual, the fingers of his free hand gripping her jaw. The sight made Sahara hunger for a man as dark as Vaughn was golden; a man as remote and contained as her cousin's mate was wild and affectionate.

Putting her hands on the rope ladder, she reached for Kaleb, this Tk who had a claim on her deeper than memory. *I'm about to enter the aerie.* It took a few steps to get used to the motion of the flexible ladder, but her body soon learned the rhythm and she was pulling herself up onto the landing half a minute later.

The aerie proved to be a single large room, with a tidy kitchen area to the right as she entered, and the shower and other facilities tucked away in the back behind sliding doors of gleaming pine. A bed made up with a pretty comforter in soft pink and white sat to the back left and on the window ledge beside it was a small basket filled with chocolates. Every feature she checked was ecologically sound, the aerie a living part of the forest.

"How did you prepare this so fast?" Sahara asked as her cousin followed her inside. "There's food in the cupboards, a new set of toiletries in the bathroom, fresh towels." It felt warm, welcoming.

"Both these aeries are new, built in anticipation of younger members of the pack wanting their own space in the coming year," her cousin said. "In the meantime, we keep them ready for guests of the pack. Vaughn and I just had to stock the food, and that was easy enough since we all keep extra supplies these days, with the growing unrest."

Her cousin's reference to the turbulence rocking the world had Sahara thinking of Kaleb again, of the games he played with a ruthless ease that made him as much a predator as the jaguar lounging in the doorway.

A jaguar who said, "There's a big family of wildcats in the area. Lynx, too. They might come by to scope you out."

"I hope they do visit." Excitement bubbled in her blood. "I can't imagine seeing them up close."

"Those might be famous last words. Cats are incurably curious—you'll have more wild visitors than you know what to do with." Vaughn paused before adding, "I guarantee none will make any aggressive moves, not with what I'm guessing is Krychek's scent all over you."

Sahara sucked in a breath and met Vaughn's incisive gaze, suddenly conscious he'd intuited the intimate nature of her relationship with Kaleb. "There's something bad in his scent?" she asked, a painful knot in her abdomen.

"No, Sahara. There's something very dangerous in it."

IT was an hour later, the skies graying, that Sahara said good-bye to Faith and Vaughn. "I'll be fine on my own, I promise," she reassured her cousin when Faith hesitated on the landing. "I have your comm and cell codes if anything goes wrong."

Faith's lips curved in a rueful smile. "Sorry, I know I'm being over-protective. I promise I'll leave you be."

"Rest and heal," Vaughn said, brushing the back of his knuckles over Sahara's cheek in an unexpected caress. "You're safe here."

Sahara watched them leave from the doorway, thinking how very, very lucky she was in her family. She had expected an interrogation about Kaleb, but Faith had asked only if Kaleb was coercing her in any way. Accepting Sahara's negative response, her cousin had promised not to tell Anthony about her relationship with Kaleb, though Faith and Vaughn would have to alert the DarkRiver alpha.

"Do you know what we did to Santano Enrique?" Vaughn had asked, expression grim.

At her nod, he'd said, "Krychek's name came up in our investigations after we executed that sick bastard—we didn't go after him because there was no indication he'd ever been near the victims we know about, but that doesn't make him innocent. Be damn careful. And if he ever hurts you in any way, you run to me."

I was there for every second of their torture and deaths.

Kaleb's gruesome confession circled in her mind, and she knew the sane thing would be to tell Vaughn and Faith, but she didn't. Because deep inside, she simply *did not believe* him capable of such heinous acts, the girl inside her mutinous and unyielding in her rebellion. Maybe that was a sign of her escalating obsession, but she wasn't yet ready to give up on him, and on the darker, uglier truth she sensed below the words he'd spoken.

So she kept her silence, and a half hour after the others left, said, *Would you like to see my treehouse?*

Are you inviting me?

Yes.

When he appeared a foot from her, dressed in black suit pants and a dark gray shirt, she felt as if she'd found a missing piece of herself. "It's almost time for breakfast. Will you have something with me?" It was a growing need she had, to care for him.

No one else ever had or ever would.

"I've eaten," he said, making no move to avoid the fingers she curved over his shoulder, just brushing the tendons of his neck. "But you should have more nutrition."

Perhaps it was the fact that she stood in an aerie far from everything she'd known, a silent indication of inner strength that belied her near breakdown when Anthony had mentioned a safe house. Perhaps it was that she fought the terror of losing her father with every breath, time more precious than diamonds. Perhaps it was the way Kaleb didn't repudiate her touch, regardless of the fact that he knew exactly what it could cost him.

Or . . . perhaps it was because her heart was heavy with a truth everyone else seemed to forget—that this deadly man had been a defenseless child when taken by Santano Enrique—but she knew the time for avoidance was over. If they were to move beyond the haunting fragility of the bond that connected them, she had to dare ask the question she'd long left unspoken. "Did you choose to witness or participate in the murders committed by Santano Enrique?"

Chapter 25

NO ANSWER.

Sahara's mind, however, wasn't so reticent, her question activating a hidden key to unlock a secret mental vault. Memories swirled within, confused and clouded by time and the mistakes made during storage by the scared girl she'd been: a girl who, in a desperate attempt to save the most important pieces of herself from the ravages of the labyrinth, had locked the vault not with words . . . but with emotion.

The personal key meant no one else could violate her memories, destroy what she held most precious. But it also meant that should Kaleb have never found her, should they have never met again, that part of her would have been forever lost. A huge risk built on the same wild faith that had kept her going for seven hellish years.

"Sahara! I'll come for you! Survive! Survive for me!"

It would take time—days, maybe weeks—to unravel the pieces, to reconstruct what had degraded, but one memory was crystalline: a younger Kaleb—*seventeen? eighteen?*—bleeding from his nose, his teeth clenched as fine blood vessels burst in his eyes and a trickle of wine red rolled down his jaw from his ear.

"I know that monster hurt you," she said, her anger a hugeness inside her. "I've *always* known that." It was a piece of knowledge so visceral, she couldn't imagine how she had suppressed it for so long. "I also knew you couldn't talk about it." It was his attempt to do so that had led to the agonizing punishment that sent dark red swimming across the black of his eyes. "Are you free to answer my question?"

Kaleb broke contact to walk outside and to the edge of the landing, the forest the misty gray of very early morning, fog licking along the ground and sending tendrils up into the trees. The softness would've given the entire scene a sense of unreality, of a dream that smudged hard edges away into nothing, but for the jagged obsidian of the man who stood staring out into the gray.

His silence was so long and so deep that the whispers of the forest surrounded them in a heavy cocoon, leaving them the only two beings in a universe that held its breath.

"Men," he said at last, body as motionless as stone and voice without inflection, "aren't supposed to be raped."

Rage roared through her. "He did that?" *No, no, not her Kaleb.* To be hurt in that way, to be subjugated, it would've destroyed this strong man.

"Not in the way the world thinks of it," Kaleb said in that dead tone she'd *never* before heard from him. "He wasn't interested in soiling his body with such base contact."

But Santano Enrique had been a cardinal Tk at the height of his powers, while Kaleb had been a boy. "He used his abilities to violate you," she said, keeping a furious rein on her anger and hurt for him.

"Yes." A chill sound, echoing with emptiness. "He was *inside me* every day, every night. I could never escape, never know when he'd shove deeper, force me to do things with my body while my mind fought itself into madness to escape."

Sahara thought of the ugliness of the violation when her shields had been stripped, and imagined herself a child with no labyrinth to use as protection . . . and no hope. She had *always* known someone was coming for her, even if she had locked away his name to protect it. Kaleb had had no one and nothing to hold on to, his parents having turned their backs on the child they'd brought into the world.

Her hatred for them a cold burn, she took Kaleb's hand.

His fingers didn't curve around hers, his eyes a dead, cold black looking out into nothingness. "I was his only audience for a very long time. The first time was four months after my seventh birthday—a belated gift, he said."

Sahara bit down hard on her lower lip. She'd known. As soon as she'd read about what Santano Enrique had done, some part of her had *known*, been unable to bear to connect the dots.

"I wasn't strong then." That same dead voice. "I went . . . away, but he brought me back. Santano always brought me back."

Horror in her veins, she parted her lips, but Kaleb continued before she could say anything. "I couldn't kill him, couldn't stop him. No matter how old and powerful I became, I couldn't stop him." There was rage now, deadly and blade sharp, of a strength that had been building for decades. "I had to watch while he slit his victims' throats after torturing each one for hours, days.

"In the final years, he found amusement in telepathing his atrocities to me; it was his way of telling me that while I might have become strong enough to lock him out of my mind on every other level, I could never escape him or the compulsion he'd planted in me. I was a powerful businessman, a feared cardinal, and I couldn't even *speak* of what he was doing, much less raise a finger against him."

The last violation, she thought. The worst violation. Even the lowliest animal had the right to fight back, regardless of the size of its opponent.

"It wasn't until after his death that I was finally able to break the compulsion—and that was when I discovered he'd had a single remaining conduit into my mind, a tiny doorway that allowed him to do just *one* thing: reinforce the compulsion to keep his secrets and never cause him harm." Rage so deep it was a quiet, deadly thing. "Even then, when I thought I was finally free, he was inside me."

Anger and pain caustic in her veins, she wove her fingers into his and shifted into his line of sight. "I'm so sorry, Kaleb." The words weren't enough, would never be enough for what he had survived.

"Don't be." A calm statement, his fingers still not responding to her touch. "He made me what I am."

Fear overwhelmed every other emotion. "You are not his creation. You made yourself." He didn't answer her. She wondered if he even heard. *"Kaleb."*

"When I was sixteen years old, he said it was time I became a man."

The rage had been tempered by a black coldness that was worse than the ice, far more dangerous than the obsidian. "She was a swan changeling only a few years older than me, her hair white as snow—the blood when I slit her throat turned it scarlet."

Her heart thudded, hard rain inside her chest, but Sahara knew what he was doing, and she wouldn't permit him to do it. Breaking the connection with his unresponsive fingers, she placed her hands on either side of his face. "Did you put that knife to her throat of your own volition?"

The blackness continued to crawl over his irises, to chill his skin. "Does it matter? I murdered her while she begged for her life."

"Yes," she whispered, holding on to this man who saw himself as a monster. "It matters."

Kaleb's answer was a sickening portrait of Enrique's evil. "He'd had free access to me since I was three years old, my shields embryonic; plenty of time to build countless back doors and switches in my mind. That night, he reached in and . . . took everything, while making certain I remained alert and aware of his actions." Chill emptiness. "It gave him pleasure to know I was screaming inside while he used my body to carve her up. Mine was the last face she saw, my hand the one that drove the knife into her flesh over and over."

"Enough," Sahara snapped, terrified that he was going away as he'd done as a child. "You come back to me." Blinking away tears, she refused to release his gaze. "That wasn't you, Kaleb. You *know* that. Mind control takes away volition and intent and will." It made the victim a flesh-and-blood marionette.

Kaleb's lashes came down and when they lifted back up, nothing had changed, her Kaleb buried under the blood of an innocent woman who had never known that the boy she saw was another victim, not her murderer.

"No," Sahara said and, rising up on the tips of her toes, pressed her mouth to his.

Kaleb always reacted to her . . . but not today. His lips remained cold, his hands by his sides. Refusing to cede victory to the serial killer for whom she hoped hell was a vicious reality, she put one hand on his nape and, continuing to cup his cheek with the other, kissed him with a slow sweetness that was an invitation, a coaxing.

Come back, she telepathed. *I need you.*

His fingers brushed her hips, his hands rising to press flat on her back. One of his hands wove into her hair a minute later, the other pushing up under the thin black of her cardigan to splay on skin. An endless kiss, their bodies pressed impossibly close.

Not breaking the intimate connection, Kaleb lifted her up in his arms and carried her inside. The comforter was soft against her back when he laid her down, his body a muscled, heavy weight that made her moan, his lips on her throat a wet heat. "Kaleb. Kaleb, Kaleb." The gasped chant was a reminder to him of who he was—not Santano Enrique's creation, but Kaleb, who touched her with a primal passion and who always kept his promises.

Sinking her teeth into his lower lip when he kissed his way up her throat and back to her mouth, she released him after a quick bite. And when she looked up, it was to see Kaleb's eyes looking down into her own. There were no stars, but the obsidian was sheened with midnight colors, beautiful and mysterious.

Her fingers clenched on the muscled heat of his back, the fine cotton of his shirt crumpling under her touch. "You came back."

Closing his hand around her throat, he stroked gently, his mouth demanding on her own. She spread her thighs to accommodate his body, her core slick and soft. When he tugged at her cardigan, she reached down and pulled it off over her head to throw it to the floor. It left her dressed in a bra of delicate lace, her breasts straining at the cups.

Kaleb released her throat to look down at her breasts . . . and her bra straps tore in half, the center of the bra ripping to have the piece of lingerie falling off her body. It was the first time he'd used his Tk in such an intimate way, and her shocked surprise turned into pure pleasure when—still holding her gaze—he ran his fingers lightly over her nipple.

This time, his name whispered from her lips in a soft moan.

Looking up, his hair falling across his forehead, he closed his hand over her breast and settled his weight more heavily on her. Then he kissed her. Until her nails dug into his back and she was so wet between her thighs that her musk perfumed the air. Through it all, he petted and stroked her upper body with a hotly possessive hand that made it clear Kaleb Krychek considered her *his*.

And still, he didn't say a word.

SAHARA under his hands, soft and silky and responsive. Sahara's touch on his back, her taste in his mouth, the scent of her arousal a drug. Sahara who said his name as if it meant everything. Sahara who was and had always been the biggest fracture in his Silence. "Sahara."

The deep blue of her eyes shimmered with emotion he couldn't read, her fingers brushing his lips then her own in a silent invitation he had no intention of refusing. Her mouth opened at the first touch of his, her body arched and her thighs locked around him. He was caged by Sahara and it was the most painfully pleasurable confinement of his life.

Gripping the back of her neck, he tasted her so deep, she'd never forget the taste of him. *Mine*, he thought, *you are mine*.

When her hands went to the buttons of his shirt, he let her open them to the waist, slide her hands inside . . . press her lips to his skin in a sweet, hot kiss that splintered the second to last of his outer shields, the cracks going outward in a spiderweb that could collapse at any instant. The part of him that lived in the void, a creature without reason or boundaries, roared with black rage at being denied again, but that part— possessive and violent and of his soul—would die for Sahara in a heart- beat, and it knew he could crush her rib cage, collapse her lungs if he lost his grip on his abilities.

Wrenching himself up onto his elbows, he drew in harsh breaths and made a futile effort to reconstruct the shields. Impossible with Sahara so soft and sensual around him, accepting him though she knew the blood that coated his hands, stained his soul. Perhaps, the twisted, broken mess in the void said, perhaps she won't turn away once she remembers the hotel room and the pain and the screams.

"How bad are your shields?" Tenderness in her eyes.

"Bad." A fraction more sensation and the rawness of his emotions would not only be exposed on the PsyNet, his telekinetic and telepathic abilities would slip the leash. But when Sahara would've relaxed her legs from around him, he reached back to hold her in place, his hand flexing on her thigh.

She tightened her grip. "Obsidian, Kaleb. Did you go obsidian?"

"No." The obsidian shields might be impenetrable and unbreakable, but as Sahara knew, they were also absolute. "I'll be cut off from the flow of information in the PsyNet for the duration." He had never disconnected from the Net to that extent, had thousands of pieces of data flowing into his mind at any second.

Sahara traced his lips with her fingertip, the lightest of caresses. "If you're not filtering Net data, can you divert that energy into maintaining a grip on your abilities?"

Kaleb did the calculations, nodded. "It'll bring the risk of a catastrophic breach down to twenty-five percent." Not great odds, but not bad, either, not with Kaleb's control.

"Is there even a hint of anything major on the horizon?"

"No."

"Can you still be reached via a telepathic call?"

"Yes."

Sliding her hand over his nape, the charms on her bracelet cool against his skin, she whispered, "Then let the PsyNet take care of itself for an hour or two, and take care of me instead."

He didn't have to choose; there was only one option.

"Not here." He couldn't be certain of the security.

Sahara gasped as they 'ported into his bed . . . then pushed aside his shirt and leaned up to place her lips on the skin she'd bared. Slamming down the obsidian shields fed of his telepathy and augmented with the kinetic energy of his Tk, he pushed up Sahara's leg to make more room for himself between her thighs—and released the leash.

Chapter 26

KALEB TUGGED SAHARA up with a grip in her hair, taking her mouth with a slow, concentrated fury that made it clear she was now the sole focus of all that merciless power and attention and will. Moaning into the kiss, she surrendered, opening herself to anything and everything he wanted.

Buttons tore as he ripped off his shirt, and then the naked heat of his chest was crushing her breasts. A slight shift and he closed one of his hands over her left breast, fondling and squeezing with unhidden possession as his tongue rasped over her own, his mouth slanting to create the perfect fit.

Fingernails digging into the heavy muscle of his back, she met him kiss for kiss.

My Kaleb, *mine.*

His thumb rubbed over her nipple, his fingers strong and sure on her flesh, his hold that of a man dead certain of his welcome. When he broke the kiss to plump up her breast in his hand before sucking the top part of it into his mouth, she cried out and attempted to get impossibly closer, the hot suction a dazzling pulse of sensation. Releasing her throbbing flesh after she was halfway to madness, he looked down at the shining wetness of her skin, her nipple furled into a tight, begging point that he plucked with his fingertips.

Her womb clenched.

Running her mouth down his throat, her need for him a feral thing, she made a vocal complaint when he lifted his body off hers. A hot look, a strong male hand in her hair as he branded her with his kiss, then drew back again to rip open the zipper of her jeans, pull them off. His belt buckle bit into her abdomen when he returned to her mouth, his erection an aggressive demand against her that made her want to squirm.

Except he was deliciously heavy, pinning her in place. No one else would she have trusted in such a position of power, no one but the most dangerous man in the world. Unable to get enough of his kiss, of the connection that was a fist punching through her diaphragm to grip her heart, she locked her ankles tight at the base of his spine and spread her fingers on his upper back.

"I want to kiss every inch of your back," she managed to say between kisses.

"Later." Thrusting his hand into the rear of her panties, he cupped her lower curves, taking her startled cry into his mouth, his voice a dangerous, seductive blade in her mind. *Soft and smooth and mine. Always mine.*

Sucking in desperate breaths when he set her lips free to kiss his way along her throat before coming back up to claim her mouth once more, she ran her nails down his back. It was harder than she'd intended, his mouth and hands doing things to her that left her devastated, the marks ones he'd wear for a day at least.

Breaking the kiss, he threw back his head.

When those obsidian eyes met hers again, they were matched by a smile that held nothing calculated about it—it was lethal . . . in a way that made her body rise toward his. But he was already moving with the powerful grace of a cardinal Tk, kissing his way down her body to tear off her panties, push her thighs apart, and rub his jaw against the ultrasensitive inner surface of her thighs.

"Kaleb!" Her mind exploded outward to slam up against his shields, her body bowing. "Don't stop," she begged. "Don't—" A soundless cry, her synapses fried, his mouth hot and demanding on her damp flesh, his hands a little rough on her thighs as he held them apart.

Sahara knew about the mechanics of sex, though the Silent didn't indulge in the act either for procreation or for pleasure, but never in her education had she been taught that there were levels of intimacy even in sex. This, what Kaleb was doing to her, it was nothing she'd ever imagined, and oh, but she *liked* it.

Arching into his mouth as he licked at her, his tongue exploring her with a thorough attention to detail that made it clear he'd be as relentless in bed as he was in every other aspect of life, she held him to her with one hand in the heavy silk of his hair. That hand clenched without her conscious volition when he would've shifted his attention from the slippery, throbbing nub at the apex of her thighs.

Lifting his head, his eyes a storm of midnight, the shadow of that lethal smile on his lips, he said, "Does that feel good?"

Her toes curled.

Nodding, she held her breath as he dipped his head . . . and gave her what she wanted, fixing his mouth on her clitoris and sucking hard, his hands clamped on her inner thighs to keep her spread for him. Every so often, he'd move his thumbs on the delicate, sensitive flesh, adding to the tumult of sensation that had her gripping at the sheets, then at the muscled warmth of his shoulders.

Even as she sobbed her ecstasy, her nerve endings shredded with the sweet, hot pain of sexual pleasure, his voice was a dark caress in her mind. *Harder? Softer? Like this? Or do you prefer this?* Each question was accompanied by an erotic demonstration, her body her lover's instrument. *What about this?* Strong white teeth grazing the swollen flesh of her clitoris . . . then pressing down the barest fraction.

Pleasure wracked her, left her a ruin.

Rising to kneel above her quivering body, he curved his hand around her throat in an act of possession that had become darkly familiar, and bent to her mouth. The taste on his lips was her own, and it was an intimacy that should've been shocking, but nothing was shocking, nothing was taboo when it came to the man in her bed.

A slave to him, her body soft with pleasure, she said, *Let me do these things to you.*

His hand releasing her throat only to close over it again. *We may have to build up to that. Even obsidian won't hold if you put your mouth on me. Not yet.*

The black velvet of his tone made her shiver, her body undulating toward him on a fresh wave of need. She had waited so long for this, for him, and now her flesh was ravenous, her soul greedy. *Please.*

Tell me what you need. He moved his hand from her throat to between her legs.

Sahara flinched as his thumb brushed her clitoris, her fingernails digging into his upper arms. *It's too sensitive.* The realization frustrated her—it felt so good when he touched her there that she wanted only to experience the sensations again. But there was something she wanted even more.

"You should know this pleasure, too," she whispered as he put his palm over her damp flesh, the rough warmth of him a subtle caress. "Teach me what feels good on your body." She ached to kiss and pet him as he was doing her, burned to see those cardinal eyes drenched in the same storm that had sucked her under.

Watching you orgasm gives me extreme pleasure, was Kaleb's unvarnished answer as his lips sought hers once more. *Feeling you sticky and damp against my tongue, my fingers, your body soft under mine, your aroused nipples rubbing against my chest, that's what feels good.*

Sahara's breath turned jagged, her breasts rising and falling as she fought not to drown under the erotic onslaught. Until this instant, she hadn't known words could be as sensual, as arousing, as touch. Even more so when she knew Kaleb wasn't saying the words with that intent—he was simply stating facts, her pleasure his own.

He tapped her clitoris again. *Still sensitive?*

Yes, she managed to answer through the acute bite of sensation.

Let's try this instead. Breaking the kiss to focus his attention lower on her body, his expression steely in its intensity, he pushed at the tightness of her entrance with his finger, and when she shivered, hands falling to fist in the sheets, worked that finger slowly inside. *Yes?* Hair tumbled over his forehead, he looked up, their eyes locking.

So much power, she thought, *such unyielding control.* It should've made her feel at a vast disadvantage. It didn't. Because this was Kaleb. "Yes." A moan of discovery as he slid his finger out, then pushed it back in just as slow. "Yes, please."

A second finger, and all at once she'd had enough, her womb contracting with an emptiness that hurt. She might not ever have done this act before, but instinct told her what experience didn't. "You," she said, and it was an order. "I need you." Only Kaleb.

His responding kiss was a naked demand, his tongue licking deep. "Spread your legs wider," he commanded when he released her mouth, withdrawing his hand and rising to rid himself of the rest of his clothing at last—to reveal a body that made her feminine core clench.

Gloriously naked, his erection heavy, he settled between the legs she'd spread for him, one of his hands on her thigh, the other palm-down beside her head. Their gazes locked again as he began to push inside her with the blunt tip of his penis, her hand on his nape, her body slick and ready but still so tight against the thick intrusion of him. A painful kind of burning had her hissing out a breath, but below that was a need that wanted, hungered.

Are you hurting?

I want this hurt.

Sweat dripped down Kaleb's temple, his jaw a brutal line, but he maintained the slow, inexorable push of his body until his erection was buried to the hilt inside her. *Sahara.* Passion-flushed cheekbones and eyes stormy with so much power it was akin to looking into the heart of a thunderstorm.

I feel . . . perfect. Tight and full to the point that it was almost pain and exactly where she was meant to be.

When he shuddered and pulled out an inch, she cried out, the friction of his rock-hard penis against her sensitized flesh an erotic shock. Kaleb thrust back in, only to repeat the withdrawal and reentry, the hand on her thigh shifting to her hip to pin her in place as he dipped his head to kiss her breasts, sucking on one of her nipples before releasing it through his teeth.

The caress made her internal muscles flutter around him. His body turned rigid, the tendons of his neck standing out starkly against his skin, the veins on his arms pulsing as his muscles went taut. But Kaleb had learned control in a vicious crucible—he didn't break even under the intensity of the sensations. Kissing her again as she hooked one of her legs over his hip, he pulled out all the way, then pushed back in with ruthless patience.

Writhing beneath him, the abrasion of her breasts against his chest a sensual counterpoint to the harsh possession of him inside her, she moaned into the kiss. He swallowed the sound and once more repeated the slow, complete withdrawal and return, stretching her swollen tissues until her clitoris throbbed. Slick as she was, her body lubricating itself in rippling waves of passion, his size made taking him an effort—a hotly erotic effort that had her breaking off the kiss to issue a breathless feminine demand. "Faster."

Are you sure? His fingers dug into her hip.

"Yes!" Gripping at his back, she attempted to arch her body toward him . . . but he was already pulling out.

Only to slam back in. Hard.

Sahara screamed, her body clenching around Kaleb's in an orgasm that felt as if it would tear her to pieces . . . and that was when Kaleb's control snapped. There was nothing practiced about the way he pounded deep into her over and over again, nothing restrained about the way he wrenched her head to the side to kiss and suck at her throat, nothing calculated about the way he bent her thigh upward then pushed it wide to facilitate a deeper taking.

It was primitive; it was rough; it was spectacular.

Coming so hard around him that her thoughts were nothing more than splinters, she held on tight to the sweat-slick muscle of his body, his heart beating a drum that matched her own and his fingers almost bruisingly tight on the bottom of the thigh he'd pushed up. *Kaleb, my Kaleb.* It was a claim passionate and possessive as pleasure tore her apart.

Kaleb came in violent silence, his breath harsh against her ear and his body rigid. The hot wet of his possession as his semen pulsed inside her made her erotically abused muscles spasm again, clenching tight around him. Jerking, he raised his head, eyes of obsidian holding her own as he drew back one final time, then thrust deep past her clenching muscles.

"Mine. You are mine."

They were the last words Sahara heard before Kaleb's kiss tore her apart, his body locked with her own as they fell.

Chapter 27

"WE'VE SHARED DNA," Kaleb murmured to the woman who lay in his arms afterward, knowing he should've told her the ugly truth before this, his only excuse being that he hadn't believed she was anywhere close to accepting him inside her body. "There may be consequences."

"No." Sahara raised her head from his chest, eyes smudged with lingering echoes of pleasure. "I made a discreet visit to another one of the M-Psy in the clinic when my father"—a hitched breath—"went in to check on a patient yesterday afternoon. I've known the medic since childhood, and she made the necessary changes in my body chemistry without any intrusive questions." Her fingers rising to trace his lips. "I knew this was inevitable."

"Good. It's better if my DNA isn't passed on."

"Why? You're smart, beautiful, powerful."

"I'm also mentally unstable and may have tendencies toward criminal insanity."

The softness faded from her expression. "Kaleb, I refuse to call anything you did under Enrique's coercion a choice. That was *his* insanity." Flat, absolute, daring him to argue with her. "I'm not without intelligence. I know you've hurt people as an adult, but I also know you would have done so with a rational motive," she said, seeing him with a clarity that was a razor.

"Power, control, money, you'd always have had a reason for your actions, whether or not those actions were justifiable." Hard words, and yet her hand remained spread over his heart. "The criminally insane don't have any rational reasons for their actions—what Enrique did? He found a sick pleasure in it. Did you?"

"No, but the seed lives in me." Nothing could alter the pitiless biological fact of it. "That night after I killed the swan," he said, speaking the truth for the first time in his life, "Santano told me that the paternal name on my birth certificate is a lie."

Unwilling to believe anything the other Tk said, Kaleb had waited until he was wealthy enough to make arrangements for anonymous DNA tests, his intent to disprove Santano's words. "I confirmed the fraud as an adult." It had taken him ten cycles of testing to accept the truth of his tainted blood.

Struggling up onto her elbow beside him, Sahara pushed back her hair, a frown marring her brow. "How can that be? DNA is cross-checked at birth to make sure of genetic lines."

"Money and power can alter anything."

He watched Sahara digest what he'd said, saw the instant of realization. "Santano Enrique," she exhaled. "That bastard was your *father*?"

"In genetics." Kaleb would claim nothing more of Enrique than he had to. "He had a theory about how to create high-Gradient offspring. He didn't, however, want that child connected to him in case the experiment failed." Santano Enrique could not have a *weak* child, could not be anything less than perfect in every way.

"Sometime after my birth, he made the decision to continue the subterfuge—mostly because it gave him a different kind of access to me." A parent who treated his child with cruel brutality would be looked at askance in the Net, but a trainer was actively encouraged to do so in the case of an offensive ability. Discipline was everything when it came to a cardinal Tk child—without it, even an infant could kill.

"The man on your birth certificate?" Sahara brushed his hair off his forehead. "Your mother?"

"Bought off, then quietly murdered while I was still a minor." He felt nothing at the thought of the people who had raised him till he was three, then abandoned him to Santano Enrique. "Low-Gradient as they were, no one noticed."

"Surely," Sahara said, "there were suspicions of a cardinal born of two low-Gradient Psy."

"Santano chose two people with the necessary recessive genes to make such a birth a rare but true possibility." He spread his fingers on her lower back, her skin delicate and warm, but with a promise of sleek muscle beneath, as if her body were remembering the dancer she'd once been . . . the dancer whose flesh had torn under a knife with a chipped blade. "I carry him in my very cells."

Sahara's jaw set in a stubborn line familiar to him from her childhood. "You may carry his genes," she said, "but you are not and never will be Enrique's son." A passionate negation that vibrated with cold fury. "If you were, you wouldn't find pleasure in touching me with care, only in causing me pain." Pressing her fingers to his lips, she shook her head. "You're Kaleb. That is your identity."

A half hour later, Sahara was intensely aware of Kaleb watching with silent eyes as she moved around his kitchen, putting together a meal for them both, the ends of the white shirt she'd borrowed from him brushing her thighs. Certain parts of her body twinged with every movement, a silent reminder of the uninhibited intimacy they'd shared in the privacy of his bed.

Kaleb, dressed only in a pair of black sweatpants, the ridged muscle of his chest shadowed in the early evening light in this part of the world, was a young god, a Greek statue come to life. Strong and gorgeous and remote.

Except he wasn't remote, wasn't cold. Not for her. Never for her.

He'd obtained the most recent update on her father minutes before and had offered to take her to the hospital. The only reason Sahara had forced herself to wait was that Leon Kyriakus remained in isolation, his immune system weakened as a result of a hostile infection caused by the dirty knife the bounty hunter had used. She didn't want to risk introducing a fatal contaminant into his system in her need to see him alive and well.

"His prognosis is good," Kaleb had said, scanning the medical report when her eyes watered too much to do so. "The injury was severe, and his recovery will be slow, but with the infection caught in time, there is no cause for concern."

To anyone else, the words might have sounded callous, unfeeling of the fear that twisted her gut, but to her, they sounded like honesty. Kaleb had never once lied to her, and if he said her father was going to make it, he was. And when Leon woke, he would be disappointed in her if, in her worry, she'd failed to do the one thing he'd asked of her the night they'd talked till dawn.

"Live your life, Sahara. Live it as big and with as much color as you can stand to bear. Don't let anyone or anything—the family, Silence, the weight of your ability, even my need to keep you close—confine you again."

So she blinked away the incipient tears, looked into the ruthless face of the man who made everything in her ignite—joy, pleasure, fear, anger, terror, hope—and took the next step on her road to an extraordinary life.

"I need to ask you something," she said, picking up a spoon to mix the nutrient drink he insisted on having in place of anything with more taste. She'd tried to swallow the question, but it was souring her stomach, making her jittery, and he'd noticed.

A silent look that told her to ask.

"Where exactly did you learn what we just did?" It came out edgier than she'd intended.

"With the way our bodies respond to one another, preparation seemed prudent."

"I see." The spoon hit the insides of the glass, her motions jagged.

Shifting to lean on the counter next to her, Kaleb cupped her jaw. When she refused to look at him, he rubbed his thumb over her lower lip. "I researched sexual intimacy the same way I research everything else. Methodically and in intricate detail."

Sahara grabbed at the edge of the counter as her mind was deluged by a telepathic cascade of erotic images, limbs entangled and fingers digging into flesh. Eyes wide, she met his. "How did you . . . ?"

"Sex," he said, rubbing his thumb over her lower lip again, "is something the other races find endlessly fascinating. Sourcing the images, literature, and recordings was child's play. A simple Internet search brought up millions of hits."

Cheeks burning from some of what had tumbled into her mind, Sahara said, "What about putting theory into practice?" If he'd shared his body with anyone else in *any* way, her anger would be as violent as her pain. Her fragmented memories, his lust for power and lack of a moral compass, none of it mattered on this most elemental level.

Here, he belonged to her.

"Practical application," he said in that cool, calm Kaleb voice, "would've been a pointless exercise, given the high likelihood I would kill anyone who dared touch me in such a way." Another brush, his eyes focused on her lips. "With you, however, I fully understand the human and changeling preoccupation with sex." This time the image he sent her would've buckled her knees if she hadn't had the support of a telekinetic.

The snapshot was of her, as she'd been in his bed not long ago, her thighs spread and her back arched, the point of view that of the man who'd had both his hands on the inner surfaces of her thighs at the time. Accurate in every detail, down to the perspiration that glimmered on her skin and the slickness between her thighs, it showcased the steel-trap memory of the cardinal Tk who was now her lover.

"That," she rasped, "is unfair. I don't have the same ammunition."

Kaleb's expression didn't alter, his tone didn't warm, but the words he spoke were very much not of Silence. "I'll send you some video files." Then he bent his head and told her they should practice kissing, voice as chill as frost . . . and eyes licked with black fire.

It was a long time later, the two of them back in her aerie, that he reached into the pocket of his black suit—his shirt a dark forest green she'd chosen out of his closet—and pulled out a small jewelry box. "This is for you."

It wasn't her birthday, but Sahara knew the box held a charm. "To mark my return?" she asked softly.

"Yes." Opening it, he retrieved the charm. "In case your father didn't get a chance to tell you, there was a transfer into your account yesterday—

tagged as the income from an investment he made for you when you were a child, to mature on your twenty-third birthday." A pause. "It was meant to mature at eighteen, giving you independent funds for education, but Leon kept extending the date."

Sahara swallowed the knot in her throat. Once again, her outwardly distant lover had demonstrated his consciousness of her emotional needs by telling her a fact others might have omitted. Holding out her wrist, she said, "Did you get me a sheath for the blade?" The charm bracelet glowed luminous in the sunlight coming through the window.

"It's too soon for the work to have been completed." His fingers closed around her wrist, his thumb over the flutter of her pulse. "You'll have to wait for next year."

Next year.

If she'd been standing, she might have staggered under the force of her relief. "And the single star?"

Eyes of inky black holding her own, the words he spoke only a fraction of their conversation. "It appears it did not suffer fatal damage."

Such a precarious equilibrium. So many lives balanced on her sanity when her mind remained in chaos. "Let me see," she whispered to this man who would've laid waste to the world in vengeance for her.

As before, she tried to crane her neck, tried to peek, but he blocked her view, his wide shoulders angled to show the nape of his neck beneath the neat black of his hair.

Lifting her free hand, she just barely touched skin. A moment of motionlessness, then nothing but masculine warmth, his fingers holding her wrist as he resettled the bracelet and let her see the newest charm.

An eagle in flight, wings spread to their greatest length.

Freedom.

Pure Psy

PSY UNIFORMLY CREMATED their dead. It was the most effective way to dispose of a corpse, and those of Vasquez's race had no need for a grave where they could mourn. However, Vasquez hadn't cremated Councilor Henry Scott's ravaged body. He'd had Henry buried in an isolated location deep in the Tatra Mountains in Europe.

He hadn't done it because he needed emotional absolution. His Silence was Pure. No, he'd buried his murdered leader so he could report back to Henry. He'd done so aware that many would consider such communication an irrational act, but with Henry gone, Vasquez trusted no one with his plans for Pure Psy. He felt more . . . stable speaking to the resting place of his lost leader than inside his own mind.

It might be, he thought now, looking down at the grave covered by a fine layer of new grass, the humans and changelings had a point on this one aspect of things. Vasquez had no argument with accepting the other races had certain qualities and strengths that might be useful to his own—however, they were not, and had never been, the equal of Psy.

His was the race with the ability to affect the very *minds* of the other races. Psy could enslave those minds if they so chose, crushing the autonomy of human families and changeling packs to erase their society itself. As such, the emotional races could not be permitted to ascend to the point where they believed themselves the rightful rulers of the planet.

It was also true that the fault for the baseless conceit recently evidenced by humans and changelings alike didn't lie with them. That responsibility belonged to the weak ones in the PsyNet, the ones who had allowed the inferior races to claw their way to a power they could not hope to understand. In this, Henry had been wrong in his decision to attack the SnowDancer and DarkRiver packs so directly.

"They are animals," he said quietly, his respect for his leader steadfast even in this disagreement. "They do not know the depth of the waters in which they play." And the humans? Weak. Defenseless as babies. "We can enter human minds at will, alter the very reality of their existence."

Silence was his only answer, but he felt the peace of knowing he was on the true path. "Our rightful place is as the caretakers of the lesser races, not as aggressors. Ill discipline must be punished, of course, but only to break them of bad habits." Blood need not be spilled when the mind could be taught to fear pain. "In time, they will become what they have always been meant to be—our obedient servants, who know we only want that which is best for them."

Before that state of grace could come to pass, however, Vasquez first had to redress the current power imbalance in the world. To do that, he had to destroy what had become a defective and decaying ruling structure, giving his race the gift of being able to begin anew.

Humans and changelings had been and would continue to be caught in the crossfire as their betters struggled for dominance, but that couldn't be helped. This was a war for the survival of the Psy race. "Collateral damage," he said, thinking of the operation that was about to put Pure Psy and the need for Silence on everyone's lips from one end of the globe to the other, "is inevitable."

Chapter 28

HAVING RESTED FOR a few hours after a night that had begun with an exhilarating climb, was shattered by an enemy intruder, and ended in Kaleb's arms, Sahara woke just after two in the afternoon. The first thing she did was call Anthony for an update on her father, to be told he remained in isolation but that the doctors were increasingly confident of his recovery. Kaleb confirmed that status when she touched his mind . . . and it struck her that though Anthony was her blood, it was her dangerous lover she trusted not to lie to her.

Thank you, she said, almost able to see him in the Moscow office where he said he was finalizing a project in spite of the late hour there, a beautiful man in a handmade suit who might as well be a knife blade; a man so complex, she knew she understood only the barest pieces; a man who had survived hell as a child and come out of it a shadowy enigma.

He belonged to her in a way she couldn't articulate, the bond between them unbreakable, but Sahara had no illusions about Kaleb. The scars of a lifetime tied to a monster could never be erased—and no one, not even she, could predict the decisions those scars would lead him to make. *You need to rest,* she said, a painful tenderness inside her. Because no matter what else he was, he was hers first.

Soon.

Black ice in her mind, but that no longer scared her. His icy control was as much a part of Kaleb as the dark possession of his kiss, and Sahara understood the need for it.

The external damage? she asked, pulse racing at the memory of her shock when she'd looked absently out the kitchen window after they'd shared their bodies—to see huge gashes in the landscape as far as the eye could see, as if the earth had been cracked like an egg.

Limited to a five-hundred-meter radius around the house. I fixed the cracks after 'porting you to DarkRiver territory.

Sahara knew she should be worried about the fact that she'd been in bed with a man who'd caused that kind of damage with a momentary and, according to him, minor loss of telekinetic control during intimacy, but she felt her lips kick up at the corners. *So we literally made the earth move?*

A slight pause, before Kaleb said, *I suggest we don't engage in sex in populated areas.*

The cool comment made her burst into laughter.

Centered by the short interplay, she ate a small, healthy meal, mindful she couldn't become complacent about her physical health, then climbed down the rope ladder to walk through her new surroundings. Her intent, however, was not to explore, but to utilize the sun-dappled peace to mend the tears in her psyche. As a result, she was soon lost in the vault of tangled memories that held the broken pieces of her.

"You look like you need a cupcake."

Sahara jumped, having heard no footsteps, not even a whisper that someone was in the vicinity.

"Sorry, didn't mean to sneak up on you," said the tall woman with hair of a red more golden than Faith's, the strands pulled back in a tight French braid. Dressed in jeans, boots, and a T-shirt, she did in fact have a pink-frosted cupcake in her hand. "I was going to eat this one, too," the woman confided, "but I've already had three and my hips are starting to groan in protest."

Sahara saw nothing but supple muscle on those hips. "Thank you," she said, taking the unexpected gift. "Are you one of the guards?" The woman's walk identified her as a feline changeling.

"Name's Mercy. DarkRiver sentinel—it's my job to make sure your perimeter remains secure at all times." She put a hand on the slight curve of her abdomen in an absent move, her watchful eyes on the forest around them.

"You're carrying a child," Sahara blurted out, realizing too late it was rude to raise so personal a topic.

"According to your cousin," Mercy said dryly, and with no indication of having taken offense, "I might be carrying half a dozen. Faith refuses to tell me if she saw triplets or quads, and I'm not asking beyond that— not sure either my or my mate's sanity can take it." A grin. "The pupcubs will no doubt kick the knowledge into me when they're ready."

"Pupcubs?"

The other woman laughed. "That's a long story involving a very sexy brown-eyed wolf and far too much hard liquor."

Hesitant but hopeful, Sahara smiled. "I have time." She liked Mercy, and unlike when she'd been a girl, she didn't have to keep her distance from someone she wanted as a friend.

Over the next hour, as they walked through the wild green of the trees, Mercy spoke of her passionate courtship with the wolf she clearly adored and who was the father of the "pupcubs" in her womb. Again and again, Sahara's eye fell on the charms Kaleb had given her . . . and she began to dig deeper into the vault for the fragmented story of her own courtship.

IT was fifteen minutes past two in the morning in Moscow when Kaleb lay down to rest. He'd only been asleep twenty minutes when he was woken by a piece of raw data that set off his subconscious alarms. He felt no sense of surprise at opening his eyes to discover that Pure Psy had attacked a university heavily attended by Psy, due to its location in the center of the busy city that was Denver.

The world-class campus was famous for its progressive students and faculty. Discussion about current events had to have been rife. And with that many bright minds in one place, no doubt sides had been taken. If Kaleb had to guess, he'd say the majority had decided against Pure Psy—but a minority had disagreed and one or more had no doubt reported the "disloyalty" to the fanatical group.

Pulling on cargo pants, a long-sleeved T-shirt, and combat boots, he teleported into the chaos, identified the individual in charge of evacuating the collapsed buildings, and made himself—and the Arrows who had 'ported in at his request—known as ready to assist. For reasons yet unidentified, Pure Psy hadn't used firebombs this time, leaving a much higher chance of survivors.

The short, plump, silver-haired human female running the show didn't blink at their arrival and began to use their skills with a quick-thinking clarity that meant no one attempted to usurp her position. "Quadrant two, at two o'clock," she said when he checked in after helping to stabilize a building that had threatened to collapse on top of injured and immobile survivors. "Equipment's picking up breathing."

A younger man who moved with the fluid grace of a changeling, the university logo on his T-shirt torn but not bloody, ran up the section before Kaleb could begin to shift the pieces of old plascrete. "Wait." He held out a hand, his skin tawny brown in the afternoon light. "I can scent them."

Kaleb contained his Tk. While he could sense a number of minds, their pain and panic blanketed the area, making it impossible to pinpoint specific locations.

Moving carefully over the broken section, the changeling nodded at Kaleb, his eyes the amber-green of a large predator, possibly one of the reclusive tigers. "Here."

Kaleb moved the jagged plascrete with care. Trapped underneath was a tall human student who appeared to have a broken clavicle and ankle. Kaleb shook his head when the changeling boy—and he was a boy, not more than nineteen—would've lifted her out. "I've alerted the paramedics. She needs care in case of spinal injuries."

The next live recovery was of a pair of Psy students, both with severe crush injuries. Three more followed. Everyone else was dead—including an older changeling whose lab coat identified her as a professor, and whose eyes the boy closed with trembling fingertips that had become tipped with claws.

"Confirm no further heat signatures!" called the human scientist who'd been scanning the wreckage with specialized radar equipment.

The changeling boy, his face drawn, nodded. "The scents are confused . . . but all I scent nearby is death."

Kaleb scanned for live minds in the immediate vicinity, found none. "It's time to check in, get a new assignment."

Two Psy paramedics ran past right then, heading for the next quadrant, a human doctor already on the scene, a changeling nurse at his elbow. Kaleb hadn't ever seen such cooperation between the three races—and he wasn't the only one who noticed. Journalists from around the world interviewed the rescued who could talk, bystanders who'd survived the initial blast, rescuers benched because of exhaustion, anyone who'd sit still for a few minutes.

Kaleb, you must be exhausted. According to the news reports, you haven't stopped since you arrived.

He was almost expecting the telepathic message. *My energy reserves are higher than that of most cardinals.* The fact was, he didn't know how long he could go for as an adult, had never been pushed to the point where he'd flatlined.

Have you eaten?

Yes. If his body failed, it wouldn't matter if his psychic reserves remained high. *I'm in no danger of overload. How is your father?*

Holding strong.

He expected her to retreat as he continued to work, but she stayed with him throughout, the telepathic pathway open but quiet.

No one but Sahara had ever cared enough about him to worry.

It wasn't until almost twenty hours later that Kaleb stopped working. According to the equipment, there were no further signs that anyone had survived, and the changelings had been over the area multiple times with the same results. Because of the number of rescue personnel in the area, Psy telepathic scans weren't as useful, but they'd been done, too.

"No further chance of survivors," was the ruling by the silver-haired female who hadn't taken a break throughout. "Thank you. All of you. Go home now, and rest. It's time for the body recovery teams to take over."

Physically spent in a way he hadn't been for longer than he could remember, Kaleb considered his next move. The cooperation today had come in the aftermath of a terrible tragedy—it would not hold if Pure Psy continued to attack racially mixed targets, particularly if those targets focused on the young.

The majority of people understood the bloodshed stemmed from a radical fringe of the Psy population, but according to the media reports flowing through the PsyNet, a small element was beginning to believe differently: that the Psy were sacrificing some of their own in order to hide their true aim—to kill large numbers of humans and changelings, setting the stage for a worldwide takeover by their race.

If that element reacted to protect their own by violent action against those they considered the enemy, the civil war in the PsyNet could tip over into a true global war. The carnage would result in a broken world, its people demoralized and without hope.

The perfect time for a new emperor to come to power.

Pure Psy

VASQUEZ WATCHED THE news feeds with a growing sense of unease. The situation was even worse than he'd believed: Psy journalists were not only praising the skills of and the assistance provided by the lesser races in the aftermath of the university strike, they were calling it a bright new dawn in interracial cooperation.

If this continued, his people would soon begin to see the animal emotions of the changelings and humans in a positive light, and the traitors in the Net would have another weapon in their fight to topple Silence. That could not be permitted to happen—and Pure Psy's next strike would make certain of it, splintering all hope of cooperation in a miasma of distrust.

The university hit had been nothing, a decoy to distract those who hunted Vasquez and his faithful soldiers. Pure Psy's true message was yet to be heard, would be written in the skies in deadly flame, the omega site going down in the history of the world.

An Arrow was rumored to be sniffing around that site, and it was a concern, but not enough to make Vasquez authorize a premature "go." The fact that a large number of Tks had been tired out by the university operation played a weightier role in his deliberations, but in the end, he decided on patience.

If he detonated now, with the final preparations not quite in place, he risked doing a grave injustice to hundreds of hours of painstaking work. His people deserved to witness the glory of what they could achieve—and in the end, it did not matter if every single Tk in the world responded to the next strike: it could not be stopped, could not be minimized.

"We will," he said to the memory of his lost leader, "arise anew from the ashes of the world."

Chapter 29

THIRTY MINUTES AFTER the head of the rescue team at the university announced no hope of further survivors, Sahara felt the prickle at the back of her neck that was Kaleb's presence. He'd showered and changed from the clothing she'd seen on the comm and wore camouflage black pants, his T-shirt an olive green.

Nothing on his face betrayed the exhaustion he had to be feeling, but Sahara had stayed up with him through the brutal hours, wasn't fooled. "You need to be asleep," she said, grabbing his hand and tugging him to her bed. "I can't believe you were stupid enough to waste energy 'porting to me."

When she reached for the bottom of his T-shirt, intending to pull it off so he could sleep more comfortably, strong hands closed over her wrists. "Would you like to sleep with me?"

Sahara went motionless at the cool question. Kaleb Krychek, she knew without asking, trusted no one beside him while he was as vulnerable as he ever became. "Yes," she whispered. "I'm tired, too."

To her frustration, he again used energy he should've been conserving to 'port them to the night-swathed Moscow house, but she didn't argue. He wouldn't be able to lower his guard enough to get real rest anywhere else. Grabbing the T-shirt he stripped off, she removed her own clothing and pulled the soft fabric over her head.

It was still warm from his body, the scent of pine and Kaleb in the weave. Shivering in tactile pleasure, Sahara decided she would always steal his T-shirts. She'd undone her braid and crawled into bed when she spied him leaving the room. "Kaleb?"

"I'll be back after I check the security system."

Unsurprised, she drew the sheet over her. Kaleb's body burned so hot, she'd need nothing else. She was half-asleep when he returned. Coming to the bed, he touched the arch of her cheekbone. "You're on my side of the bed." It was a quiet reprimand.

Sahara smiled, sleepy and content, rolling over to surrender the spot that put him between her and the terrace sliders. "All secure?" she asked, dead certain nothing and no one would ever hurt her with Kaleb in the vicinity.

"Yes." His weight in the bed, but no touch.

The ache for skin-to-skin contact was a dull throb in every cell of her body, but she bit down on her lower lip to stifle the request on the tip of her tongue. Kaleb's power reserves had to be at minimal by now, which meant his shielding capacity—

He curved his body behind her own, one arm sliding under her head, the other around her waist, as his thigh pushed between her own.

"Your shields—"

"Intact. I'm only physically tired. My psychic reserves are full."

Impossible, Sahara thought, but sensing his body begin to shut down with the same icy discipline he used in every other aspect of his life bar one, she kept her silence and fell into the soft hush of sleep seconds behind Kaleb.

KALEB woke first, to discover his hand under Sahara's T-shirt, his fingers curved over the warm heaviness of one of her breasts. Leaving it exactly where it was, the erotic weight a deep pleasure, he quickly scanned the information that had filtered into his mind while he slept; he forwarded two items of business for his aide to handle, while taking note of the increasing disquiet in the Net.

Nothing required his urgent attention.

Slamming down the obsidian shields, he got rid of the sheet, then kicked off his sweatpants to press his nakedness against the lace-covered curves of Sahara's lower body, the T-shirt bunched up at her waist. It made her sigh in her sleep and wiggle closer. Nudging aside the silken black strands at her neck, he pressed his lips to her sensitive throat, abdomen tightening when her thighs squeezed down his.

He had watched videos of people copulating in this position, analyzed the mechanics of it, while seeing no reason to pick it over any other. Now he realized there were two very good reasons—it gave the male free access to the female *and* near total control of the sexual act.

Kaleb liked control in all things.

"Sahara." A graze of teeth on her neck that made her shiver. "Wake up."

She stretched sinuously against him, body pliant, no fear or surprise in her at their intimate entanglement . . . only an increasing dampness in the lace that pressed against his thigh. "How does this work?" It was a sleepy question, her foot lifting to rub over the back of his calf.

Kaleb rifled through his image files to find one that showed her exactly what he wanted. "Like this."

Sahara whimpered but pulled off the T-shirt in silent acquiescence. Throwing it aside, she brushed her hair off her face, then curled her arm over her shoulder until her fingers brushed his nape, the charms on her bracelet cool against his skin. It left her entire body exposed for him to touch, for him to possess, her breasts lifted lush and high on her chest for his private viewing. His body rock-hard, he stroked one hand over the sweetly sensitive skin of her thigh before pulling it up and back to hook over his own, his fingers pressing into the delicate flesh.

His other hand he curled gently around her throat.

"Are you ready?" he asked, though he could feel her molten stickiness against his thigh.

"Yes."

"Show me."

"I—how?"

"Use your own fingers."

Color pulsed under her skin.

"No taboos, no rules here," he said, wanting her with him through every step of this erotic exploration. "This is our place, our time." *Finally* it was their time.

Sahara wet her lips, eyes of midnight blue drenched in passion. "Our bed."

Squeezing the base of his penis with a telekinetic ring, he reined in the driving urge to thrust inside her. "And my Sahara." Always his.

Sahara shivered and moved her hand down the concave slope of her stomach to splay her fingers over her navel. When she hesitated, he kissed her throat again. "No taboos."

Her hand ventured lower, the tips of her fingers disappearing under the creamy lace of her panties. Breath turning shallow at the visual stimuli that hit every single one of his pleasure centers, he watched her hand move under the lace as she stroked herself. His abdomen was rigid, his chest tight, the pleasure almost pain by the time she withdrew her fingers, the digits slick and shiny.

"Make me yours, Kaleb."

The throaty request, falling from lips plump and wet, snapped the ring of black ice. Slipping his hand under her thigh after repositioning his own, he spread her further and, tearing away her panties with a negligible use of his Tk, pushed inside her. She was tight. He was slow, deliberate. Moaning, Sahara dug her nails into his nape, her breasts flushed, her nipples lush beads he wanted to roll against his tongue.

Since he couldn't indulge in the latter, he covered one of her breasts with a telekinetic hand, stroking down to squeeze her nipple. She clenched around him, her wetness molten. It took Kaleb's brain a microsecond to make the connection. Giving her neglected breast the same treatment, he rubbed at her clitoris with a phantom finger, while never faltering in the slow, steady rhythm of sexual intercourse that had his testicles drawn up tight against his body, the pain exquisite.

Sensing her body begin to tighten, he parted her labia using telekinesis and squeezed her clitoris.

"Kaleb!" Sahara convulsed around his erection, her entire body shaking with the strength of her orgasm.

Kaleb had intended to continue the slow pace that was an exercise in erotic control, but his brain short-circuited at the possessive clenching of Sahara's intimate muscles. Pushing her onto her front, her face turned sideways on the pillow, he fisted one hand tightly in her hair and slammed into her in a brutally deep and fast rhythm, her body tight and slick and of the woman who was and had always been his. It felt like madness, creeping red on the horizon.

Hurting her, the part of him that lived in the void screamed, *I'm hurting her!*

His muscles locked, his mind trying to force his body to pull out of her and failing. He didn't want to break the rawness of the connection, her skin as sweat-slick as his own, her body a hot, silken fist. "I'm hurting you," he managed to ground out.

"No, you're not!" Punching her fist on the pillow, Sahara undulated her lower body toward him. *Move!*

The feminine demand was the only thing he needed to hear. Pounding into her, he saw her fingers clench tight on the sheets, her lips part on a breathless cry, and then she was coming around him once more, the pulses harder, more viciously possessive. Caught in the vise of her pleasure, his back arched as white lightning tore through his spine.

The bed slammed back to the ground.

Hard.

So did every other item in the room.

SAHARA was attempting to gasp in air when a fragment of memory untangled itself from the vault.

"Did you steal this?"

"No. I earned it."

Her bracelet, she'd been talking of her bracelet with the man whose muscled body covered her back, both of them breathing as if they'd run a marathon. Never, she thought, had she asked him what he'd done to earn it; that wasn't a choice she had any intention of altering. Whatever price Kaleb had paid for the platinum that encircled her wrist, he had done so for her, and she would honor it.

His chest sliding against her back, Kaleb pushed up a fraction. *Can you breathe?*

No, but it has nothing to do with your weight. Come back. Fingers flexing as he obeyed, she released a shuddering exhale and tried to shape words with her mouth. It took her at least two minutes. "I want to do that again."

"I'm not sure our bodies can take it."

The icy tone made her toes curl—she knew full well he only went that cold with her when he was fighting to leash himself. Then he kissed her neck and she knew he'd lost the fight. To her shock, they did manage to have sex again, her on her front, Kaleb's chest rubbing over her back, though he used his Tk to lessen the pressure of his weight. This time, it was slow and deep from start to finish.

"It feels like a full-body kiss," she whispered as her inner muscles began to clench in a quieter but no less potent pleasure.

Lips at her throat, Kaleb rocked her through the orgasm, then filled her in a burst of liquid heat.

They were both drenched in sweat and sticky with sex, but Sahara had no intention of moving. In fact, she wasn't certain her bones hadn't melted. So it was as well her lover was a cardinal Tk who could 'port them into the shower.

SHOWERED and dressed in fresh jeans and a soft pink cardigan from the closet she had in her original room, Sahara went hunting in the kitchen while Kaleb dressed in preparation for a comm meeting. The charcoal gray suit teamed with a steel blue shirt and charcoal tie was one of her favorites. There was something incredibly sexy about a man so lethal that civilized dress only served to highlight the danger, not lessen it.

Discovering a stash of frozen meals he must've stocked for use after a high-calorie burn, she put several in the thermal device in the corner. The flavors would be bland by the standards outside the PsyNet, but right now, she could eat a small mammal. Stomach fluttering at the reminder of exactly how she'd used up the kilojoules, she was pouring piping hot pasta into a dish when Kaleb walked in, the fingers of his right hand slotting in his left cuff link.

Hair combed and tie knotted, no trace of passion in his expression, he was Kaleb Krychek, cardinal Tk and former Councilor, once more. The transformation was so complete that it shook her, making her conscious of the level at which he could compartmentalize—and leaving her with the troubling question of exactly how much of himself he ever showed her.

Then he touched his finger to the arch of her cheekbone, and the fear splintered, because only her Kaleb touched her in that way.

Sitting down to eat, neither one of them spoke until they'd almost completed the meal.

"My father just came out of isolation," she said, having received the update while she was heating up the meals, relief a shuddering emotion inside her. "Anthony called."

"I can take you to him."

"Your meeting?"

A slight pause. "My aide is rescheduling it now."

Sahara wasn't the least surprised that Kaleb had put her first. He always did. "Thank you," she said through the painful burn of a tenderness she wasn't certain he'd ever accept. "But"—she met those incredible night-sky eyes—"I need to ask you a question first."

Kaleb dosed her water with a vitamin and mineral tablet. "Ask."

"How could you possibly not have been wiped out by what you did at the university?" Cardinals might be gifted, but their abilities were still finite. "You had enough energy left over to 'port us both to the other side of the world."

Waiting until she'd drunk half her fortified water, he said, "Do you know about the Amplification Effect?"

She shook her head and, because she didn't like the distance in his expression, reached out to tangle her fingers with his.

"Per the effect," he said, not repudiating the touch, "an individual with two midlevel abilities, for example 4.7 in telepathy and 3.9 in psychometry, can sometimes use one to amplify the strength of the other, pushing themselves into the 8 or higher range." He paused to finish a high-energy nutrient bar. "No one has ever considered if the effect would hold true if an individual had two *cardinal*-level abilities."

Sahara couldn't imagine the storm of his power. To be a cardinal was to be off the scale. To be a *dual* cardinal was incomprehensible. "What happens if you amplify?"

"My dual-cardinal status already makes me stronger than other cardinals, by an unknown factor." No arrogance, only cold fact. "I believe there must be a low level of unconscious amplification taking place at all times. That's why my abilities didn't flatline at the university, and have, in fact, never flatlined."

Teleporting away the wrapper of the nutrient bar, he said, "As a very young child, I once lifted the wreckage of a bullet train off a trapped survivor—even a cardinal child shouldn't have been capable of that."

Sahara struggled to understand what he was saying. "Have you ever consciously amplified your abilities?"

"As a test, yes. Amplification impacts my telekinesis, not my telepathy. I could conceivably reach the earth's core with the resulting power, destroy the planet from the inside out."

She had no words, not for a long time, her fingers twined with those of a man who held the fate of the world in his grasp. "Kaleb?"

He didn't answer, but she knew she held his attention.

"Promise me something."

"Yes?"

"That you won't destroy the Net." If he struck out, she knew it wouldn't be against the humans or the changelings, but against his own kind; against the ones who had taken her—and almost broken him.

"I told you," he responded in the same coolly pragmatic tone he'd used for the entirety of their conversation. "I've decided against it."

"That's not what I asked." She held the obsidian of his gaze. "I want you to promise to *never* destroy the Net." No matter what happened or didn't happen to her.

A pause filled with a thousand unspoken words . . . and the words he did speak, they made the tiny hairs on the back of her neck rise. "Some things need to be broken to become stronger."

Chapter 30

"DO YOU THINK," she whispered, "that holds true for me?"

He went very, very still. "No. You should've never been hurt."

Something in those words, in the dead rage of his tone, made her mind open the doorway to a second vault hidden inside the first. She entered and flinched, a sea of viscous red spreading across her irises. Her breath caught in her throat, dots swam in front of her eyes . . . and Sahara realized she'd stopped breathing, her heart losing its rhythm.

A hand on the back of her neck, a man with eyes of obsidian on his haunches in front of her chair. "It's gone, done. He's dead."

He's dead.

Her lungs expanded in a rush of air, her subconscious understanding—*reveling* in—his words, even if her conscious mind did not. Her chest still hurt, shards of glass in her veins as she reached out to touch the hard line of his jaw. "Something bad happened to me, didn't it?" Worse than the captivity, worse than the torture after she created the labyrinth.

Kaleb knew he'd made a major tactical error. But he'd promised Sahara he'd never lie to her, so he said, "Yes," and waited.

"I'm not ready yet." Her hand fell to his shoulder. "Not strong enough yet. But I will be soon."

He had no doubts about that. "Do you want to go to your father now?" he asked, wanting her mind off the one subject that held the potential to destroy the bond between them.

If she ran, he hoped she would do as he'd asked and make sure she didn't leave him alive. Because without Sahara, the world would learn

what a child became when his trainer wove nightmares into his mind—
of knives slicing into flesh, of women begging for their lives—then put
the blade into his hand.

"This is my legacy. You will continue what I have begun."

"Kaleb." Sahara's fingers in his hair, her eyes seeing too deep. "Don't
leave me again. Don't go away."

She'd said those words to him before. And his answer, it was the
same. "I won't. I'll always be here. For you." Only for her.

Her eyes mysterious with thoughts unvoiced, she stepped into his
arms when he rose, her hold fierce. It was the greatest of ironies that the
only person who had ever held him as if he mattered was the one person
who did not need to hold him at all. If Sahara called, he would come.

Always.

"Let me take you to your father." Using Leon Kyriakus as the lock, he
completed the transfer.

They came in beside the bed where Sahara's father lay surrounded by
complex machines that regulated his body while he healed. Face crumpling, Sahara left Kaleb's arms to take the older man's hand, sinking into
a chair placed beside the bed. "Father."

Eye on the small window that allowed the NightStar guard on watch
outside to look in on occasion, Kaleb shifted out of view, positioning
himself against the wall beside the old-fashioned inward-opening door.
If the female—whom he identified from the back as a high-level telepath
skilled in mental combat, her petite size distinctive among Anthony's
most trusted security people—had spotted him during the 'port, Kaleb
would've dealt with it. Since she hadn't, there was no cause to add further stress to the situation.

The guard proved herself by opening the door thirty seconds later,
the ebony of her skin dulled by the pane of glass that lay between her and
Kaleb. Clearly recognizing Sahara, the armed woman didn't dispute her
right to be there, but asked, "The teleporter who brought you?"

"I have direct telepathic access to him. He'll take me back when it's
time."

Satisfied with the soft-voiced answer, the guard closed the door behind herself and took up her sentinel position once more. Kaleb stayed in the shadows, thinking about the complexity of the lie Sahara had told—which wasn't a lie at all, simply a statement that invited the guard to draw the conclusion that the teleporter had departed the premises.

Sahara, with her intellect and her talent for shaping language to serve her needs, was much further along in her recovery than she realized. Today she'd shied from the bloodiest of the memories that connected them, but the clock was ticking down at rapid speed. Body and spirit, mind and heart, it was unlikely to be long before she faced the past with the same stubborn will that she had survived it.

He had known it would come down to this, to a day of final reckoning.

What he didn't know was if they would survive it.

SAHARA spent the majority of the next two days at her father's bedside, Vasic 'porting her in and out. The Arrow did the task with quick efficiency, but he made Sahara uncomfortable, his Silence a cold gray frost. Kaleb, however, threatened to cause too much friction with her family, and right now, she wanted the focus on her father; he'd woken up at last, was able to speak.

As well, Kaleb had a critical item on his agenda—hunting Pure Psy.

Sahara hugged her arms around herself as she stood on the landing outside her aerie, looking out into the falling dark of night at the end of the second day. She should've long since asked the question that continued to haunt her: *Just how far would Kaleb go to seize control of the Net?*

It made her sick to even consider that he'd work with Pure Psy, but if she looked at the situation through the filter of cold, hard logic, the partnership made perfect sense.

"Some things need to be broken to become stronger."

The fanatical group had proved itself skilled at destruction, and as evidenced by the single star on her bracelet, Kaleb had no loyalty to the PsyNet.

None.

She couldn't blame him for it—how could anyone expect a child to have faith in a system that had left him at the mercy of a monster? Now that tormented child was a deadly man, and though Sahara loved him in ways that tore at her soul, the aching resonance of old emotion tangling with the stark beauty of the fragile new trust that had grown between them, she also understood his choices might be untenable.

Yet when he came to her that night, she couldn't bear to ask the question. If she was wrong, it would wound him—and the wound would be all the worse because he'd encase it in black ice and refuse to acknowledge the damage. If she was right, it would force her to act in a way she never wanted to act. To erase Kaleb from the world . . . No, she didn't have the strength to face that choice.

A little more time, she bargained with herself. *Only a few more days. Pure Psy will need to regroup after a major operation like the university strike. I have time yet to love him.*

"I've drained the bounty account," he told her from his position leaning against the outer wall of the aerie, his tie off and his white shirt unbuttoned at the collar. "The information will have already begun to leak. You're safe."

His protectiveness stabbed at her heart. If he had crossed the line, if she had to use her ability to end him, it would break her. And this time, she wouldn't come back. "That means I can leave the forest," she said around the rock in her throat. "No one in the wider world has any reason to recognize me."

Kaleb slipped one of his hands into the inside pocket of his suit jacket, the charcoal fabric sitting perfectly on shoulders that might yet bear the marks she'd made on his body two days before. "A means of defense," he said, having retrieved a sleek little gun. "This is considered one of the most dangerous weapons in the world, because even a child can point and shoot and hit his target." Showing her the controls, he handed it over. "Make sure the safety is on at all times unless you want to debilitate or kill."

Sahara forced herself to handle the deadly piece, knowing he was right. Her ability wouldn't protect her if an aggressor shot at her from a distance. "I expected you to attempt to stop me from leaving the protective zone inside DarkRiver land."

"I told you, Sahara, I will never hurt you."

Fingers trembling, she placed her free hand over his heart. "Thank you for keeping your promise, for coming for me."

His response was to tuck her hair behind her ear, the action as possessive as it was gentle, his face so darkly handsome as to steal her breath. No man should be as hard, as beautiful as her Kaleb.

"There's something else," she said, voice husky. "You can release me from your shields—mine are now operational."

Kaleb stilled, the primal creature that lived in the void rigid in its attempt to maintain control. "Your Silence is broken. You'll become a target for Pure Psy the instant you reappear in the Net." He would never permit her to be so vulnerable.

Sahara's hand spread on his heart. "Take a look at my shields."

He did so and beheld a mind so Silent, it had not even the finest of hairline fractures. Intrigued, he examined it from every angle and could find no errors that might give her away, nothing that would make anyone take a second look, the lie told with flawless skill.

"This isn't your work." Sahara was gifted in many things, but advanced shield mechanics of this complexity was a highly specialized field that required years of practice. "Sascha Duncan," he said, and saw from Sahara's wide-eyed surprise that he was right.

Councilor Nikita Duncan's daughter was not only a defector and mated to the alpha of DarkRiver, she was the best shield technician Kaleb had ever seen. He had acquired some of his most useful tricks by covertly monitoring her while she'd been part of the Net.

"She's enhanced her technique." Unexpected, given that Sascha Duncan was infamously no longer in the Net—or perhaps not. This region had seen a significant rise in the number of Psy with fractured or suspect conditioning. Those individuals would need a way to hide in plain sight.

Leaning to his right, Sahara put the gun on the window ledge, and he could tell she was uncomfortable with the weapon. As long as she used it when necessary, that didn't matter.

"It's not a shield but a shell," she told him, her hand sliding to his waist as she straightened, "its sole function to mask my broken Silence. My natural protective shields are hidden beneath, and they're tougher than most people's. They always were."

Yes, her natural shields were formidable, a side effect of her ability— but she'd been sixteen and already compromised by severe trauma when taken captive, while Tatiana had been an adult in full control of her scalpel-sharp telepathy. An inequitable contest from the start. "Total restoration?"

A nod that sent her hair sliding over the hand he'd curved around the side of the slender column of her neck, the strands cool and heavy. "Yes, faster than I predicted. It helped that no one was tearing away new growth before it could take root."

Kaleb decided he needed to increase the misery of Tatiana's punishment. Perhaps he'd introduce insects into her environment. It was amazing how much terror such small creatures could cause.

"What are you thinking?" Sahara's eyes were suddenly acute, as if she'd glimpsed the darkness that lived in him.

He told her, felt her flinch. "I managed to kill all the insects," he said, thinking of the tiny, lightless closet in which he'd once spent three days for no reason but that Santano wanted to remind Kaleb who held the power, "and I was only ten."

"No." Sahara cupped his face, her own grim with an anger he knew wasn't directed at him. "You do not do this, you do not become that monster's legacy."

"You are my legacy."

"Tatiana is evil," she continued over the chill sound of memory, "and she'll do more evil if she's free, so I won't argue against her imprisonment, but no torture. Not of the physical kind and not of the mental. You're strong enough to tie up her mind without isolating it as you've done now."

Kaleb thought of the seven years he'd been alone in the dark, of the horror of a sixteen-year-old girl forced to imprison her own mind to survive, and said, "I'll consider it." In deference to Sahara's request, he wouldn't torture Tatiana as he'd been deliberating, but seven years would have to pass before he'd review the state of her mental imprisonment.

Sahara shook her head, her expression fierce. "Do you think I don't see you?"

"I know you do." It was the greatest, most inexplicable gift of his life that she saw him and didn't turn away. "This one thing," he said, "I won't give you. This vengeance is mine to exact."

Sahara pressed a lingering kiss to his jaw, a single tear escaping her closed eyelids. "What would we have become if we'd been free?"

Kaleb didn't know the answer to that whispered question, couldn't imagine an existence other than the one that had shaped him, but there was one request he could honor.

Chapter 31

THE OBSIDIAN SHIELDS around Sahara's mind slid away to leave her exposed to the PsyNet. She hadn't been on the psychic plane for so long that the sheer vastness of the mental network made her pulse roar, her mouth dry.

Sahara. Starless eyes connecting with her own as her lids flew open. *I can reinitiate my protection if you aren't ready.*

No. She took a trembling breath, her hand spreading on the tensile muscle of his chest. *It's overwhelming . . . but it's also freedom.*

Freedom can be intoxicating. Be careful.

You won't abandon me?

This telepathic channel will never be closed. "Slow and easy," he said aloud, his fingers playing with the eagle charm on her bracelet. "You need to strengthen your wings before you can fly."

Holding on to him, she looked into the Net again, each mind a glittering point of light in the psychic network that connected millions of Psy around the world. In the spaces in between flowed fine silver streams—data shared by those minds—until the landscape was a sea of sparkling silver, the waves ebbing and flowing in a beauty that closed her throat.

Another strand of memory worked loose of the vault.

"Why does everyone call it a starscape?" She frowned. "That doesn't make any sense."

"Path me an image of what you see," Kaleb said, his face young, the line of his jaw not yet refined to masculine hardness.

Sahara did so, her feet hanging off the high branch of the tree at the back of the NightStar compound.

When Kaleb turned to her, his eyes held a wonder that was so rare it made her go motionless. "I don't see what you see. I don't think anyone does."

"Do you want to travel through it?" Kaleb asked, and the fine thread of her past wove into a present where that beautiful boy with a healing gash on his cheek had become a powerful man, his hand spread protectively on her lower back.

"Can I do so anonymously?" she asked, even as a section of her mind continued to disentangle the memories inside her, desperate to unravel the mystery of Kaleb before she asked the question no part of her wanted to ask. "Tatiana and Enrique both probably hoarded the truth about me, but just in case."

A set of telepathic instructions flowed into her mind, and two minutes later, she drew what was effectively a cloak around her roaming mind and stepped out into the PsyNet.

Would you like to see something interesting? Kaleb asked almost an hour later.

Drunk on the pleasure of being free on the psychic plane, Sahara had to be careful not to surf the data streams with too much abandon, lest she give herself away. *Yes!*

Can you see me?

Yes. His cloaked presence was a shadow she could barely make out through the psychic filter he'd instructed her to build into her own cloak. Now he took her deep, to a part of the Net devoid of stars, but no less alive for it, the silver thick and calm, as if she and Kaleb stood in a bay.

Delighted, she dipped a finger in the sea and came away with streamers of information wrapped around her psychic skin. The filaments waved as if in a breeze, each one a random piece of data. Astonished by the sight, she sent Kaleb a snapshot. *I couldn't do this before!*

Outside the aerie, his hand clenched on the back of her top, the fabric a fine green knit. *It's been a long time since I saw the Net through your eyes.*

She nuzzled at his throat, her arms around his body under his jacket. *This place is wonderful.* Dipping her fingers into the silver water on the

psychic plane, she scooped up shimmering handfuls of data with a joy-
ous laugh, throwing them up to create a sparkling rain. *Thank you for
showing me.*

This isn't it. Taking her to the center of the bay, he held out a psychic
hand. *You have to connect so I can get you through.*

She accepted the connection without hesitation, and they slipped
through a fissure in the Net she couldn't see, to come out into a stunning
blackness—the data in this part of the Net was so heavily compressed
that it had become a faceted jewel.

"This is effectively the backup drive of the PsyNet," Kaleb said,
switching from telepathy to psychic speech with a confidence that told
her nothing would leak from this place. "If the Net ever fails, the data
can be reintegrated to within twenty-four hours of the terminal event."

Fascinated, she attempted to concentrate on a single minuscule block
of data, but it was of such complexity as to be impossible to comprehend.
"How did you find this?"

"The NetMind showed me." He brought her to the center of the data
archive and to a sphere that gleamed with a constantly shifting slick of
color, an iridescent mirage that reminded her of the midnight colors she
saw in his eyes when he let go of the leash. "This is the restart button for
the Net, meant to sanitize it from the core."

Horror cracked black fractures in her wonder. "Why does that even
exist?"

"Because I created it."

KALEB disconnected from the Net on Sahara's heels, her face a strained
white where she looked up at him. "That's how you planned to kill
everyone."

"Originally," he said. "I later wrote in an algorithm to spare those
under the age of sixteen." He'd never had a childhood; Sahara had come
to womanhood in a cage. It seemed fitting to spare the children they had
never had a chance to be.

Sahara shook her head in a mute refusal to accept what he would've done.

"It was intended as a last option." To be initiated only if they had stolen her from him forever. "Seizing control of the Net will be intensely more satisfying."

"You're the wrong person to be in charge of so many lives," Sahara said, her arms still locked around his body. "You have no allegiance to the Net."

Kaleb was in no way insulted by her judgment. He knew what he was, knew that his experience at Enrique's hand had permanently warped the fabric of his personality. But— "My allegiance is yours, and you need the Net to thrive."

Huge, dark eyes, one of her hands coming around to lie on his heart again. "What are you doing to me, Kaleb?"

"Someone," he said, closing his hand over her own, "has to make the ruthless decisions or the Net will die anyway." He showed her images of the rotting places where nothing could survive, reminded her of the infection that had taken hold in the psychic fabric that connected every Psy on the planet but for the renegades. "Our race is on the verge of extinction."

Sahara's fingers flexed, her expression somber. "Our people have voluntarily crippled themselves. Of course that damage will be reflected in the Net. The only thing that might reverse the—" Her eyes widened. "You're planning the fall of Silence."

"It can't fall for all, but for the majority it must." If it didn't and the rot continued to grow, the poisonous biofeedback would equal a slow death for millions upon millions.

"A sudden fall will cause massive psychic shock," Sahara argued. "Thousands upon thousands could die."

"Acceptable collateral damage." Kaleb had no problem with losing a quarter or even half of the population. "Those who remain will be the strongest, most resilient."

Sahara shook her head. "You can't mean that."

"It's a practical solution. Slicing off the diseased and the weak will mean our race has a stronger foundation on which to grow."

"*I* fall into that category." A fierce response that spoke to the steel that ran through her body. "I'm weak yet, still broken in so many ways."

He knew what she was trying to do, but—"I don't have empathy, Sahara. I can't feel for those who are going to die. It would be akin to asking a falcon to take flight when his wings had long been hacked off."

He remembered the bone-shaking fear he'd felt as a three-year-old thrown into the hell that was Santano Enrique's "training." He also remembered the day he'd embraced the full weight of the conditioning. Better to feel nothing, he had thought with a calm unnatural for the boy he'd been, than to scream in horror every minute of his existence.

"You," he said, "are the single exception to that rule." The oldest, deepest, most beautiful flaw in his Silence. "Without you, I would be a monster."

SAHARA lay in bed hours after Kaleb left her to meet with the Arrows, the calm way he'd told her of his lack of empathy colliding with her fears about his possible collusion with Pure Psy to leave her scared in a way that went so deep, it was in her very cells. Not of him. For him. For her Kaleb, who had never, ever let her down.

It didn't matter that she didn't have the memories to support that truth—she knew it the same way she knew the sky was blue and the rain wet, a fact so absolute it was beyond question.

"I will *fight* for you."

With that determined vow, she sat up and pushed the window open to look out into the night-cloaked forest, the heavy darkness as impenetrable as Kaleb's eyes when he wanted them to be. Was he right? Had his capacity for empathy been destroyed during the nightmare of his childhood? She wanted to disbelieve him, to assume it was simply buried deep, but then she thought of the damage done to her by Tatiana, and, heart hurting, considered the choices a vulnerable boy may have made to survive . . . and accepted he might be telling the absolute truth.

Even as she struggled with that realization, part of her mind continued to tug strands of memory free from the vault . . . and suddenly an entire chunk of her past came loose without warning.

She was cutting through the park again, her school satchel banging lightly against her hip. There were two younger students ahead of her, both on bicycles, but they disappeared around the corner a second later. Sahara twisted to fiddle with the strap of her satchel, her aim to confirm there was no one behind her, either.

The pathway was empty.

Picking up her pace, she waited until she was in the single surveillance blind spot along this route, then slipped off the path and into the bushes. It took her half a minute of rapid walking to reach the grove of trees to the right of the path. No one would call it a forest, but the small wood was thick enough to provide cover. More important, it was out of range of the security cameras.

Sahara didn't think anyone watched the cameras twenty-four/seven. Their main purpose was to act as a deterrent against antisocial behavior. If, however, someone ever became suspicious of her actions to the extent of tracking her movements, that individual would find exactly nothing. She'd arrive home via another route, making it appear as if she'd decided to walk off the approved route. A fact that would get her a stern lecture about safety but carry no other consequences.

"Where are you?" she whispered when she reached the tree that was theirs. Without him to take her home, she could only wait for eleven minutes. That was the safe window where no one would miss her. If he was late—

But no, there he was.

Having teleported near another tree, he walked toward her, his eyes a brilliant cardinal starlight that she saw in her dreams, his body tall and of a young man, not the boy she'd known over half her life. He was harder than her, ruthless in a way she knew she'd never be, and the fact that he was almost twenty-two to her near-sixteen had nothing to do with it. He'd been the same way six years ago.

Here, however, they were equals, and beneath the disturbing coldness she glimpsed in him too often now, he was still her Kaleb. The one whose Silence appeared as pristine as her own while hiding a chaos of emotion so violent, she knew he could be beyond dangerous should his control ever slip. But never to her. Not ever to her.

Dropping her satchel, she ran into his arms. His own locked around her, squeezing so tight, she could barely breathe. "It's all right," she whispered, her hands in his hair. "It's all right." Over and over again, she said those words, attempting to comfort the man she loved when love was a crime that could get them both sentenced to living death.

Yet even as she spoke, she knew it wasn't all right, that the reason for his hurt was a trap he couldn't escape—and her beautiful Kaleb had never been meant for a cage. It terrified her that he'd go too far in the maddening fight to get out and she'd never again feel the steel of his arms around her. "I'm here. I'm here."

He just held her, in that way he had of doing during the worst times. She had no need to hear the details to know that he'd had to become even harder, more pitiless simply to survive. If it kept on in this way, she thought, her Kaleb would one day be lost behind a wall of black ice. Angry pain had her tightening her hold, her forbidden emotions hidden behind shields Kaleb had automatically augmented to protect her from exposure on the PsyNet. He'd been doing it for years, ever since he first realized her Silence simply wasn't sticking, the psychic taste of him as familiar to her as her own.

Never once had he failed to protect her. But she could do nothing to stop him from being hurt over and over again, the helplessness a fury inside her. "I'm here." She held on even tighter, refusing to surrender him to the ugliness that was Santano Enrique. If the black ice did form, she would shatter it with her bare hands. He was never going to shut her out, shut himself away in the darkness. Sahara wouldn't allow it.

Today he held her for almost the entirety of their stolen time together, and then he stepped back. "You shouldn't meet me anymore." No stars in the black, his voice dead in its tonelessness. "I'll hurt you."

It was a thought so incomprehensible, she didn't know why he'd said it, why he'd wound himself in that way. "You'd never hurt me."

"Don't be so certain."

Chapter 32

SAHARA FELL OUT of the memory to find her cheeks wet and her hands fisted to bloodless severity, anger a jagged blade in her chest. She had loved him. *So* much. Enough to defy her family. Enough to chance the psychic brainwipe of rehabilitation. Enough to fight for him even when he warned her off.

She had loved him until it was the defining fact of her existence.

Life, she thought, rubbing her hand over her heart, had come full circle. Because as the girl she'd been had loved him, so did the woman she'd become, her heart branded with his name. No matter what the future held, the terrible choice she might yet have to make, no one else would ever be to her what Kaleb—

Another unraveling of memory, dragging her further back into the past.

"Please show Kaleb around the grounds, Sahara." Anthony nodded at the boy who sat straight backed and expressionless in a chair beside a man Sahara disliked on sight. She knew not to say that, however. She was only seven, her Silence brittle, so she wouldn't be in big trouble for blurting out her immediate and violent distaste, but she'd still be in trouble, probably have to do twice her normal quota of mental exercises.

Better to keep her mouth shut.

The man she didn't like shot her a glance out of cardinal eyes that weren't pretty like the boy's, but flat, dead. "That child," he said, dismissing her as if she were a piece of furniture, "is too young to provide conversation that will in any way interest Kaleb. He can remain."

"I don't conduct business with children present," Anthony responded in a calm tone that Sahara knew meant her uncle wasn't about to change his mind. "We can schedule another appointment next month to discuss the forecasting services required by your company."

Steepling his fingers, the not-nice man turned his head toward the boy whose name was Kaleb. "Go. Behave yourself."

To Sahara, the words sounded like a threat.

Walking with Kaleb around the grounds, Sahara pointed out the things her father had told her she must point out to a guest. "Such independent social interaction with non–family members is an important part of your education," he'd said. "If your backsight eventually leads you to a career in Justice, you'll need to interact with a wide range of personalities, both Psy and not. I've told Anthony you're ready to act as a guide for those of your age and slightly older."

Sahara was pretty sure the boy called Kaleb fell outside that age group, but Anthony probably didn't have any choice but to use her since the older children wouldn't get out of school for another hour.

She was telling Kaleb about the hydroponic garden when she glanced up and saw fine lines radiating out from his eyes, bracketing his mouth. "My father's an M," she said. "We can go see him."

Kaleb stared at her with eyes that had lost their stars. "Why?"

Sahara was sure he had a hurt somewhere, but she knew it wasn't polite to say things like that to someone she didn't know. So she said, "He has interesting scanners in his office."

"I've seen medical scanners before."

Figuring Kaleb wanted to see his own medic and not a stranger, Sahara said, "Okay," and kept going . . . only she didn't walk as fast, and she didn't take him up the slope to the recreation center the grown-ups used for exercise. If they went there, the manager would want Kaleb to try the new machines, and she didn't think he should while he was hurt.

"There's fish in the pond," she said, after they'd covered all the areas visitors were permitted to view. "Do you want to see?"

Kaleb followed her in silence, but he went down on one knee to watch the orange fish in the pond in the center of the park within the NightStar compound. "Why was this created?"

Sahara barely stopped her shrug in time. Someone of her age, she'd been told multiple times, should've already conquered the habit. "I heard Father say it was an 'approved meditation aid,'" she parroted without quite understanding the words. "The F-Psy who live here use it." Her cousin Faith didn't live in the compound. She had a separate house, like all the really strong foreseers.

"Are you an F?"

"Not really. I'm subdesignation B. That means I have backsight." It wasn't as interesting as being an F, but Sahara thought she might like catching bad people for Justice. "What are you?"

"A Tk."

Excited—though she tried not to let it show, in case he told on her—she said, "Can you do any tricks?" One of the telepaths in her class had just a tiny bit of Tk and she could write on the electronic board without moving from her seat in the class; the teachers made her do that so she'd practice her telekinesis.

Kaleb didn't say anything and it took Sahara a few seconds to realize she wasn't touching the ground anymore, her body floating several inches off the grass. Eyes wide, she stood up, her feet on nothing, then, checking to make sure no one was watching, jumped up and down without ever hitting the ground.

"That was wonderful," she whispered when he set her down, then felt bad she'd forgotten about his pain. "I'm sorry. Did it hurt you to do that?"

Shaking his head, Kaleb played a finger through the water of the pond, making the lazy fish pretend to move. "Your Silence is flawed for your age group."

Suddenly aware she'd forgotten to fake Silence because he was nice even if he didn't talk a lot, Sahara bit down on her lower lip. "Are you going to tell on me?"

"No."

And he never had, Sahara thought, sitting on a corner of her bed, her back braced against the wall and her arms wrapped around her knees as she thought of the boy with such haunting pain in his eyes. Instead, he'd taught her how to be more careful . . . and he'd visited her.

"Hello."

Surprised, Sahara looked up from the wide stump where she sat. No one ever came this way, her home backing onto a stand of trees that ended at the perimeter fence. Pretty cardinal eyes in an expressionless face met her own.

"Hi!" Knowing her father was busy in his study on the other side of the house, she put down the datapad that held her despised math homework. "Is that man here again?" She hesitated, then said what was in her heart, since Kaleb had kept his word and not reported her terrible Silence. "I don't like him."

Kaleb shook his head. "I came to see you." A pause. "I don't know any other children who talk to me."

"That must be lonely." She broke off half her nutrition bar, held it out. "I know you probably think I'm a baby, but you can be my friend if you like." Shifting on the stump when he accepted the snack, she made a space for him.

"I don't think you're a baby." He took a seat beside her. "I think you're smart and you see things other people don't." This time, the pause was longer, his gaze focused on something she couldn't see. "I don't like him, either."

Another thread pulling free of the vault almost before she'd assimilated the last, another memory, this one tinged with laughter.

Sahara poked out her tongue at the datapad on her lap. She might be eleven and much better at pretending to be Silent in public, but she still hated math. She'd tried to tell her teachers not to put her into accelerated lessons when it came to this one subject, but they kept pointing out the fact that her IQ scores placed her learning capacity in the gifted range. According to them, all she had to do was try harder. "Hah!"

When Kaleb appeared beside the stump where she always did her homework, she smiled in relief. "I have to finish this by Friday," she told him. "Or I'll be put into an after-school math tutorial." It wasn't the tutorial part that horrified her—it was the thought of doing even more math!

"Here." He took a seat beside her, a greenish bruise below the curve of his left cheekbone.

Sahara kicked her heel back into the stump to force herself not to ask about the bruise, the impact painful on her bare skin. She knew the answer to her question and she knew there was nothing she could do about it, the knowledge bubbling acid in her stomach. "What's this?" Putting aside her datapad and tightening her abdomen against the futile surge of anger, she took the hard-copy book he held out.

"You're a tactile learner," he said, *as she opened the pages to see that it was a math textbook. "I thought this might help you remember the equations better." Reaching into a pocket, he put two ink pens between them.*

"Why don't you just tell me the answers?" she asked brightly. "Then we can talk about much more interesting things."

Kaleb simply looked at her with those beautiful starlight eyes that were too often an empty black these days, holding a numbness that made her chest hurt.

Sighing, but happy because he hadn't gone away again, she picked up the blue pen and began to do the equations on the first page, making sure to write down her entire painstaking process. When she was done, Kaleb went over her work, showing her where she'd made errors of logic so she wouldn't make the same ones again.

"Can you write down the correct processes, too?" she asked him. "I can use them as study aids while I do my homework." No matter what the teachers tried, Sahara never learned as well at school as she did with Kaleb when it came to math. He knew exactly how to explain things to her.

Nodding, he went down the page with a black pen, his writing strong and neat. "Did you have a dance lesson today?"

She said, "Yes," then ran over to the side of the house to peek at the window to her father's study. He was still there, working on a paper for the Psy-Med Journal. *Smiling, she ran back to Kaleb. "I learned a new step."* Bubbles of happiness in her blood. *"Want to see?"*

Closing the math textbook, he set it on the stump and nodded. Then, as the birds flew home to their nests and the sky turned a dusky orange, she danced, the grass soft beneath her bare feet and Kaleb her quiet audience.

Sahara's heart warmed at the innocence of the memory, at her absolute trust in the boy-becoming-a-man who had understood that for her, dancing was like breathing, their friendship iron strong. It had only grown stronger as the years passed, but Kaleb had had to be so careful— Enrique had him on a very tight psychic leash, but the older he grew, the better he became at slipping that leash for small periods of time.

Secret, everything had been secret.

Her stomach clenched without warning at the whispered thought, bile coating her throat.

Staggering out of bed, she made it to the bathroom before falling to her hands and knees to retch, her abdomen and throat hurting from the force of the convulsive shudders that tore through her body to leave her shivering on the floor. When she could move again, she cleaned up the mess, brushed her teeth, then showered under a red-hot spray before wrapping a towel around her body and walking to sit back down on the bed.

Droplets of water trickled over her neck and between her breasts, but she made no move to mop them up, her mind on her fragmented past. It didn't take a genius intellect to realize the bad thing that had happened to her was somehow connected to Kaleb, an event her mind continued to rebel against remembering, regardless of how hard she tried.

All it got her was the promise of another episode like the one she'd just suffered.

Frustrated but conscious she couldn't expect absolute recall all at once, she gave up the fruitless exercise after twenty minutes and got up. Pulling on underwear, a pair of jeans, and a V-necked cashmere pullover in an azure blue shade that Faith had gifted her, the texture exquisite against her skin, she dried and braided her hair.

Her next task was to check on her father. Hearing that he was in a natural, deep sleep had her smiling after she disconnected the comm link. She could've gone for a walk under the moonlight, but what she really needed was to be close to Kaleb, her heart chilled by the malevolence that hovered over her.

Is your meeting over? she asked over the extraordinarily pure connection that spoke of his telepathic strength.

Yes. I'm working from the house—what do you need?

Swallowing at the question that said so much about what he felt for her, she sent her answer. *To come to you.*

Kaleb appeared by her side an instant later, dressed in the same suit he'd been wearing earlier, minus the jacket, his collar open and sleeves rolled up. "Is something wrong?"

"No." Stepping into his arms, she held on tight. "Can we sit on the terrace?"

Skin hot through the fine fabric of his shirt, he took her home and sat down in the lounger with her between his legs, her body curled up against him under the early afternoon sunlight on this side of the world. It took time for the masculine heat of him to melt the ice, for her body to stretch out until she lay with her back to his chest, his arms around her and one of his legs bent slightly at the knee outside her own.

"You made me float beside the koi pond."

Tension infiltrated his muscles at her quiet words. "You remembered."

"Yes." She curled her hand around his biceps. "How we met, how you came to visit me."

"Do you," he said, the tension fading, "remember what you asked me to do on your fifteenth birthday?"

Sahara went to shake her head but the memory was suddenly there, as if it had simply been waiting for her to notice.

Chapter 33

SAHARA'S LAUGH WAS sunlight in his veins. "I asked you to kiss me. And you said no!" Tipping up her head, she pretended to scowl at him. "I finally had to make the first move."

"In my defense, I was twenty-one to your fifteen. It would've been inappropriate." Stroking his hand around her throat, he angled her head so he could taste her lips. That she'd come to him after what he'd told her at the aerie, it was a miracle. The fact that her mind continued to withhold the bloody truth from her was another.

"It took me a year to build up the courage," she murmured against his mouth, lips curved and fingers laced behind his neck.

"Your determination," he said, pushing up the softness of her pullover to place his hands on the silken warmth of her abdomen, "has never been anything less than steely." She'd caught him as he bent over her wrist to affix the dancer charm to her bracelet. He'd been so startled at the shockingly intimate contact, he hadn't broken away, and the taste of Sahara had entered his bloodstream, a brand he'd wear for the rest of his life.

Color had painted her cheeks in the aftermath. "Sixteen and twenty-two isn't a significant gap." It had been a mutinous statement. "Five more years and I'll be twenty-one, and a legal adult with full rights. We can file a conception and fertilization contract, and once we have a child, we can agree to joint parenting and live—"

"Yes," he'd said, interrupting the rush of words because she had no need to convince him to accept a trust of which he would never be deserving, but that he intended to take and protect to his last breath.

A dawning smile. "We'll have a home," she'd whispered, "where I can kiss you as often as I like."

But that had been their first, their only kiss. Two days later, Sahara had screamed until her voice broke, her blood slick on her brutalized skin.

"I'm sorry," he said, the memory one he'd carry to his grave, "that I'm not the man you remember. Too many things happened while you were gone." If she'd been with him through that time, the bright light in the nightmare, he might have battled to retain some sliver of his "humanity." But they had stolen her from him, stolen the only being in the universe about whom he cared, and in so doing, they'd changed the course of the world.

Sahara's fingers tightened on his arm. "You're mine." Simple, quiet words that were a punch to the chest. "I will fight for you, today, tomorrow, and all the tomorrows to come."

In the intensity of the silence that followed as they simply held on to one another, as if to mitigate a separation that had scarred them both, he saw her eyes close, her breathing even. She'd fallen asleep in his arms. The first time she'd done that, she'd been eleven years old, their relationship a friendship that had become integral to his sanity.

Tired from her dance lessons, she'd leaned against him as they sat in front of the stump, and the next thing he knew, she was fast asleep. No one had ever shown him such trust. He hadn't dared move for the entire time he was able to spend with her, waking her with the gentlest of telepathic hails when it was time for him to go.

He could still remember the smudgy blue of her eyes when she'd wakened, the way she'd accepted his presence without surprise or fear. As if that was his place. With her. Rubbing at her eyes, she'd said, "Will you come tomorrow?"

"Yes."

He'd always said yes to her, to the girl who had given him a sense of belonging, a sense of *home*. As she'd grown and realized where he went when he left her, what was done to him, those eyes had turned bruised. But never had she turned away from him, no matter how broken he was when he came to her.

"*I'll tell,*" she'd said at twelve, her face set. "*He's hurting you even if you won't say how, and I won't be quiet about it anymore!*"

"*You can't. There's no evidence.*" Santano had made certain of that. And should a J-Psy be called in to check Kaleb's memories—"*I'll have a fatal accident before he allows anyone close enough to examine me.*"

Tears of rage, face red. "*I hate that monster! I hate him.*"

In the end, her loyalty and love for him had cost her everything. "I'm sorry," he said again, touching his fingers to the tiny scar on her cheekbone. "No one will ever again cause you harm." He'd already executed three of the guards who had helped to imprison and torture her.

All had hidden like the rats they were when they understood they were being hunted, but Kaleb was patient. He'd find each and every one. And he'd break their minds before he broke their necks.

THREE days later, Sahara waved good-bye to her father on the comm and watched him turn away to get to work. He'd been discharged a day earlier and was already in the clinic office, looking over patient files in direct violation of the orders given him by his own medic. There was no doubt where she'd inherited her will—a will Kaleb had teased to a shattering point the previous night.

After he'd sat distractingly shirtless beside her as she viewed one of his research videos. Every so often, he'd looked up from his datapad to point out a technical aspect of what the naked people on-screen were doing, his voice cool and expression clinical. She'd lasted exactly seventeen minutes before pouncing on him.

Blushing at how very unclinical he'd been with her, she turned off the comm and headed down the rope ladder to meet Faith and Mercy for a shopping trip to San Francisco. It was time for her to explore her new life, and the idea of doing it with friends was sweetly wonderful. Both

her cousin and the witty, kind DarkRiver sentinel had become an important part of her life, and she intended to nurture that relationship, come
what may.

"I need to think about what I'm going to do," she said to them in the
SUV, turning slightly to involve Faith in the discussion. Her cousin had
insisted Sahara take the front passenger seat when Mercy picked them
up, since the scenery would be new to her. "With my life, I mean."

"You don't have to decide that right now." Faith frowned over her
carry cup of coffee, the scent luscious enough to make Sahara question
her own dislike of the bitter liquid. "If anyone's earned downtime,
it's you."

"That's what I thought"—Sahara made a face—"but that's not my
personality." It never had been. "Now that I'm healthier, my brain's going
a hundred miles an hour." She'd already inhaled multiple textbooks on
her favorite subjects.

Mercy grinned. "Leopards, as they say, don't change their spots."

After the laughter, they spoke of her options, whether she might
want to go back to school or if she'd prefer to do something less academic
for a while. It was a valuable conversation, one that gave her plenty of
food for thought.

"I was worried I'd be overwhelmed," she confessed upon arriving in
the busy city by the water that was San Francisco, "but I love the noise
and the color and the people!"

It was a couple of hours later, as they were walking into a small Ital-
ian restaurant for lunch—after stashing their shopping in the SUV—
that three things happened in quick succession. Someone shot at Faith
and missed, the bullet smashing a window; Mercy spun to cover Faith
with predatory grace while yelling at Sahara to duck; and bony hands
gripped Sahara around her upper arms.

Then the restaurant was gone, and she was in what appeared to be a
small, empty warehouse, dust motes dancing in the streaks of sunlight
slanting through the old wooden boards that made up the walls.

"I assume you're after the bounty?" she said in a calm tone in spite
of her racing heart, stifling her first instinct—which was to call Kaleb.

Since she wasn't dead or bleeding, it meant the man behind her, his gloved hands already off her skin, wanted her alive, so there was a chance she could defuse the situation without violence.

The kidnapper shifted to face Sahara. He was thin and relatively short, only two or three inches above her in height, but he not only moved with an economy that shouted skill, he had a gleaming black laser pistol in his hand. "The bounty is gone," she said at his continued silence, her own gun snug in the ankle holster covered by her jeans.

"I have a private client." Curt words that added to the impression of a honed professional. "As long as you cooperate, I have no intention of causing you bodily harm."

Glancing around the warehouse, she spotted an overturned crate a meter away. "May I sit?"

A brisk nod as, keeping her in his line of sight, he moved to a paper-thin portable computer set up on what appeared to be a cheap card table.

"Are you checking to see if your client has wired the payment?"

No answer. But while he believed her docile and resigned to her fate, Sahara watched him. It soon became apparent that he was moving with a deliberate care she hadn't noticed at first glance. The man was weak, close to his limit—either he'd teleported her to a location far outside his range, or he'd had to 'port several times in close succession in order to pull off the shot at Faith followed by the grab.

"How," she said, working through her options, "did you locate me?"

"That knowledge can't assist you now."

"I'd like to know where my security failed." True, except she didn't need him to tell her. "An intellectual exercise."

A slight pause before, surprisingly, he gave her an answer. "According to my employer, it was certain NightStar would put you in a secure location. There was only an outside chance you'd be with your cousin, but I decided it merited forty-eight hours of my time. Since DarkRiver's territory is large, I determined to surveil the parking lot of the pack's city HQ with the intention of tailing Faith."

Chance, Sahara thought, was a tricky beast. "Luck is certainly on your side today." Rising, she took a few slow steps toward him, aware of his eyes tracking her every move, his fingers curved around the gun at his side. "May I?" she said and nodded at the water bottle beside the computer.

"Here." He handed it to her, confident of the protection afforded by his gloves.

That was his mistake and part of what made Sahara so dangerous.

A split second after her fingers brushed his, the kidnapper handed her his gun, his eyes blurry with confusion. "What am I doing here?"

"You got lost." Weaving a new memory for him, she sent him to sleep on the floor. When he woke, it would be with a recollection of an altercation that required he lie low for a week.

Sahara hated the idea of violating anyone's mind, but this bounty hunter had lost the protection offered by her abhorrence for mental invasion when he decided to abduct her. Slipping in and out of his mind as if it were her own, she logged on to his computer using his password and erased everything that referenced the deal, whether in his e-mail or in his bank accounts. It helped that he was organized, his mind filing the data about her in a discrete section, but it still took time.

Rather than attempting to overwrite the hard drive, she decided to take the computer with her. That meant another memory insertion where the kidnapper's phantom opponent in this altercation threw the small backpack containing his computer under a passing truck, the pieces that remained fit only for the recycler.

Kaleb, she said afterward, conscious it was past midnight in Moscow. *Are you awake?*

Yes. What do you need?

For you not to kill someone.

He appeared beside her a second later, taking in the situation with a single glance. "Why shouldn't I kill him?" An ice-cold question.

"Because I've handled it. He's more useful to us alive." Once she'd touched a mind, Sahara could slip back in and take total control regardless of distance or time, turning the individual into a flesh-and-blood puppet who had not even a suspicion that his decisions weren't his own.

The idea of doing such a thing revolted her, but that didn't mean it wasn't true. Resulting from an unknown genetic mutation that meant it had no official classification, her ability was one that would be the bogeyman of her race should they know about her. No mind was safe from Sahara's, no shield impenetrable, no offensive ability capable of stopping her if she got close enough just *once*.

She left behind no trace of her interference, the memories she implanted as real as true memories. And she was undetectable when she worked. Should she desire, she could make a Councilor dance to her tune, a CEO sign over his properties, a man slit his own throat while smiling. And while she'd never had cause to test how many minds she could control at one time, the trusted NightStar telepath who'd worked with her to understand her ability when it first came to light, had posited it to be in the triple digits.

It was the ugliest of abilities to have for a woman whose own mind had been torn apart, but she had come to terms with it during the periods of lucidity built into the labyrinth. The decisions she'd made and the rules she'd laid down for herself all revolved around a central question: *If she ever had a child, could she look into that child's eyes without feeling ashamed at what she had done?*

Nothing about her actions today breached that test.

"Who hired him?" Kaleb asked, his gaze on the kidnapper, the stars eclipsed by lethal black.

"I've handled it," she repeated rather than responding to the question and, when he didn't shift his gaze, decided to play hardball. "If you don't respect my wishes, I simply won't call you next time."

The line of his jaw remained a blade, but he turned his attention off the bounty hunter. "Who?"

"According to his memories, Tatiana."

"Impossible. She's exactly where I put her."

"Then someone in her organization smart enough to work out what I can do, and cocky enough to deceive and undercut his boss." If the rumors about the other woman's rise to power were correct, it truly was a case of what the humans called karma.

Not wasting any further time or energy thinking about Tatiana, she looked into the face of the cardinal telekinetic who she knew was having to exercise harsh self-control not to send the man at their feet to an early grave. "Let's go home, Kaleb," she said, brushing her fingers over his jaw in a silent reminder of who he was to her.

Chapter 34

THE FIRST THING she did once they were on the starlit terrace in Moscow was put down the laptop, borrow Kaleb's phone, having forgotten her own at the aerie, and call Faith. "I'm safe," she assured her cousin. "You? Mercy? Her babies?"

"We're fine. Mercy ate the paramedics alive when I made her get a checkup," Faith said with an affectionate laugh. "Then Riley turned up and she decided to cooperate because he was crazy with worry—but she was right. There wasn't a scratch on her and, in her expert former hellion-child opinion, the pupcubs enjoyed the excitement."

Relieved, Sahara cut Faith off before her cousin could ask for her exact whereabouts, and promised to be home by the time night fell in San Francisco.

"You need to eat," Kaleb ordered when she returned the phone, pointing out the high-density nutrition bars that had appeared on the small table beside the lounger. "You're not healthy enough yet to afford to miss meals."

"I'm starving," she admitted and took a seat on the edge of the lounger. Kicking off her shoes and removing the ankle holster, she picked up one of the nutrition bars. "My ability might feel effortless, but it burns psychic energy." So did 'pathing to Kaleb, but she'd already worked that into her calorie requirements.

Leaning his back against the railing, Kaleb didn't speak until she'd finished the bar and washed it down with water. "You've become more confident about your power." His expression was shadowed, his voice icy with approval. "I never agreed with your distaste for it."

"I was young." She grinned when a second nutrition bar floated pointedly in front of her face. "And you've always been overprotective." Taking the bar, she tore it open.

"You matter to me."

So simple. So honest. So powerful.

Rubbing a hand over her heart, she shared her secrets with the one person who would never betray or use her. That he was the same man who planned to create an empire that spanned the globe was no contradiction. "My ability has matured." It had been erratic at sixteen, one of the reasons Tatiana had been able to imprison her mind. And once imprisoned, Sahara had been unable to break out—it turned out she could get through any shield except one created around her *own* mind.

It was her greatest weakness, a natural balance to the power she wielded.

No one could so easily entomb her now, but seven years ago, she'd been a scared girl and Tatiana a powerful adult telepath trained in psychic aggression. Enrique, too, must've played a role in her mental imprisonment—the nausea that roiled in her stomach at the mere thought of him was proof enough of that.

"Once I was trapped inside the shields Tatiana created," Sahara told Kaleb, "she suffocated my ability, too, except for short periods of 'freedom' when she wanted me to use it." The other woman's aim had been to break Sahara down until she was Tatiana's pet and could be trusted not to use her abilities against the other woman.

"But the enforced concentration of my power," she continued, "had the effect of accelerating my growth in a way Tatiana never suspected." Sahara had hidden the development in the labyrinth, aware Tatiana couldn't stand the insane chaos. "I no longer have to touch skin for the initial contact—I just have to be close."

"That eliminates a dangerous vulnerability," Kaleb said, his tone so arctic, she knew he was thinking about the ugly thing that had happened to her. "Previously, if someone managed to incapacitate your body, it rendered you helpless, so long as he made certain not to accidentally touch your skin."

Shivering, she hugged herself. "Please sit by me. I can't stand to see you alone in the dark."

He came to her, but rather than sitting on the lounger beside her, he sat down in front of her, his back against her legs. Spreading her thighs, she tugged him closer, her fingers weaving through the silk of his hair.

"I am," he said quietly, "more at home in the dark than the light."

"I know." It was a painful wonder, to sit with him under a diamond-studded sky and know that he was hers. For this moment, the civil war, his broken conscience, her suspicions of the indefensible lines he might have crossed, none of it mattered. There was only the velvet night and the primal warmth of him so close. "It's the aloneness I can't stand."

Picking up one of the hands she'd dropped to his shoulders, he brought it to his mouth, pressing a tender kiss to the center of her palm. "I can feel you inside me, always."

Her eyes burning, she leaned down to wrap her arms around him, her cheek kissing his. "I did discover something else deeply problematic," she told him. "The telepath who helped me with my training didn't realize it, and neither did I, possibly because all my tests were on willing subjects." Sitting back up, she began to play her fingers through his hair again. "I take no risks when I enter a mind, rifle through memories and rearrange or erase them, or when I insert new ones."

Kaleb ran his hand along the back of her calf. "That's not why Tatiana wanted you. She can penetrate shields herself, though compared to your scalpel, she's working with a hammer and chisel."

"No, it was the mind control, of course." Tatiana could do that, too, but for her it meant a twenty-four/seven commitment that drained her psychic and physical energy to the point of leaving her a skeletal shell. And that was to control a single mind. "She planned to use me to rise to greater and greater power."

Insidious as her ability was, it meant all the more when Kaleb leaned back into her stroking hands. He had never once flinched from her after she admitted what she could do. All he'd asked, she remembered as her fingernails scraped gently over his scalp, was that she never go inside his mind.

"I don't want you to see what I've done."

It was a promise so embedded in her psyche, she hadn't been tempted to break it even when she hadn't known herself, Kaleb's trust a precious jewel that could never be replicated.

"What," he said now, his eyelashes throwing shadows onto his cheeks, he'd relaxed so totally, "did you discover?"

A curling warmth deep inside her, Sahara leaned down to press a soft, sweet kiss to his jaw. "In the early days after my abduction, Tatiana would disguise me, then manipulate a situation to get me close enough to an individual to take an initial imprint. Then sometime later, she'd ask me to slip into that individual's mind and make them do a small thing, silly even." She swallowed. "I justified each as being a harmless test in order to buy time."

Kaleb's eyes stayed shut, his hand slipping under the hem of her jeans to close around her bare ankle. "You made choices that kept you alive." It was clear he saw no reason for her to feel guilty.

Rubbing her cheek against his once more, she said, "What it took me too long to realize was that each time I returned to a mind to control it, I lost a piece of me." And she had no way of controlling the memories that would be erased. "If I'd continued, I would've eventually ended up a blank slate, a weapon for Tatiana to direct at will." Shuddering, she tightened her arms around Kaleb.

His lashes lifted, eyes of stunning obsidian looking into hers. "Are you certain about not torturing Tatiana? I can break her for you, make her beg."

Sahara knew that to be a deadly serious offer. A tiny part of her was tempted—she wasn't a saint, and Tatiana had brutalized her to the point where she'd forgotten what it was to be a sentient being—but the temptation was nowhere near the depth of her feelings for Kaleb. He lived in the dark, but she wouldn't allow him to be swallowed by it, wouldn't *use* him as Tatiana had intended to use her.

"No torture." Sitting up again, she began to massage his shoulders for the sheer pleasure of touching him. "We need to concentrate on discovering the identity of the person who orchestrated the kidnapping attempt.

"I'll take care of it."

"I have the right skill set to discover the truth without anyone being the wiser," she said in response to Kaleb's flat statement. "I'm certain it must be one of the guards, since no one else was close enough to work out what I can do—and I have no problems with infiltrating their thoughts." Not given their active participation in Tatiana's evil.

"No."

Sahara argued with rational calm, then in a furious temper, but Kaleb was immovable. "I will not permit you anywhere near someone who might cause you harm."

Making incoherent sounds of frustration, she nonetheless admitted this was one battle she had well and truly lost. Kaleb was never going to be a man she could control, and she couldn't expect to win every argument—but there was one point on which *she* had no intention of budging. "Promise me you won't return to the warehouse and execute the bounty hunter."

"Since you can't take control of him without causing permanent damage to your memories, your line of reasoning about him being more useful alive is no longer valid."

That was why she had to get a promise. "Forget about that. I don't want his death on my conscience."

A small pause. "I won't go back and kill him unless he proves a renewed threat."

"That, I can accept." Her breath caught as he changed position slightly, his shoulders brushing the sensitive skin of her inner thighs— just as his cell phone rang.

Answering it, he listened then said, "Time?" A slight pause. "I'll be there." He slid away the phone without further words.

"A meeting?" she asked, using her hands to massage the heavy muscle of his shoulders again, having sensed his pleasure in the act before they'd begun to argue. "It must be an important deal for an in-person discussion."

"It's not business," Kaleb replied, angling his neck to the side so Sahara could reach a tight spot. No one else would he allow this close to his jugular. But Sahara? "Harder," he said, undoing two more buttons on his shirt so she could slide her hands inside the open collar.

"Like this?" It was an intimate question as she exerted just the right pressure.

"Hmm." Stroking his thumb over the curve of her anklebone, he let his eyelashes close, his body languid. It was a state he only ever found with Sahara, and in all previous instances, it had been after sex.

"There's a small bottle of oil on the bathroom counter in the aerie," Sahara said softly, continuing to touch him with a sensual possessiveness that made even the part that lived in the void, dark and violent, turn lazily quiescent. "It was part of the pack of toiletries set out for me. Can you get it?"

Catching the detailed telepathic image she sent to him, of the bottle and exactly where it was in relation to the rest of the bathroom, he retrieved it without effort. An instant later, a scent he identified as vanilla drifted onto the air, Sahara's hands no longer on his skin. "Take off your shirt so I don't get oil on it."

Kaleb had no desire to move, but he did as she asked. The feel of her warm hands on him, the oil making it easier for her to glide over his skin, dig deeper into his muscles, was his reward. Tactile sensation, he thought, had certain addictive qualities. But only when it was Sahara whose thighs bracketed his shoulders, Sahara whose voice was a murmur in the dark as she told him of the pleasure she found in touching him.

"In your reading on current events," he said several minutes later, before his increasing arousal could blur his senses, "did you come across references to an insurgent named the Ghost?"

"You want to talk politics *now*, when I'm doing my best to seduce you?"

The husky, laughing question had him tugging at her arm until she got the message and came around to straddle him. "You have no need to seduce me." He was hers. Always. "The process, however, is enjoyable." True physical intimacy, he thought, had far more nuances than he'd previously understood, having conflated it automatically with sex.

Sahara's lips curved. "I'll just keep going, then." A slow kiss as proprietary as the hands she returned to his shoulders when she drew back.

"As for your question . . . according to several *Beacon* back issues," she said, a thoughtful cast to her expression, "prior to the Council's dissolution, the Ghost was responsible for a number of information leaks that put the Councilors into the position of having to explain themselves.

"He was also," she said, running her thumbs down the tendons in Kaleb's neck, "rumored to be involved in the explosion of a lab that was allegedly working on a bioneural chip to force people to be Silent." Sahara shivered, clearly horrified by the idea. "My impression is that he's responsible for fomenting dissent in the Net against the entire Council superstructure, fracturing their power base from the inside out—and that his goal is the fall of Silence."

"Yes." Kaleb was unsurprised she'd already managed to gather so much data—Sahara Kyriakus had been born with a mind both thirsty for knowledge and able to process it at high speeds. "The Ghost is a dangerous individual to anyone in power."

Sahara's hands went motionless, the deep blue of her eyes troubled. "Kaleb, you can't hurt this person. So many of your goals align with the Ghost's—this rebel is fighting against the rot at the core of our race, and so are you. You can work together."

"There can't be two powers in the Net, Sahara." It would only fracture and divide the populace. "The Ghost has a stay of execution for the present, but his time is coming to an end."

Chapter 35

SAHARA SHOOK HER head, her voice grim. "If you harm the Ghost, you risk inciting another wave of rebellion, this time directly against you."

Again, she displayed how well she knew him, using logic rather than any emotional plea for the safety and well-being of their race, a plea she knew would fall on deaf ears. "It won't come to that." The death of the rebel would cause an acute and violent disturbance in the fabric of the PsyNet, and that, Kaleb would not permit. Not when the Net would soon belong to him. "The Ghost will simply fade from the limelight at a certain nonnegotiable point."

"Fade?" Sahara's fingers dug into his muscles as she continued to caress him regardless of their discord. "Kaleb, everything I've read tells me this rebel has survived *years* of being hunted. He's not the type to quietly disappear, even if it's you giving the order."

"He'll listen to reason. The Ghost's actions," he said over Sahara's inarticulate sound of disbelief, "show him to be an eminently rational individual."

"Really?" It was a comment rife with disagreement. "Putting that aside, how do you even propose to find him? He's a shadow."

"I already know his identity, and have since he made his first move."

Hands fisting on his shoulders, Sahara shook her head. "I don't think he'll fall in with your plans. This Ghost seems to be just as relentless and driven as—" A sudden pause, her eyes narrowing. "You," she whispered. "It's *you*!"

"Of course it's me," Kaleb said and took the mock punch Sahara aimed at his jaw, her skin soft against his. "No one else has access to the depth of data at the Ghost's fingers, and the ability to be anywhere in the world in a split second."

Sahara attempted to look stern, but she was too delighted by the fact Kaleb had just played a game with her—with cool eyes and an icy tone that had blinded her to what he was telling her. He was right: the Ghost could be no one but the cardinal Tk who held her. Else, Kaleb would've eliminated him long before the rebel became such a dangerous adversary in the Net. It was a truth as inexorable as the staggering power at his command.

The one question that remained and that she would not ask was *why*.

She knew the answer, knew it was written in blood and born of the sadistic pain survived by a gifted, scared child who'd had no one to whom he could turn. "Is that what the call was about?" she asked instead, leashing her anger because this night, it was *theirs*. She would permit no echo of evil to taint it. "You have fellow rebels?"

"Yes," he said, tugging her forward for a kiss.

Opening her mouth for him, Sahara decided further discussion could wait. Right now, she wanted only to drown in the taste of Kaleb. No other male could ever match the visceral passion he aroused in her, and she'd met her share during her time with DarkRiver. Sensual and strong, affectionate and tactile, the leopard males laughed easily and considered play a normal part of life. The soldiers who patrolled her area were friendly, and a number had flirted openly with her, would've gone further had she offered any encouragement.

Sahara hadn't—because it was only Kaleb she wanted. "I was very smart at sixteen," she murmured, leaning down to kiss his throat, the scent of vanilla warmed against his skin and intertwined with his own natural scent making her breath catch. "I claimed the sexiest man in the world as my own." Perhaps he was irrevocably damaged, scarred to the point that she'd have to destroy them both in order to save their very race . . . but she would not take that step until all hope was lost, her Kaleb fatally fractured at the vicious hands of a long-dead madman.

"I want to feel your skin against mine," he said, his body still languorous in a way rare for Kaleb as he tugged off her pullover and got rid of her bra.

Then, as the stars glittered overhead and the world spun another hour closer to what might be a catastrophic global war, Sahara kissed her lover. Pressed against the ridged muscle of him, his hands strong against her back, she threw back her head as he went for her throat. Pleasure rippled through her in a sultry wave, the shooting star that passed across her vision a shimmer she grabbed onto with both hands.

We've earned this, earned our future! A fierce cry in silence. *Just give us our time.*

It was the simplest of wishes, but as Kaleb took her mouth with the relentless demand of his own, one of his hands rising to cup the back of her head, she knew it might also be one of the most impossible.

AN hour after he'd taken her under starlight, her body a flow of feminine curves, Kaleb didn't fight Sahara's decision to return to the aerie. Faith was no doubt waiting for her, and Kaleb had plans for the night of which Sahara would not approve.

Tatiana was huddled feverish and dirty in the hole where he'd left her, her hands bandaged using the rudimentary medical supplies. Blood on the walls made it appear she'd attempted to climb her way out, or perhaps she'd lost her sense of reason and pounded at the concrete until it shredded her flesh and tore off her nails.

Keeping a vigilant eye on his shields, he leaned against the wall across from her. "I thought you could use some company."

Eyes flat and vicious as a snake's looked at him, Tatiana's Silence beginning to flake away at the edges. That disintegration didn't impact her mind. "You need something. What's the bargain?"

"There is no bargain." Never would be. "You'll tell me what I want to know, or I'll break a bone in your body." This didn't count as torture to Kaleb's mind—that would be if he was hurting her for no reason but to watch her scream. "I'm sure the infection won't take long to set in, in your current damp accommodations."

Fear crawled over her skin. Oh, she hid it well, but the one thing he'd always known about Tatiana was that she was a bully. And bullies never did well when they no longer had the upper hand. Santano had apparently begged for his life when the changelings came for him. One day, Kaleb would gain access to the recorded footage the packs had of the execution, then he'd sit back and watch until every instant of Santano's torment was burned into his memory banks.

"Who else in your organization," he said to the woman who was just like Santano where it mattered, "did you trust with the knowledge of Sahara's ability?"

A twist of her lips. "Someone else is hunting Sahara Kyriakus? It'll be an easy capture. She's always been far too weak to actually use her power as it's designed to be used."

Kaleb didn't argue, didn't negotiate. He simply broke the smallest finger of her right hand. Screaming, Tatiana cradled the hand to her chest. "You're mad," she gritted out after she could talk again. "Truly mad."

"What I am," Kaleb said, "is a man of my word. Now, would you like to answer the question?"

"I trusted no one." Right then, she was the Tatiana the Net knew, ruthless, amoral, and willing to do whatever it took to win. "I would've been a fool to do so, given the temptation at hand—if and when Sahara regained full use of her faculties, a single intelligent individual could use her to take over the entire PsyNet. Why would I risk sharing that information?"

Truth, he judged. "Who in your employ is smart enough to work it out?"

"There was a guard," Tatiana said, her finger already swollen. "David Sezer. He showed a little too much interest in Sahara. I had him reassigned after he was caught in the cell with her against my personal directive."

Kaleb felt the chill darkness in him stretch awake, drawing the DarkMind's eager presence. "That seems unusually magnanimous of you." On the psychic plane, he "stroked" the DarkMind into patience— it would get the violence for which it hungered.

"I concluded that his Silence was flawed and that he'd been attracted by the opportunity to abuse a vulnerable female."

The darkness grew icier. "You didn't make certain?"

"Shield penetration takes energy and David was no one important. As he hadn't managed to touch Sahara and was otherwise useful, I made the decision to keep him on. He did, however, come into an inheritance a year ago that would give him the financial resources to hire a hunter." A sneer. "If he thinks he can use Sahara, he's delusional. Even pathetically weak as she is, the girl is stronger than him."

Kaleb rifled through PsyNet databases as the DarkMind curled around him. It took him a short two minutes to locate one David Sezer attached to a secondary branch of the Rika-Smythe corporation. "Did anyone else with 'flawed' conditioning get close to Sahara?" Sahara was small, her physical strength nowhere close to that of a full-grown male's—and she'd been drugged, her abilities suppressed on top of that. Easy prey.

"No."

Catching the skitter in Tatiana's eyes, he snapped another finger. The reverberating echo of her scream had no impact on him. "Who hurt her?"

Bent over, her body wracked by shudders as she threw up, Tatiana couldn't immediately answer, but he was patient. "We had to gain her cooperation." A voice raw with pain and fear. "Force was utilized."

He *would not* kill her, no matter the provocation. It would be far too merciful. "Tell me where you keep the records of Sahara's captivity, and I'll leave," he said in a pleasant tone he knew disturbed people on the deepest level. "Otherwise, we'll be spending several hours together." He teleported in a scalpel—she didn't know of his promise to Sahara, didn't know that her victim's conscience was the only reason he wasn't torturing her right this instant. "I learned many things at Santano's knee."

Fear a sheen of sweat on her face, she scrabbled backward into a corner. "A vault in the PsyNet. I'll have to telepath the location and pass codes."

Kaleb smiled, knowing she wasn't as broken as she was attempting to appear. "No, you won't. Talk."

Tatiana talked and, when she was done, said, "You truly were Enrique's protégé, weren't you?" in the tone of someone making a discovery. "You helped him brutalize the changeling females he murdered."

Judging she was in no danger of dying from the slight fever and her minor injuries, he left without wasting another word on her. Locating the vault wasn't a problem, but he took care in downloading the data. Tatiana didn't disappoint him—the booby traps were clever and meant to be fatal.

Once he had the data, he asked the NetMind to erase every other trace of it from existence, including the automatic copy in the PsyNet backup drive—which Kaleb had named the Obsidian Archive. No one else would ever know what had been done to Sahara during the years Tatiana had her in a cage. He would permit no one to look at her with pity in their eyes when she deserved only pride for her courage and strength.

That done, he began to read the files, noting the name of every individual involved in the sessions meant to break Sahara's will. Three of them he'd already executed after tracking them through other methods, and another one was going slowly and terribly mad, thanks to Kaleb's secondary ability. The remaining two were minor players he told the DarkMind to suffocate in its blackness and consume.

David Sezer was the only one left, and the birds were beginning to sing outside when Kaleb decided it was time to pay the other male a personal visit. It was three hours later, once he'd showered and dressed after taking care of that matter, that he went to meet the two people other than Sahara who had a claim on his loyalty.

It was nothing akin to what he felt for her, but it was enough for him to teleport into the night shadow of San Francisco, the clouds hiding the sickle moon from view. Sliding into the last pew in the church where Father Xavier Perez welcomed all who came, he spoke to the back of the former Arrow who sat in front of him. Never did the other man look at his face, but he knew it was to Kaleb that he spoke.

"You want to discuss Pure Psy," Kaleb guessed. The three of them—Xavier, Judd, and Kaleb—had long been bound by a mutual desire to collapse the rotten power structure of the Net, but where Judd and Xavier wanted to save the innocents of all races caught up in the rot, Kaleb had fought only for Sahara.

That he *had* saved a number of lives during their fight, helped some of those innocents, had been a consequence rather than an aim. Then again, perhaps Judd and Xavier had had a deeper impact on him than any one of them believed; after all, he had spared the children in his plan to wipe the Psy off the face of the planet if his search for Sahara ended with the knowledge of her death.

He'd told her about Judd, about Xavier, and about the details of their strategic war, in the quiet minutes after he and Sahara had had sex under the starlit Moscow sky, his heart beating in time with hers as she lay warm and sated against him. The only person with whom he had ever understood friendship had seen that in his relationship with the two men. He had accepted her judgment, knowing Sahara comprehended far more about emotion than he ever would.

"No," Judd said now. "Not Pure Psy. I need information on Ming."

Kaleb thought about why his fellow rebel would need data on the former Councilor. "He's become too big a threat to Sienna." Judd's niece might be the only individual on the planet as dangerous as Kaleb, but since she had no desire to impinge on his territory, nor he on hers, he'd left her alone.

That, and his loyalty to the fallen Arrow in front of him.

"Ming's fixated on her," Judd confirmed. "She managed to hurt him the last time they came in contact, and Ming never forgets a threat." He raised a hand in a silent hello as Xavier walked down the center of the church toward them, while Kaleb drew back into the shadows. It was safer for Xavier not to know his identity.

Unlike Judd, the priest had never been trained to be lethal.

Sliding into the pew beside Judd, Xavier said, "We've worked for a better world all this time, believing the ugliness that was the Council needed to be excised from the Net, and now it appears that the Net is fracturing, with fatal results. I do not wish to bathe in the blood of innocents."

"Innocents were never our targets," Judd said, his next words directed at Kaleb. "Has that changed?"

"Do you remember when you asked me if there was one person in the PsyNet who mattered to me?"

"Yes."

"That person has asked me not to destroy the Net." Like the scars that marked him, the rot would be nearly impossible to eradicate without first sanitizing the network. But he knew he couldn't do that and still have Sahara look at him the way she'd done on the terrace, a softness to her that made him believe he might understand happiness. "Your innocents are safe from me."

"I'm glad." Quiet words from the former Arrow.

"Would you have attempted to execute me if I'd answered otherwise?" While Judd's Tk wasn't as powerful as Kaleb's, he was fiercely intelligent, might just have achieved his aim.

"Yes," came the brutal answer. "It would've destroyed a piece of me to end your life, but I would've done it."

Chapter 36

KALEB FELT NO sense of betrayal; he'd known the answer before he asked the question. He also knew the other man would've done everything in his power to save Kaleb before he attempted to assassinate him. Judd had somehow survived the cruel life of an Arrow with his conscience, if not intact, then not totally destroyed.

Not long ago, Kaleb had watched the other man laughing with his mate and considered such an existence beyond his understanding or reach. Even should he find Sahara, he'd believed himself too damaged to give her what Judd gave his mate. Yet tonight, Sahara had kissed him, fought with him, laughed that familiar husky laugh when he not only bent, but broke every single one of the metal railings during their slow, lazy sex under the stars.

If Judd and Xavier had helped him remain sane enough to give Sahara what she needed, then he owed them a debt that could never be discharged. "Ming," he said, "is in France.

"Champagne region as before," he added, having updated the data the previous day, "though he's shifted his base of operations. I'm in the process of tracking that base, but he's tactically minded and careful." Ming also knew how to lay traps with blade-sharp teeth.

"The confirmation he's in the region is enough. We have certain sources in the area."

"You can't kill him yet. I need to stabilize the Net enough that his death won't cripple it." Even with the Council in ruins, each of the former Councilors held so much economic and psychic power that a violent or sudden death could cause a deadly shock wave.

The ripples had been minor when Kaleb assassinated a Councilor just over a year and a half ago, but the PsyNet had been stable then, not teetering on the brink of collapse. The backlash from the loss had been absorbed with no more than a few minor incidents. "A shock wave right now could be catastrophic."

"It'll take time to set things up," Judd said. "I'll give you a twenty-minute warning before we move, so you can be on alert for any structural weaknesses in the Net."

"How do you plan to reach Ming?"

"The same way the packs reached Santano Enrique," was the cool response.

Kaleb knew he'd get nothing more. As Kaleb's first loyalty was to Sahara, Judd's was to his mate and the changeling wolf pack he now called family. It was a measure of the trust that had grown between them that Kaleb allowed the matter to rest.

Xavier spoke into the silence. "We sit in a house of God and speak of murder. What does that make us?"

"Men who understand that there is evil in the world," Judd answered. "The data I passed on—did it help you track down your Nina?"

Nina, Kaleb knew, had been Xavier's love before a Psy attack tore them apart.

The priest's breath shuddered out of his chest. "The information points to a tiny village in the mountains of my homeland. I am . . . afraid to go there. I must gather my courage to face the truth, and perhaps my Nina's hatred."

They spoke of other matters then, Kaleb leaving an hour later, just before Judd. Waiting in the shadows until the former Arrow was out of sight, he returned to the church to find Xavier where he'd left him.

"I expected you," the priest said without turning around.

Kaleb took a seat behind the other male. "Did you?"

"A man who has lost his only love knows when he hears the same loss in another's voice." Xavier shook his head, the near black of his skin gilded gold by the candlelight. "Has your Nina returned? Is she the one who asks you to have mercy on the innocent?"

"Yes." Leaning forward, he crossed his arms on the back of Xavier's pew. "I don't know how to love her." He would die for her, kill for her, but he did not understand the emotion he had always sensed she needed from him, even when she'd been a bright-eyed sixteen.

"Love is the greatest form of loyalty, one that places the happiness of the beloved over that of the lover," Xavier said with a peace that was an integral aspect of him, even in his confusion. "And you know loyalty."

"I will," Kaleb said as the candles burned around them, "think on what you've said." He paused. "Xavier, I can take you to your Nina." It could be done without the other man ever glimpsing Kaleb's face.

"Thank you, friend." Xavier's voice shook. "But I think I must do this the hard way. I must earn her."

Leaving the priest to his thoughts, Kaleb went to Sahara after he exited the church, simply to watch her sleep. To see her safe and alive, the need he had to ensure her well-being one that would never fade. And though he made not a sound, thick lashes lifted to reveal eyes of sleepy dark blue. "Kaleb?" Scooting over, she raised the blanket with a mumbled invitation. "C'mere. 'S cold out."

He hadn't meant to stay, but he slept that night in the arms of the only person in the entire world to whom it mattered if he was cold . . . and he thought that perhaps he might understand not only love, but joy.

Maybe it was that thought that ignited long-dormant neurons in his brain, but for the first time in over seven years, he dreamed not of blood and pain and cruelty, but of the day a girl with eyes of darkest blue had forever altered the course of his existence.

HE sat motionless in the chair beside Santano, his feet flat on the floor and his eyes trained straight ahead. He'd already noted everything about Anthony Kyriakus's office, particularly the two doors and the large windows that spilled sunlight into the room and onto his legs.

He had no windows like that in his room at the remote training facility where he lived, and logic said it made the office vulnerable to attack, but the design also had good points. The biggest was that it gave Anthony an uninter-rupted view of the main gates that guarded the sprawling compound that housed most of the PsyClan NightStar.

In the reports that Santano had given Kaleb to read as part of his political studies, it said that "strong familial loyalty" was a characteristic NightStar trait. Kaleb had no family, hadn't understood the concept of loyalty the first time he'd read about it—but after researching it, he'd realized it meant being connected to someone who would care if he lived or died, someone who would fight for and with him, someone who didn't want to hurt him.

He had never experienced any of those things.

"Shall we begin?" Santano said to Anthony, placing a datapad on the desk between them. "I brought a copy of the relevant files."

"A moment." Anthony glanced at the small girl who stood in the main door-way, her hands clasped neatly in front of her. "Please show Kaleb around the grounds, Sahara."

Kaleb didn't move, even when Anthony nodded at him in silent permis-sion. He knew Santano wouldn't allow him to interact with anyone outside of the Tk's control—Kaleb didn't have to be an adult to know it was all part of his trainer's strategy to break him down, erase his will. It was the same reason the other Tk had burned a large part of Kaleb's back minutes before they tele-ported to the NightStar compound.

It had been—was—excruciatingly painful, but Kaleb hadn't made a sound, his expression impassive. He'd learned long ago never to react; that only fed the ugliness that lived inside Councilor Santano Enrique, an ugliness no one else ever seemed to see.

"That child," the other cardinal now said, after a dismissive look at the girl in the doorway, "is too young to provide conversation that will in any way interest Kaleb. He can remain."

Kaleb waited for Anthony to back down. Everyone did. Santano was a Councilor, while Anthony was merely the head of a family.

Except Anthony, his tone as firm as his gaze, said, "I don't conduct business with children present. We can schedule another appointment next month to discuss the forecasting services required by your company."

Rather than rising to make an immediate departure, Santano steepled his fingers and turned his head toward Kaleb. "Go. Behave yourself." A wrenching tug on the psychic leash around Kaleb's mind, the compulsions that kept him silent about Santano's perversions in full effect.

Ignoring the additional pain, Kaleb walked to the door and into the compound with the girl called Sahara. They were in the hydroponic vegetable garden when she suddenly said, "My father's an M. We can go see him."

Kaleb froze. "Why?"

Sahara's face held an expression he recognized as concern, but she said, "He has interesting scanners in his office," and he knew it for a ruse to get him to the medical center.

"I've seen medical scanners before." It was an answer forced out by the compulsions.

Searching his face, Sahara finally nodded, "Okay," and carried on.

It wasn't until ten minutes later that he realized she'd slowed the pace and ignored at least one slope . . . because she knew he was wounded. No one else had ever done anything to help him and he didn't understand why she did, what she expected to gain.

"There's fish in the pond," she said at the end of the tour. "Do you want to see?"

Kaleb nodded to delay his return to the office . . . and to extend his time with this girl who saw his pain when no one else did. "Why was this created?" he asked once they reached the large pond bordered with smooth rocks.

Sahara knelt down beside him with a slight betraying movement of her shoulders that said she'd been about to shrug. "I heard Father say it was an 'approved meditation aid,'" she said, her khaki-colored pants wet by a droplet of water as she dipped her hand in the pond and swirled. "The F-Psy who live here use it."

"Are you an F?" he asked, echoing her movements in the water.

"Not really." Nothing in her said she was troubled by her lack of status in a family so well-known for its foreseers. "I'm subdesignation B. That means I have backsight."

Flicking her hand dry, she looked at him with eyes of a deep, distinctive blue vivid against the thick black of hair contained in two neat braids. "What are you?"

"A Tk."

Her cheeks flushed pink, her eyes shining. "Can you do any tricks?"

Accessing the part of his telekinesis that Santano hadn't strangled when he wrenched the leash, Kaleb thought about what Sahara might consider a good trick and lifted her small body off the ground.

Eyes wide when she realized she was floating, she stood up and, after glancing furtively around, jumped up and down on the cushion of air, the sun sparking off hidden strands of red-gold in her hair. Waiting until she'd sat back down and was stable, he lowered her gently to the grass.

"That was wonderful," she said, her lips curving into a smile before worry darkened her expression. "I'm sorry. Did it hurt you to do that?"

Kaleb shook his head at the unexpected question. He'd lain bloodied and broken in front of Santano and his pet medics, but not one had ever looked at him like Sahara was doing—as if he was a person and not a thing. "Your Silence is flawed for your age group," he said, the water cool under his fingertips as he swirled it again.

Folding her arms, Sahara bit down on her lower lip. "Are you going to tell on me?"

"No." He had no loyalty to anything or anyone, nothing worth betraying this girl who made him forget she'd been ordered to spend time with him.

When she waved surreptitiously at him as he left, he decided he had to come back, had to find out what she would do if she was free to choose whether or not to talk to him.

It took him almost two weeks to slip away from the training facility. He used Sahara's face as a teleport lock, arriving in the backyard of a small home to find her sitting on a wide stump. Her feet were bare and her braids messy, a frown of concentration on her forehead as she stared at a datapad.

"Hello," he said, and waited for her to scream that an intruder had breached the security of the compound.

Except . . . she broke out into a huge smile. "Hi!" Setting down the datapad, she said, "Is that man here again?" Her smile faded. "I don't like him."

Kaleb shook his head, a strange sensation in his chest at not being rejected. "I came to see you." He thought about not adding the next part, but it seemed wrong to lie to Sahara when she'd trusted him with her own thoughts. "I don't know any other children who talk to me."

"That must be lonely." Taking a squashed nutrition bar from her pocket, she broke it in half and held out a piece toward him. "I know you probably think I'm a baby, but you can be my friend if you like."

When he accepted the offering, she shifted on the stump to make a space for him.

Taking the seat, he said, "I don't think you're a baby. I think you're smart and you see things other people don't." Countless adults had seen him after Santano tortured him, but none had ever noticed that he was hurt. Worse, none had ever seen Santano for what he was. "I don't like him, either."

Sahara chewed on her half of the nutrition bar and banged the back of her feet on the stump. "Oh, good."

He wasn't aware of what he was about to say until the words were out. "You have to be more careful." If someone like Santano found out how bad Sahara's Silence was for her age group, they'd put her into intensive conditioning and crush her with pain until her responses were "correct." Until she wasn't Sahara anymore. "You smiled at me."

"That's because I like you." It was a statement so absolute, he couldn't not believe.

"I can help make your PsyNet shields stronger," he said, a sensation inside him that he thought might be the beginning of loyalty. "So you're not exposed there." He'd have to take care, but the ugly things Santano had planted in his mind only reported back if he used too much energy.

"You'd do that? Thanks, Kaleb!" She threw her arms around him.

It was the first time he could ever remember being held.

Chapter 37

SAHARA WOKE TO find Kaleb watching her, his eyes of starlight. "What are you thinking?" she asked in an intimate whisper, her legs tangled with his and one of his arms acting as a muscular pillow for her head.

He tumbled her gently onto her back, his body pressing down on hers. "How you taught me to climb trees."

Delighted at the idea, she wrapped her arms around his neck. "Was I a good teacher?"

"Yes, but you kept trying to trade your teaching skills for answers to your math homework."

The cool comment made her grin and demand further stories about her aborted career as an extortionist. He gave her what she demanded—and she hoped that these wonderful memories, innocent and bright, were safe in the vault, that she'd soon be able to access them herself.

"You even made a plaque to commemorate my first successful climb of the biggest tree in the compound," Kaleb added. "It's in my study."

Sahara frowned. "I don't . . ." Laughing as she realized what he was talking about, she nuzzled at his throat. "The piece of wood with your name?"

Fingers weaving into her hair, he held her to him. "You worked on it for weeks," he said, as another related memory tugged free of the vault.

"Here."

Kaleb took the small, battered book from her hand. "What's this?"

"Poetry." Sahara saw from his expression that he had no idea what to make

of that and clasped her hands nervously behind her back. "I know the lines seem nonsensical, but they always make me think."

Perhaps, she thought, her heart hurting, the sheer perplexing nature of the rhymes would help him see that the world wasn't simply full of horror and pain, that there were strangely wonderful things, too. It worried her how much darkness she saw creeping into him day by day, hour by hour, and she'd fight the slow loss of her Kaleb any way she could. Even if it was with whimsical poems about fantastical creatures.

"Thank you," he said, opening the cover to see the homemade birthday card she'd put inside. His hands treated both the card and the book with care, as if they were precious. Kaleb always treated her gifts as precious.

"I'm sorry it's not in very good condition." She'd bought it with part of her stationery allowance, after managing to fix a broken datapad so she didn't have to replace it.

Kaleb's eyes were filled with stars when he looked at her. "It's perfect. Even if I am certain I'll be as bad at understanding poetry as you are at math."

The memory fading, Sahara smiled at the dangerous man in bed with her. "Did you read the poems I gave you?" she asked softly, thankful to the girl she'd been for fighting for Kaleb with every weapon in her arsenal, no matter how small.

"First, I had to learn French," he said, to her shout of laughter. "They were still incomprehensible. I told you that, and next time, you gave me a seventeenth-century romance." His hair fell across his forehead as he dipped his head. "You had to decipher it for me."

Laughing even harder, she cupped his face, their foreheads touching. They talked for several more minutes after she finally caught her breath, until Kaleb had to leave—but not before he gave her a molten kiss that was a promise. Feeling as if her body were one big smile, she tidied up the aerie, then called her father for a chat. Of course, he was already at the medical center. "I don't suppose you'll be going home early," she said, worried he was overdoing it.

Leon Kyriakus gave her a steady look out of eyes of deep blue. "No, but I have confined myself to writing academic papers in the afternoons. Does that make you happy?"

"Yes," she said, not the least bit sorry for hounding him about his health.

After she hung up, Sahara decided it was time to go back into San Francisco. She intended to be careful about it, but she had earned her freedom and no bounty hunter was going to steal that from her. She also wanted to run some informal tests to gauge the development—or lack—of her ability with languages.

Catching a ride with Mercy when the other woman swung by after a routine perimeter check, she rubbed the eagle charm on her bracelet.

"Not that I don't appreciate the company," Mercy said as they drove out, "but why didn't you hop in with Vaughn? I saw him leaving as I came in."

Blowing out a breath, Sahara fixed the knitted cap that hid her hair. "He's developed a distinctive protective streak when it comes to me." There was no way her cousin's mate would've left her alone in the city, and it was something she needed to do, to prove to herself that she could.

Mercy, by contrast, raised an eyebrow when Sahara asked to be dropped off near Fisherman's Wharf, but didn't attempt to stop her. "According to my orders, we're meant to provide a safe harbor, not imprison you. And if that gun I glimpsed at your ankle's what I think it is, you're smart enough not to need a babysitter.

"Still, put this number into your phone." She passed over a card. "Any trouble while you're there, call that and a packmate will come get you— our city HQ isn't far." A wry smile. "I mean in case you don't feel like being teleported by the scariest man on the planet."

Sahara was still smiling an hour later, her mind lingering on the way that scary man had held her against his heart throughout the night, when she noticed the gathering crowd in front of one of the large public comm screens on Pier 39. Unlike with a sports game or musical performance, the group was deathly silent.

A single look showed her why.

A night-draped Hong Kong was burning, the smoke so thick, it was a roiling cloud over the glittering steel metropolis that was home to a majority Psy population and a minority human one, their combined numbers near to four million.

With the skyscrapers so close together, and the fact that the flames seemed impervious to the fire-retardant building materials used in most inner-city areas, the death toll could be in the hundreds of thousands. Horrified, she lifted her hand to her mouth, just as an emblem flashed on the right-hand side of the screen: a black star with a white *P* at its center.

"... *whether or not it is a purposeful echo,*" the Psy reporter was shouting into the camera in an effort to be heard over the cacophony of rescue vehicles and the voracious roar of the flames.

On the other side of the screen flashed a single silver star.

"*The silver star is Councilor Kaleb Krychek's highly recognizable emblem. With their new symbol, Pure Psy appears to be issuing a direct challenge to the man who has stopped or mitigated a number of their recent attacks.*"

"*Our contacts in fire rescue tell us this fire is unlike anything they've seen. Their normal methods are having zero effect, and the size of the blaze means it's too dangerous to be contained by even a team of Tks without Councilor Krychek's assistance. He is the only individual who may have the power to contain, if not end, this inferno.*"

Sahara's heart stopped at the reporter's final words.

The one question she hadn't been able to ask Kaleb now burned red-hot across her irises, as fear for him—because she knew without a doubt that he'd soon be in the burning city if he wasn't already—mingled with terror for what he might've done. She couldn't bear to think that his soul was that pitiless, couldn't bear to accept that she was too late, her heart clenching so hard within her chest that it was a physical pain that threatened to bring her to her knees . . . but the one thing she couldn't avoid, couldn't refuse to hear, was the evidence of his own words.

"*I don't have empathy, Sahara. I can't feel for those who are going to die. It would be akin to asking a falcon to take flight when his wings had long been hacked off.*"

KALEB had planned to sit out the next major Pure Psy attack. It would not do for people to become suspicious of his motives. The situation in

Hong Kong, however, threatened to be so cataclysmic as to require a drastic change of plans.

Ordering his own teams in the region to respond, as well as giving the same command to all available telekinetic Arrows, he arrived to discover that Ming, the only other former Councilor with significant personal military might, had appeared with a Tk team. An interesting move for the telepath who ordinarily preferred to keep his face out of the media, and one that showed Ming was learning this war would not be won in the shadows.

Too bad he'd already lost it.

Acknowledging the other man with a nod, Kaleb turned to Aden, the blast of heat from the fire roaring a block away causing sweat to bead on his temples and plaster his long-sleeved T-shirt to his back. Aden shoved back sweat-damp hair before he spoke. He'd already been in the city for a meeting with other members of the squad based in the region and had reacted quickly to hook himself into the communications network.

"It's obvious Pure Psy has a source for high-grade military-spec explosive charges," the Arrow told him as the last of the Tks close enough to 'port in without exhausting themselves completed the transfer. "This operation had to have been put in place over months. The entire central core of the city was mined to blow, but the initial blasts only did minor damage—it's the fire that's the real assault."

Kaleb looked at the images Aden had obtained of the devastated city center. The flames burned white-hot with an abnormal green tinge. "Fire retardant?"

"No effect." Aden touched his finger to his ear. "Report from one of the fire crews—sky drops of water and retardant are both failing."

Ming, having examined the same images, said, "They'll continue to fail. These flames are distinctive of 'scorch' charges, meant for use in erasing isolated targets surrounded by large areas of rock or desert or water. Once lit, the fire will burn until every possible consumable is gone."

Meaning after it engulfed Hong Kong Island, it would sprawl outward in any direction not marked by a water boundary. "The primary bridges and tunnels to Kowloon," Kaleb said, pointing to a team of four Tks. "Collapse them, then take care of the secondary access routes and any physical links to outlying islands." The other bridges weren't as sturdy, with a lesser risk the fire would crawl across, but they needed to go as well.

"The squad," Aden said as the four-man team left, "is unaware of such a weapon."

"It was developed two decades ago," Ming replied, "and shelved because of its ferocity. Given its lack of subtlety, I deemed it of no use to the squad."

And that, Kaleb thought, was why Ming had lost the Arrows. He had treated them not as the highly intelligent, dangerous men and women they were, but as his personal army of assassins. It had been a fatal mistake. "Vasic," Kaleb said to Aden's thus far silent partner, "did you do a telekinetic test?" Not every fire reacted the same way to their ability to manipulate the destructive energies.

"Yes. It's a viable option, but"—the teleporter's gray eyes locked with Kaleb's—"the size of the blaze means it'll be unstoppable without direct intervention by a Tk of your strength."

Not answering the unasked question, Kaleb took charge of the amassed telekinetics. No one, not even Ming, demurred. As Vasic had pointed out, Kaleb could do things they couldn't even as a group. "Rescue must be a secondary aim," he said, and it was a ruthless decision that needed to be made. "If we can stifle the flames, the non-Tk teams can go in to provide assistance."

"This is a map of the area currently on fire or under threat," Aden said, putting a small device on the road where they stood. A touch of his finger and a holographic map sprang up. "The central core is gone, no hope of survivors."

It had to be significantly over a thousand degrees in that core, Kaleb thought. No one could survive such an inferno without specialist equipment and clothing, a single breath burning the throat and lungs to ash.

"This swath of homes"—Aden marked out a rough circle around the

leading edge of the flames using a holo-compatible pen—"has been successfully evacuated."

"Can we push the fire inward?" Ming asked, putting his hands
together as if around a neck. "Strangle it of fuel?"

Aden was the one who answered, though Kaleb guessed the response
was Vasic's. "Not with the core burning as violently as it is—we'd concentrate the entire energy of the fire in one area, risk creating a massive
firebomb."

Kaleb agreed with Aden's conclusion, which left a single option. "We
go outward," he said and drew a second rough circle inside the first, the
real-life distance between the two approximately five hundred meters.
"One team inside the fire, the second in the evacuated zone, the aim to
compress the fire in between and suffocate it." The large surface area of
the ring would mitigate, if not eliminate, the risk in concentrating the
energy to that extent.

"I'll go in first, into the core." Kaleb shrugged into the fireproof gear
Vasic had 'ported in for him, the Arrows already suited up. "Soon as I'm
in, I'll push the fire outward. Your task"—he pointed to the Tks who'd
be positioned in the evacuated zone—"is to make sure the fire spreads no
further. Ming?"

The telepath nodded as the rest of the group started to get into their
gear. "I'll coordinate external placements to ensure total coverage."

"Easiest way for the internal team to get in position," Aden said, "is
to run in the five hundred meters from the external ring." Getting no
arguments from his Arrows against what would be a hellish run through
deadly flame, he continued. "Once Kaleb has pushed the fire to this
point"—he tapped the inner circle—"you keep it there. If you can't stifle
it, then you let it burn out. Understood?"

A sea of curt nods.

"If," Kaleb added, "you feel the ring is about to fail, I want you *all* to
'port to the external perimeter to make sure the fire doesn't spread. I'll
hold the internal section. Otherwise, I'll assist in stifling the flames as
soon as the ring is stable." Glancing around to make sure the message
had been heard, he said, "Get in position."

The Tks began to 'port out to the external points using images provided by the fire and medical teams working around the city.

Kaleb, however, had no available image to use to get inside the blazing core. Which was why Aden and Vasic flew him up in a jet-chopper, hovering right over the center of the fire. Using high-definition binoculars, he captured a viable mental image and 'ported . . . just as the jet-chopper exploded from the proximity of the heat.

Aden?

We're fine. Vasic was monitoring the fuel tank.

Consumed by the white-hot core, the heat so violent as to create a dangerous level of warmth even inside his fire gear, Kaleb knelt down on one knee and spread his arms outward, palms pushing against the flames that crawled over every inch of his body.

The suits won't last the expected sixty minutes, he told Aden. *Anyone caught in a backdraft will have forty minutes maximum.*

I'll warn the others.

A single calm breath of the air reserves built into the suit, his mind a sea of black ice . . . he unleashed the force of the power that lived in him.

Chapter 38

"INCREDIBLE."

Sahara echoed the anonymous gasped judgment in frozen silence as the comm station successfully linked to a satellite that had zoomed in on Hong Kong, showing its viewers what was happening in the metropolis: the impossible. From the noxious core that reporters had stated was burning at a staggering five thousand degrees *at least*, according to the most recent estimates by scientific experts, the flames were being pushed outward in a perfect sphere, while the ragged edge of the fire remained stationary, as if held in stasis.

Fear gripped her chest, ice in her veins, but she bit down hard on her lower lip to fight the urge to reach out to the man she knew had been in that cauldron of flame until he shoved it outward. To distract him now could mean his death. Instead, she watched an event so phenomenal even the news anchors had gone quiet, the only sounds that of the seals in the bay and the seagulls overhead.

The blackness inside the conflagration continued to grow as the fire was pushed farther and farther away from the core. And then it came to a halt, a perfect ring of flame in the center of the island that burned a violent white against the night sky in that part of the world.

For two minutes, nothing happened.

Then the fire began to collapse in on itself, slowly but surely, as if it were being compressed by invisible walls. Exactly twenty-seven minutes later, the last flame went out, the glittering lights outside the fire zone making the smoking, darkened core so much more blatant a scar.

Squeezing her arms around herself, Sahara walked away from the comm screen and surrendered to need at last, reaching out across the vast distance that separated them, and hoping Kaleb would pick up her psychic signal with his far greater reach as he always did. If he didn't, if there was only silence . . . no, he was fine. He had to be fine. *Kaleb? Are you all right?*

IT took Kaleb a second to understand the question.

No one had cared if he lived or died for over seven years, and he found he didn't know what to do with the knowledge that Sahara did, as she'd always done. As if his life was worth something quite separate from hers.

Halting with the fire suit hanging off his hips, his upper body drenched in sweat, he said, *I'm uninjured,* all the while aware that Sahara was wrong in her belief. His life was one that should've ended in the cradle, the genetic legacy inside him stifled like the fire had been, while he was too young to understand what it made him.

Now the only value he had was in keeping Sahara safe.

You promised me you'd never lie to me, she said, the words holding a weight of emotion he could feel even through the distance that separated them.

I never have. It was the one untainted point of honor in his life. *What do you want to know?*

The pause was long, her question a psychic whisper. *Did you help create this incident?*

The black ice shuddered, fractured. *No.*

I'm sorry.

Don't be. It was a rational question given my history.

But I hurt you, and no one has the right to do that. Fierce words. *Not even me.*

Another fracture in the ice, this one deeper. *Pure Psy did reach out to me, but our goals don't align.* He glanced around at the rubble of Hong Kong Island, thinking of how Vasquez had refused a face-to-face meet, suspicious of Kaleb's motives. He'd been right to be. Kaleb would've executed the other man on sight. *You know my stance on Silence—and I have never had anything against the humans or changelings.*

Turning to the leader of the Arrows when Aden jogged over, he listened to the damage report and update on rescue efforts. "Am I needed?"

At Aden's nod, he removed the fire gear and threw it on the pile where the Arrows were shedding their own. His cargo pants were as sweat soaked as his T-shirt, but there was no point in changing. The fire might be dead, but the heat hadn't yet seeped out of the ruins of the city.

Take care, Kaleb. A kiss against his mind. *It would break my heart if you were hurt.*

The city lay devastated around Kaleb as he jogged in the direction Aden had pointed him, yet he saw only the midnight blue eyes of the woman who, as her earlier question proved, knew exactly what he was capable of, but claimed him all the same. Always Sahara had seen him. And always she had refused to walk away.

The last time, it had cost her seven years of her life. This time, he'd lay the world itself at her feet. *I'll come to you when this is over.*

I'll be waiting.

The promise kept him going through the grim hours that followed, his main task to assist in maintaining the structural integrity of buildings while rescuers, including changeling teams who had come in via watercraft, combed the floors for survivors, their heightened sense of smell a priceless advantage. For every burned and barely alive survivor, they found ten corpses.

"We saved millions of lives," Vasic said once the final telekinetic task had been completed, "and yet it doesn't seem enough when you see them bringing out curled-up bodies, skin blackened from the fire."

Kaleb thought of the ash that was all that remained in the core, no bodies, no bones. "Vasquez intended this to be a demonstration of Pure Psy's power." He'd studied the leader of the fringe group, knew how his mind worked. "That's why he deliberately chose a high-profile island rather than a larger landmass."

"He knew we'd collapse the bridges and the water would've acted as a natural firebreak, containing the fire to within Hong Kong Island." Vasic nodded. "A logical plan, but instead of proving Pure Psy's power, he gave you a stage on which to demonstrate yours."

Kaleb would answer questions, justify his actions to only Sahara. As he'd noted earlier, however, Ming's mistake had been in thinking of the Arrows as his servants rather than his partners. "Pure Psy," he said, giving Vasic an oblique response to his unasked question, "must be extinguished. Tell Aden that is no longer the Arrows' top priority, but the squad's only one."

Vasic, his eyes on the charred and broken remnants of a once-tall skyscraper, said, "Kill or capture?"

"Kill." The Arrows might believe Kaleb's intent was to get rid of the group after they'd outlived their usefulness, but that wasn't a supposition he could refute with any expectation of being believed. The lethal squad would do its own investigations, make up its own mind— the one thing they would no longer find, of course, was evidence of Kaleb's plan to annihilate the Net.

"My personal teams have already taken care of destroying a number of Pure Psy's munitions and supply bases." He'd initiated the sweep after the university bombing and considered the resulting actions successful, but as this strike showed, the group was more organized than anyone had previously realized. "I need the squad to put extreme pressure on their leadership."

"You think they'll make mistakes."

"Everyone does if pushed hard enough." It was a lesson he'd learned in a cheap hotel room over seven years ago and never forgotten. "I've been tracking three members of their leadership across the Net with the aim of unearthing Vasquez—I'm sending you the information in a telepathic file. Interrogate if possible; otherwise, execute."

"You risk losing Vasquez."

"It's become obvious to me over the past forty-eight hours that he's been very, very careful not to connect himself directly to any one of these individuals. I'd been intending to pursue other options in any case."

"I've passed the file to Aden," Vasic said. "These operatives will be eliminated within the next day. We also have leads on four others."

In no doubt that the Arrows would take care of that matter, Kaleb turned his attention to something else. "Where's Ming?"

"He left minutes after the fire was suffocated." A pause. "Ming knew about the scorch charges, when even the squad didn't."

Kaleb had already considered that interesting fact. "If Ming did supply Pure Psy, he had to know I would be the only one capable of stopping the attack." And the other man would never give Kaleb such a huge platform on which to showcase his strength.

"Pure Psy may have gone off script. Ming's team could have handled a smaller fire."

"Yes." Kaleb watched two men carry a body out of the nearest building. The dead who still had flesh on their bones were being rapidly processed, else the city would become a hothouse for bacteria that fed on necrotizing flesh.

"Keep me informed of your progress," Kaleb said as another body was brought out. "I'll funnel through the data I unearth." He was already scanning the Net for any clue that might lead to the faceless man at the head of the fanatical group. It was time Vasquez learned that there could only be one power in the Net and the position had already been claimed.

SAHARA knew Kaleb wouldn't show his pain, but she also knew she had wounded him. So when he appeared on her balcony over twenty-four hours after he'd left, freshly showered but with uncharacteristic lines of strain marring his features, she walked up to him, took his face in her hands, and said, "Forgive me."

"You never have to ask." He closed his hands over her wrists, his hair blue-black in the morning sunshine. "There is nothing you can do that I won't forgive."

Sahara wrapped her arms around his neck and held on tight. "And there is nothing you can ever do that will make me turn away from you," she whispered. "I love you, Kaleb." It was an inexorable, beautiful truth.

"You shouldn't say that." Kaleb's arms came around her, his hold almost punishingly tight. "I'm capable of terrible things. I *would've* killed millions if I hadn't found you."

"I can say whatever I like." She pressed kisses along his jaw to his mouth. "And just because I love you doesn't mean I'll condone the untenable." Loving him didn't make her blind to his flaws. "I will continue to fight to pull you into the light."

Kaleb's eyes were that beautiful obsidian sheened with midnight color. "It may be a battle for the ages."

Her lips curved in a shaky smile. "That's okay. Someone once told me I'm the most stubborn individual he knew."

He bent until their foreheads touched. "And you were only nine at the time. I consider myself warned."

Gently caressing the back of his neck with her fingers, she spoke with her lips on his. "I don't ever again want to worry about something like this." A raw confession. "I need you to tell me everything you're involved in, so I don't have to wonder, don't have to guess."

Kaleb was silent for several minutes before saying, "I planned to have a changeling pack track you by scent if you ran from me."

Sahara widened her eyes as a smile tugged at her lips. "How astonishing. I didn't realize you were that possessive."

He didn't respond playfully to her tease as one of the leopard males might have; he reacted as only Kaleb would. "I theorized your ability might be limited to those of our race."

"I've never had reason to test it," she said, fascinated all over again by the complexities of his mind, "so you may be right." Continuing to caress his nape, she waited, knowing that small confession had been a test to see how she'd take the rest.

"I did something to Tatiana you're not going to be happy to hear."

He'd promised her no torture, and Kaleb didn't break his promises . . . but that left all kinds of loopholes for an intelligence as ruthless as his. "Tell me," she said, accepting that this relationship was never going to be simple. "Tell me everything."

They spoke for hours, in which he told her about Tatiana and about many other things, including the fact that he'd killed Marshall Hyde, the senior member of the Council at the time. "It was a flawless operation that no one ever connected to me," he said, holding her close where they sat on the floor of the aerie with their backs against the bed.

"Why him?" Sahara asked, not shocked in the least. Council politics was notoriously bloody, and Kaleb had become a Councilor at twenty-seven. No one did that without being ready to play the game in cold blood. "Ming would seem the better target if it was about taking control of the Council."

"It had nothing to do with the fact that he was a Councilor." Kaleb's voice chilled. "Marshall knew what Santano was, what he was doing to me, that I was nothing but a kind of toy he had created as an experiment."

His fingers fisted in her hair. *"Just make certain your proclivities don't affect your duties. That's what I heard Marshall say to Enrique when I was seven; that's when I decided I would kill him and destroy his precious Council. Best way to do that was to become a part of it."*

"If he knew and did nothing," Sahara said, so angry her body vibrated with it, "it made him as culpable and as depraved as Enrique. I would've killed him, too."

"No," he said, "you wouldn't."

Sahara shook her head. "For what he did to you? Yes. I am fully capable of erasing the memories of anyone that monstrous to leave them a walking dead shell. I did it once," she said, needing him to understand that she wasn't lily-white. "It was a guard who'd hurt me so much." The orders may have come from Tatiana, but the male had done his task with a relish that betrayed the ugly truth about Silence. "He came too close and I took everything, every memory, every wish, every dream, leaving him a shell with no past and no future."

"I know," Kaleb said, icy approval in his tone. "Tatiana documented the incident in her files."

"Then you know I've walked in the darkness," she said, hand fisting on his heart and voice fierce. "I won't ever judge you for doing the same." No one had any right to do that. *No one.*

The world had abdicated that privilege when it abandoned a child to a monster. "I will fight you endlessly if I think you're wrong," she said, taking his lips in a passionate, possessive kiss, "but I will *never* judge you."

The stars returned to his eyes when she didn't flinch from him, and he told her about something that had nothing to do with hatred, but rather the opposite—how the Ghost had first met his fellow rebels Judd Lauren and Xavier Perez. "Judd thinks I approached him because he was a trained assassin who had already begun to quietly rebel against the status quo, the perfect partner for the Ghost."

"That wasn't the reason?" Sahara asked, straddling his thighs so she could watch him as he spoke.

"It was only a peripheral one." Kaleb put one of his hands on her own thigh, his thumb brushing the inner seam of her jeans. "The real one was that he never forgot his family. Regardless of the risks, he did everything in his power to protect them."

Unspoken was a truth Judd couldn't have known—that in the other man's refusal to give up on his family, Kaleb had seen an echo of his own relentless hunt for Sahara. "Xavier was Judd's connection first," he continued, "and I didn't see the point of bringing him in when Judd suggested it. What could a human offer, after all?"

Compelled by the story of how these three disparate men—cardinal telekinetic, assassin, priest—had come together, she leaned forward, her arms around his neck. "What changed your mind?"

"The Ghost had a conversation with Father Xavier Perez." Eyes of obsidian potent with memory. "He understands evil better than any other person I've ever known. We disagree in how to eliminate it, but we do not disagree that it exists."

"I hope I can one day meet them both," Sahara said, knowing she owed Judd Lauren and Xavier Perez in a way the two men would never understand. They'd not only kept her Kaleb from walking always alone, they had questioned his choices, and in so doing, kept him from becoming the darkness that lived in him. "Will you continue to maintain your shadow identity?"

"It may come in useful on occasion." His hand around her throat, drawing her closer. "The Ghost is a hero to many people, while Kaleb Krychek is a threat. So perhaps the Ghost will endorse Krychek after a suitable period."

Laughing at the calculation on his face, she bit down on his lip. "Do you ever think in straight lines?"

"Only when it comes to you."

It wasn't until she was about to fall asleep in his arms that she realized he'd deftly avoided going anywhere near one particular subject, the same subject her mind still kept from her. Sahara had a dark suspicion she knew what it was—but given the reaction of her body the last time she'd tried to access that particular memory, she made the decision not to force the issue.

It was, she thought as sleep took her under, going to take every ounce of her intelligence to dance with Kaleb. Spreading her hand over his heart, she smiled and thought of a phrase she'd heard one of the DarkRiver guards use when issuing a friendly challenge to a packmate: *Game on.*

PSYNET BEACON: BREAKING NEWS

Hong Kong fire contained. Unknown number of casualties—estimates range from two to three hundred thousand dead.

UPDATED Pure Psy sends letter to all major comm networks. Text as follows.*

Absolution in Purity

We take total, unmitigated responsibility for the Hong Kong strike. It has never been our intention to hide what we do—because what we do is necessary to awaken our people to the reality of our ruined society.

Our actions could not have been successfully completed had the world been under the leadership of a strong Council. It is the weak who lead us now, and that weakness will destroy us all. Silence is the only way to counter what has proved to be a fatal flaw.

Without Silence, this is who we will be—a people without protection or will, a people who can be picked off by the inferior races until the world is ruled by savages. We will not permit such a future to come to pass.

This is a call to arms to all who believe in Silence, in the superiority of our race.

Join us.

PSYNET BEACON: LIVE NETSTREAM

The letter is nonsensical gibberish. Where in the Protocol does it mandate wholesale slaughter?

Y. Schulz
(Munich)

It is not the "inferior races" who masterminded this attack, but our own. Does that not make us the savages?

R. Gueye
(Riyadh)

Whatever their actions, one thing is incontestable: Pure Psy is not afraid to speak the truth. We have lost our place as the leaders of the world and it is the fault of those at the top. Though Councilor Krychek, at least, has shown significant power. Such a man could rule not only the PsyNet but the world. It is my belief that, together, Councilor Krychek and Pure Psy would make an invincible ruling junta.

K. Choi
(Kingston)

Kaleb Krychek's actions in assisting to save lives in Hong Kong are to be commended. As a cardinal Tk, he did not have to get involved. That he did speaks highly of his ability and willingness to protect the people he no doubt seeks to rule.

J. Jantunen
(Nadi)

It is clear Kaleb Krychek is using these unfortunate events in order to con-solidate his power base. Which leads to the question of whether he is, in fact, behind the attacks and is the puppet master who manipulates Pure Psy's destructive strings.

No name given
(Hohhot)

Our race can stand tall today—when the worst happened, our people did not flinch. Kaleb Krychek and his men are to be commended, as are Ming LeBon and his team.
    Pure Psy, on the other hand, must be eradicated. They are a pustule on the face of our society.

B. Oliveira
(Santiago)

A number of the individuals clad in black with the single star on their left shoulders who assisted in the aftermath of this attack, and several previous ones, are rumored to be part of the shadowy and powerful Arrow Squad, rather than simply Kaleb Krychek's personal forces.
    If so, and if they now belong to Kaleb Krychek, he already has the PsyNet within his grasp. As we have seen today, he could take it by sheer

brute force. That he hasn't makes me hypothesize he seeks a rational solution, and such thinking is something I can support, in a way I cannot support the irrational violence of Pure Psy.

T. Saowaluk
(Vancouver)

The "Pure" should be burned in the same fires as those that consumed their victims. If they have no reason to hide their actions, why aren't they standing in front of us, willing to publicly own their cause?

G. Barrie
(Tasiilaq)

Pure Psy

"FOOLS." VASQUEZ DROPPED out of the PsyNet after reading a sampling of the thousands upon thousands of citizen opinions that had come in since Hong Kong burned.

The vast majority were virulently anti–Pure Psy, which only went to show the extent of the decay corrupting their society. Rather than seeing in Pure Psy their chance for redemption, the populace saw only what their weak minds had been programmed to see—Psy who weren't toeing the line, weren't being the sheep they were meant to be.

It had reached the point that the Silence of his faithful was being questioned. That could not be permit—

Sir! The mental voice of one of his trusted deputies, the tone urgent. *I've walked into a trap! Krychek's men are closing in.*

Do not allow them to take you! Vasquez ordered. *You know too much.*

I won't let you down, sir.

Two minutes later, came a final message—*Absolution in Purity*—and then the nothingness that indicated the deputy had ended his life rather than risk betraying the cause.

Vasquez deleted the man's name from his mental list. It was the fourth name he'd crossed off in the past thirty-six hours, all belonging to individuals high in the Pure Psy command structure. If he'd had any doubt that the Arrows had been shot at Pure Psy, it had just been erased.

There was a decision to be made, and it was not one he had thought to make so soon, but their enemies were getting too close. For Pure Psy to achieve its goals, it must survive to continue the fight, because without Pure Psy's leadership to lead the Psy race out of the darkness, their people would soon be extinct.

Sending out a simple code via a single-use cell phone that he dismantled straight afterward, he made his way to a comm unit he would destroy as soon as this was done. All of his surviving deputies called in one after the other within the next minute, each utilizing a single-use mobile comm. He could see their faces, but they couldn't see him or one another, which meant they could not give up their fellow soldiers if caught.

None spoke, aware they had only a two-minute window.

"We are being hunted," he told them. "And our enemy is strong. It's time to initiate the Phoenix Code."

Men and women alike, they gave brisk nods, and he knew the task would be done. That was why he had handpicked each deputy, chanced trusting them with critical parts of his plan. It was the only option. "Do not delay. You've already lost four of your brethren. You must put your pieces in play and disappear."

Knowing the caliber of the opponents on their trail, he knew that speed alone wouldn't be enough. "I, together with a small team, will personally instigate a diversion to assist you. Make use of it." It was of concern that the plan for the diversion was one he'd had to put together in haste and without the necessary reconnaissance, but things did not always go according to plan in a war. "You have your orders."

"Sir."

Chapter 39

KALEB TELEPORTED INTO hell.

Screams echoed through the air; dusty, bloody children with huge, helpless eyes sat in the debris; first responders tried to make order out of chaos. But there could be no easy order out of this. At first glance, it appeared Pure Psy, the fanatical group having already claimed responsibility, had lost any sense of reason, any sense of their "mission," and attacked no target that could advance their cause.

The Worldwide Student Caucus in Geneva was a weeklong event, held for the best and brightest students from around the world, ages spanning twelve to eighteen. Supervised and challenged by teachers who were experts in their fields, they came to discuss advances in science, engineering, the arts, music, and medicine.

The caucus had been created by the educational branch of a lobby group but now received funding from governments across the world. Every country sent at least one student, many on scholarships funded by large corporations that hoped to one day lure some of these bright minds into their workforce. None of those corporations, however, were permitted to influence the curriculum carefully chosen by an independent body of educators. Kaleb knew all that because Sahara had been invited to the caucus at fourteen.

Deemed too divisive in the quest for pure knowledge, the two subjects *not* on the agenda were politics and religion. There could have been no formal discussion here that threatened Pure Psy. Yet, according to field estimates, more than a quarter of the students and faculty were dead, the majority of the rest injured or trapped.

They weren't the only casualties—the blast had come at half past noon, when hundreds of people from the nearby office towers had been in restaurants in the pedestrian mall that surrounded the convention center, some with small children they'd picked up from day-care centers attached to their places of work.

Kaleb was already shifting debris to uncover trapped survivors as he took in the carnage. In the first five minutes he worked, he heard French, German, English, and Russian, as well as a number of languages he couldn't identify . . . and realized that Pure Psy had targeted the caucus for a very rational reason: to create an inciting incident that would affect every country on the planet.

If the situation wasn't immediately managed, someone, somewhere, would interpret this as a personal attack and launch a counterstrike against the Psy. The ensuing war would engulf every country, every race, every individual. And when the dust finally settled, it was the survivors who'd create the new world.

"Some things need to be broken to become stronger."

The fact that Pure Psy was working from the same playbook he himself had done was not lost on him. But Kaleb would allow no one to sow the seeds of destruction—not now, when Sahara had asked him to find another way to create a better world. And children . . . children should always be off the agenda.

As he should've been. As Sahara should've been.

Aden, he said, having set the Arrow on a particular task, *do you have the information?*

I've examined one of the devices that failed to detonate. It's standard—no improvements to extend range or casualties. Placement of the devices was also haphazard, else we'd be dealing with triple or quadruple the casualties.

It could be a sign of Pure Psy crumbling under the pressure the Arrows and Kaleb had put on them in the two days since the Hong Kong fires were contained, but it seemed too fast a result. Why would the group sacrifice such a high-visibility target with a clumsy strike? Aden was right—done correctly, the entire convention center could've been collapsed on the delegates, and with the convention having begun just the day before last, Pure Psy would've had four more days to put their plan in place.

Wait, Aden said. *Initial death estimates are being revised downward by a significant degree. Fifty percent of the delegates were away from the convention center for a scheduled day of visits to laboratories, museums, and specialist firms.*

Half their targets out of range? It left hundreds of potential casualties, but Pure Psy had always gone for maximum damage. This was too big a mistake. And given Vasquez's intelligence and training, that meant it wasn't a mistake. *This is a diversion, meant to occupy our attention while they set up something bigger,* he said, 'porting an injured girl directly to the triage station at one end of the blast zone. *I need trackers now. The team that put this in place will be a skeletal one with few resources. We need to run them down, and this time, I want them alive for interrogation.*

I'm pulling Abbot and Sione, Aden replied. *They're the best trackers on the squad.*

Kaleb agreed with that assessment, but finding the Pure Psy strike team wasn't the only problem. Already reports were trickling into the PsyNet of ordinary Psy being harassed in countries around the world, as hotheads screamed for vengeance for the blood of their young, forgetting that the Psy had also lost a number of their own young. If he was to head off a global war, he had to do so now, and in such a way that no one would be left in any doubt that Pure Psy was a fringe element and did not represent the Psy race as a whole.

Entering the PsyNet, he blasted a message that would be heard in every corner of the psychic network, carried by the violent wave of his power

PURE PSY ARE MASS MURDERERS WITH NO CLAIM TO SILENCE AND AS OF THIS NOTICE THE MOST WANTED FUGITIVES IN THE WORLD. IF YOU KNOW OF ANYONE

WITH AN AFFILIATION TO PURE PSY, CONTACT A
MEMBER OF COUNCILOR KALEB KRYCHEK'S PERSONAL
OFFICE.

THE SENTENCE FOR ANY INVOLVEMENT IN THESE
ATTACKS WILL BE DEATH. THE SENTENCE FOR HAR-
BORING PURE PSY WILL BE TOTAL REHABILITATION OF
THE ENTIRE FAMILY UNIT. THERE WILL BE NO MERCY
GRANTED FOR CRIMES THAT CAN HAVE NO RATIONALE
EITHER IN SILENCE OR IN EMOTION.

He streamed live images of the broken bodies of the children he continued to 'port to the medics or to morgues, and he stamped the trans-
mission with a glowing platinum star that could not be duplicated or
erased.

If Pure Psy wanted to challenge him, they had to be prepared to pay
the price.

Silver, he said, dropping out of the Net. *Alert the offices.*

It's already in progress. A pause. *Sir. My family is sending our telekinetics
to Geneva in high-speed airjets, to act under your authority. They are not teleport capable, but they can take over some of the rescue work so the Arrows and
your teams can focus on the hunt for the fugitives.*

Understood. Kaleb sent the information to Aden while continuing to
talk to Silver. *More medical teams will be needed. Geneva sent a large group
to assist in treating the burn victims in Hong Kong, as did a number of other
nearby regions.* All of those medics would be exhausted and unable to
assist here, even if Kaleb diverted Tks to pick them up.

The problem, of course, was that a large percentage of the world's
strongest Tks were also exhausted after Hong Kong, leaving a dangerous
gap. *Find out who has spare medics close enough to be useful, and get them here
any way you can.*

The M-Psy Union is sending me a list, Silver answered. *I'm also coordi-
nating with major changeling groups and the Human Alliance to get all useful
personnel to Geneva.*

I didn't realize you had a contact within the Alliance.

I don't—their security chief just made the contact. A pause of several minutes. *Sir, the Alliance heard about your broadcast and have thrown their public support behind the call to apprehend Pure Psy.*

Good. It would ameliorate the world's growing anger if they saw the races working together to hunt down the perpetrators.

They also have a large medical warehouse less than an hour's flight away, Silver continued. *An airjet is already in the air with equipment and necessary drugs.*

Switching telepathic channels when he felt Sahara's touch, he listened as she said, *I heard your message, and I called Vaughn to tell him. He says it's being communicated to all groups with whom the pack has any kind of a link.*

Kaleb knew he had no need to explain the importance of that communication given DarkRiver's strategic position, not to Sahara, his lover with her brilliant mind.

The pack has a man in the area, she added five minutes later. *He's confirmed the local changeling trackers are happy to work with Psy teams to find the bombers. Changeling rescue and healing/medical teams should also be reaching you within twenty minutes.*

Focusing on lifting a massive piece of the outer wall that had fallen inward, he took a second to reply. *Silver's direct line is in the cell phone I gave you. Route her into all communications dealing with rescue and medical so she can coordinate available resources.*

I'll get the number. She disappeared for a minute before returning. *Kaleb, the Forgotten also have someone in the area who might be able to assist. She'll come in with the DarkRiver male and requests no one attempt to shadow her as she works.*

The Forgotten, having dropped out of the PsyNet at the inception of Silence, had been marrying humans and mating with changelings for over a hundred years. As a result, Kaleb was well aware they had some very interesting new abilities in their genetic line, abilities they preferred to keep under the radar. *No one will interfere with her.*

Seeing a bloody but breathing child curled up in a cavity formed by pieces of debris that had saved his small body from being crushed, Kaleb called out for a paramedic. A minute later, and two feet deeper, he found a child who hadn't been as lucky, her eyes staring blindly into death, grit across her irises. Going down on one knee, he brought her eyelids down in an act that he knew came from the voice in the void.

All the while, he could feel Sahara tucked against his mind, staying with him as she'd done at the university, and in the aftermath of the inferno that had engulfed Hong Kong Island.

Never again, he thought, would he be alone in the dark.

SAHARA'S heart ached at the indefinable emotion she sensed from Kaleb across their telepathic bond. He would speak to her about it when he was ready, of that she had not a single doubt in her mind. Her dangerous lover was learning that she'd become even more stubborn than she'd been at sixteen—she had claimed Kaleb and she would not turn away, no matter what.

Now she met the cat-green eyes of the DarkRiver alpha. Lucas Hunter had turned up at her aerie soon after the news of the bombing went live, his eyes glowing against the early morning darkness on this side of the world. The pack, he'd told her, had no one connected to the Net, and so she was their information source when it came to what was happening on the psychic plane.

"I'm linking in with Kaleb's aide, Silver," she said, and he nodded at her from where he was talking on the phone with the leader of the Forgotten, the four slashing lines on the right side of his face a silent reminder of the predator that lived beneath his skin.

Kaleb's ice-blonde aide, her hair in a flawless twist, was expecting her call. "Do the groups to which you have access," Silver said without further ado, "have any translators willing to assist the medics? We can comm them in—with a number of the on-site translators dead or critically injured, there aren't enough to help the medics and keep the survivors calm. Multiple languages needed, some of them esoteric."

"I'm a translator," Sahara said. "All languages." It seemed a safe enough claim, given the tests she'd been running on herself while out and about

in the city. Anytime she heard an unfamiliar language, she'd listen . . .
and then she'd understand, without ever activating her ability.

Whatever it was she could do, it worked on the subconscious level. "A
minor psychic gift," she explained to Silver. "No official designation."

The aide's eyes sharpened. "That's useful enough that I can justify
diverting a Tk to pick you up."

"I'll take over as liaison," Lucas said, entering into the comm frame
so Silver could see him. "Give us a couple of minutes to organize an
image your teleporter can use as a lock."

Soon afterward, Sahara was in the trees a short distance from her
aerie, and Lucas was tying a brightly colored rope around the trunk of an
otherwise nondescript pine—just because the pack wanted to help didn't
mean they intended for a strange Tk to have a permanent image lock
inside their territory.

Taking a snapshot with her cell phone, she sent it to Silver, as Lucas
said, "Good luck," his eyes grim.

Vasic was the Tk who teleported in—not surprising, given the
distance—and as a result, she was in Geneva seconds later.

"Thank God," the man in charge of the field hospital said when she
told him what she could do. Slapping the symbol of the Rosetta Stone on
her shoulder, he pointed her in the direction of a boy on a stretcher about
ten feet away. "Obscure mother tongue. He must have something of one
of the major world languages, but he's lost it in the shock."

It took Sahara half a minute to comprehend what the boy was saying.
"It's okay," she reassured him when he began to cry at the realization that
she understood him. "You're not alone anymore. Now, you need to tell
the doctor some things so she can help you."

That was the first of many similar conversations she had over the
hours that followed, as Geneva went from light to dark, the stars bright
overhead. Someone brought her a meal when she began to fade, and that
kept her going until the early morning hours. Deciding to crash for an
hour to head off a collapse, she curled up on one of the cots set up for
rescue personnel. *Have you eaten?* she asked the cardinal Tk who, she
knew, would not sleep.

I've had nutrition bars delivered to me throughout the day.

No one, she thought, wanted to lose any of the already depleted telekinetics—but Kaleb was in a league of his own. *Take care with the structural damage. Some of the areas are really unstable.*

Though he had to know that far better than her, he didn't reject her concern. *I'll be careful.*

Will you wake me in an hour?

Yes. Rest now.

"COUNCILOR."

Turning at the voice, Kaleb found an older woman holding a bottle of the energy drink he'd been downing twice an hour to fuel his body. "Thank you."

"I can take the bottle once you're done." A polite enough offer, but her eyes didn't move off the bottle in his hand.

Kaleb's instincts went on immediate and high alert. Pinning the woman's body in place using telekinesis and compressing her jaw to keep her silent, he unscrewed the bottle to take a sniff. Nothing smelled off. *Vasic, a second.*

The Arrow walked around the corner soon afterward. *I'm near flame-out. I'll need to rest for three hours at least before I can continue.*

Kaleb nodded. "Can you quickly test this?"

Holding up his left arm, Vasic slid back a small screen on the computronic gauntlet fused to his body. "One drop."

Kaleb placed the sample on the test surface.

Chapter 40

"IT'S A COMPLEX poison," Vasic said in less than a minute, "would've incapacitated you almost immediately." His eyes shifted to the would-be assassin. "At which point, she would've killed you with the garrote in her bracelet." Removing the bracelet, he snapped out the thin metal wire designed to cut off a target's air supply with silent efficiency.

"Who sent you?" Kaleb asked, releasing the woman's jaw so she could reply.

"Do what you will, Councilor Krychek," was the icy response. "My mind is set to implode at any attempt at an intrusion."

"Interesting." Having already told the DarkMind to entrap her so she couldn't connect to anyone on the psychic plane, he pinched a nerve that made her slump to the ground, then ordered another of his men on the scene to blindfold and tie her up. "Put her somewhere out of the way. I'll deal with her later."

He 'ported the poisonous drink into a biohazard container on-site, just as Vasic said, "The explosives used at this site have been traced back to a Council depot in Europe under Ming's control."

Kaleb had always believed Ming to be the martial mastermind behind Henry Scott during the time the now-dead Councilor headed Pure Psy, but this type of indiscriminate violence didn't fit Ming's modus operandi. Neither did Pure Psy's racial agenda. It was far too irrational and Ming was nothing if not rational; that was part of what made him so dangerous.

However, Ming was also fully capable of playing a deep game, Pure

Psy likely nothing but a pawn to help further an agenda of which the fanatical group knew nothing. "I'll have one of my men tug that thread," he said to Vasic, "see what comes of it. I want the squad to remain on Pure Psy."

It wasn't until six hours later, having done everything he could to assist in the search for survivors, that Kaleb had time to deal with the woman who had attempted to poison him. But first he wanted to see Sahara. Locking on her image, he found her alone in the tent that had functioned as a canteen for survivors and those working in the field hospital. She was tidying up the detritus, the area quiet and calm.

From his telepathic conversations with her during the past hours, he knew the majority of the survivors were now in hospitals in Geneva and nearby cities. Each also had the support of at least one individual from his or her own country, the multilingual representatives having been flown in from around the world on high-speed jets courtesy of an airline controlled by Nikita Duncan.

The ex-Councilor wasn't famous for being a humanitarian, but she was smart enough to know the action would paint her in a positive light when the dust settled. It was an intelligent, calculated move worthy of the woman who had lasted more than a decade on the Council. Nikita, he thought, would always find a way to come out alive on the other side.

Anthony Kyriakus, too, had made his mark. An unidentified Night-Star foreseer had seen a vision of further bombings in Luxembourg and Paris with enough specificity for both to be averted. "It is unfortunate that we could not do the same for other recent tragedies," had been the statement of the NightStar press officer when questioned by media in the aftermath. "Nonbusiness foresight is a new area for NightStar, and we are learning that not all events can be foreseen or averted."

Some things, Kaleb thought as Sahara looked up and saw him, had to be survived.

"Kaleb!" She flew into his arms.

Holding her close, her breath warm on his cheek, her body slender but strong against his, he felt as if he'd come home. He didn't know how long they stood locked together, but when they did draw apart, he kept his promise to not withhold anything from her and told her about the attempted poisoning.

Sahara hissed out a breath, eyes incandescent with fury. "Take me to her." *No one hurts you.*

"Only a retrieval, Sahara," he said, gripping her chin. "Nothing else, nothing that will affect your memories." *I need you to remember me.*

"She's not worth a piece of my life." A scathing judgment. "Now take me to her."

This time, he did as ordered. Sahara didn't speak, simply stepped close enough that her hand was an inch from the blindfolded woman's face, then nodded at him. He 'ported them directly to the Moscow house. Should her language skills be needed again, he'd take her back, but the nonspecialist volunteers were capable of handling the cleanup.

"That *woman* is one of Ming's people," she said, heading into the kitchen to get them both energy supplements. "A low-level operative who was in the area. It wasn't a well-planned operation, but a chance opportunity Ming decided to utilize."

"He knows I'm on the verge of taking over the Net."

Sahara stirred cherry flavoring into her drink, after passing him an undoctored glass. "What will you do to him?"

"Nothing." Seeing her open disbelief, he traced the shape of her upper lip with his finger. "There are others who have deeper grievances against Ming. It'll be handled."

"Kaleb, you don't trust anyone except me . . . and your two friends." Sahara nudged at him to finish his drink. "Is it the fallen Arrow who has the prior claim?"

"Not Judd alone. He's simply the one with whom I have a connection." Kaleb put down his empty glass. "I'd be extremely surprised if Ming doesn't end up torn apart by changeling claws and teeth."

Sahara halted with her own drink halfway to her mouth. "Change-lings?"

"Judd's niece is someone Ming wants dead or in his control. She's also mated to the alpha of SnowDancer, considered the most dangerous changeling pack in the world." Kaleb tapped her glass until Sahara lifted it to her mouth. "Man like that won't rest until he's eradicated the threat against his woman." Kaleb wondered if the wolf alpha would be surprised to find he had something in common with Kaleb Krychek. "Hungry?"

Sahara wrinkled her nose. "Shower first."

They'd just reached the bedroom when his cell phone rang. It was Aden on the other end. "Vasquez is proving his intelligence," were the Arrow's opening words. "His entire team split up after Geneva and scattered in different directions. We captured one; two others suicided when cornered. There are signs two more remain at large."

An impressive result, but they both knew it wasn't enough. "Vasquez?"

"Signs point to him being here, but he slipped away." Though Aden's voice betrayed nothing, his frustration level had to be high—in the icy way of any Arrow denied his target. "Interrogation of the captive did yield one piece of data; he was assigned to the Luxembourg site with a member of the team we haven't yet captured. Luxembourg and Paris, however, were also both meant to be distractions."

"The prisoner didn't know why Pure Psy needed the distractions, did he?" Vasquez *was* smart, smart enough to keep information on a need-to-know basis.

"No," Aden confirmed. "But whatever it is, it's happening soon, and it's important enough that a lieutenant we were about to capture threw herself off the side of a building rather than surrender."

No organization could afford to lose its entire leadership, and now not only had Vasquez risked exposure, his top people were sacrificing themselves to protect their secret. "Leave the teams who have live leads in the field," he said to Aden. "I want you to rest, along with a rapid response team. We move the instant Vasquez surfaces or Pure Psy makes a move."

"Agreed."

Hanging up, he relayed the information to Sahara. "Vasquez might have gone under," he said, "but his options for safe harbor are limited and shrinking by the minute."

We wanted to protect our people. We didn't want the blood of children on our hands.

It was a refrain Kaleb had seen over and over again in the reports Silver had forwarded him, of minor players who had either turned themselves in after his warning blasted through the Net or been turned in by others. "The populace isn't so Silent," he said, watching Sahara peel off her T-shirt, "as to not be horrified by the growing atrocities."

She dropped the T-shirt to the floor and kicked off her shoes. "It makes me hope," she said softly, "that we have inside us the capacity to build a better future."

Kaleb didn't understand hope, but he knew he would do everything in his power to give Sahara the future that was a fragile dream in her eyes as she walked toward him, bare to the skin. Reaching him, she tugged up his long-sleeved black T-shirt, then undid his belt.

"I'll wait for you in the shower," she whispered, pressing a kiss to the center of his chest. "I think, after so many years, no one can begrudge us for stealing a little time."

His eyes caressed every inch of her as she walked away from him with the grace of the dancer she'd always been . . . and he knew she was healing in the deepest of ways. Ripping off the rest of his clothing, he stepped into the shower behind her, his hands at her hips. The hot water pounded over them, but the beat of his heart was louder, deeper, stronger.

Bending his head to her neck, he kissed her throat, his hands rising to cup her breasts. She arched into him with a shudder, her hands slippery on his thighs, his Sahara who had never turned away from him. Picking up her arms, he brought them around his neck, then poured some of the liquid soap into his hands. She moved with a sinuous sensuality against him as he slicked the soap over her skin, the foam trickling down her legs.

"Put your hands on the wall."

She obeyed his quiet order with a smile that was at once sultry and possessive. "Have you gone obsidian?" Hands flat on the tile, she moaned as he stroked the soap over her back and onto the curves of her buttocks.

"Yes." He took his time with the task, before going down on his haunches to run the soap over her legs.

His kiss to her inner thigh made her gasp and turn around. Tugging him to his feet, she let the spray hit her back and held out her hand for the soap. "You're dirty, too."

Somehow, those simple words took on a far different nuance in this context. Curving his hand around her neck, he took a kiss from those soft, wet lips, her tongue hot in his mouth and her body pressed against his erection. When she broke the kiss, it was to clasp her hands around that pulsing hardness, her firm grip as possessive as her eyes had been.

"I," she whispered, moving her hands in tight strokes that had him gritting his teeth, "have been doing some research of my own."

His mind threatened to blank as she went down in front of him, her breasts wet, her hands spread on his thighs . . . and her mouth red-hot as she took him inside her. Pleasure engulfed him in a tidal wave, dark and vicious, and he knew this time, his Tk wouldn't only be tearing up the fields outside.

TWENTY minutes and a storm of wracking pleasure later, Sahara pushed her damp hair off her face where she lay on her stomach in their bed and ran her hand over the chest of the man who lay beside her, his breathing rough. "I just checked the PsyNet," she said, her own breathing not exactly even. "This region just experienced a medium-sized earthquake."

Kaleb turned his head on the pillow. "It was located deep underground, I made sure of that. No real damage."

It should've been surreal, lying in bed with a man who had just caused an earthquake, but this was Kaleb and he was hers. "The poor scientists," she said, "are going to be scratching their heads over the sudden seismic activity in this region over the next few decades."

Kaleb's lips didn't curve, but she saw the wicked smile in his eyes as he said, "You took me by surprise."

"Good." Lax and sated, her mind on the rage of his power, she went to ask him how he'd controlled it as a child, then realized what she'd be bringing into this bed, the blood and the horror and the one event they'd both shied from facing. Body and mind, she was ready to handle it, but not today, when Kaleb appeared as young as she'd ever seen him.

Instead, she drew a design on his arm with her finger and said, "Food, then rest." The afternoon sun might be bright beyond the terrace sliders, but neither one of them had had enough sleep over the past two days. More, they needed to maintain their strength.

She didn't have to be an F to know the war wasn't yet over.

KALEB woke in the middle of the night to a telepathic hail from Aden. *An individual we believe to be Vasquez has been tracked to California by an Arrow team and independently by the Forgotten tracker and her changeling partner. Past experience makes it highly probable that San Francisco is his destination and his target.*

Yes. The city had become a focal point for Psy who were fractured, making it anathema to Pure Psy. Even more provocative was the fact that the changelings, humans, and Psy in the region had worked together to repel the last attack by the fanatical group. *Send me all the data.*

Scanning it as it came in, he looked down at the woman who slept with her head on his chest, her hair tumbling over the arm he had around her waist. "Sahara."

"Mmm." Hand flexing against him, she ran her foot over his shin before snuggling back down to sleep.

He felt something inside him that was so gentle it was painful, something that awoke only for Sahara. Maybe it was the emotion called tenderness. Running his hand up the line of her spine, he curved it over her nape. "It's time to get up."

"No." In spite of the bad-tempered mumble, her lashes flickered against him. "Why?"

He saw the last of the sleep fade from her face as he told her. "But," she said, sitting up, "from everything I've read, Pure Psy suffered a decisive defeat in the region at a time when they had an army. Why would they risk a return with such a ragtag team?"

"There are two options," Kaleb answered, his eyes on the beautiful woman who sat nude beside him in a silent indication of bone-deep trust, the sheets pooled at her waist.

"The first"—he curved his hand around her hip—"is that Pure Psy does have an army waiting in the wings, and this is the major strike they've been planning." It would make sense, the previous defeat a cause of shame for the group. "However, I've been keeping an eye on the region, and there are no signs of any offensive force in or around the area."

"So that leaves the second option." Sahara frowned, her fingers running absently over the ridges of his abdomen. "That Vasquez wants to cause as much chaos as possible to cover this unknown other action?"

Kaleb clenched his stomach muscles as her hand drifted lower. "A man working alone," he said, stroking the curve of her hip once before he forced himself to get out of bed, "or only with a small covert team, can create it on a large scale, especially if we take Vasquez's training into account."

Pulling on a pair of black sweatpants that hung loosely on his hips, he considered the situation and the necessary response. "We need to corner Vasquez in the city, but entering changeling territory without an invitation risks creating a political situation"—a fact Vasquez could be counting on to delay any pursuit—"so we get that invitation. I'll contact Judd."

Chapter 41

"ANTHONY," SAHARA SAID, tucking her hair behind her ears. "I can call him. He'll be able to advise Nikita—they've both made it clear Pure Psy is unwelcome in their region, and they may have on-the-ground data you can't access."

At Kaleb's nod, she turned to make an audio-only call on the mobile comm beside the bed, while he used his cell phone to contact Judd—and for the first time, their conversation was not between the Ghost and a former Arrow, but between Kaleb Krychek and a SnowDancer lieutenant. When the other man ended the conversation, it was to speak to his alpha, as well as get word to the leopard alpha. "I'll call you back in five minutes," he said and hung up.

In the interim, Kaleb contacted Enforcement's central command in the United States and asked them to issue updated bulletins to their officers in California and the surrounding states. "Warn them not to approach if Vasquez is sighted," Kaleb said. "He's a high-level telepath trained in hand-to-hand combat and sniper-grade shooting."

"Does this request come via the Council?" the commissioner asked.

"No. The Council is gone. This comes directly from me—I trust Enforcement has no difficulty with that."

"Enforcement has no issue cooperating in the hunt for the criminal Andrea Vasquez. Future cooperation, however, will depend on the circumstances."

"Very well, Commissioner." Kaleb had so many moles inside Enforcement he could get anything he wanted at a moment's notice, but he saw no reason not to be civil.

Hanging up, he glanced at Sahara. "Anthony is getting in touch with Nikita," she said, zipping up a hooded sweatshirt over the jeans and T-shirt she'd pulled on. "He didn't say, but I'm guessing he'll also connect with the others in the region, changeling and human." A questioning look. "Your invitation?"

Kaleb began to dress. "Pending." The fact was, he'd be going in with or without it. Vasquez was too big a threat to leave to even the packs' capable hands.

His phone rang on the heels of that thought. "You and the Arrows are cleared," Judd told him. "Strategy meeting at DarkRiver's Chinatown HQ, twenty minutes."

Since the SnowDancer den was some distance from that location, Kaleb guessed Judd and the wolf alpha would be teleporting to the meeting. "I'll be there." Hanging up, he finished getting into clothing indistinguishable from the black combat uniforms worn by the Arrow Squad, the clothing made of bulletproof material that would also repel a certain level of laser fire.

Unbeknownst to Sahara, all her jeans, as well as the hooded sweatshirt she was currently wearing, had the same properties as the combat gear. He hadn't been able to swap out her T-shirts and other tops as yet, but one of his companies was currently working on a superfine version of the rougher, heavier combat fabric. "Keep that sweatshirt on throughout," he told her, and when she smiled at him, he realized she'd already figured out what he'd done.

Her intelligence had always been one of the most attractive things about her.

"Can you get me to a location like this?" she asked as he took a seat on the bed to put on his boots, sending him an image of a busy concourse, people moving every which way. "I think I might be able to help gather information."

What she was proposing, he understood when she sent him another image, would be akin to standing in the middle of the data streams of the PsyNet, except on the physical plane. She'd pick up hundreds, thousands of random thoughts as people passed by.

"It's getting close to crossing a moral line," she said with a solemn expression, "but it could mean saving countless lives. And since I have no intention of ever taking control of the minds that brush past me, it's a decision I can live with."

"Are you sure?" Sahara's conscience was a powerful force, one that could crush her from the inside out if she took the wrong path.

She nodded. "I must have this ability for a reason—and this conscience, too. I have to trust in myself and my intention to do no harm." Blowing out a breath, she said, "It might end up being a fruitless exercise anyway."

"It stands as much a chance of success as any other." Vasquez was a man trained to be a shadow, and San Francisco was a city of millions. "You need protection. I'll organize an Arrow escort." Kaleb would trust her safety to no one he didn't think capable of repelling Vasquez.

But Sahara, fingers working to weave her hair into a neat braid, shook her head. "An Arrow will stand out in such a changeling-heavy city— they may be trained in covert ops, but there's no doubt they're lethal, and it puts people instinctively on edge. I saw that in Geneva."

He got to his feet. "You want a changeling guard."

"It's safer. People will assume I'm a human packmate," she pointed out. "I don't look, act, or sound like the stereotypical image of Psy."

It was a clever and more than plausible argument. "You risk exposing your abilities to the changelings." The more people who knew, the greater the chance of a leak.

Sahara wrapped an elastic tie around the end of her braid. "I won't tell them what I'm doing. I'll say I'm putting myself in prime position to have a useful flash of backsight."

The part of him that lived in the void, possessive and obsessively protective, wanted to state a vocal negative to her plan . . . but paradoxically, that same part would fight to the death for her freedom. "Even a hint of trouble and you call me."

"Done." Rising on tiptoe, her hands on his shoulders, she claimed a kiss, her gaze tender. "I won't underestimate Vasquez."

Trusting her promise in a way he trusted no one else, he said, "According to Aden's latest report, Vasquez is already on the ground. The central skytrain station is a better option for you than the airport."

FIFTEEN minutes after the conversation with Kaleb, Sahara glanced at the amber-blond male who stood with her. Both of them leaned casually against one of the thick columns that ran along the center of the massive station, just another two bored travelers waiting for a long-distance connection. Adding to that impression were the duffel bags at their feet, the battered fabric thrown into harsh relief by the bright afternoon sun pouring through the massive skylights.

"You're too good-looking for this," she said to Vaughn. It was happy chance that he'd already been at DarkRiver HQ when she'd requested an escort. "That woman almost missed her skytrain, she was so busy eating you up with her big, brown eyes." Sahara fluttered her lashes as the hapless brunette had done.

Vaughn shot her an unsmiling look, but she saw the amusement that prowled behind it. "Get to work, Ms. Kyriakus."

"I need a little time to get my zen on, as Mercy would say." She nudged his arm with her shoulder, comfortable with him in a way she was with very few men aside from Kaleb. "Was it Faith? The unnamed NightStar foreseer who saw Luxembourg and Paris?"

A small nod, Vaughn's lazily feline posture attracting another admiring glance to which he seemed oblivious, though she knew those eyes of jaguar-gold missed nothing. As Kaleb would probably snap the neck of any other woman who tried to touch him without invitation, she knew Vaughn would respond with claws and teeth. Skin privileges, she thought, were not to be assumed lightly with men of this caliber.

"Better for NightStar to handle the press and imply the F was one under their command," Vaughn added, "than to draw further specific attention to Faith." Reaching out, he tugged the front of her ball cap a little further down.

He'd given her the cap when he met her and Kaleb in the deserted service corridor Kaleb had used as a teleport lock. According to him, the cap, branded with the logo of the champion local baseball team, would make her far less apt to attract attention, even if she spent hours in the station. Since she'd already seen a number of other people with the same cap, she couldn't argue.

"How's Leon?"

"Good. Really good." Sahara spoke to her father every day and had already planned a visit in the coming days, no matter what. But first, she had to do what she could to help stop another wave of violence. "Okay"— a deep breath—"I'm ready."

It was the first time she'd attempted anything of this magnitude, and from what she'd heard of telepaths who had allowed their shields to drop in similar situations, she had to brace herself for a crushing blast of noise as a thousand different minds crashed into her own. Ninety-nine percent of individuals, Psy, human, or changeling, had a "public" mind, an upper level of inconsequential thought that was rarely shielded; that would be bad enough, but Sahara intended to scan the next layer down.

Here I go, she said to the Tk who was her own.

I won't let you drown.

Holding on to that promise, she opened her senses the smallest fraction, ready to shut everything down the instant she hit overload. Except—

Oh!

It wasn't the same as with the telepaths. Her ability was unique, her mind created to filter data from other minds in a streamlined fashion. The thoughts of passersby were clearly delineated, her mind visualizing each individual as a separate, understandable strand . . . shimmering silver for Psy, a haunting, luminous blue for humans, and a stunning wild green for changelings.

It was a multihued sea as extraordinarily beautiful as the PsyNet.

Not feeling the least stretched, she expanded her senses bit by bit and had to bite the inside of her cheek to stifle her excitement. Her reach wasn't only two to three inches around her body. It was far, *far* wider. At fifty percent strength, she could understand the thoughts of every individual passing within the walls of the station . . . including those of the change-ling next to her, and changeling shields were meant to be impenetrable.

What she caught made her want to grin—Vaughn was humming a nonsense tune clearly meant to obfuscate his thoughts. It worked, and it told her Faith had her suspicions about Sahara's abilities. That didn't worry her. Her cousin would never betray her. Now, after consciously blocking Vaughn's mind, she began to scan and discard thoughts at a speed that turned the strands into a silver-blue jetstream vibrant with sparks of wild green.

KALEB didn't teleport inside DarkRiver's HQ after leaving Sahara and Vaughn at the station. He walked through the door in a gesture of good-will that had him receiving a curt nod of welcome from the leopard alpha. The green-eyed male was around Kaleb's height, with the sleek, muscular build so common in the feline changelings.

"Krychek. You've beaten Anthony here."

The head of NightStar walked in two minutes later and Lucas ges-tured for them to follow him into a large meeting room dominated by an oval-shaped table that currently held seven people. Kaleb caught Judd's eye, noting the other man sat beside the wolf alpha, Hawke. Next to Hawke was a male Kaleb ID'ed as Nathan Ryder, DarkRiver's most senior lieutenant.

Nikita was on the other side of the table, next to Max Shannon, her security chief. According to Kaleb's informants, Max's wife, Sophia, an ex-J with a huge network of contacts, had also quietly become one of Nikita's most trusted advisers. Her reliance on the couple was a fact many in Nikita's organization struggled to understand, since Max and Sophia were apparently as often in conflict with Nikita as they were in agreement.

Kaleb understood. He didn't employ the weak, either.

Now Max Shannon caught his gaze and nodded in a silent thank-you.

Kaleb thought to tell the other man theirs was a debt he might one day collect, but didn't for the same reason he'd helped save Sophia's life from a madman over half a year ago. He hadn't been able to help the one woman who was everything to him, his mind a place of angry darkness, but in saving Sophia, he had gained, if not redemption, then an instant of grace in the darkness.

Sahara, he'd thought, would've been proud of him for his actions that day.

Accepting the thanks with the slightest incline of his head, he turned his attention to Teijan, alpha of the Rats and head of the best spy organization in the region. Opposite the sharply dressed alpha was a man Kaleb couldn't immediately identify, until he realized the copper-skinned male had cut off his formerly long hair: Adam Garrett of the Wind-Haven falcons.

"Your assistance," he said to the falcon as he took a seat, "may be invaluable in pinpointing possible targets." A falcon could fly lower than any aircraft, follow suspicious movements at the turn of a wing.

"My people are already doing sweeps," Adam replied, "working in partnership with teams on the ground. Nothing as yet."

The Enforcement vice commissioner for the city entered the room right then and took a seat. The middle-aged Psy woman, her skin an unusual papery white, was followed by an elderly human male of Asian descent identified as Jim Wong, representative of the shopkeepers in the warren of Chinatown, their reach extending citywide through a network of family, friends, and customers. At his heels came a tall black male the DarkRiver alpha introduced as the liaison from the Human Alliance.

The silence was taut, as people who would never normally term one another allies found themselves facing each other across the glossy wood of the table. It was, Kaleb mused, a sight that would inflame Pure Psy.

"Everyone's here," Lucas Hunter said after shutting the door, the savage markings on his face echoed by the look in his eyes. "Let's get straight to it—we need to narrow down the list of possible targets."

"The offices of the mayor," the vice commissioner suggested.

Kaleb shook his head. "It doesn't have as much shock value as a school, a nursery, or a hospital." Pure Psy wanted to cause pain and loss and anger that would turn humans and changelings against the Psy. "Vasquez intends to cause a war that'll leave only the 'pure' standing."

It was Hawke who next spoke, his ice blue eyes and silver-gold hair those of the predator within—a predator who now had Ming in his sights. "I have to agree with Krychek," the wolf alpha said. "But we've already put all obviously vulnerable institutions on high alert, beefed up security, and Vasquez had to have realized that would happen. I think he'll go for a softer target."

"Hawke's right." The Rat alpha leaned forward on the table, his dark eyes quick and watchful. "We've picked up *nothing* that even hints Pure Psy's managed to infiltrate San Francisco like they did Hong Kong—I have enough faith in my people to state categorically that Vasquez is working without a foundation. Whatever he's planning, it's going to be quick and dirty."

"The scorch charges used in Hong Kong," Judd said, evidencing his connections. "Even a limited number could do serious damage to the city."

"They're too unstable to transport without proper containers: specifically, lead-lined boxes." Kaleb knew that because he'd made it a point to access the hidden files on the charges. "All sightings of the operative we believe to be Vasquez state he's moving with nothing but a small backpack. He could, however, have access to other weaponry if he was smart enough to hide a small cache in the city at some stage in the past—in a public locker hired under another name, for example." Nothing that would set off alarm bells, even with the packs' tight security.

"So"—Lucas Hunter's voice was grim as he spoke—"soft target, high possibility of casualties, intense political fallout, those are the parameters."

"Airports and skytrain stations fit," Nikita said, "and have been alerted by my security team"—a nod of confirmation from Max—"but they're more difficult to monitor, given the constant foot traffic."

Kaleb. Sahara's telepathic voice vibrated with anger and fear com-

bined. *Something is about to happen here. I just caught a thought about timing "the purification" for rush hour.*

  Have you identified the individual concerned?

  *No. It appears this level of perception does have a cost. I can understand the
thoughts of everyone in the station, but with my senses extended to cover such
a large area, I can't shift focus fast enough to zero in on a mind while a particular thought is in progress. However, whoever it was was thinking specifically about the layout of the station and how to achieve "maximum strategic
impact."*

Chapter 42

"THE CENTRAL SKYTRAIN station is a target," Kaleb said aloud, interrupting the conversation in progress. "Rush hour today."

Nikita turned cool eyes in his direction. "If we focus our resources on the wrong target or targets, we risk exposing other vulnerable locations."

"The information is highly reliable." He switched his attention to the leopard alpha. "Do you have enough people to quietly evacuate the schools and check the hospitals for threats? We can't risk tipping our hand."

"It's already being done. Anthony's and Nikita's teams are working with the packs and Mr. Wong's network." Lucas glanced down the table. "Vice Commissioner, is Enforcement sweeping the shopping malls and movie theaters?"

She checked the datapad in front of her. "No threats detected as yet. We cannot, however, clear these locations *and* assist with the central skytrain station."

"The Arrows and I can handle the station." Kaleb had already sent the order to Aden's rapid response team.

The changeling alphas looked to one another, an unspoken communication passing between them, before Lucas said, "Agreed, but we'll give you some of our trackers. If the attack is anything chemical based, they may be able to catch the scent."

Kaleb knew those trackers would also be keeping an eye on him and the Arrows, but that was to be expected. Acceding to the stipulation with a nod, he said, *We're on our way,* to the woman who stood in the center of what could become a death zone.

SAHARA spotted Kaleb entering the station, though he was wearing a baseball cap, sunglasses, and a UC Berkeley sweatshirt. *Nice outfit,* she teased, immediately blocking his mind from her continuing scans.

My face is well-known, but people will see what they expect to see.

And no one, she thought, expected to see Kaleb Krychek in a central city skytrain station, much less wearing an old sweatshirt and battered cap.

Listen for any hint of alarm, he told her. *The Arrows are better at blending in than you realize, but Vasquez is trained to spot covert operatives.*

I'll 'path the instant I sense anything. She could not fail in her task. If this building went down, not only would hundreds of innocent people die, *Kaleb* might die.

It was ten minutes later that she heard from him again. *The changelings aren't scenting any chemical explosives. The bombs may be small and well hidden, or we may be looking at something quieter; Pure Psy has been known to use poison gas.*

The connection between them open, she heard him give telepathic orders for all airflow conduits to be checked. *I'm taking the main fans,* he said to her. *They're outside, high on the building, but I have a line of sight.*

Sweat dampened her palms at the idea he might be teleporting into danger. *Be careful.*

Always.

She had to force herself to remain in the alcove where she'd been concealed for the past half hour. When she glanced over at the jaguar who'd kept her company throughout, it was to catch an impatient look on his face. "I'm sorry you have to babysit me. I know you'd rather be doing something else."

To her surprise, his lips curved. "I'm not impatient about watching you—I'm frustrated because I can't scent anything that might give us a clue."

It's the air. Kaleb's voice sliced into her mind. *A concentrated dose of poisonous gas attached to the conduit below one of the main fans and timed to go off at rush hour.*

Sahara's throat went dry, her mind seeing the busy station go silent as people fell where they stood. *Have you teleported it out?*

No. It's very cleverly rigged. There's a risk it'll disperse before transport is complete. I need a tech; the wolves have a skilled female who came in with their tracking team—she's at DarkRiver HQ helping coordinate information. Ask Vaughn to contact her.

The tech was on the roof with Kaleb soon afterward, 'ported there by a dark-haired telekinetic Sahara hadn't met, but guessed to be Judd Lauren from what Kaleb had told her of his friend's allegiance to the wolves. A minute later, Vaughn received a call and asked her to follow him to the nearest set of public restrooms.

"Anyone in the women's?" he asked.

Peeking in, she shook her head.

Vaughn entered and went through it stall by stall. "Women's West 2 cleared," he said into his cell phone just as an older woman with red cheeks pushed through the door.

"Excuse me." She sniffed. "I know you young people like your 'unusual environments,' but really." With that, she bustled into one of the stalls and slammed the metal door with a loud bang.

Sahara kept her mouth shut until Vaughn cleared the men's restroom and indicated they had to move on to the next set. "'Unusual environments'?" she murmured, doing her best to appear innocent. "Did she mean to imply something sexual? Where, other than the bedroom, do people exchange intimate skin privileges?"

"Talk to Faith."

"She's not here."

"You're just like an annoying little sister, you know that?" A sadness in his voice, in his eyes, that was old and worn. "Always asking questions."

Seeing the smile that balanced the sorrow, Sahara decided not to pull back. "So?"

The smile grew wider, deep grooves forming in his cheeks. "So, talk to Faith."

Having arrived at their destination, Sahara checked to make sure the coast was clear. Except this time, she pressed her hand against the door once inside to make sure they didn't inadvertently shock anyone else. "You're checking for small incendiary devices?"

A nod. "The Arrows found one at the other end of the station—cheap and easy to make, small range but big noise. Vasquez might have seeded the station with them to fool people into believing the entire place was mined to blow."

"To delay rescue efforts once people began to collapse from the gas." Intelligent in the most psychopathic of ways.

"Ye—" Vaughn's sudden silence told her he'd found something. "Stay behind the wall until I give the all clear."

Sahara didn't argue, well aware that, protective as he'd become of her, Vaughn wouldn't be able to focus if she flouted his command. Earlier, he'd thrust a chocolate bar into her hand with an order that she eat the whole thing. "Psychic muscles use energy," he'd said. "And don't even try to argue. Faith doesn't get away with that and neither will you."

Sahara had taken great pleasure in pointing out that he was acting exactly like Kaleb. His growl would've raised every hair on her body if she hadn't been grinning and eating chocolate at the time.

"Done," he said now, three minutes after he'd asked her to stay behind the wall. Placing the remnants of the device into his duffel bag, he rose. "Let's go."

They had just stepped outside when—

"—may have been compromised. Push go!"

Sahara was speaking to Kaleb even as the final word echoed in her mind. *They know! Kaleb!* So close to the poison, he'd never survive the exposure.

A minuscule pause that sent her heart into her throat before Kaleb said, *It's all right. We've defused the poison bomb. I'm in the process of tele-porting the container out now.*

There were three small booms on the heels of Kaleb's words, but though people hesitated, looking around for answers, no one panicked. Acting as planned in the event of a possible panic situation, the Arrows ducked their heads and merged into the flurry of people in the station, as changeling teams moved in to cordon off the damaged areas.

Since Vaughn was one of those changelings, she heard him feed the curious a story about teenagers playing with banned fireworks. The explanation wasn't wholly believed, but the travelers, regardless of race, relaxed as soon as they realized the changelings had the situation under control. It gave Sahara a glimpse of exactly how much San Francisco had become a changeling—specifically leopard—city.

In the end, that was the only damage done that day, but Vasquez, faceless and unidentifiable, remained in the wind. Accepting Kaleb's offer of a teleport, the changeling trackers used the faint scent found at the fan to begin their hunt, each changeling accompanied by an Arrow who could scan for and block possible psychic attacks.

Not strong or fast enough to keep up, Sahara decided to stay at the station. "In case Vasquez or his men decide to circle back," she said to Kaleb.

He nodded, his eyes connecting with Vaughn's. "Take care of her."

The jaguar male's responding nod was quiet, the grim look he laid on Sahara after Kaleb left not the least unexpected. "He's not the kind of man you want to be involved with."

Sahara made a face at him. "That would be my business."

"Sorry, doesn't work like that." Folding his arms, he leaned back against the wall, eyes fully jaguar. "You're family now, little sister."

"And look how safe you are," she said, hands on her hips. "I'm sorry, anyone who turns into a predatory cat with big teeth and claws can't exactly throw stones."

Vaughn narrowed his eyes at her. "I will hurt him if he puts a single bruise on you."

"You won't have to," Sahara said softly. "He'd end himself before causing me harm." As he'd once almost done . . . her beautiful Kaleb who had bled so much she'd thought he'd do permanent damage to his brain.

"No! Don't! Kaleb, stop!"

• • •

IT was a long day that merged into an even longer night. Kaleb stayed with the changeling trackers . . . and Sahara stayed with him. She'd left the station when it became night-quiet and gone to DarkRiver's HQ, but remained connected to Kaleb on the telepathic plane. It was a quiet reminder that he mattered, that someone would miss him if he was gone.

Ahead of him, one of the trackers—a wolf named Drew—held up a hand. Kaleb scanned the area and pinpointed a number of Psy minds in the vicinity, but there was nothing to tell him if one belonged to the individual who'd left the scent, whether it had been Vasquez or one of his skeleton team. Then a gunshot rang out from the four-level garage to the left and he had a far smaller area to scan.

Unable to teleport to the location without a clear visual, he ran to a vehicle in front of the structure, then reached for both Judd and Aden with his mind. *I need cover.*

Go. Laser fire erupted from all sides, interspersed with the harder sounds of gunfire.

I can bring in more people, he said to Judd once his back hit the inside wall of the garage. *No hostiles on this level.*

We'll stay out here, draw his attention. Looks like a single shooter.

Kaleb was already moving, taking extra care to ensure his footfalls didn't echo. He was almost to the fourth level when the world went silent. *Judd, update.*

He stopped without warning. May have realized you're there.

Kaleb increased his speed, aware Vasquez—if it was the leader of Pure Psy, and not one of his subordinates—had the skill to rappel down the side of the structure and once again elude capture. The bullet came out of nowhere, glancing off his upper arm. Gritting his teeth against the bruising pain, he rolled behind the protective bulk of a gleaming black all-wheel drive.

Kaleb!

He didn't know how Sahara had sensed the blow. *Bulletproof fabric did its job. I'm fine.* His arm remained functional.

Risking a look around the corner, he twisted back as another bullet snapped past his head, but the quick glimpse combined with the trajectory of the bullet gave him what he needed to zero in on the location of the shooter. He rose to his haunches as the all-wheel drive took multiple shots from both a projectile weapon and a laser, safety glass cascading around him. Shaking it off, he spread his hands, palms out, and *shoved* every single car on this level of the garage forward in a lethal wave that left the shooter with nowhere to go.

The guns went wild as the shooter tried to take Kaleb down and cut off the flow of his telekinetic power. Kaleb easily avoided the bullets . . . until one ricocheted off a metal sign on the wall to punch into his thigh with an impact that told him it had been designed to penetrate bullet-proof fabric. It did. The violent pain might have interrupted the concentration of another Tk, but Kaleb had learned to work through worse as a boy.

Gritting his teeth, he slammed the cars into the back wall, the metal scraping along the sides of the parking garage to leave deep gouges. Then came silence. Total and possibly dangerous. Sweeping out with his telepathic senses, he found a living Psy mind, but it was flickering, for lack of a better word, critically injured. He had to shift three crushed cars to get to the shooter, who lay crumpled between the wall and the twisted hulks of metal, his guns crushed, his lower body sticky and red, bones in splinters.

The only way Kaleb could know if this physically unremarkable male was Vasquez would be to tear into his mind. But even with the blood pooling around his lower body, thick and dark, the man had a look in his eyes that told Kaleb his mind was apt to be rigged to collapse if breached.

Removing the man's knife and anything else he could use to speed up his own death, Kaleb 'ported to Sahara, after sending her a warning message, tugged the hood of her sweatshirt up over her head to shadow her face, and 'ported back with her.

Sounds had begun to echo through the garage by the time they arrived, the rest of the team doing a level-by-level sweep to make sure there was no one else hiding in the structure.

"No questions?" the critically injured male rasped on their return, blood bubbling out of the corners of his mouth.

Kaleb's leg was bleeding badly now, the viscous liquid having soaked into the tough fabric of his pants and trickled into his boot, but he would finish this. "You're unlikely to answer them."

The man's lashes came down, settled, then lifted to show he was still alive and conscious. "So you'll stand there and watch me die, not even attempt a retraction?" Contempt in those words.

It is Andrea Vasquez, Sahara said along their familiar telepathic pathway. *But this was not his final strike. That is what he calls the Phoenix Code: he's split Pure Psy into multiple cells, each with the goal of collapsing as much of the PsyNet as possible, until only the "pure" remain—his belief system, as well as those of his followers, has altered until they now truly think that those who are "pure" are stronger. Anyone who dies was therefore not pure.*

The tautology of that belief did more to disprove Pure Psy's "rational" rhetoric than any reasoned argument.

Geneva, Sahara continued, *Luxembourg, Paris, San Francisco, they were all intended to give his people time to scatter and hide deep, only to arise anew once the dust has settled. While their goal to rid the Net of the impure is paramount, their secondary aim is to instigate a worldwide war that will eliminate the weak and the "inferior."*

His legacy, as he thinks of it, is an organization with so many heads that it will be impossible to decapitate: a true hydra.

Chapter 43

VASQUEZ'S PLAN WAS all the more terrible for its simplicity. It was too bad for the leader of Pure Psy that, at last count, the Arrows had taken down seventy-five percent of his lieutenants and were now moving on to the next layer. Even a multiheaded hydra needed some type of a command structure, and Kaleb had no intention of permitting the remaining lieutenants to set up any kind of a power base.

As for the weaker members—they might be troublesome, but only to the extent an insect is to a dragon. Eventually, they'd all be crushed.

"You would sentence your race to annihilation," he said to Vasquez, and it wasn't a judgment. How could it be when he had once considered destroying the PsyNet? No, it was a question, one Vasquez understood.

"We will rise as the phoenix from the ashes. Better, stronger, purer." His eyes met Kaleb's, the sclera red with burst blood cells. "You understand."

"Yes." And because he did, because he saw in Vasquez who he might've been but for Sahara, he crouched down to grip the other man's hand so he did not have to go into death as alone as he'd been in life. Neither did he tell Vasquez that the plan he'd sacrificed himself to put in place would never come to fruition.

It was the only peace he could offer.

The leader of Pure Psy coughed up bloody froth, his voice a raw whisper as his blood-slick fingers tightened on Kaleb's. "The Psy have always been meant to rule. When it is over, we will be the only power that remains." A final rattling gasp, his eyes fading to stare out into the nothingness of death.

Andrea Vasquez was dead and with him, his dream of a world enslaved by the Psy.

Closing the man's eyelids, Kaleb rose to pull Sahara close. "We may have won this battle, but now comes a far harder one—to rebuild a society that is so fundamentally broken it has begun to cannibalize itself."

"Which you need to be alive to do," came the furious response. "The bulletproof fabric *did its job*?" She was staring at his thigh as she repeated his earlier assurance.

Only to Sahara would he explain himself. "That was a later shot."

Ignoring him, she twisted around as the first of the wider team cleared the level. "Judd can—"

"No." He teleported them directly to a private medical facility staffed by those who would not dare betray Kaleb, not only because he paid them very well, but because the agonizing punishment involved should they speak his secrets would in no way be worth it.

Pushing back her hood, Sahara began issuing orders to the medics. *Stay still*, was her snapped telepathic command to him when the head M-Psy reached for a scanner.

Kaleb obeyed.

"Projectile weapon. Bullet hasn't exited." The M-Psy put the scanner aside to pick up a surgical tool. "Sir, you may wish to deaden your pain centers."

Kaleb had done that when he was shot. "Go."

The M-Psy began to work with an efficiency that was a silent testament as to why she was in Kaleb's employ. Reaching out, Sahara went as if to brush Kaleb's hair off his forehead, then dropped her hand after a quick look at the medic. *Sorry.*

It's all right. There is no risk here.

Be quiet. Folding her arms, she stood stiff and silent and watchful as the medic put the retrieved bullet in a tray and used another piece of equipment to speed up the healing process.

"This procedure is complete, sir," the M-Psy said some time later. "You may have slight tenderness in the area, but it shouldn't last more than a day or so." She looked up after putting down the tool she'd been using. "Are you wounded anywhere else?"

"Scan my upper left arm." It was possible the impact of the glancing bullet had caused injuries of which he was unaware.

"No tearing or fractures," the M-Psy said after the scan was complete, "but significant bruising. I can work on it—"

"No, that's fine." Kaleb barely felt the injury and he wanted to be alone with Sahara.

"Yes, sir." Removing her gloves to leave them on the tray, the medic left without further words.

Noting from Sahara's unchanged stance that she was in no mood to talk, he teleported them directly into what had become their bedroom at the Moscow house. He'd already discarded his torn and dirty sweatshirt into the same medical incinerator he'd sent the bloodied equipment the medic had used, and now ripped off his long-sleeved bulletproof top in preparation for a shower, after kicking off his boots and socks.

Not saying a word, Sahara picked up his arm to examine the place where the first bullet had grazed him. His skin was beginning to turn the mottled shade that denoted it would be a heavy bruise, but was otherwise undamaged. She didn't say anything. Instead, she reached down to pull aside the fabric of his cargo pants where the medic had sliced it to work on the wound.

Delicate as air, her fingers danced over the spot. "Does it hurt?"

A strange sensation whispered through his veins now that she'd spoken to him again. "No. It wasn't a bad wound."

The look she gave him was murderous . . . but he saw her lower lip tremble.

At last he understood, realized he'd made her afraid. "I'm sorry."

Swallowing, she rose on tiptoe to wrap her arms around his neck. He bent to make it easier for her to hold him, entrapping her in his arms. "I'm sorry," he said again, remembering what it had done to him to lose her, and seeing in her response the same bone-numbing terror.

"If the bullet had hit your femoral artery, you'd be dead." Trembling voice, tears wet against his skin. "A quarter of an inch to the—"

"No," he said, needing to make this right. "I would've teleported immediately to the medics in that case." Changing his hold, he carried her to the bed and sat down with her in his lap, uncaring of the dried blood on his pants.

Tightening her hold, she buried her face against him. He didn't know what else to do, how to comfort her, so he simply held her, held the only person in the world who had ever cried for him.

The first time had been six months after their first meeting, when she'd noticed the blue-black bruises on one of his arms after he'd forgotten about them and pushed up the sleeves of his sweatshirt. Having no idea what to do, he'd warned her she'd be in trouble if she was caught crying, but no matter what he said, she kept crying silent tears and patting at his arm.

"I can't fix you. I'm sorry. I can't."

She was patting him like that again, her hand gently caressing the hurt spot on his upper arm. So he said the same thing that had finally stopped her tears that day. "Please stop crying. If you do, I'll make you fly."

"I'll make you fly."

Memory powered through Sahara in a single slamming punch, and all at once, she was sitting on the edge of a small, hidden pond in the farthest corner of the NightStar grounds, colorful koi moving lazily beneath the clear surface and the taste of salt on her lips.

"What?" she whispered to the boy who sat a foot in front of her, his arm telling her a story his voice never would.

"See." He held up the beautiful blue pebble she had given him after finding it in the small box of stones her father had given her as an educational tool. He'd told her to look up the properties of the stones, but Sahara had also read about the nonscientific meanings. Lapis lazuli, the text she'd accessed had said, was a stone meant to represent friendship.

Now the blue stone rose high into the air. *"Like that."*

Smiling, Sahara caught the stone, wiping the backs of her hands over her cheeks, and memory segued into reality.

Drawing back to look into eyes gone ebony, she cupped his face. "That was a fun day, wasn't it?" He *had* made her fly, after they stole away into a secluded section where no one would see them.

"You wanted to sit on the highest branch of the biggest pine in the woods."

Sahara laughed through the remnants of her tears. "You let me." Delighted, she'd sat up there without a care in the world, legs hanging off the sides as she waved to Kaleb. "I think you were terrified I would fall off."

"I may have been . . . uncertain of your balance."

Sahara's laughter faded as other memories came into clear focus, other times he'd been hurt and tried to hide it from her. "How," she whispered, "did you manage to contain all that power as a boy without the pain controls? Why was the monster never afraid you'd strike out at him?"

Kaleb went motionless, and she wanted to call back her words, stifle them as she'd done before, but some secrets were poisonous, and it was time they faced the bloody night that had scarred them both. And that night began in a childhood that had been a nightmare of pain and loneliness and horror.

"Together," she whispered, telling him he wasn't alone in the darkness, would never be alone. "Now and forever."

Eyes of impenetrable black in that beautiful face, but his arm slipped around her waist, his palm warm on her lower back even through the sweatshirt. "Santano placed the telepathic equivalent of a choking leash in my mind," he said at last. "As a cardinal himself, he could constrict that leash at any time to cut off my power."

Sahara kept a vicious grip on her anger. "You broke it as an adult?"

"It was more a case of the leash disintegrating under the force of my strength as my abilities matured . . . but not fast enough." His hand fisted on her back. "And even when I thought I was free, I wasn't; he could always make me watch."

Sahara could erase those memories, heal his pain that much at least, but in so doing, she'd forever taint the indefinable trust between them. "He tried to break you," she said, fierce in her pride, "but you didn't only survive, you thrived to become a power unlike any the world has ever seen."

Kissed by the passionate fury of this woman who loved him enough to fight his demons, Kaleb knew he had to finish this, had to tell her everything. "Don't you wonder how he found out about you? When we were so careful?" When Kaleb had been dead certain he'd built a secret compartment in his mind that Santano couldn't reach.

Sahara didn't flinch, didn't turn away. "A child has no shields and he was a cardinal," she said, the deep blue of her eyes an endless midnight. "There is no blame."

"You don't understand."

"What?" Hand over his heart, she said, "That he did to me what he did to so many changeling women?"

He froze, every cell as hard as ice. "Yes." With that brutal confirmation, he put her gently aside, rose, and shoved open the doors that led to the terrace.

Outside, the sky was black with rain heavy clouds, the air gray, the chill wind slapping against his bare upper half. Walking to the broken metal railings, he began to rip them out with methodical precision, piling the remnants in one corner of the terrace. He was aware of Sahara standing in the doorway, eyes on him, but she didn't say anything until he'd finished demolishing the fence he'd put in place.

Stepping to the very edge of the terrace, he stared out into the darkness. "It turned out Santano knew about you for years," he said, the padding of her feet on the wood as she crossed to him hammer blows against his ribs, "but he didn't interfere. He later told me you kept me stable, so you were useful." *Useful.* The most beautiful thing in his life had been useful to Councilor Santano Enrique. "Because of me, he knew you existed."

Sahara's hand on his back. "You warned me to be careful," she said with a confidence that told him the memory was crisp, clear. "You said I should never, ever be alone with that monster. Kaleb, you were bleeding so badly that day, I was afraid you'd cause serious damage to your brain—you *fought* the compulsions so hard for me."

Kaleb watched rocks tumbling down into the gorge and knew he was the cause, his rage seeking an outlet. "It wasn't enough. Not when he dug deeper into my mind and realized your true ability—and how quickly you were learning to discipline it. It wasn't simply that you might be capable of seeing all his secrets one day soon, but that you had the contacts to be heard."

Kaleb had begged Enrique not to touch her, the only time in his life he had ever begged. He'd been willing to give up the final ragged shreds of his soul if that was what it took, but Enrique had other plans. "He told me it was time he reminded me that he *owned* me."

Sahara wrapped her arms around him from behind. "He wanted you to hurt me."

Chapter 44

KALEB CONTINUED TO stare out into the darkness, every muscle in his body locked tight, until he was made of stone. "You've remembered everything about that night."

"Almost," she said, pressing a kiss to his back. "It's been coming to me in pieces over the past twenty-four hours. I have most of it now."

"Why aren't you afraid of me if you remember? Why are you still here?"

"Because you're mine."

The stone fractured, his hands rising to close over her own. "He knew if I hurt you, it would break the defiance that kept me Kaleb rather than his creature."

"*Cut her.*" *The knife being pushed into his hand.* "*You're like me, have always been like me. Do what comes naturally.*"

Sahara twisted around to face him, careless of her safety. When he pulled her from the edge with a sharp rebuke, she smiled and said, "I knew you wouldn't let me fall." Reaching for his left arm as her trust smashed the stone to pieces, she traced the mark on the inside of his forearm. "It's almost like a brand," she murmured. "Or a burn that was never treated, and the design, it's familiar."

"It's the insignia from the old-fashioned wall radiator in the hotel room Santano chose for that night." He dared touch his free hand to her hair, felt the ice inside him melt when she turned her face into the caress, her lips pressing a sweet kiss to the center of his palm. "The room was cheap and isolated and hundreds of miles from your home. It was also covered in DNA by the time he finished. That's why he set it on fire after wiping the entire place down with bleach."

Meticulous, the other Tk had been the worst combination of intelligence and deadly pathology. The fire that night might've been overlooked as vandalism . . . except after Santano teleported Sahara away to a secret location while choking off Kaleb's ability to go to her, the leash yet holding, he'd teleported in the body of a changeling girl he'd killed three weeks earlier and kept on ice.

"It amuses me to watch the rats chasing their tail," he'd said with the arrogance of a man who had been getting away with murder for years, his victims scattered across every corner of the world. *"Let's throw them this bone and see what they do with it."*

The fire damage to the girl's body had ruled out DNA identification—Enforcement had finally identified her using dental records, thanks to the dedication of the detective in charge. That detective had also connected the murder to those of two of Santano's other victims through the marks left on the bone by the knife Santano had used that year, and because at the time, the monster had been "experimenting" with decapitation.

While the fact that it was Santano Enrique who'd been behind those three murders wasn't public knowledge, enough people suspected his involvement in the still-unsolved crimes that there was a possibility someone, someday, would make the connection between the scar on Kaleb's arm and that burned-out hotel room. The heavy iron radiator, after all, had been one of the few pieces that survived without any major damage. Its distinctiveness may have been the reason journalists repeatedly used the image when talking of the crimes, the shot having leaked from Enforcement files.

It was why Kaleb never bared his forearm in public.

He had no concern with being branded as apprentice to a serial killer. When he'd first joined the Council, it would have been problematic in light of Santano's recent execution, could've led to a challenge from the others. He'd needed to be on the Council then. That no longer applied; nobody could touch him. Now he cared only about what public exposure would do to Sahara. No one had any right, even unknowingly, to push that nightmare in her face.

"I'll get it removed tomorrow," he said, and knew it was time to admit his failure. "I couldn't do it until I found you, until I protected you as I didn't then." She'd been hurt right in front of him, over and *over* again.

"Enrique did something to the radiator," Sahara murmured, her fingers gentle on the raised edges of the burn. "With his kinetic energy. It glowed red-hot—" Her head jerked up. "He held your arm against that insignia so long that your arm stopped working, the burn was so deep."

"It didn't hurt." Dulling his pain receptors, he hadn't made a sound, not willing to give Santano the satisfaction. "Nothing hurt except being forced to watch him cut you and not able to move so much as a muscle." Santano had made him helpless to come to the aid of the one person who was his everything, the one person who had never once let him down, the one person who thought there was something good in him.

That *had* broken him . . . then it had made him a nightmare.

It wasn't the result Santano had intended.

"Kaleb." Sahara kissed the mark on his forearm, her lips butterfly soft. "You know what I see when I see this? I see a man who fought so hard for me that he scared a monster. You know I was meant to die that night."

Sahara could hear Enrique's voice whispering in her ear, ugly and excited as he told her of his plans to have Kaleb take her life. Except Kaleb had refused to buckle under the compulsions Enrique had planted in him. "You hit him with a telekinetic blow, hard enough to crash him into the wall."

"No," Kaleb said flatly. "I didn't do anything to stop him." His hand shook where it touched her hair. "I hurt you—I can still hear you screaming at me to stop."

"You hurt *Enrique*, not me!" Sahara grabbed at his upper arms, unable to bear that he'd believed such a soul-destroying lie for seven long years. "You came close to killing him."

Seeing total incomprehension in the eyes of endless black that had lost their beautiful obsidian sheen, she cupped his face and sent him the

images—nuanced, *real*—from her memory. Having been locked inside
the vault within the vault where she'd hidden her sense of self in an effort
to protect it from the ravages of the labyrinth, the memory was pristine,
every detail of that nightmare room picked out in intricate detail.

*SAHARA tried not to scream as Santano Enrique dug his blade into the upper
curve of her breast, knowing her pain was savaging Kaleb. The monster had
pinned him against the wall using invisible telekinetic manacles, forced his
head toward the bed so he couldn't miss seeing Enrique torture her.*

*Kaleb could've closed his eyes, shut out the horror, but he didn't. She'd
known he wouldn't, even when she silently implored him to look away. Her
Kaleb would never leave her alone with a monster.*

*The scream broke out of her in spite of her every attempt to contain it, her
body unable to fight the pain after so many cuts that her skin was a slick of red
in the light of the two bedside lamps that spotlighted Enrique's evil. He waited
for the scream to fade before continuing to cut. "Do you know why I chose this
place? Cheap as it is, the rooms are all soundproofed—and even if they weren't,
there are no other guests at this time of year."*

*Sahara had worked that out long before. "Please stop," she rasped out, her
throat raw.*

*Enrique dug his blade in deeper. He thought she was begging for surcease.
She wasn't. Her words were for Kaleb, her beautiful, strong Kaleb who held
her gaze with a violent silence that was a black rage, his own eyes bleeding as
he fought to break the compulsion that leashed his powers, fought to come to her.*

*She knew he was putting deadly pressure on his brain, but he wouldn't
listen to her—and she couldn't reach him with her mind, Enrique having done
something to both of them to block their telepathy. He just continued to fight
with a brutal intensity, his face a mask of blood.*

*"Stop," she whispered again, trying in vain to reach for him with hands
Enrique had bound with Tk. "Don't." She couldn't bear to see him hurting
himself, couldn't bear to think he might do fatal damage. How could she exist
in a world without Kaleb?*

"Begging will do you no good," the monster said. Playing his hand desulto-

rily over her brutalized flesh, his fingers smearing wet blood over dried, Enrique leaned in close. To her, his breath was fetid, repulsive as his mind, as he whispered, "You mark his final rite of passage. It will be the sweetest kill of his life, a high he'll forever attempt to re-create."

Pain wracked Sahara, her heart breaking for the boy become a man who had done everything in his power to keep her safe since the day they'd met. "It's all right," she whispered so low that Enrique didn't hear as he got off the bed and moved to Kaleb.

But Kaleb heard, he understood, his eyes black pools of nothingness, hard and dead, and of rage.

"It's all right, Kaleb," she repeated again, but those stone-hard eyes repudiated her words, the blood beginning to drip from his ears as his brain was crushed between the twin forces of his incredible will and Enrique's malevolence.

"Cut her," Enrique ordered, thrusting the bloody knife into Kaleb's hand and forcing his fingers to close over the instrument of so much pain. "You're like me, have always been like me." A sly look over his shoulder at Sahara before he turned back to Kaleb. "Do what comes naturally."

Kaleb's fingers flexed in a jagged spasm, the blade falling to the carpet with a dull thud.

The change in Enrique's face occurred within a split second, the slyness replaced by something Sahara knew was pure evil. It lived within the monster always, was hidden by the facade of faultless Silence. There was no facade now, no barrier between Kaleb and the ugliness that was Santano Enrique as the monster said, "You think you can defy me?"

Sahara cried out as Kaleb was slammed down to his knees so hard the bed vibrated from the impact. An instant later, his shirt-clad arm was pressed to the old-fashioned radiator on the wall next to him. At first, she didn't understand what it was she was seeing. . . . then the radiator glowed red-hot.

"No! Don't!" she tried to scream as the metal melted through his shirt and into his flesh . . . and blood began to drip from his nose. "Kaleb, stop!" He was killing himself in front of her. "Please, Kaleb. Please!"

Her voice was all but gone, but his eyes locked with her own, his head moving in the slightest negative shake. She didn't need telepathy to understand him, understand what he was asking her to do. Of everything that had happened that night, this was the hardest, but she swallowed the tears that burned her eyes until they became a painful knot inside her chest, and she stopped talking.

If Kaleb could be silent as the scent of burned flesh filled the air, and his blood dripped onto the white of his shirt, then she could keep her tears from falling. Santano Enrique might have drawn their blood, might even take their lives, but the monster would get no more of their pain. It battered and bruised her heart when Enrique kicked Kaleb in the chest with a booted foot, hard enough that something cracked and Kaleb coughed blood, but she kept her face turned toward Kaleb so he wouldn't be alone, and she didn't cry, even as her vision began to waver from blood loss.

That was when Enrique glanced back at her . . . and the radiator stopped glowing, Kaleb's arm hanging limply at his side. "Since you've rejected my offer," the monster said, "I'll have the pleasure of ending your Sahara's life— and the time, it appears, must be now. She's growing weaker and it would be such a waste if she didn't feel her death." He picked up the knife. "A pity our little party could not continue for longer."

"Stop," Kaleb said, coughing up more blood to draw in a hard-won breath. "I'll give you anything you want if you set her free. Complete obedience, no defiance."

He was bargaining his soul for her life. Sahara wanted to tell him no, that she would never accept that bargain, but she was having trouble forming words.

"Everything?" Santano asked. "Would you crawl? Become my compliant pet?"

Kaleb answered without hesitation. "Yes."

The monster's laugh was a harsh sound that scratched her mind. "How touching." Wrenching back Kaleb's head with a telekinetic hand, he said, "But this time, I'll decline. I told you—it's time you remembered that I own you." Shifting on his heel, Enrique faced the bed. "I'll cut her up piece by piece while you watch." A look back at Kaleb. "It'll be much more satisfying to break you to the choke than to have you submit."

So weak now that the world threatened to fade in front of her eyes, Sahara bit down on her tongue to keep herself from unconsciousness. That might equal an easier death, but she would not leave Kaleb like this, would fight to the last beat of her heart, the last gasp of air in her lungs.

Eyes stinging from the pain of the self-inflicted hurt, she brought the world back into sharp focus to see Kaleb staring at Enrique as the other Tk walked to the bed. The tendons in Kaleb's neck stood out in stark relief, the bones in his face pushing white against skin, the bloody tears that dropped from the corners of his eyes thicker now, more viscous as he breathed in shallow gasps through broken ribs.

Reaching her, Enrique got onto the bed, careful not to touch her skin. "I think," he murmured, "I'll cut off your lips fir—"

The older cardinal was suddenly thrown across the room to smash up against the door. A bone snapped with an audible crack, and she thought it might've been his ulna coming into contact with the doorknob. As he struggled up, he was slammed back again, his head thudding against the wood, the sound hard and wet at the same time.

Her telekinetic bindings came free.

So weak she couldn't feel her legs, she tried to crawl off the bed, the bracelet Kaleb had given her coated in shades of bloody rust where it lay warm against her skin. If she could touch any part of the monster's body with her own . . .

But Enrique, his shoulder hanging in a way that told her it had been dislocated or broken, shoved out his good hand and suddenly her body was being bent backward in half, her muscles and bones wrenched to the breaking point. Her knee popped, tendons tore, and darkness beckoned on the horizon, her scream a silent agony.

"Sahara!"

No, she wanted to say to Kaleb, don't let him distract you! But it was too late. Sucking in breaths of jagged glass as Enrique released her back onto the bed, she watched in horror as Kaleb was slammed up into the ceiling, then back down, both his legs shattering on impact and blood pouring out of his mouth. He convulsed for a hellish five seconds and when he stopped, she knew the monster had won the bloody psychic battle, caged her strong, smart, beautiful Kaleb again.

She tried to go to him, but only her fingers twitched, her heartbeat so sluggish, she knew she was dying.

"Don't!" Kaleb yelled, crawling to her in spite of his broken legs and shattered ribs, in spite of the fact that his eyes were a sea of red as he fought the evil thing the monster had done to his mind and his ability to come to her, his every movement a testament to his will. "Don't you give up!"

Her fingers inched toward his on a last, stubborn surge of strength. "I won't," she promised in silence as her vision began to fade. Anything else would hurt him and she would never hurt her Kaleb. "I won't." The very tips of his fingers brushed her own as he gripped the edge of the bed, his blood sliding against her own.

Then she was being lifted up and away from him with brute telekinetic strength, and the monster was saying, "I've changed my mind," through harsh, whistling breaths. "I think I'll make her into my pet in your stead."

"Sahara!" A rage of sound. "I'll come for you! Survive! Survive for me!"

They were the last words she heard before her mind went black.

Chapter 45

"DID YOU SEE?" she asked. "He was having trouble breathing, Kaleb. You broke something inside him and the only reason he was able to grab control was that you tried to protect me."

Kaleb didn't reject her memories, but said, "I can hear you scream, feel the knife against my palm, the blood smeared on my fingertips, see Santano picking you up and teleporting away. There's nothing in between."

"You told me he had back doors into your mind," Sahara said, fighting for him to believe the truth. "He was clearly able to do something to make you forget the most important part of that night."

Continuing to hold his face between her palms, she said, "You *scared* him." She vividly remembered the tone in Enrique's voice that night, the shock that anyone had the power to cause him harm. "That is the only reason he decided to let me live." With those words, she understood the terrible, painful truth. "He used me as an extra leash to make sure you stayed in line, didn't he? As long as you didn't fight the compulsion, as long as you remained his audience, he wouldn't arrange for my death."

When he didn't answer, she tried to shake him. "Talk to me!" But on this point, Kaleb wouldn't open his mouth. She didn't need him to. She knew. She *knew*. "You allowed that monster to rape your mind for years to protect me—even when you had to know it could all be for nothing, that I could already be dead." Dashing away tears with an impatient hand, she said, "How dare you say you didn't do anything! You did everything."

"It wasn't enough." Finally his eyes met hers again. "You were imprisoned and hurt until you had to entomb your mind to survive." Rage in his every breath, his hands fisting in her hair. "I want to mutilate and torture every person on the planet who in any way supported Santano or Tatiana, break them until they beg and crawl. Then I want to tell them it'll never end."

Sahara dug her fingers into his arms. "You do not do this," she said, and it was an order. "You *do not* let that monster destroy the life we are going to have together. You are mine, not his. You have *always* been mine."

The claiming was so absolute, it dared him to fight. Kaleb had no intention of doing so. Shuddering, he crushed her to him. "Yes," he said, battling the rage because if he gave in to it, he would lose Sahara. "I'm yours. I will always be yours."

Her lips on his jaw, on his cheek, her love fierce. "Remember that. Each action, every action you take, it has my name on it."

When her mouth touched his, he gripped her jaw to kiss her with a violence he might have worried would terrify her, except that her nails were digging into his nape as she fought to get even closer. Breaking the zip of her sweatshirt, he pushed it off, tearing at the T-shirt to bare her skin. Her bra met the same fate.

"Kaleb, Kaleb, Kaleb." It was a husky, addicting litany as she kissed him wherever she could reach, her breasts rubbing against his chest, uncaring of the sweat and the blood that marked his body. "I want you. I want you so much."

He tore the rest of her clothing to shreds using his telekinesis. His own didn't last much longer. Taking her to the polished wood of the terrace, he flipped them so he was the one on the bottom. She rose on him, a goddess anointed by the rain that had begun to fall in a hushed whisper, the hair that had cascaded over his hands when he pulled off the elastic band cool, sensual silk. Hands braced on his chest, the charms on her bracelet brushing his skin, she rose over him, her breasts slick with the rain that beaded on her nipples.

"I might," she whispered, "need a little help." A shy, sultry smile that invited him to play with her. "This may be one of the more advanced techniques."

Gripping his stone-hard flesh with one hand, he guided her onto him, the scalding heat of her making his back bow, the rain seeming to turn to steam when it hit his skin. Sahara made an intensely feminine sound of pleasure as she took him to the hilt, the curves of her body soft against him, her breathing choppy. When he stroked his hands up over her thighs to cup her buttocks, his fingers digging into silken wet flesh, she shivered and began to draw herself up.

Realizing her knees were pushing against the wood of the terrace, he gave her a telekinetic cushion, wanting her here, under the stormy sky. His lover didn't stop what she was doing, the sweet, tight slide of her body on his an agony to which he willingly surrendered . . . for two strokes. Gripping her waist, he held her down, grinding his body against her delicate flesh until she clenched convulsively around the part of him she held possessively inside, her pleasure molten honey.

"*Kaleb.*"

He flipped her onto her back on that breathless moan, making sure she never touched the wood. Her legs locked around his hips, her arms around his neck, her passion as wild as the rain that had turned hard, pounding against his back. Taking her mouth, tasting her with his tongue, he broke the kiss to thrust in and out of her in a driving rhythm, the water dripping off his lashes to hit her cheeks.

"Everything, Kaleb," she gasped, her nails the sweetest pain on his shoulders, "give me everything."

"You have it." All his secrets, anything she wanted. Even his scarred, maimed heart. "I love you."

Eyes of deep, deep blue locking with his, a single tear rolling down her face. "I know," Sahara said, her heart breaking that he'd said the words for her. Hurt and brutalized beyond belief, shown not even an ounce of love until they met, it wouldn't have surprised her if he'd believed himself incapable of the emotion.

She knew he was more than capable of it, felt it in his every breath, his every touch, his every promise. That he knew he had the capacity for it . . . it was everything. "Tell me again."

Both arms under her body, his hands curved over her shoulders as he held her in place for deep, hard thrusts that made her intimate muscles clench in sheer pleasure, he paused, his hair dark against his forehead, his eyes holding the colors of twilight, and his body a sculpture of male beauty. "I love you. I will always love you."

Lightning, jagged and dangerous and beautiful, flashed overhead as he began to move again, his mouth seeking hers to lock them together. Around them, the rain was a thundering cocoon, theirs a private world. Kiss after kiss, stroke after stroke, they couldn't get enough, would never get enough.

He was so strong and hot and out of control, one of his hands now at her throat in a caress that her body instantly associated with erotic possession. She felt the orgasm approaching, tried to fight it off because she wanted more of this, didn't want it to end, but it was too late, the pleasure tearing through them both in a wave of sensation as wild as the lightning that split the skies.

Only this time, it wasn't limited to their bodies. Their minds collided on the psychic plane, their thoughts crashing together in a splintering of astonishing color that made her cry tears that became rain as she saw all the pieces of him. "I love you, Kaleb."

KALEB'S hand was tangled up in the wet heaviness of Sahara's hair as she lay half on, half off his chest, their legs intertwined and every inch of skin slick with rain. Neither one of them wanted to go inside, in spite of the continuing downpour, but he'd put a heavy telekinetic shield over them to protect Sahara from what was in fact icy cold water.

Inside the shield, the temperature was considerably higher, Kaleb's ability to create and manipulate kinetic energy being used in a way most trainers would consider wasteful. It wasn't. Not if it kept Sahara warm.

"What was that?" she asked, chest rising and falling as her lungs struggled to drag in air. "At the end?"

"Our minds connected." It was an experience he'd never forget, Sahara's love and spirit an intensity of light deep inside him, a candle flame that lit up the void. Damaged and twisted and scarred beyond all hope of repair, the part of him that *was* the void touched the candle flame in wonder, astonished that it was for him.

For *him*. For Kaleb.

This was purity, this painfully beautiful thing Sahara felt for him, and it was a truth Pure Psy would never comprehend. But—"I'm sorry for what you must've seen."

"I saw wild, dangerous beauty. I saw devotion. I saw *you*." Lifting her head off his chest, she fisted one hand against her heart. "I can feel you deep inside, a midnight star so impossibly strong and loving and *mine*." Her voice trembled. "I'm so glad you're mine. I won't ever let you go."

This time, it was Kaleb who said, "I know," devastated at being so wanted. "You are just a little possessive."

Sahara laughed, her eyes wet as, inside him, the candle flame continued to burn, the light a warm, enduring gold. But there was more. On the psychic plane outside their minds, a fine thread of midnight, distinguishable from the black of the Net only by the glittering obsidian facets of it, had woven intimately with one of golden light, the tie going from his mind to Sahara's. "We've bonded." *Look.*

Sahara's eyes turned inward, her smile luminous. *"Kaleb."* Laughing in open delight, she pressed kisses along his jaw, halting only when the fingers of one of her hands brushed the scar on his forearm. "Are you determined to erase this?"

"I won't risk you." He telepathed her the reasons why as the rain turned slowly to a misty haze, the connection between their minds so clear it was beyond even his telepathic strength. "And whatever you see in it, I'll never see the same." For him, it would always be a reminder of the day he'd lost her.

"All right." Shimmering droplets on her eyelashes, stars caught in transition. "But will you replace it with something for me?"

"Anything." His body was hers.

Brushing her fingers over his lips, she said, "You gave me an eagle. I want to give you one, too." A tender kiss pressed to the scar. "I want us to fly together."

"You saw me, all of me," he said, dragging her up to his mouth. "You know I'm never going to be good." After seizing control of the Net, he'd do whatever it took to maintain it. No one and nothing was ever again going to imprison either one of them.

"A good man," she said, her lips against his, "wouldn't have survived what you did, wouldn't have been able to find me. To fight evil, you have to understand the dark. We both do."

"You'll have to be my conscience." He knew his flaws, and he knew the parts of him that were irrevocably broken. "Mine isn't going to grow back."

Pushing off wet strands of hair from his forehead, Sahara held his gaze. "Have I ever let anything slide? That won't change." A slow smile. "I intend to have a thousand fights with you."

He thought of a lifetime of having Sahara's stubborn will in his life and knew that she was his reward for surviving.

"Kaleb?" When he met her gaze, she touched one of the fine silvery scars on her own body, and his anger ignited anew, rage swirling in his veins. "No," she whispered with a shake of her head. "You don't think of him when you see these. You think of *me*. A fighter, a survivor, your lover." It was an order . . . and one he realized he would have no hesitation in following, the marks her badges of honor.

Leaning up, he kissed one on her shoulder as she'd kissed the scar on his arm. "Only you," he said, the vow a final one. "My fierce, intelligent, lovely Sahara who spit in a monster's eye."

"Kaleb."

They were lost in one another in the minutes that followed, touching and caressing and simply being together.

"Our bond," he said afterward, "it'll be visible in the Net if I drop the shield I placed over it." It had been an instinctive act from his mind, the feral response to protect something indescribably precious. "Twenty-four hours—that's how long I plan to keep the shield in place."

Worry shadowed Sahara's smile and he knew she understood what he intended to do. "Are the people ready?"

"Some will never be ready, but it's time." The disease rotting the fabric of the Net was growing stronger, more virulent with every passing hour. "The only other option is a slow death."

Sahara thought of the dark places Kaleb had shown her, the dead places, and knew he was right. "You need the time to speak to the Arrows, don't you?"

"Yes. I have to find out if they'll fight me or support me when I announce the fall of Silence. I don't want to execute men and women who are more like me than any others in the Net, but I will if necessary."

If the squad fought him, Sahara thought, the resulting conflict would be far more devastating than anything Pure Psy had done. "The Arrows are intelligent; they must see Silence is rotten at the core."

"It's difficult to fight over a century of unyielding tradition."

Kaleb's words had Sahara thinking of the teleporter with the cold gray eyes. Could a man like Vasic exist in a world without Silence? It might be an impossible demand. Her heart hurt for him, for the choices he had never had, and she wished there was an easy answer, some way to give him a path out of the darkness.

Then the midnight star pulsed inside her, and it was a silent reminder that life wasn't easy. Sometimes, it demanded heart's blood and gave back only unbearable pain. Sometimes, it broke you. "When you're broken," she whispered to the man who would save the world for her, "you can't see hope. *We* must be their hope."

Kaleb held her close as she tucked her head under his chin. "You want me to drop the shielding around our bond when I talk to them."

"It'll be a risk, I know. They could immediately turn on us, but, Kaleb, that could've been us in another life." The idea of never meeting Kaleb, never loving him, made her heart thud in a panicked rhythm. "You're as lethal as any Arrow, but you made it out. Let them see that life isn't only pain and survival."

"Even if they join us, we won't save all of them." It was a grim truth.

"Then," Sahara said, the fingers of one hand locking tightly with Kaleb's, "we save the ones we can. Together."

"Always."

Chapter 46

ADEN WAS STANDING under a heavy desert moon, the dunes desolate waves of silver and shadow, when Kaleb appeared beside him. He'd realized long ago that, like Vasic, the cardinal could go to people as well as places, but the other man had never before been so confrontational about his ability. He had, Aden thought, been courting the Arrows.

Clearly, the courtship was over.

"Vasic is practicing the weapons capability of his gauntlet?" Krychek asked, his eyes on the churned-up sand around Aden's partner, Vasic having chosen a position midway down the dune that was Aden's watchtower.

"Yes," he said, and refused Vasic's telepathic offer of assistance at the same time. If Krychek had come with hostile intent, he'd have struck already. "It's meant to integrate with his base telekinetic strength, but there are glitches."

Vasic teleported in and shot a small, personal laser missile at a target they'd set up on another dune a hundred meters away. It not only went haywire, it doubled back toward the teleporter. Not showing any indication of being concerned, Vasic pressed something on the gauntlet and the missile exploded in midair.

"I'd say the glitches are significant," was Kaleb's cool appraisal. "He shouldn't have been implanted with the device if it's at this level of development. Its usefulness doesn't balance the risk."

Aden found himself in the unusual position of being caught unprepared. Because Kaleb had just repeated Aden's own argument when he'd tried to talk Vasic out of volunteering for the risky procedure. "There was no way," he said after a slight pause, "for the scientists to progress further without implanting it onto a live subject."

"Can it be removed?"

"No, it's fused too deeply to his body." Aden watched as Vasic launched another missile. "You didn't track us down to watch Vasic target practice," he said as this missile did exactly what it was meant to do, sand exploding in a silver geyser.

"Why are you here?" Kaleb asked instead of answering the implied question. "There's nothing you can do to stop an accident."

Aden had no intention of answering with the truth. "I'm here to monitor the tests, provide a backup account of the results."

Kaleb was quiet for a long time, the two of them watching the arcing blue flare of weapons fire as Vasic tested another setting on the gauntlet. When he spoke, Kaleb again said the unexpected. "You're here so that if something goes wrong, Vasic doesn't die alone. He's so close to the edge, you aren't certain he won't engineer a fatal accident."

There were very few people in the world who knew Vasic that well. Kaleb Krychek was not one of them, and yet he'd come to the right conclusion. Turning toward the man who was dressed in black combat pants and a black T-shirt, a large thin-skin bandage on the inside of his left forearm and scuffed boots on his feet, Aden said, "What do you want?"

Kaleb shifted to face him. "To know if I'm going to have to leave you dead on the desert sands."

"What makes you so certain you could?"

The white stars in the cardinal Tk's eyes gleamed as hard as diamonds. "You could incapacitate or kill me if you had the element of surprise, but in brute strength, I have no equal."

"Vasic has a lock on your position." His partner had taken that action the instant Kaleb first appeared. "He can have a gun to your head in the space between one breath and the next. And I am no medic." The only reason he told Kaleb that was because he was certain the other man already knew the true nature of his abilities.

Unlike Ming, Kaleb took nothing at face value, especially not a field medic who held the loyalty of the entire squad. "To be complacent in the presence of a cardinal Tk of opaque objectives and fluid allegiance," Aden added, "would be stupid in the extreme."

"That's why I'd rather not kill you," was Kaleb's response. "It's easy enough to find a trained assassin—an intelligent fighter capable of foresight, and flexible enough to alter his plans given the circumstances, is a far more rare thing." Shifting on his heel, the cardinal began to walk down the dune. "There's something your partner needs to see."

Aden followed in silence, unable to predict what Kaleb would do next. When the cardinal asked both Aden and Vasic to meet him on the PsyNet, they did so without argument. Once there, the other man said, "I need you to step inside the first layer of my shields."

Again, neither one of them hesitated; Krychek's shields were byzantine, but Aden and Vasic were more than capable of breaking out of this layer without problems. Aden had actually broken *into* it when the squad had first begun to consider shifting their loyalty to Kaleb—in a strictly limited sense that made it clear the Arrows were no one's lapdogs.

Then, he'd seen nothing, the outermost layer of Kaleb's shielding nothing but a redundancy that acted as an alarm bell in case of incursion. Today, he saw a psychic bond that went from Kaleb's mind to another one he didn't recognize, the colors of the bond faceted obsidian and a radiant light gold.

Force, coercion, manipulation, indications of psychic fraud, he searched for any hint of that in the connection that broke every rule of Silence, and found nothing. It was an organic construct, growing from two minds that had reached out for one another across the void, the light embracing the dark, the dark protective around the light.

Almost before Aden understood what it was he was seeing, he and Vasic were shoved out by a wave of naked power, shields of impenetrable obsidian slamming down over Kaleb's mind and that of the unidentified other.

"You're emotionally linked to someone," Aden said back in the desert, thrown enough by what he'd seen that the words spilled out past his normally airtight guards.

Was it real? Vasic asked at the same time, as if distrustful of his own perception.

Yes.

"My true allegiance," Kaleb said on the heels of Aden's telepathic answer, "has never been fluid."

It was Vasic who next spoke, the desert wind so quiet around them that it disturbed not a single grain of sand. "That bond cannot exist in a Silent world."

"No."

At last, Aden understood why Kaleb had come tonight, why the cardinal needed to know if he would have to drench the sands with their blood. "The Arrows," Aden began, "were created at the dawn of Silence, our mandate to protect the Protocol at all costs."

Kaleb said nothing, his face so remote, it was impossible to believe he had the capacity to bond with anyone.

"The first Arrow," Aden continued, "was told that Silence was the Psy race's only hope, that without it, we would fall into madness and insanity until our people were nothing but a terrible memory. Zaid believed. We all believed."

"It wasn't a total lie." Kaleb's gaze met Vasic's. "Not all of us would have survived to adulthood, or maintained a kind of sanity at least, without some level of conditioning."

"No," Vasic said, "it wasn't—*isn't*—a total lie, but the core is rotten."

"That's why it must be excised." A ruthless proclamation from a man who had always seemed the embodiment of the Protocol: cold, powerful, without ties of any kind. "Silence must fall. Will the Arrows fall with it?"

"The Arrow Squad," Aden said, "must always exist." For those like Vasic and Judd—and Kaleb. The ones who were too dangerous to live in the ordinary world; the ones the rest of their people would fear if the outliers were not first trained to hide their lethal nature; the ones who would always be needed to protect their people. "It cannot fall."

Kaleb's answer was blunt. "Then it must adapt."

It would be the most difficult journey any Arrow had ever taken, and Aden knew some would splinter before this was all over. But, his men and women were ready. The squad had known it might one day have to break from Silence, from the Net itself—though that Net was their life-blood, a psychic home they had fought to protect for over a hundred years . . . even as it killed them.

Arrow after Arrow had been lost as a result of decisions made by those who saw them as disposable, perfect soldiers who were thrown out the instant they became too fractured to be of use. The squad didn't wish to abandon their people, but they had been willing to do so, to defect, to protect those of their number who weren't yet fatally damaged.

Having seen the life Judd had made for himself, Aden had cautiously expected that, given the chance, the younger Arrows—the ones still on the right side of the abyss—might be able to build the same: a life that didn't involve only death and isolation and an existence forever in the shadows. Yet if Kaleb Krychek had been able to bond with another living being . . . Perhaps Aden had sold his Arrows short. Perhaps salvation could come for even the most broken among them.

"We'll adapt," Aden said, the heavy moon standing sentinel above, "but one thing will never change—we'll follow only those orders with which we agree." The time for blind obedience, for faith in a leader who was not one of their own, had passed. "And should you ever become a threat to the squad, we'll turn on you without hesitation."

"I would expect nothing less." Kaleb slid his hands into the pockets of his combat pants. "You understand if the latter ever happens," he added, "I'll show no mercy."

Vasic said the words on Aden's tongue. "The Arrows expect mercy from no one."

There was no further discussion, the bargain made, the future irrevocably altered.

Looking at the streak of light that marked the passage of an airjet in the star-studded night sky, Aden thought of the cold at that altitude. Icy, inimical to life. But it was in that same hostile environment that snowflakes formed on the windows of slower craft, creations of delicate filigree . . . beauty born in the bitterest cold.

IN the hours that followed Kaleb's meeting with the Arrows, a *very* select number of people received a visit from Kaleb Krychek—and two men received one from the Ghost, their meeting place the last two pews of a small Second Reformation church, the lights turned off in this one section. Neither Judd nor Xavier was surprised at the news of the upcoming revolution in the Net.

"The wave," Judd said, "has crested. To swim or to drown, those are the only two options."

Xavier's words were quieter, held more worry. "So, we've achieved our aim—the Council is no more, and Silence is about to fall. And yet I think the task is just beginning." Looking up as a parishioner entered, Xavier rose to speak to the frail, elderly man, while Kaleb turned his face deeper into the shadows.

"It's not safe for Xavier to be connected to Kaleb Krychek," Judd said once the priest was far enough away that he wouldn't overhear the words, "but no one will blink an eye at the fact that Judd Lauren knows another Tk. If you need me, I'll be there."

"The same applies." Kaleb didn't quite understand how he had come to have the loyalty of these two men, but he knew he'd guard their trust with his own. "I'll make sure Xavier remains safe." He paused. "I paid a quiet visit"—unknown, unseen—"to the mountain village where his Nina is meant to be." It was an act that would gain Kaleb nothing, but he thought he had done it out of friendship, to save Xavier pain should it be a false trail.

Judd's laugh was soft. "So did I."

"Shall we tell Xavier?"

"No, he leaves for the mountains tomorrow. I think some things a man must experience to believe."

Kaleb thought of the candle flame in the void, of a bond beautiful and unbreakable, and knew Judd spoke the truth.

. . .

WHEN he returned home at last, all the pieces in place, it was to find Sahara standing in front of the house, her eyes on grasslands kissed by the pearl gray light of the time before true daylight, the mist still licking the ground. Wearing a pretty white top and a flowing ankle-length skirt of summer yellow flecked with tiny flowers in myriad shades, the skirt embellished with two layers of ruffles created of the fabric, she looked like a piece of sunshine racing ahead of the dawn.

"Kaleb." She ran into his arms.

"What are you doing out here?" He didn't speak of the meetings he'd attended; she'd been with him everywhere but the church—terming that a discussion with friends. It was Sahara who had known Vasic was close to broken; as for Aden, she'd agreed with Kaleb that the telepath was a man who could become a powerful ally if they could earn his trust.

"I was waiting for you." Fingers weaving through his hair, she drew him in for a kiss that reminded him he was hers and *no one* else's.

The past, she told him with her every touch, had no claim on either one of them.

Breaking the kiss when he would've drawn her closer, she said, "Don't tempt me," and nudged him toward a chair she must've brought from inside the house. "I've been working on something I want you to see. We still have time, don't we?"

"A half hour," he said. "But first"—he lifted his arm, the bandage gone, the skin no longer red thanks to two minutes with an M-Psy—"I had it done a few hours ago." The same M had excised the original burn with a skill that had left Kaleb with only the faintest scar now obscured by black ink. As for the medic, since she had kept her silence in all the years of her employ, he had no doubts she'd do the same now.

Sahara traced the ink with a trembling finger before she bent to press her lips to the tattoo, her touch tender, her eyes dark with emotion. "I've branded you."

"You did that a long time ago."

"I did, didn't I?" A tear he kissed off her cheek, one of his hands curving around her throat.

"I told you," she whispered against his lips, "I was very smart at sixteen. Now sit."

When he did, Sahara stepped back, stretched out her arms . . . and then she was dancing, her limbs flowing with a grace and a beauty that made it appear as if she had wings. He couldn't breathe, wasn't sure his heart beat until she stopped and went down on her knees in front of the chair, her hands on his thighs.

"That's all I have so far." It was a laughing confession. "I know I'm rusty."

Chest painful, he said, "You were beautiful." Strong and whole and a luminous repudiation of everything the monsters had tried to do to them both. "Again. Please."

The mist swirled around her in fragile streamers as she granted his request, her body seemingly weightless. When he gave her a cushion of air as he'd done when she'd been a girl, her eyes sparkled and she flew higher, her hair a midnight rain down her back, his Sahara for whom he would've burned down an entire civilization . . . except that she'd asked him to save it.

"Kaleb!" Chest heaving, she held out her hands, her voice coaxing. "One dance."

"I can't dance," he said, even as he rose to walk to her.

"I'll teach you." Taking one of his hands, she placed it on her hip. "And"—a slender hand on his shoulder, the fingers of the other intertwined with his—"I won't even try to get answers to math problems."

Kissing her smile until it was in his blood, he processed her telepathic instructions with the brain of a Tk for whom movement was like breathing and took the first steps. Sahara gasped in delight, and then she was fluid lightning in his arms, their bodies forming a single unit as they moved across the grass.

On the horizon, the first rays of a dazzling dawn splashed the sky with color.

Dawn

AS DAWN BROKE on a new day, former Councilor Kaleb Krychek, his mind linked to a mysterious woman identified as Sahara Kyriakus, told the PsyNet that Silence was no longer the guiding protocol of their race.

The Arrows, the guardians of Silence for over a century, stood by him.

The ragged remnants of Pure Psy, scattered across the planet, vowed to fight the fall to the death, to destroy the world and seed it for a better one.

Hundreds of thousands of fractured Psy went to their knees, their hearts breaking at the freedom to be what they had always been meant to be. Others huddled in confusion, waiting for someone to tell them what to do. And the weakest, they struggled not to break under a wave of change that threatened to drown.

There will be those who seek to exploit this time of change, read the decree that blazed with a single platinum star at the top, bracketed by two smaller emblems representing Nikita Duncan and Anthony Kyriakus, and underlined by a black arrow, *but we will respond with deadly force against anyone, regardless of status, rank, or ability, who attempts to seize control of any part of the Net.*

Our people have survived one civil war. A second will not be permitted.

The statement of authority, of control, was a beacon not only to the weak and the confused, but to those who hoped for a better future. It gave them a structure to cling to, the violence of Kaleb Krychek's power a paradoxically stabilizing force. No one, whispered men and women from one end of the globe to the other, would dare stand against him.

For another people, such knowledge might have made them fear for their freedom, but as birds who have had their wings clipped cannot fly, no matter how wide the sky, a people trapped in bondage for over a hundred years cannot be given total freedom without a fatal cost. Structure, power, discipline, this was what they needed, Kaleb's steel hand the only thing that halted a deadly wave of shock from ending the lives of millions.

The transition will not be easy, ended the decree, *and it will not be without cost. But we are not cowards to hide from the powers that define us. We are Psy and we are capable of greatness.*

It is time to step out of the dark.

Nalini Singh was born in Fiji and raised in New Zealand. She spent three years living and working in Japan, and travelling around Asia before returning to New Zealand.

She has worked as a lawyer, a librarian, a candy factory general hand, a bank temp and an English teacher, not necessarily in that order.

Learn more about her and her novels at: www.nalinisingh.com